Come Gentle Spring

BOOKS BY JESSE STUART

Man with a Bull-Tongue Plow
Head o' W-Hollow
Beyond Dark Hills
Trees of Heaven
Men of the Mountains
Taps for Private Tussie
Mongrel Mettle
Album of Destiny
Foretaste of Glory
Tales from the Plum Grove Hills
The Thread That Runs So True
Hie to the Hunters
Clearing in the Sky
Kentucky Is My Land
The Good Spirit of Laurel Ridge
The Year of My Rebirth
Plowshare in Heaven
God's Oddling
Hold April
A Jesse Stuart Reader
Save Every Lamb
Daughter of the Legend
My Land Has a Voice
Mr. Gallion's School

FOR BOYS AND GIRLS

Penny's Worth of Character
The Beatinest Boy
Red Mule
The Rightful Owner
Andy Finds a Way

Jesse Stuart

COME GENTLE SPRING

McGRAW-HILL BOOK COMPANY

NEW YORK ST. LOUIS SAN FRANCISCO TORONTO

First Published in *Esquire Magazine:*

"Uncle Fonse Laughed," copyright © 1936 by Esquire, Inc., renewed 1964. "Fast-Train Ike," copyright © 1937 by Esquire, Inc., renewed 1965. "The Land Beyond the River," copyright © 1937 by Esquire, Inc., renewed 1965. "The War and Cousin Lum," copyright © 1937 by Esquire, Inc., renewed 1965. "The Last Round Up," copyright © 1940 by Esquire, Inc., renewed 1968. "King of the Hills," copyright © 1942 by Esquire, Inc. "Come Gentle Spring," copyright © 1954 by Esquire, Inc.

The author wishes to acknowledge with gratitude the cooperation of the following additional publishers and publications in whose volumes the material herein first appeared. "Two Worlds," *Georgia Review;* "A Christmas Present for Uncle Bob," *Philippines Free Press;* "The Rainy Day at Big Lost Creek," *Country Gentleman.*

COME GENTLE SPRING

Copyright © 1969 by Jesse Stuart. All Rights Reserved.
Printed in the United States of America.
No part of this publication may be reproduced, stored
in a retrieval system, or transmitted, in any form
or by any means, electronic, mechanical,
photocopying, recording or otherwise, without the prior
written permission of McGraw-Hill, Inc.

Library of Congress Catalog Card Number: 75-76825

First Edition 62243

Contents

1. Come Gentle Spring 1
2. Two Worlds 12
3. The Weakling 21
4. A Christmas Present for Uncle Bob 31
5. The Old Law Wasn't Strong Enough 45
6. Love in the Spring 55
7. The Water Penalty 70
8. Our Wiff and Daniel Boone 82
9. Pa's a Man's Man All Right 97
10. Mad Davids and a Mechanical Goliath 120
11. The Last Round Up 130
12. A Land Beyond the River 143
13. Powderday's Red Hen 164
14. Fast-Train Ike 176
15. Uncle Fonse Laughed 195
16. Does the Army Always Get Its Man? 210
17. Seventy-Six Days 220
18. The Rainy Day at Big Lost Creek 234
19. The War and Cousin Lum 252
20. King of the Hills 272

Come Gentle Spring

TOM Eden stood before the cracked mirror hanging in the hall and pushed back his hair with a coarse-tooth comb. The hair was as white as wild blackberry blossoms and as thick as a sheep's wool. Then he took a fine-tooth comb from the rack beneath the mirror and began to comb his long white beard.

"Are you about ready to go, Tom?" the elderly woman asked as she limped from the kitchen.

"Yep, I am, Bridget," he replied.

Tom continued to look in the mirror and comb his beard that was as fine as young corn silk in August.

"It breaks my heart, Tom," she sobbed. "Think you can sell it?"

"Yep, I've got Lacie Littleton's promise," he said.

Her wrinkled face was serious.

"You know the understandin' with Lacie," he told her. "I'm lettin' him have this place cheaper than I would anybody else because he'll let us live here until one of us goes!"

"Sad thoughts, Tom," Bridget said, wiping her eyes with the corner of her apron. "We've been together a long time."

"That's right," Tom said as he put the comb back in the rack.

"But I'm a-goin' to Blakesburg this mornin' to see the people in that old-age-pension office."

Bridget turned so Tom couldn't see her eyes.

"Take it easy, Bridget," Tom spoke bravely. "We've faced harder things than this before. We can face this, Bridget."

"It's a long walk for you, Tom," she said.

"Only five miles," he said. "And I might get a ride. I got one the last time I went to Blakesburg."

Tom lifted his old familiar poke-shaped hat from a nail on the wall and set it slowly on top of his white hair. The hat looked like a black cone-shaped roof above a white circular wall. He picked up his walking stick that he kept leaned beside the door. It was a hickory stick he had cut green and bent one end before the fire and seasoned it to a shape to fit his hand.

He started walking down the Sweetwater Valley Road that automobiles occasionally drove over now. Tom remembered when he was a boy people walked or rode horseback down Sweetwater. He remembered that he helped his father make the first road and build the first four wooden bridges so a team and wagon could go over this road. As he walked along, he stopped and looked back to see if an automobile was coming. He hoped to get a ride. But he chuckled to himself when one didn't come. He reminisced how, as a young man, he used to run the length of the Valley.

When he reached the mouth of Sweetwater Valley, he was on the Sandy Turnpike, where he stopped and looked up the road to see if an automobile was coming. *Any other time one would be along*, he thought. *I ust to walk it and i'gollies I can walk it yet.*

Cars zoomed past Tom all the way to Blakesburg but none stopped to give him a ride. When he reached Blakesburg he went straight to the courthouse and to the office where he had been once before.

"Well, I'm back, Mr. Gardner," he said to a young man sitting at a desk with a typewriter before him. "Remember me—Tom Eden? I was here once before and you said I'd haf to sell my farm to get the old-age pension!"

"Oh, yes, Mr. Eden, I do remember you," Mr. Gardner said,

smiling at the old man with the cone-shaped black hat sitting like a black mushroom on top a large white stem. "Have you sold your farm yet, Mr. Eden?"

"Nope, not yet," he said. "That's the reason I'm in here. I want to be sure this thing'll work before I sell it. I don't want to be left out in the cold. Bridget and I haf to have a place to live!"

"Well, we can take your application," Mr. Gardner said. "And as soon as you sell your farm, we can get the pension through for you. Now, we've got to ask you a few questions."

"You ast me a lot of questions when I was in here before," he said.

"We have so many applicants I don't remember the answer to your questions," Mr. Gardner said. "You'll have to answer 'em again for us."

"Oh, that's all right, Mr. Gardner," Tom said, smiling. "I jist never got over all the questions ye ast me. I told Bridget about 'em and she laughed too."

"How old are you, Mr. Eden?"

"I'll be ninety-three August eighth."

"How old is Mrs. Eden?"

"Bridget is young," he said, smiling. "She's eighty-seven."

"You all deserve an old-age pension."

"Yep, but I never wanted the damned thing," Tom said. "Looks like Bridget and I jist about haf to take it. We didn't want to sell our home. But as I told her this mornin' when I left, she and I are tired. Everything out there is tired. Old Rock, our mule who is twenty-one years old, is tired and stands around in the sun a-restin' a leg at a time. Our old barn is so tired it leans. Even our fence posts are so tired they sag, and our house is tired, and even the old hills I farmed so long are so tired they're a-slippin' down into the road to rest a spell. I farmed last summer and I told Rock that'd be the last time he and I'd plow the hills together."

"I believe, Mr. Eden, you told me you didn't have any children?" Mr. Gardner said.

"That's right," Tom replied.

"We'll get a good pension for you and Mrs. Eden," the young

man said. "You're as deserving as anybody who has ever come to this office. Each one of you will draw twenty-nine dollars a month."

"Sounds like a fortune," Tom said. "But I still hate to sell our home to get it. And Bridget does too. We can sell our farm to a neighbor and he promises to let us live on in the house until one of us goes."

"Well, of course, Mr. Eden," said the young man as he continued to fill out the applications, "we don't make the laws. It's a state law you can't get an old-age pension if you own land."

"Oh, I'm not blamin' you," he said.

"Now everything is fixed up here, Mr. Eden," the young man said. "You sell your farm and show us the transaction and we'll put this pension right through for you."

Tom left the courthouse in a hurry. He walked to the railroad tracks on the outskirts of Blakesburg and a truck with two men in the cab pulled up and stopped. The driver looked up and down the tracks for trains. Tom pointed up the Sandy Turnpike with his cane, and the driver motioned for him to climb in the cab. With considerable effort, he pulled himself up and rode to the mouth of Sweetwater Valley.

Lucky a-comin' home, he muttered to himself. *Bridget won't be expectin' me this soon.*

That afternoon Bridget and Tom walked up the hill to see Lacie. Lacie was working in his tobacco when the two old people arrived. He stopped work when he saw them and walked up the hill.

"Well, did you get your pension?" Lacie asked.

Lacie was short, broad-shouldered and muscular. He had blue eyes, a beardy, sun-tanned face, and his clothes smelled of green tobacco.

"We got the pensions, all right, if we sell the farm," Tom said.

"That's wonderful," Lacie said grinning. "We'll go right now. How did you go in this mornin'?"

"Walked in this mornin' and catched a truck back to Sweetwater," Tom replied.

"You're a very spry old man to get a pension," Lacie teased him. "Last year when I saw you plowin' Rock on that steep hill, I said to myself: 'Old Tom will be plowin' the same corn patches when he reaches a hundred!' "

"Lacie, there's one thing I want to ask ye," Bridget said, as the early September wind moved the white hair under her bonnet. "I want to know if we can stay on in the house until one of us goes!"

"Oh, yes, Mrs. Eden," Lacie said.

"But something might come up that you'll want us out," she said. "That's the house I went into as a bride sixty-eight years ago and I don't want to leave there now. If you don't put this in the deed, I won't sign and sell to get a pension."

"We'll put it in the deed that you stay in the house until one of you go," Lacie said.

"Well, I trust you, Lacie," Tom said, "but business is business, and that'll be better. Bridget never wants to leave and I don't neither."

"All right, you won't have to walk to Blakesburg now," Lacie bragged. "I'll get the truck and we'll be down there in a few minutes and get everything fixed up."

That afternoon Lacie took them to Blakesburg in his truck and they made a deed in attorney Oscar Timmons' office. Lacie agreed to pay them $2500 for their seventy-two acres of hill land with a house, barn and two-acre tobacco base. Bridget had Oscar Timmons read the deed over to them so she would be sure they could live in the house until only one was left. Bridget signed the deed and Tom made his cross in the presence of witnesses and a notary signed for him. Lacie Littleton paid them $1000 and agreed to pay $50 a month until he had paid for the farm.

The following week, Tom looked out his window and saw Lacie standing in the barn. He was looking up at the rafters. Tom got his cane and walked over to the barn.

"That barn will have to be strengthened before it'll hold my terbacker," Lacie said.

"But what'll I do with the hay I got up there in the loft? Where'll I put old Rock?"

"This barn is mine, Tom, and I'll have to have it," Lacie said. "Where you put your mule and your hay is your problem. This is my barn now. There's nothin' in the deed that says I can't use this barn, pasture these pastures, cut this timber and farm this land!"

"Oh, so . . . ," Tom stammered. But he couldn't speak his thoughts. He turned and walked back to the house, stabbing his hickory walking stick into the soft ground. *What will Bridget think?* he thought.

When Tom reached the porch, Bridget knew something was wrong.

"He's a-goin' to fill the barn with terbacker, Bridget," he mumbled softly. "Where'll I put old Rock? Where'll I put my feed fer 'im? Old Rock's had a stall in that barn twenty-one years. He was raised there."

"It's trouble, Tom," Bridget told him. "We no longer own this place. We've just got the house."

"Bridget, I never thought about him a-takin' over the barn."

"But we had to sell it to get our pension, Tom."

"This is awful, Bridget."

Bridget held his shaking arm as they went inside the house together. That night they sat and talked about what to do with old Rock and the hay. And the following day, Tom took the floor up from an old smokehouse and made a stall there for Rock. Then he went over to the barn and threw the hay down from the loft and carried it by forkloads and stacked it near the smokehouse.

"Tom, it would be better to sell Rock," Bridget said.

"But I can't sell that mule, Bridget," he said. "He's old and tired and who would be good to 'im now? He can't do enough work fer his keeps. I want to keep 'im until he dies. We've plowed many a acre of steep hill together."

A few days later Lacie came back and brought a man with him. They fetched tools to cut tierpoles to put through the barn so he could hang his tobacco. When he saw the hay had been moved, he was pleased. But when he found the floor removed from the smokehouse and a mule stall fixed within, his face flushed with anger. Lacie and the man he had brought to help him put the floor back in the smokehouse. When Tom and Bridget saw what they were doing, they stayed inside the house.

"Maybe Millard will take the mule," Bridget said. "He'll be good to old Rock. We'll get him to haul the hay to his barn and keep 'im this winter."

That afternoon Tom walked down on the Sandy River to see Millard Artner about keeping his mule for the winter. Millard, a young man of seventy, had been a neighbor to Tom all his life. When Tom told Millard what had happened, he agreed to take Rock and keep him for the winter. Tom was pleased when he led Rock with a halter down to Millard Artner's barn. "You'll have a good stall and plenty of feed," he told Rock, patting his nose with his old wrinkled hand. Old Rock seemed to understand what his master was telling him. Millard Artner came with his wagon and team and hauled the hay and corn down to his barn for Rock while Lacie and his helper cleaned the barn and lined it with tierpoles. They also braced the walls of the leaning barn.

In middle September when Lacie cut his tobacco, he hauled the first load down from the hill into Sweetwater Valley. Instead of going down to the lane that passed the house to the barn, he cut the fence, crossed the little meadow where Tom had always cut his hay. This was a closer way to the barn. When Tom saw him do this, he went back to the house to tell Bridget. "He's makin' a road across my little meader when there's already a road to this barn. This is goin' to finish me, Bridget."

Then Tom took from his coat pocket a long stiff check filled with small perforated lines. He held the check off at arms' length and looked at it. "I'm a-tearin' this thing up," he said. "I'm a-tearin' it smack in two." He took each end of the long check in each gnarled old wrinkled hand.

"Oh, no, ye can't do that, Tom," Bridget said as she grabbed his arm. "That's the state's business and that's dangerous. And that means we can spend the rest of our days. . . ."

"In hell," Tom interrupted. "That's what it is. I'll give them back this pension if I can get my land back. I never was a man to rule back on a trade either. But I'm sick, Bridget."

"Wonder if Lacie'd sell this farm back to us?" she said. "Why don't we see 'im? We've not spent the money he's paid us."

Tom put the stiff check back in his coat pocket.

"Maybe we could," he said, feeling relieved. "Pay back the state too. We've only spent one draw from the state!"

The following morning was filled with softness and October mist. The tobacco hanging in the barn was soft and pliable now. It was ready in case Lacie came to bulk his tobacco down and prepare it for stripping. When Tom saw him go into the barn just after the break of day, he walked over toward the barn without his walking stick. His step was firm and his face was beaming.

"Lacie," he said soon as he stepped inside the barn door, "I wonder if ye'd sell this farm back to me? Bridget and I have talked it over and we don't want the old-age pension. We'd rather have our land back. Would you deal back with us, the way we dealt with ye? We can pay back every dollar that ye have paid us."

"And then you'd haf to pay me some more," Lacie said, looking straight at the old man. "I wouldn't take a cent less than $4000 for this farm with this two-acre terbacker base and the good barn that I have here now! Not a cent less."

"We couldn't do that," Tom said, hanging his head in disappointment. "That's a lot of profit."

"But the land's gone up," Lacie said.

"Mighty fast," Tom grumbled.

"I don't want to trade at any price," Lacie said. "I'm satisfied with things as they are."

Lacie began lifting tobacco sticks from the tierpoles. Tom turned and walked away.

By his window, Tom sat and watched Lacie knock the rusty wire from the sagging posts and move it over and staple the wire to green trees.

"Too lazy to set posts," he said. "He's a-ruinin' the young trees I kept fire from. He's a wasteful man."

Before the tobacco was hauled to the market, Tom and Bridget saw strange cattle in their pasture and bundles of fodder spread where grass grew in summer. The ugly fodder stalks lay there stripped of blades and moldering in the faint winter sun.

In November Tom and Bridget took their crosscut saw down to a dead maple that had been rooted over by the wind. Each autumn they had been a familiar sight sawing wood beside the road. Tom would cut up the small branches with an ax while Bridget held them across the chop block. And they would saw up the trunk of the tree, each quarreling over who was bearing down on the end of the crosscut. Many people had stopped to watch them cut wood. And each season they'd have many cords of wood cut and ricked for winter burning. When Tom and Bridget started working on the maple, Lacie drove up.

"I'd rather, Tom, you wouldn't cut that tree," Lacie said, bringing his team to a stop. "I've planned to cut that tree for wood."

"Shucks, this old dead tree," Tom said, looking up at Lacie. "It's not worth anything."

"Worth as much to me as it is to you. And besides," he growled, "it's mine. With all I'm payin' ye on this farm and with two pension checks comin' in, looks like you could buy coal."

"We didn't know it'd be like this," Bridget said.

Tom picked up his ax. Bridget got one handle of the crosscut and he held the other. They walked away like two small children forced to leave their playhouse. Bridget once looked at young Lacie Littleton propped up high on his wagon as he drove his team down the road.

"This house is all we have," Bridget said.

"I'll see a lawyer," Tom told her.

"No need to see a lawyer," she told him. "We have only the house, Tom."

"House, yard and garden," he said.

"Maybe," she said.

"It said in the deed we got this place until one of us was left," he said.

But the snows came and drifted in Sweetwater Valley. Tom couldn't put on his poke-shaped black hat over his white head and with a walking stick wade the deep snow to Blakesburg.

Then January came and a sun broke through the black mountains of overcast and melted snow water filled Sweetwater Creek. And, soon as the snow had left the bleak, forsaken, tired land, Lacie appeared in the garden. He started tearing down palings and stacking them. Tom rose from his chair by the window, grabbed his walking stick and lifted it high above his head. "I'll show 'im," he shouted.

"No, Tom," Bridget spoke softly.

"But I rove the palings from a white oak," he shouted. "I put them there twenty-five years ago. The fence might be tired, but I want it to stand around my garden."

Bridget led him to his chair. He slumped down, relaxing his legs and resting his hands on the chair arms.

"I can't stand to see our garden go," he said.

That day, just before noon, Lacie saw Bridget, bundled in a coat, in boots and with a scarf over her head, walk down Sweetwater Valley. Bridget didn't speak or turn her head his way. And after a couple of hours he saw her return and go into the house.

When Lacie was throwing the last palings on the fire, Millard Artner and Doctor Torris got out of the doctor's car. They, too, hurried inside the house. Lacie didn't stop to ask what was wrong. He had heard from Bill Eversole Tom had the flu. And often when he fed his cattle fodder, he saw Millard Artner leave in the morning. And he saw others come and go.

February came and passed and Millard came and went from Tom's and Bridget's house. And the neighbors often came and stayed awhile and went away. Every time Lacie was on the place, he saw activity of people around the house. And in early March Lacie came and plowed the garden for tobacco. He plowed the little meadow that Tom had never plowed. One day after Millard had gone and he was sure there were no other visitors, Lacie let his team rest and went over to the house. He knocked on the door.

"Oh, so it's you," Bridget said, when she opened the door.

"I just wanted to ask how Tom was," Lacie said.

"You've been a long time about askin'," she told him. "Go plow our garden and our meader and bring more misery to Tom as he watches ye through the winder."

April came, and the wild plums that grew along Sweetwater blossomed in wild profusion. Blossoms hung from the slender stems like weighty pods of snow. Higher up on the rugged slope, directly in front of the house, there were sails of redbud blossoms. There were white sails of dogwood blossoms, too, that rustled in the wind. When Lacie saw Tom's head against the window, his hair was the color of the wild plum blossoms.

Mornings later when Lacie looked at the window he didn't see Tom's white head. While he looked at the window, Millard opened the door and walked across the garden.

"Lacie, this house belongs to you now," Millard said. "Tom didn't wake this mornin'."

Lacie tried to stammer something but the words wouldn't come. He watched Millard walk across the garden to the Sweetwater Road. Then Lacie turned to look in a different direction. He saw the last blossom leave the top of the tallest plum and zigzag slowly down on the bright April wind until it reached the ground.

Two Worlds

WHEN Grandpa Shelton walked in front of me along the path he was so broad I had to look around on either side to see what was ahead. There wasn't much ahead to see except our flock of sheep upon the slope near the sky. Then, there were brown sandstones and dark stumps scattered over our sheep pasture.

"He was a great man," Grandpa said.

"Yes, he was all right, Grandpa," I agreed.

"But I said a great man," Grandpa spoke firmly.

Grandpa weighed two hundred and forty-three pounds. He wasn't fat. He was an even six feet tall, his shoulders twice as broad as his hips and when he took a step he didn't raise his foot very high. He shuffled along up the steep winding path. His arms, hanging down by his sides, moved like slow pendulums. His hands dropped almost to his knees. His hair was as thick and white as clean sheep wool. He was seventy-five years old. I was fifteen, six feet, one hundred and sixty-five pounds. I had one year in Blakesburg High School and I had made first string guard on the Blakesburg High School Tigers. And because of all the trouble that went on in my home, I had read all the books I could find in the Blakesburg High School Library about the Civil War.

Grandpa wouldn't call it the Civil War nor the War Between the States. He called this war The Decent Rebellion.

"I want you on my side, Shan," he said. "I'd rather have you, a Powderday by name, on my side as any Shelton grandson I have. I've lived here with your Ma and Pa twelve years now. I've seen you grow up. And I've taught you to work, my son!"

Grandpa had taught me to work. My father, Mick Powderday, left home at five in the morning. Walked five miles over the mountain to the railroad tracks and there he joined a crew of section hands who pumped a hand-car another five miles to work. He worked ten hours a day and on short winter days he didn't get home until after dark. He worked six days a week. During the summer and on days when I wasn't in school, I worked with Grandpa.

"Say Robert E. Lee was a great man," Grandpa said. "You know he was! You've had a year in high school now. You have read a lot of books. You ought to know!"

But I didn't say anything. I followed behind Grandpa. I didn't want to face him and look into his kind blue eyes. I loved my mother's father. I had never known a kinder man. I knew if I agreed with my Grandfather that Robert E. Lee was a great man that when my father came in from work on the railroad section Grandpa would tell him I was on his side. And I knew this would hurt my Grandfather, old Mick Powderday, a Scotsman, and a Union soldier who slept somewhere in an unmarked grave.

When my Grandfathers met once, they looked at one another and never spoke. Grandpa Powderday was another six-feet-two, two-hundred-thirty-pound, broad-shouldered man. He had enlisted when Abraham Lincoln called for seventy-five thousand men to carry on the war. He was a mountaineer who didn't like slavery. Said he wanted to be as free as the hawk that circled in the skies and he wanted everybody else to be.

The Powderdays had fought in mountain clan warfare, had killed and had been killed until but few of them were left. Grandpa had to flee from the high mountain country to where we live now. But he had become dissatisfied with the Little Sandy River Country and he had gone back to his native Big Sandy

River Country, where he had been killed by his enemies and buried at night. His unmarked grave was now lost. Two of my Powderday cousins, Uncle Joe's boys, claimed they got his killers. Two men died the day he was killed.

"I almost got you named Robert E. Lee Powderday," Grandpa said. "Your Pa held out to name you Ulysses S. Grant Powderday and of course when your Ma and Pa quarreled for three days over which name to call you I stopped insisting about your name. They compromised and named you Shan after my son, your Uncle, and after your Pa's boyhood friend!"

"I'm glad they didn't name me after either one," I said. "I'm glad they compromised and called me Shan. I like my name."

What trouble I would have had in our divided house, I thought, if I had been named after either of the generals that led the Northern and the Southern Armies in the Civil War. I had had to walk a tight-rope since I had been born. I had had enough trouble in my home to make me a natural diplomat. Whatever my mother was, my father wasn't. My mother was a Baptist and a Democrat. My father was a Methodist and a Republican. Although my father wasn't a devout Christian, let anybody say anything against the Methodists and he had a fight on his hands. He was a devout Republican and when he ran once for school trustee, my Grandfather Shelton, who lived in our home, wouldn't vote for him. He voted for a stranger who was a Democrat, John Higgins, who beat my father by one vote.

"Why do you love Grandpa Shelton?" I once asked my father.

"Shan, Old Dad is the kindest, finest man I've ever known," my father said. His words leaped from his mouth. "And your Grandpa Shelton is no killer! The Sheltons are good people. They're mountaineers and there's no record where a Shelton ever killed a man! I wish we Powderdays could say that, Shan! You're born of a fine mother!"

"But Grandpa rode with Morgan's Men," I said. "He was in a shooting war!"

"But no fighter, Shan," my father said. "The Sheltons never owned a slave. Your Grandpa, a big boy at fourteen, enlisted and rode with Morgan's Wild Riders. He never killed anybody. A Shelton won't kill. He came as nigh as a pea of getting killed! He had a bullet put through his hat that just grazed his head and left a little scar."

I knew that my father loved my mother even if they did get into quarrels over North and South, over the Democrats and Republicans and the Methodists and the Baptists, that would last a week. One summer when Mom's people from Elliott County were visiting us, they were all so large chairs creaked when they moved as they sat in our front yard under the poplar trees. Aunt Nance, Grandpa's sister, said she believed only a Baptist could enter Heaven. My father, a small wiry man with a sliced-beet-red face, a long nose and a pair of big blue eyes, got up from his chair, never said a word but walked to the barn and never returned to the house until Mom's relatives left. This was his reply to Aunt Nance.

"Shan, our tools haven't done a thing since we put them away last night," Grandpa said.

I was glad he had turned the subject from Grant and Lee. We had reached the giant rock in our sheep pasture, the one the sheep had climbed upon to trim their hoofs. They'd never climb upon this giant rock again. Grandpa and I had split this rock into sections. I had never known before that a man could split a rock as big as this one. My father didn't think it could be split either. We were scoring and hewing rocks to build a chimney in the center of a new house Grandpa and I were building on our farm.

Grandpa and I had gone over my father's fifty-acre farm looking at rock cliffs and the big single rocks that had broken loose from the cliffs and had rolled down on a flat or to the foot of a hill. Here high upon this hill Grandpa had chosen this old familiar rock where I had once sat with a rifle watching for squirrels in the hickory trees that grew around it. My sisters had made playhouses on this rock. But when Grandpa looked at it carefully he observed rock seams through it. "It's a rock that will split," he said. "Here's where we'll get stones for our chimney."

Now, Grandpa picked up his sixteen-pound hammer and his

steel wedges he'd had Britch Meyers, the Blakesburg blacksmith, to make and temper to suit him from junked car axles. The steel had to be hard and tempered just right to split and cut rocks, so Grandpa said. Grandpa had taught me to cut timber, to make crossties, clapboards for house and barn roofs and to hew and score logs for a house. He was the greatest chopper I had ever seen. Now I was getting a new education. I'd never known before Grandpa was a stone mason who could split and hew stones.

He set the wedge in a seam of the stone. He hammered it carefully with a light hammer until it was set. He told me the spot to set another wedge in the seam. After we had set a half dozen wedges spaced equidistant from one end of the rock to the other, Grandpa went from one wedge to the other, hitting each one a lick with the big hammer.

"See, Shan, this way we split the rock the right way. We don't want it to sliver!"

After Grandpa walked up and down hitting one wedge after another, the slab of rock let loose and turned over on its side—a slab as smooth as a big timber sawed at the mill. My Grandfather Shelton was an artist when it came to splitting a rock.

"Our hard work will come when we start splitting the slabs into squares," he said.

Up here, I could look from the biggest hill on my father's farm over into the Ohio River Valley. I could see the broad Ohio River, in this August morning sunlight, move like a silver serpent down the valley toward the Mississippi on to the Gulf of Mexico and then to the Atlantic Ocean. Beyond the river I could see the palisades and foothills and this was Ohio. A part of another world for my Grandfather. This was the North. About five miles away in Kentucky on this high hill top, here splitting rocks, Grandpa and I were in his World the South—only that river down there in the valley divided Grandpa's world.

Maybe working up here where we're in one world and can see the other is why Grandpa has been bringing up Grant and Lee to me so much, I thought. Once when he stopped hammering on the wedges to wipe sweat from his brow, he looked toward Ohio, then pushed at the wind with his big hand, shrugged his shoulder and turned his back to Ohio. "That's not the county," he said. "That's not it! Shan, we're too close!"

Grandpa had once ridden into Ohio with Morgan's Wild Riders. They had been given a hot reception. That was where he had the bullet put through his hat. They were repulsed more than once as they rode into villages and towns. But Morgan and his men had spread terror in Ohio and had caused panic and fear. They had invaded the North.

My father had always followed William Howard Taft of Ohio and later his son Robert Taft. He had looked to them for political deliverance which he never found in our state of Kentucky. We were a one-party system where a small Republican minority voted and always lost. He wouldn't have known how to accept victory. All he'd ever known was political defeat. But he never quit hoping for victory.

He had subscribed for a Taft newspaper, published in Cincinnati, which leaned heavily toward the Republicans. This paper reached us by train two days late. Since my father couldn't read and Mom could read but wouldn't read this paper that favored Republicans, I read the paper to him while he sat, listened and sanctioned with an "amen" everything good said about the Republicans. He always wanted me to read loud enough for Mom to hear.

To him the Ohio River was no big boundary. It flowed through a country and not between two worlds. There had been times in his life when he had talked about moving to Ohio, but my mother told him when he moved he would go alone, that she would stay in Kentucky with her seven children.

Now working with Grandpa up where the air was cool and thin, splitting rocks for the chimney and looking around us at the wild roses blooming in our sheep pasture because wild roses were something sheep wouldn't eat, I realized more than ever how I lived in a divided world. Here I had been born to divided parents. I had grown up with two good parents whom I loved. But I had heard them quarrel over the North and South, over Lee and Grant, over the Democrats and Republicans, over the Methodists and Baptists until I thought the roof of our house would be lifted up and float away. I sometimes wished it had gone off to scare them. I wished it would rise and float away everytime they quarreled, which was so often we would have lived in a house without a roof.

And here I'd been born on the border between the North and South. My brothers and I were sons and our sisters daughters of two worlds. Each world was a powerful voice beckoning us to follow. We were children of indecision! Two great voices called until we didn't know which world we would join and which we would forsake. My oldest sister leaned to Mom's and Grandpa's world.

I played neutral with Grandpa. He couldn't get me to say that Robert E. Lee was the greatest man who ever lived in America. And I wouldn't say that Abraham Lincoln was the greatest man and that Ulysses S. Grant was the greatest General. My father argued on every occasion he was attacked that they were. I loved Grandpa. I didn't want to offend him. I loved my mother more than anyone. I didn't want to hurt her.

And I would not hurt my father, who had taken me by the hand when I was six, and we'd walked five miles to see baseball games. I'd seen him play baseball too until he got too old, and section labor had made him too stiff to play. I'd opossum-hunted with my father and always carried the opossums in a sack. I'd fished with him in the Little Sandy, where we never caught a fish. I'd worked with him in the garden and the cornfield. He'd taught me many things. I'd never go against him and his fighting father, Old Mick, who would never be considered as fine a man as my Grandfather Shelton. I couldn't go against any of them. So I played neutral and became a diplomat. This was the only way out.

When Grandpa chipped stone squares with tempered chisels he'd had Britch Meyers to make, he cut the groove deeper and deeper. He waited until he cut the groove over an inch deep in the rock, then he let me follow him with a chisel, cutting the groove still deeper. When we had cut the groove as deep as we could, we turned the slab over with hickory poles. Turning a slab over that weighed a ton with hickory poles furthered my education. Grandpa put a rock heel under a pole twenty feet or more and when he put his two hundred and forty-three pounds down on the end of the pole he lifted it a few inches and I put rocks under the slab to hold each lift. Slowly he built it up, turned it over and Grandpa then marked the other side. Then he cut grooves to correspond to grooves cut on the other side. This way we cut the rock into perfect squares. After we had the slabs cut into squares, Grandpa smoothed each square with a dull double-bitted axe and with chisels. By his showing me how I learned to hew stone with a double-bitted axe and chisels. I'd never known before a double-bitted axe tempered to the right hardness could cut rock. I'd always thought an axe was to be used chopping wood. But my Grandpa was a smart man, a powerful man who went to work at sunrise, quit at sunset. We never stopped work only long enough to eat a lunch Mom had prepared for us.

But Grandpa wasn't always pleasant to work with. When a rock slivered, he would say, "Dam that Grant-wroughted thing!" He blamed his mistakes and bad luck on Grant and threw his sledge hammer over the hill, wiped sweat from his brow, then asked me to go fetch his hammer back. I would go get his hammer. When my father walked back, tired from his day on the railroad section, he would come to see our rocks.

"Dad, there was never a worker like you," my father would say. "You're a young man at seventy-five. I've never seen prettier rocks!"

Then, my father would laugh as he looked at Grandpa, whose clothes were as wet as if he'd waded into the Little Sandy River up to his neck. My father's clothes would be as wet as Grandpa's. Even though my father and Grandpa lived in two worlds, if Grant and Lee, Democrat and Republican, Baptist and Methodist were not mentioned, they got along fine together.

They went opossum-hunting together. And when our mountain cur treed an opossum up a slick barked poplar tree without a branch for thirty feet, Grandpa would want to climb the tree to get the opossum. My father would laugh at big Grandpa scaling up the tree to get the opossum. He could climb better than my father but not as well as I could.

Only one thing my father wouldn't let Grandpa do was work his horses. He said Grandpa was stronger than a horse and he couldn't judge, because of his own great strength, how much a horse could stand. He was afraid Grandpa would hurt his horses.

My Grandpa Shelton and I cut the houselogs, scored and hewed them and split and hewed rocks for the chimney and for two fireplaces in one summer. We had cut board trees, sawed cuts, bolted the timber, and rove the boards in the dark of the moon. Grandpa said rive them in the dark of the moon they didn't curl on the roof in the sun. We had the sprawling six-room house (all the rooms were large) up so we could move into our new house by late September. Our house wasn't finished but we moved into it anyway.

So all the time we had worked together he had never got me to say that Robert E. Lee was the greatest man in the world and that Ulysses S. Grant was the worst General America had ever had. I had remained neutral. And he had never got me committed to his side. I had come through unscathed and was not on either side. And I wondered, since I knew we had the best father and the best mother ever children could have, why we had been the victims of being born between two worlds and on the border of the South and North. One thing I believed would come from our predicament of our having to practice diplomacy young, that we would grow to womanhood and manhood and be tolerant and to know how to get along with people. We have been such experts. Due to our early training, we could be called a family of diplomats.

The Weakling

I GOT up from my soft warm bed and walked over to the window. When I raised the window blind I saw the hills covered with snow. The snow on our smokehouse roof looked to be a foot deep. The branches on the white oaks in our yard were bent with snow. I could see the redbirds picking seeds from the dead ragweeds on the bank above our house.

"I'll show Ma and Pa I'm not a weakling," I thought. "I'll show them I can take it on the chin. I'll show them I got sand in my craw. I'm going hunting today. I can't help it if I am a weakling."

Then I raised my window where the cold January wind blew in and I felt it go through my pajamas onto my body. I took in deep breaths of icy wind. I pounded my ribs with my fists over my rheumatic heart. My heart fluttered like a bird. I got a little cold but I stood it like a man. I was tired of being called "The Weakling" among the Meadows boys.

Then I changed from my pajamas to my heavy fleece-lined underwear and my heavy wool socks. I slipped on heavy corduroy hunting britches and a wool shirt. I slipped my feet into my heavy lace boots. I pulled my single-barrel shotgun from the nails on the joist. I carried it in my right hand. I had my coat in my left hand. I went downstairs to breakfast.

When I went in the kitchen you ought to have heard Pa, brother Doc, and brother Harmon laugh. Harmon dropped his cup of coffee on the table and broke it, he got so tickled. Pa bent over the table and looked at his plate and laughed. Doc looked at his plate and laughed. Ma stopped frying more eggs in the skillet and looked at me.

"Where do you think you're going, Orbie, on a morning like this?" Pa asked.

"I'm going out and knock down a few cottontails," I replied.

Then Doc and Harmon started laughing again and holding their forks of ham near their opened mouths. They couldn't put the big bites into their mouths for laughing.

"What's so funny about going out to hunt on a day like this?" I asked.

"You can't make it on a day like this," Pa said. "Orbie, for sixty-one years I've been a country doctor among these hills. I know when a man's got a constitution and when he's a weakling. I know you've got a rheumatic heart!"

"That's just it, Pa," I said. "Stop right where you are! Don't say anything any more about my being a weakling. I'm tired of hearing it. I'm the weakling! Doc and Harmon are my strong brothers! Don't speak to me again about being a weakling. If my ticker stops this minute I'll never take another one of your pills. I'm through with this family. I'll show you all as soon as I eat my breakfast. I'm goin' hunting! I'm doing as I please from now on! I'm over twenty-one, am I not?"

"Yes, Orbie, you're twenty-two years old," Pa said. "You're your own man. If you want to get out and freeze to death on a day like this, just go to it! But remember I've warned you!"

"Yes, Pa," I said.

Doc and Harmon didn't finish their breakfasts for laughing. I went to the dabbling pan. I poured cold water out of the water bucket into the dabbling pan. I started to wash my face.

"Orbie, don't you want me to pour you some hot water out of the teakettle?" Ma asked. "You can't stand water that cold!"

"I'm tired of your waiting on me because you think I'm a weakling," I told my mother. "You and Pa think you've got only two men in this family! I'm here to tell you that you've got three this morning. Don't ever say 'Poor little Orbie's got a rheumatic heart' again to another person in this neighborhood."

Ma stood and looked at me with a fork in her hand. It was straight talk to Ma, but I meant it. I was riled. Then I turned to Pa.

"Pa, you go around telling about how tough Grandpa was. You've said that you saw him wash his face on cold winter mornings and throw the water up in the air from the pan. When the water hit the ground it was ice. Now come to the door and watch this."

When Pa saw the water freeze before it hit the snow, his eyes got big and shiny as silver dollars. Doc and Harmon stopped laughing at me. Now they smoked their pipes and looked at me while I ate my breakfast.

Soon as I washed down my last bites of ham, eggs, and hot buttered biscuits with two cups of hot black coffee, I got up from the table and put on my heavy hunting coat. I put on my mittens lined with rabbit fur. I started out at the door.

"Don't let him go, Ephriam," Ma said.

"He can't help himself," I told my mother. "I'm twenty-two, Ma. I'm my own man!"

"Let young Samson go," Pa said. "Wait for the coldest day in the year and then turn from a weakling to Samson! He thinks he's the man Pap was! But, Pap was a real man!"

"So am I," I said. "But I've got two lazy weakly brothers!"

"What do you say?" Doc asked me.

"You heard me," I told him. I slammed the door behind me.

"He'll freeze to death," I heard Harmon say.

"His heart won't let him climb the hills," I heard my mother say. But I didn't care what they said. "I would as soon be dead," I thought, "as to be called a weakling. I'd rather be in a grave without tombstones at my head and feet."

"I'll find rabbits sitting under the roots of turned-up trees," I thought. So I didn't call the hunting hounds. "I'll find rabbits under the edges of caved-in banks and in bunches of ragweeds and bull grass. I'll shoot their heads off and give them an easy death. They'll never know what happened. They'll die in their sleep. I'll fill this hunting coat with rabbits. I'll show my family that I'm no weakling."

The snow was nearly to the top of my boots. It was slow walking to pull through this deep snow. The wind was filled with flying frost. It was a cold wind that stung my face like yellow jackets had stung me in the apple orchard in July and August. The icy wind chilled me through my heavy clothes but I went on. I was not going to turn back. I was on my way to Shultz Creek. I was going up among the high hills at the head of Shultz to the slopes covered with broomsedge—the best place in the world for rabbits on cold winter days.

I climbed the hill behind our house. I held to sprouts on the steep hillside as I went up to the rock cliffs. I had to rest, then I would try again. I'd climb until my heart would start beating fast. Then I'd rest until my heart slowed down.

"Pa was right," I thought, "but why does he say I'm a weakling? Why does Harmon think I can't hunt? Just because he and Doc go out with Pa and they bring in birds and rabbits isn't any reason I can't do the same thing!"

I would get mad every time I thought about the way they left me at home. Then there was Ma pitying me to all the neighbor women. It made my blood boil.

The first thing I saw was a crow. He was flying low, fighting the strong wind, just above the tops of the frozen oak trees. I held my single-barrel to my shoulder. I cut down at him. I spilled him. He went flopping his wings to the ground on the steep bluff below me. I didn't go down to pick him up. I reloaded my gun and climbed to the top of the ridge. I was under a grove of pine trees now. The snow was not so deep here. It was easier walking too. I couldn't see our house below the cliffs. The air was still white with frost. The frozen oaks creaked above me. I didn't see a rabbit. All I heard was the hungry moan of the biting icy wind in the pine tops above my head. The flying frost was so thick in the air I could hardly see my way. I looked around the roots of trees for rabbits. I looked around the rocks and the sawbriar stools.

"They must be in their holes today," I thought. "I don't see anything stirring but crows, redbirds, and snow birds."

I didn't know where I was. I just followed the ridge toward Shultz. I had been on this ridge many times before. It didn't look natural to me now. The bull grass was snowed under. The ragweed patches were weighted with snow. I saw a red fox's track. It did me good to think a fox's track was close to me. I lit my pipe and smoked. I talked to myself. I followed the ridge for hours.

"About the right place to turn to my left and go down on Shultz Creek," I thought.

When I left the path I went into a snowdrift to my waist. I had a time getting out. My heart beat fast. I rested on the bank of snow. After I rested I stepped in my same tracks back to the ridge road. I was glad to get back. The wind swept across the ridge. It drifted big heaps of snow. I felt sleepy, tired, and sick.

"What if I freeze to death here," I thought. "Only the crows, hound dogs, buzzards, and foxes will find me. They won't find me until the snow melts and I thaw out. The buzzards, crows, hound dogs, and foxes will pick me clean and just leave my naked bones on this mountain."

Night closed in on me. I could reach out with my hand and get a handful of the darkness. I was sleepy. I laid down to rest. I closed my eyes. My bed was soft.

"I can't sleep here," I thought. "What will Pa and Ma think when I get home and don't have a rabbit! Harmon and Doc will laugh again at me. I must get up and knock down a dozen cottontails. I must be lazy. I am not tired."

I got up from a warm bed of leaves. The sun was shining. I was out in the pasture field not far from the house. I didn't want them to hear me shooting. I walked down among the ferns on a steep bank. I saw a rabbit's ears behind a bunch of ferns. I leveled my gun and clipped off his head. I reloaded my gun and started to pick up the rabbit for my hunting coat. Two rabbits were kicking on the ground.

"Two at one shot," I thought. "Not many times does a hunter kill two rabbits with one shell."

I put them in my hunting coat. I felt now like I was a man and a hunter. I started to walk around the bluff. I kicked a bunch of ferns. A pheasant flew up. I leveled my gun and shot. Just seemed like its life went out in a second. I picked the pheasant up and put it in my hunting coat.

"I was going to Shultz to hunt rabbits when right here in our cow pasture is plenty of game," I thought.

A rabbit jumped from under my feet. I aimed carefully as it leaped a bunch of briars. It tumbled to the ground. When I started to pick it up I saw a rabbit looking at me from a bunch of bull grass. I shot it. I picked up the two rabbits and put them in my hunting coat.

"Poor rabbits," I thought, "why don't they run for their lives? Why don't I miss them? I'm killing them right and left."

I shot away all the shells I had and I'd not missed a shot. I killed nineteen rabbits, thirteen birds, and two ringneck pheasants. I killed all these on the bluff above the little creek in our cow pasture. This part of our pasture was green with ferns. The rest of the pasture was brown with dead leaves and broomsedge.

I wiped the sweat from my face for I was warm now. I had such a heavy load of pheasants, quail, and rabbits to carry. I didn't think I'd ever get to the house.

"What will Pa and Ma think about their Orbie now," I thought. "Wonder if Harmon and Doc will think I'm a weakling."

A lot of thoughts went through my mind.

"When I went out to hunt, the snow was on the ground," I thought. "I'm going home now with my hunting coat filled with game. I am tramping on the dead leaves. It is autumn. The sun is shining on the dead leaves. It is a warm day and I am warm. I had a heart that would flutter like a bird. I can run now with a heavy load. My heart doesn't flutter. I'll run to the top of the hill with my load just to see. And I went off running just to see. The sweat streamed from my face but my heart never fluttered like a disturbed bird when a snake climbed up a tree to her nest to get her young.

"He's coming to, Pa," she said. "He's opening his eyes."

"Let 'im die, Temp," said a husky voice. "He's a Meadows, I believe. He's got that long nose and long stuck-out chin. If a Meadows is brought back to life in this house I'll never get over it! Erf Stillwell from Shultz giving life back to a Meadows? No, never!"

I looked above me. I never saw a prettier girl. Her black eyes, like shaded pools of deep water, were looking down at me. I could see she was shedding some tears. The tears shone like drops of dew on the grass in the early morning sunlight. Her hair was as black as the black oak bark. It fell around her shoulders.

"Where am I?" I asked.

"You're at Erf Stillwell's," said the same coarse voice that had said if I was a Meadows let me die. "Who are you anyhow?"

"Give me some water," I said, "then I will tell you who I am."

"Get him some water, Temp," said the coarse-voiced man who was standing over me now and looking down. "Let him tell us who he is."

"Stillwell's," I thought. "Am I dead? I started hunting in the deep snow. I went to sleep. I woke up and it was autumn. I killed a load of pheasants, quails, and rabbits. Now I'm waking up again with a girl over me looking down at my face shedding tears. Where am I? I must be dead. What is all of this about?"

"Am I dead?" I asked.

"You're not dead yet," said the old man, looking at me with a pair of mean eyes set in a wrinkled face. "You're at Stillwell's house, young man. Don't you know Erf Stillwell from Shultz?"

"I don't believe I do," I replied.

"You're a Meadows, aren't you?"

"Just a minute, Pa," Temp said.

I took the glass of water from her hand. I held it to my lips and it tasted good.

"I want more," I said.

"Not now," she said. Her voice was the softest voice I had ever heard.

"This seems like a dream," I said.

"You're on Shultz," she told me. "You're at Stillwell's. And, isn't your name Meadows?"

"Yes," I told her. "Why? How do you know?"

"Let him die, Temp," said the old man. "I'm the last Stillwell of flesh and blood. He's of the blood that shot my Oscar."

This big man stood over me. The fire danced in his black eyes. His beard was gray. His hair was long. His fists were big and gnarled with age like the roots on an old tree. I wanted to jump up and run but I couldn't run. I was lost.

"You've got the wrong Meadows," I said. "I've never shot a man in my life."

"My Oscar died," he said. "He was shot in the back. Enoch Meadows' boy waited until he turned around, then he shot my Oscar. Are you Enoch Meadows' boy?"

"I'm Ephriam Meadows' boy," I said.

"You're old Doc's boy, are you?"

"Yes, Pa's a country doctor," I said. "He tries to save lives. Our men folks have never killed anybody."

I was afraid to tell Erf Stillwell that Enoch Meadows was my father's twin brother.

"I'll declare, young man, I'm glad to hear this," he said.

"I'm glad too," Temp said.

"Glad you're not old Enoch Meadows' boy," Erf Stillwell said. "It's a good thing you're not of that family. You wouldn't live to tell the story."

"How did I get here?" I asked.

"Must I tell him, Pa?" Temp said.

"Yes, tell 'im, Temp," Erf Stillwell replied.

"My father and I were going over the Shultz Ridge to the store," she explained. "I saw a gun sticking out of a snowdrift. My father and I kicked away the snow. We found you. The snow had covered you. We were scared. We thought you were dead. There wasn't a track around you. I felt your heart. It was beating. We carried you and finally got you down to the house. Believe me, you are rugged and you can stand a lot of cold."

"Do you think so?"

"I told Temp you were as tough as a pine knot," Erf Stillwell said. "To think you'd hunt on a day like this! It takes nerve."

"Pa and Ma and my brothers call me a weakling," I said.

"You're no weakling," Erf Stillwell said. "You're what I call a man. You are as rugged as the old man used to be."

I felt so good I got up and sat on the side of the bed.

"Is your name Tempest?" I asked.

"Yes," she replied.

"She was born on a stormy night," Erf Stillwell said. "We called her Tempest for the storm. I call her Temp for short. The night Temp was born the thunder rocked the house. The lightning lit up these hills plain as daylight."

"I'm not goin' back," I thought. "I'm staying here if I can. She's the prettiest girl I have ever seen in my life. And she has saved my life. I'm a rugged man too! I'm like Grandpa. I'll make my home here among the hills on Shultz. I'm not a weakling any more. Folks will think I'm dead in the snow. Let them hunt the hills over for me. They can't track me for the wind has covered my tracks."

"This has been a hunt, a great hunt," I said. "I have found the life I'm looking for. I want to stay here."

"We can keep 'im, can't we, Temp?"

"Yes, we sure can," Temp said, smiling at me.

"I'll help you farm the corn," I said. "I can take it on the chin. I've got sand in my craw. I'm a Samson."

"We need a Samson in the field," Erf Stillwell said. "The plow will make a man of you."

"I'm glad I found you," Temp said, smiling again.

"I still believe I'm dead," I said. "I can't believe this is Shultz."

"See the creek down there," she said. "See the high hills over there covered with snow! See the dark timber on the far hill! See the pines on the ridge! You are alive. You are with us!"

But then there was a knock on the door. Erf Stillwell went to the door. When he opened the door there stood Harmon and Doc.

"Thank God we've found you alive," Doc said. "We couldn't track you for the winds have drifted the snow."

"We went to every house along the way looking for you, Orbie," Harmon said.

"How are you?" Doc asked.

"All right," I replied. "Why would you think I wouldn't be all right?"

"How did you get here?" Harmon asked. "Why are you sitting on the side of the bed?"

"Don't tell them, Temp," I said.

"We'll leave you for now and go home and tell Pa and Ma we've found you," Doc said. "Can we leave our brother with you until this spell breaks?"

"You can leave me here forever," I said.

"Yes, of course," Erf Stillwell said.

"If I can't stay forever let me stay a week," I said.

"But we will be back for you, Orbie," Doc said. "I see you're in a good warm house. And you're with friends! We must get home to tell we've found you!"

When they left Erf Stillwell's house I was glad to see them go. They would never say again, not after this, that I was a weakling. I had shown them and everybody else that I wasn't. I might have been a little crazy to go hunting on a day like this but I was no weakling.

A Christmas Present for Uncle Bob

"SON," Grandpa said to me, "we're not a-goin' to spend Christmas here!"

"Where're we a-goin' to spend Christmas, Grandpa?" I asked, following Grandpa to the barn.

Thoughts started stirring in my head like hornets stirring in their nest after being hit with a rock. I couldn't understand what Grandpa meant. He'd asked Pa, his eleventh child by his first wife, if I could come over and spend Christmas with him and Grandma. He told Pa that Christmas was lonely since his children had grown up and left the nest and that he liked to have his grandchildren around him at Christmastime.

"Well, Son," Grandpa said, stopping on the snow-hardened path, "I've only got one brother living. You know, yer Uncle Bob. And he keeps on a-complainin' that I never come to see him anymore. He said I had not spent Christmas with 'im for forty years and that I had not given 'im a present!"

"Are you a-goin' to see 'im, Grandpa?"

"Yep, thought I would!" Grandpa said. "And I'm a-takin' him a little present."

Then I didn't ask Grandpa another question as he stood looking at me with two dark eyes that looked sharp as briar-points from under shaggy eyebrows. Though the cold wind was whipping down Rove Creek like a draft through a windowless mountain shack, Grandpa didn't seem to mind. But it chilled my face for I didn't have the beard on my face to keep it warm like Grandpa had. But I didn't have to put up with a lot of icicles forming on my face like Grandpa did. Every now and then he had to break amber-colored icicles from the long beard that hid the watch chain on his vest. That was when Grandpa was chewing his plug tobacco and didn't spit straight or the wind blew the spittle back against his beard. However, the icicles that formed on the long horns of his gray mustache were never large and they were never amber-colored.

"But who will stay with Grandma?" I said, my teeth chattering.

"She'll stay with Mickie," Grandpa said.

Grandpa never called Pa by his right name. His right name was Mick. That was Grandpa's name, too. But Grandpa changed Pa's name a little since he had another son by my second Grandma with the same name. I had a Grandpa Mick Powderday, an Uncle Mick Powderday and Pa's name was Mick Powderday. And that's why Grandpa always called Pa Mickie and Uncle Mick Little Mick.

"Then, I can go with you if Grandma goes home," I said.

"Sure, sure," Grandpa said. "You could go with me if she didn't. Your Grandma has stayed alone many times before. . . . But this a-bein' Christmas time," he went on, "I thought she'd be better off with a little company around."

Then I thought of the long trip. It was sixty-nine miles to Dentonville, the big town of a thousand people where Uncle Bob lived.

"You'll like the trip, Son," Grandpa said as I stood looking down at the snow thoughtfully. "See, I've got the sled fixed up. New dogwood half-soles. It just runs over the snow like greased lightnin'. I've got the sled-bed filled with straw. And I've got red tassels for the mules' bridles and bells to jingle on their harness. Got a big lap-robe to spread over us and keep us warm, too."

When Grandpa told me how he was going, I was ready to go. I forgot Uncle Bob.

"I wouldn't miss the trip for anything," I said. "I sure want to go!"

"Run back to the shack and put on your sheepskin-lined coat," Grandpa said. "Put on your wool socks and your boots. Warm yourself before the fire. I'll have everything ready by the time you're ready."

Then I ran back into the house where Grandma was sitting smoking her pipe before the fire.

"So, you're a-goin' with 'im?" Grandma said.

"Yes," I said, wondering why Grandma had said this to me.

I sat up close to the big open fireplace where the big log blazed in many colors of flame. The heat from this roaring wood fire soon drove the cold from my body. But while I sat there Grandma didn't say another word to me. She smoked her pipe and looked into the fire and dreamed. When I got up to get my sheepskin-lined coat, my boots, sock-cap and gloves, she got up from her big rocker and knocked the ashes from her long-stemmed clay pipe on the jam-rock. Then she picked up the long-handled shovel and started banking the fire.

"Are you going with us, Grandma?" I asked.

"Nope," she said. "I'm goin' over to yer Ma's and Pa's. I wouldn't take that trip to Bob's for no amount of money!"

"But Grandpa's a-goin' to take Uncle Bob a Christmas present," I said.

"What's Mick got to buy a Christmas present with?" Grandma said. "Spends his pension money fer licker soon as he gits it. He's a-goin' to take Bob a gallon of white-lightnin' or somethin' like that, I 'spect."

"I don't know what he's a-goin' to take," I said.

"They want to get together for another spree," Grandma said. "It'll be like it was the last time they got together! Drunk and a-talkin' over old times and a lot of carryin' on."

I had my boots on now and then I slid into my big coat and pulled my sock-cap down my ears.

"You look like an Eskimo," Grandma said. She laughed when she looked at me. "But you'll need to be dressed like this in sicha weather! Mick a-takin' a child out in weather like this! And ye'll be two days on the road," Grandma sighed. "I don't know what's a-gettin' into Mick in his old days!"

"But I want to go, Grandma," I said. "I put my hands down into my rabbit-fur-lined gloves.

"Then go," Grandma said. "I'll tell your Pap about where you've gone. Maybe your Pap can do something with his Pap if he's a mind!"

When Grandma said these words they were almost muffled by the sound of jingling bells! It sounded like the way I used to think the harness on Santa Claus' reindeers sounded as they dashed over the clapboard shacks in the mountains bringing presents to good little boys and girls. And when I heard the jingling of the harness bells I shot out the door like wind before a storm. And there was Grandpa sitting on the front seat with a big lap robe over him. He had the whip across his shoulder and sat up there like Santa Claus, with the mules prancing and wanting to go. Honest, Grandpa looked a lot like the pictures I'd seen of Santa Claus! His long white beard came down to the lap robe and the upper part of his cheeks where the beard didn't grow were ruddy as ripe apples.

"Son, climb in," Grandpa said. "It's a fine day for a sled!"

The cold wind, filled with little hard pieces of flying frost, almost blew me down from the sled as I climbed in and spread the lap robe over me. Then Grandpa gave the mules the reins and we were off almost as fast as reindeers could have pulled us. I didn't tell Grandpa what Grandma had said about whiskey he was taking Uncle Bob. I didn't care if Grandpa was taking Uncle Bob a gallon of white-lightnin'. I didn't care if they did get drunk. Not now.

And I didn't mind the wind as I had when I followed Grandpa toward the barn. Not anything mattered now, not even the amber-colored icicles growing from his horns of mustache. For we were going down the narrow-gauge Rove Creek Hollow at a good speed. When we passed the shacks along the roads with our bells jingling, people came to the doors and windows, perhaps to see if Santa Claus was a-coming with his reindeers. And it made Grandpa feel good. He'd wave his big gloved hand that was almost as big as a ham of meat! Grandpa must have thought he was Santa Claus when he was just taking one present to his brother sixty-nine miles away!

As we rode pleasantly along, I thought of the days when I was a little boy, how Pa used to tell me that I could do something in life as great as Uncle Bob. He told me over and over again what a struggle Uncle Bob had in his young days to become a doctor. "He's just one of the old-fashioned country doctors," Pa would say. "But that 'was somethin.' " Then, I'd ask Pa why he hadn't become a Doctor like Uncle Bob and Pa would tell me that he had let his chance slip by when he was a young man and now it was too late for he was an old man with a family. And Pa would say over and over again to the strangers who came to our house his Uncle Bob was the only one of the Powderdays that had ever amounted to anything.

Then he would tell how Uncle Bob got tired of plowing the cornfield, looking at the south end of a mule on a steep mountain slope. How he started reading all the books he could borrow and took a teachers' examination and got a third-class certificate to teach school. He got thirty dollars a month and they had three-months' school terms in those days. But this wasn't what Uncle Bob wanted. He wanted to become a doctor. So he took the money and studied medicine three months a year for three years, teaching a school between each term of medicine. Finally he got his diploma and came back to doctor his fellow mountaineers. He heard of Denton County where there wasn't a really medical-doctor. There were many herb-doctors, faith healers and "granny" women to deliver babies. And Uncle Bob went there to compete with them. He found it hard at first but his fame spread. Soon Doctor Bob Powderday's fame spread when he probed in a man and got a bullet no one else could find. The man would have died if the bullet hadn't been removed.

When Uncle Bob first put out his shingle in Dentonville the Blairs and the Comptons were fighting each other in Denton

County, trying to wipe each other out. And Uncle Bob came in handy for he saved many a Blair, making him well enough to fight again; and he saved many of the Comptons and their in-laws who were fighting to exterminate the Blairs. Since he was the only doctor he worked for both sides and no one dared to harm him. And because there was so much shooting in Denton County, thirty-four had been killed in one year, Uncle Bob became a "specialist" on probing for bullets. As Uncle Bob had told Pa the last time we visited him, he had found his life's work in Denton County to be very exciting and he wouldn't think of ever moving back to Lantern County. He said Lantern County was too dead a place since they averaged one shooting a month and Lantern County had two doctors.

I said after my first and last visit, seven years ago, when Pa took me to see Uncle Bob, that I would never go back again. I remembered now, as we rode the snow, how I didn't like Uncle Bob. Pa had told me all the wonderful stories about him: how he had amounted to so much in life and when I saw him, he looked more like a failure to me. He lived in one of the best homes in Dentonville, county seat of Denton County. I remembered he told Pa the town was in the center of the county, right in the center of his trade and he could ride to any part of the county by muleback in less than twelve hours. He told Pa Dentonville was the center of all the shooting.

But his weather-boarded and painted house among the paintless shacks and his big yard filled with trees didn't make him look like a success to me. He wore a shabby unpressed suit that bagged at the knees and his beard was longer than Grandpa's and his mustache looked like bicycle handlebars. When I first saw him he was walking around with a big pistol in his hand. I wondered at first what he was going to do with the pistol. But I didn't have long to wait to find out. What Uncle Bob did sort of gagged Pa and it made me scream and try to take off and leave his place forever.

It happened when Uncle Bob went into the smokehouse on the corner of his lot and dragged out an embalmed cadaver that he called "Old Charlie." When I saw his dead man staring at me with lightless eyes I started to take off and Uncle Bob laughed like a roaring wind as Pa run me down and held me. Uncle Bob propped "Old Charlie" against a tree and then he counted his steps, twelve of them, and then he pulled his pistol and let "Old Charlie" have a bullet square between the eyes.

"That's a-hittin' 'im, Uncle Bob!" Pa said excitedly as he held onto me while I screamed and tried to tear loose.

Then Uncle Bob shot "Old Charlie" again, again, again and again.

"I'll show you how to probe for a bullet," Uncle Bob said as he put his smoking pistol back in a holster. "It's hard to get a body around here anymore, Mickie. People are funny about their dead. They want to put 'im away but 'Old Charlie' was a stranger killed in the coal mines and I went there and picked 'im up because he didn't have any kinfolk to put 'im away. And," Uncle Bob went on, "Old Charlie's saved many a Blair and a Compton. Come on watch me probe!"

Uncle Bob pulled a long knife and started to go to work!

"I don't want to watch Uncle Bob probe," I said.

"Let 'im go, Mickie," Uncle Bob said. "Don't hold 'im any longer. He'll soon get used to this if he stays around here!"

Pa turned me loose and I went over the hill where the cherries were red in the bushy-topped low trees and the grapes were big and blue-water-colored and luscious on the vines. I looked back once and I saw Uncle Bob hide the neck of a horse-quart under his gray mustache. Then I heard him gurgle, gurgle, gurgle and say "aham" and lick his mustache with his long red tongue and pass the bottle to Pa.

"Good stuff," Pa said, giving Uncle Bob his horse-quart. "I needed this, Uncle Bob!"

"I always need a snort too, before I probe," Uncle Bob said.

The grapes and the cherries I was eating were good. And I thought I had something to brag about. So I said, "Gee, these cherries are sweet and the grapes are delicious!"

"Ought to be," Uncle Bob laughed as he held a long-bladed knife in his hand. "There's been enough ashes from cadavers buried around the roots of them cherry trees and grapevines."

When Uncle Bob said this I spit the cherries from my mouth,

gagged and came down the tree. Uncle Bob thought it was awful funny for he laughed and laughed and Pa even laughed. Uncle Bob laughed until he had to wait awhile because he was shaking so before he could probe for bullets. . . . All these thoughts came to me as we drove along over the snow. I had tried to forget them when we left the house. I had set my mind against these thoughts, but they became alive in my head like hornets disturbed in their nest.

After we left Rove Creek we hit the Big Sandy Road and we traveled all day along this river except for a brief stop at a little tavern in Maceville, where we got a hot meal for ourselves and where we fed and watered our mules. Often we slid along where we could see the river frozen over and a lot of people, old and young, skating on the ice with their many colored scarfs flying in the wind. But when they heard our bells tingling and saw the red tassels flying in the wind from the mules' harness they stopped skating and looked toward us. And they started hollowering, "Santa Claus" at Grandpa.

Before we put up for the night in Burtonsville, a little mountain town wedged down between two big mountains, the bright sickle moon came early into the sky. The dark clouds cleared away and the empty fields of snow under the wan starlight and the pale moonlight looked bright as day. I'd never enjoyed a day more in my life.

"This is half-way," Grandpa said, as we drove up to the little hotel. "Tomorrow we'll finish this happy journey."

After we'd seen that our mules were fed and housed in good stalls for the night and that the sled was in the barn, Grandpa and I went inside the hotel and removed our heavy coats. Then we sat down to a good hot meal. I was awfully hungry and after we'd finished eating Grandpa smoked his evenin' cigar before we went to bed.

Grandpa was as hot in his long red-woolen night shirt as the pot-bellied stove in the Plum Grove schoolhouse. I must've got against him in the night for I dreamed it was a hot day in July and I was picking peaches and carrying them off the hill from the orchard in a round bushel basket. I thought I'd stop under the shade of the yellow locust trees and wipe the sweat from my face with a big bandana. And I'd pick up the peaches again and I'd start sweating.

And then I dreamed Uncle Bob came from behind the peach tree that was bending with ripe fruit and he said it was the ashes of his cadavers that made the peaches big, red and mellow. He said this just as I was about to take a big bite from the side of a delicious peach. And I threw the peach on the ground. And then Uncle Bob, Dr. Robert Powderday, rubbed a long skinny pale hand over his long white whiskers while with the other hand he reached down on his hip and pulled a long blue pistol from the holster. And when he aimed the pistol at my forehead as he laughed like a roar of July wind through the wilted peach tree leaves. And then the pistol cracked and I told Uncle Bob that he didn't hit me. But he held the smoking pistol in one hand and reached down into the sheath on his other hip and pulled a long bright-bladed knife.

"I'll probe for bullets anyhow," he said. "I'll save another Blair, another Compton! A doctor never gets through with his learnin'. He must always know how to probe!"

And when Uncle Bob came toward me with the knife, laughing as he came, I started to take off. I was running through the peach orchard with my empty basket on my arm and the peach tree limbs were hitting me in the face with their pods of wilted leaves that felt like water-soaked dish rags dabbing against my hot face.

"God Almighty, Son," Grandpa said, sitting up in bed. "What's the matter with ye? Have ye got the fidgets?"

I'd kicked all the cover off Grandpa and I was sitting up in bed hot as a roasted potato.

"I was dreamin' of Uncle Bob," I said. "I thought he'd shot me and started probing for the bullet."

"Go back to sleep and get some rest," Grandpa said. He laid back down and pulled the quilts upon him. "You'll freeze a man to death the way ye kick the kiver."

Then I snuggled up against Grandpa and was off to a dreamless sleep. Next thing I knew Grandpa was shaking and telling me to get dressed in a hurry for breakfast was ready. He said the mules were fed, harnessed and ready for us as soon as we had finished breakfast. It didn't take me long to wash up, dress myself and get down to breakfast. But it was so early that I didn't eat much. It was four in the morning and it hadn't been long enough since we'd had supper.

I'll never forget how Grandpa took the reins and we drove away by the light of the morning stars. Harness bells were tinkling and the sled runners were creaking and we could hear them plainly for the morning wind was still. We heard birds chattering in the foddershocks as we drove past cornfields where the wigwamed shocks sagged beneath the snow. We turned left up Tug Pork and then we cut right again and went up Denton Creek.

"We'll be thar by noon if we keep on a-havin' sicha good luck," Grandpa said. He gave me the lines to hold while he lit a big cigar, "Old Bob'll be shocked to see us! And the little present I have fer 'im 'll make 'im laugh with joy!"

I wanted to forget the crazy dream and the crazy thoughts I'd been having about Uncle Bob. I never wanted them to be stirred up in my head again. So I didn't think about Uncle Bob, or ask about the present Grandpa was takin' him. I looked over the empty fields where I saw snowbirds around the foddershocks and the dead ragweed stems hunting ragweed seeds for their breakfasts. And I watched the foggy breaths of the mules fade on the bright crisp December air as we drove over a piece of road where we went through a tunnel. I'd remembered this road and I remembered that on the other side was Dentonville.

"Wonderful," Grandpa said when the mules had dragged our sled over the piece of snowless road.

We'd come into the edge of Dentonville where there were a lot of little shotgun houses without paint sitting up around on the side of the mountain. As Grandpa turned the mules up Main Street our tingling bells brought everybody out of his house in Dentonville. People had looked at us from their shotgun porches and from the little windows where the houses had windows. I never saw as many faces as I saw in this town. And everybody yelled "Santa Claus" when they saw Grandpa with his long white beard, his crimson cheeks where the beard didn't cover and his whip in his hand. We turned right and drove up to the painted weather-boarded house with leafless cherry trees and naked grape arbors in the big front yard.

"Mickie, you old skalawag," Uncle Bob shouted as he ran out on the porch. "Yegads, I thought you's Santa Claus comin' to this house!"

And then Uncle Bob gave a big laugh like the roar of December wind that was rising and blowing like a draft down this narrow-gauged valley as he hurried out to our sled.

"Maybe I am Santa Claus," Grandpa said, laughing louder than he did when our Murt mule reached over and bit Dick on the ear and made Dick squeal just before we went into the tunnel.

"How are you, Mickie?" Uncle Bob said, reaching Grandpa his big hand.

"Well as common, Bob," Grandpa said.

"I never expected you to get back to Dentonville again," Uncle Bob said.

"You can blame the weather for this," Grandpa said, shaking Uncle Bob's hand. "We had enough snow for a long sled ride and no sign of the snow's meltin'. So I thought I'd come and fetch you a present!"

"It's not that white-lightnin' that Steve Pratt made like you brought me before?" Uncle Bob asked. He laughed louder than the December wind in the barren cherry trees as he let loose of Grandpa's hand.

"No, this is a better present than that," Grandpa said.

"I'll never forget that 'lightnin'," Uncle Bob said. "It took all the hide off the roof of my mouth and burnt me all the way down. I could exactly tell where that stuff lit in my craw!"

Then Grandpa and Uncle Bob laughed and slapped one another on the back.

"And there's my little fraid Uncle," Uncle Bob said, noticing me for the first time. "I wonder if he remembers the last time he was here and I probed on 'Old Charlie'?"

"I sure do," I said.

"Well, well," Uncle Bob said, "Mickie, you and the boy get

out and come in! I'll have Ronnie to unharness the mules and put 'em in the barn and feed 'em."

"Who's Ronnie?" Grandpa said.

"Well, he's not a Blair and he ain't a Compton," Uncle Bob said. "He's a neutral boy I picked up in this county to feed my horses and keep my bridles, buggy and saddles mended. Sometimes he drives me out where I have a patient plugged with a bullet!"

"You mean the fight's still a-goin' on?" Grandpa said.

"That's why I had to hire a neutral boy," Uncle Bob said. "I couldn't afford to hire a man from either clan. I'd be takin' sides. It wouldn't work!"

"Gee, that's bad," Grandpa said, shaking his head. "Remember how the Powderdays fit the Van Horns? Never had a man to die a natural death back in them days! I think of how poor Pap finally got it with a double-barrel!"

"Yep, it's bad," Uncle Bob said. "Once the soldiers came in and they declared martial law! Fight stopped while they were here. Soon as they went away it broke out again like leaves come on trees after April rains!"

"Are you doin' any more probing?" I asked Uncle Bob.

"Not anymore, son," he said. "Can't get a cadaver. People are so foolish about their dead anymore! Can't find any strangers killed in the mines! Those killed in the mines have kinfolks around to bury them!"

Then Uncle Bob laughed and Grandpa laughed fit to die. I don't know who laughed the loudest and I didn't see anything funny to laugh about.

"Oh, Ronnie," Uncle Bob yelled, "come get the mules!"

Then Grandpa got out of the sled and I followed Grandpa, who walked stiffly because he'd sat so long in one place. But he walked back alongside the sled and started clearing away the straw.

"Tell Ronnie to come on," Grandpa said. I looked down on the bottom of the sled-bed where I saw a box shaped like a guitar. It was little on one end and big up near the other.

"I've got you a real present, Brother Bob," Grandpa said. "It's a lot better than the white-lightnin' I fetched you!"

Uncle Bob looked funny. He didn't know what Grandpa was doing with such a funny box. But when Grandpa unstapled the hasp and lifted the lid that was fastened on hinges, Uncle Bob knew.

"Oh, Mickie," he raised his voice. "Where did you get 'im! It's a life-safer and I need him!"

"If I'd known that," I said, feeling sick, "I'd never been in that sled."

"Where'd you get 'im, Mickie?" Uncle Bob asked, laughing like I'd never heard a man laugh before.

"A stranger that came to Lanternville last Stock Sale Day," Grandpa said. "He was a-standin' as close to me as you are when he raised his head and let out a little squeal like a pig and just fell over dead as Collins' ram. And I asked fer 'im right thar if nobody claimed him. Waited a week after he's embalmed and nobody claimed him. All I had to pay was the embalming cost. So I fetched 'im to you! Christmas closed at hand so I saved him for you for a present!"

"What a present, what a present," Uncle Bob said. "You couldn't have fetched me a better one. I need to exercise my hands a little on probing again with this shootin' between the Comptons and Blairs gettin' hotter than it's ever been."

Then Uncle Bob got one side of the box and Grandpa got the other up near the head. Ronnie and I tailed the little end as we walked across to the little house on the corner of the big yard.

"This wouldn't be a Christmas present for me," I said.

"Nor me either," Ronnie said. His jersey-colored hair was tangled by the wind.

"But a Christmas present, whether it's big or small, is something you want most," Uncle Bob said. "This is the greatest Christmas present I ever got in my life!"

And Uncle Bob's eyes lit up like candle flames in the night and his lips curving in a smile separating his whiskers and his big handlebar mustache. I'd never seen a happier man than Uncle Bob. Grandpa was happy because he'd made Uncle Bob so happy with the last present he may ever give his brother. Grandpa was eighty-five and Uncle Bob was older. I didn't know how much. And since they were pleased, I was pleased and Ronnie had to be pleased.

The Old Law Wasn't Strong Enough

"DON'T do that, Flem," Grandpa said. "You ought to have more feelin' than to harm a pig! It doesn't know any better than to come in the house."

"I've never been ust to pigs in the house," I told Grandpa. Then he looked at me with his cold blue eyes. They shone like icicles in the sun in the oil lamplight's yellow glow. "That pig run against my leg and nearly knocked me down."

I had kicked his pig hard enough with the toe of my brogan shoe to break a panel of its ribs. Knowin' what my Grandpa had planned to do, I had come early to help him with his plans.

"Felix, you're gettin' above your raisin' when you can't stand to be in the house with my pet pig," Grandpa said. He limped from the kitchen into the dogtrot with a five-gallon can of coal oil in his hand. I had carried the can of oil from the woodshed to the dogtrot from him.

Then I picked up a two-gallon can of coal oil which I had also fetched from the woodshed. I carried the can out into the dog-trot to prepare for the night's work that was to come. I can't figure Grandpa out, I thought. Grandpa is kind to dogs, chickens, pigs, mules and cows but he'll kill our enemy.

When I reached the dogtrot with my can of coal oil, Grandpa

was talkin' to a crowd of our kinfolks who had arrived and who had gathered around. "Old Okie shot me, didn't he?" Grandpa said in a loud voice. He waved his big arms in the lamp-lighted dogtrot. "Are you, my blood-kin, too low-lifed to let him get by? All of you are the leaves from my tree! You are the sprouts from my acorns. My leg gets worse every year! Soon I won't be able to go without a crutch. I want to get this job done while I'm still able to walk on two legs!"

"We're with you, Pap," Uncle Jarvis said. He looked at Grandpa with mean eyes. He fondled the barrel of his gun with his rough calloused hand. Uncle Jarvis was a timber cutter with broad shoulders and long arms. He could sink a double-bitted ax deeper into a hardwood oak than any man of our clan. He could sink it to the eye of the ax every time he swung the ax over his shoulder with a lick.

"We've come to hep you, Pap," Uncle Seymour said while he ran his big pale hand up and down his rifle barrel. Uncle Seymour was a coalminer with blue-slate stains around his fingernails that were hard for lye-soap and water to remove.

"My sons, be careful," Grandma said. She came out to the dogtrot smoking her long-stemmed clay pipe. "You know how suddenly death can come to one of you in these mountains. You can be bushwhacked and kilt."

"But they're inside, Ma," Uncle Purvey said. "They're in the house feastin' tonight. They won't be expecting us. We've got our plans laid. We can't miss."

Uncle Purvey was a coalminer too, with blue-slate stains around his fingernails.

"They feast at hog-killin' time, Ma," Uncle Kale said. "They feast on backbones and spare ribs and drink their moonshine."

Uncle Kale was tall and his frame was spare of flesh. He was the farmer among my uncles who plowed the steep slopes with a span of mules. He looked like a gnarled tough-butted white oak growing on a poor mountain slope.

"If my plans work, I know we got 'em this time, Sibbie," Grandpa said to Grandma. "It won't be like it was before. They won't be cuttin' notches on their gun stocks. We'll be cuttin' the notches on ours. They cut a notch for me when they shot me in the leg."

"But Grover and Jad sleepin' on The Hill over the last fracas," Grandma said. Her lips trembled as she spoke. "The two notches counted for them. When I get to thinkin' about my sons I feel like takin' a gun and goin' with you!"

"But you can't do that, Mother," Uncle Bill Simpson said.

Uncle Bill wasn't any blood kin to us but he married Aunt Vie, Grandpa's and Grandma's youngest girl. This made him a part of our clan. This made it his duty to come to help us fight the Sizemores. He was carryin' two buckshot under his skin he had got from the last fracas. Uncle Bill Simpson wasn't exactly like we were about this warfare but he was obliged to help out. When Uncle Grover and Uncle Jad were killed and Grandpa was mortally wounded in the leg, Uncle Bill Simpson had to come to Grandpa's aid. Aunt Vie had seen to it that her husband went to help her father. And when he talked to Grandma, he always called her mother.

I looked at my uncles when they talked to Grandpa and Grandma. Each one carried a rifle. Each one had from one to two pistol butts stickin' from a holster on his hip or from his hip pocket. Each one had his can of kerosene that I had to fetch from the woodshed to the dogtrot in preparation for this night.

"Kill 'em and burn 'em hair and limb," Grandpa said. "Don't leave a one to sprout the Sizemore seed! Do it while I'm a livin' man and when the time comes for me to die, I'll die a happy man to know that I helped to rid these hills of Sizemores."

"That's the only way to treat Sizemores, Pap," Uncle Cy said.

Now, Uncle Cy was the quiet one, who always listened while others talked. He was the smallest of my uncles, who trapped, dug wild roots and raised a garden to make a living. He was considered the most dangerous of all of our clan.

"Let's be off to get 'em," Grandpa said. He started limpin' down the dogtrot with his can of coal oil in one hand and his long rifle in the other.

"Don't take too many chances, Mort," Grandma warned Grandpa. She drew a cloud of smoke from her long pipestem as her five sons and her son-in-law followed down the dogtrot.

"Why didn't Felix come too?" Grandma asked me as I started to follow.

"Because Pa don't believe in killin'," I said.

"It's because that mother of yourn is a Sizemore," Grandma said. "She ain't much akin to old Okie Sizemore's mean set but she's got some of their blood in her veins. To think my son Felix won't come to his father's aid and to avenge his dead brothers on The Hill!"

I didn't say another word to Grandma. I was afraid she wouldn't let me go along. I hurried down the dogtrot. I wanted to see what was going to happen.

It was a moonless night and Grandpa led the way, since he knew the paths we were to take.

"The Sizemores always have their hog-killin' feasts in old Okie's big log house," Grandpa said. "They think the big thick walls is safe against bullets. When old Okie built his house he scored and hewed the logs and notched them down until they laid on one another. He didn't leave cracks to chink and daub. And he made big thick shutters to cover the few winders. He keeps 'em closed at night. He tried to build a bulletproof house. But we'll have a surprise for his clan tonight. We won't be tryin' to shoot through the cracks or winders."

We climbed up a path through our orchard so narrow that we had to follow each other. When one talked it was just above a whisper. When a coal oil can rubbed against a brush it made a strange noise. Maybe it just seemed like a strange noise to me on this night. I could hear Grandpa gettin' his breath hard as we neared the hilltop where we reached the ridgeroad. And my uncles were breathin' hard as mules when they snaked heavy saw logs up hill slopes from the timber woods.

"Let's wind a minute," Grandpa whispered when we reached the ridgeroad. "It'll be easier goin' from here. It's my leg gettin' weaker and weaker as the days pass."

Uncle Bill filled his pipe and pulled a match from his hatband, where he stuck a row of matches to keep 'em dry. When he struck the match on his overall pants leg, Grandpa whispered, "Put that fire out, Bill! We don't want to get shot! You never know where a Sizemore is lurkin' on a dark night!"

Grandpa wouldn't let anybody smoke as we walked out the ridgeroad. But one thing Grandpa did let my uncles do, for he did it himself. Soon as we reached the path that led down the finger of a hill toward the Sizemore's house, Grandpa pulled a horse-quart from his hip and passed it around after he'd taken the first big swig.

"That's what it takes to bring out all the nerve there is in a man," Grandpa said. Then he passed the quart to Uncle Jarvis and he swigged and passed it to Uncle Seymour. It went from uncle to uncle while dreams went through my head.

Now where we stopped was the place I had met Subrina Sizemore when she had gone to the pasture to drive the cows home to the milkgap to be milked in the evening. I had come to our pasture to get our cows and take them home to be milked. There was no war between us. Near the oak where we had stopped, I had held her in my arms. I had kissed her.

Grandpa, Grandma and my uncles didn't know this. If they had known about my love for her and my dreams of marrying her someday, I wouldn't have been along tonight. I knew she would be at the feast. I hoped and prayed no harm would come to her. I'd do my best to save her. And this was the reason I had come along. I didn't carry a gun. All I did was help them with the kerosene.

Now I tried to think what it would be like to see flames shooting from a house with Subrina in it. I thought of her hair, as soft and the same golden color as August cornsilks and her eyes as blue as mountain water over gravels in a deep blue stream. And her eyelashes were like the wild ferns that grew on stream banks and leaned toward the water. She was as slender and as straight as a young sapling and as soft as the young sassafras leaves in early spring. I couldn't bear the thoughts of her going up in smoke and flame and be left ashes among the ashes of the Sizemore's big log fortress for the mountain winds to scatter over our rugged earth.

She spoke honey words to me. She loved me and I loved her. And I would marry her too if I could even if she was my fourth, fifth or sixth cousin on my mother's side.

After they had finished drinking all the moonshine from the horse-quart Uncle Kale, the last to sip, threw the empty bottle on the ground.

"Not a whisper among you," Grandpa said as he started walking on and we followed.

After we had walked a short distance, Grandpa stopped in the middle of the path. We eased up close to him so we could hear him whisper.

"I brought six big coffee sacks along," Grandpa whispered. "While the Sizemores feast, all of you but Kale take your sacks right down there and fill 'em with dry leaves and broomsage. Carry 'em right down there and dump your sacks around Sizemore's fort. Kale will go with me to stand guard while you work. We'll show you where to put the leaves and broomsage. They're in that house, all right. And we'll get 'em! An eye for an eye, a tooth for a tooth! I believe in the old Law, only it wasn't made strong enough!"

We put our coal oil cans together and my uncles laid their rifles down by the oil cans. They carried their pistols for fear some of the Sizemores might hear us.

"They're through with their feast by now," Grandpa whispered. "They are full of backbones and spareribs and now they're drinkin' their hooch. Now's the right time to work before the mornin' moon comes up."

While we filled our sacks Grandpa and Uncle Kale went down to the house. Grandpa must have soon made friends with Okie Sizemore's hounds. I heard them bark a few times. Then I heard the hounds' friendly whines.

We carried load after load of dry leaves and broomsage and emptied our loads against the big walls. We must have worked over an hour. Grandpa and Uncle Kale stood guard while we worked. And when we brought a load Uncle Kale would show us where to place it while Grandpa stood with his rifle cocked facin' the front door. We weren't takin' any chances for we could hear loud talkin' and laughin' inside. The Sizemores were makin' merry after their feastin' with their drinkin'!

We put a layer of dry leaves and broomsage all around the walls of the house and spread them about ten feet into the yard. Okie Sizemore's gang of hounds found our leaves a comfortable bed to sleep on. When Grandpa whispered we had carried enough leaves and broomsage, that all the groundwork was laid, we went back and got our cans of kerosene and rifles. We sprinkled kerosene from the spouts of our cans over the leaves and broomsage. We had to walk as quietly as possible in our heavy brogan shoes over the dry rustlin' leaves. And when Okie's hounds felt the damp fluid from the cans, they left their beds.

"I'm glad they've done that," Grandpa whispered to Uncle Kale. "I'd hate to hurt one of old Okie's hounds. They can't help what he's done. A poor hound dog ain't inhuman. And they can't fight back like a man can. It would be a pity to kill his hounds."

After we'd poured the coal oil over the leaves and broomsage, we walked as quietly as we could over to Grandpa to take more orders.

"Everybody got his gun ready?" Grandpa whispered.

There was not an answer. That meant everybody was ready. And it was so still I could hear my uncles' and Grandpa's breathing. And in the distance I could see the big moon just edging up over the dark mountain ridges.

"We've just timed this thing right," Grandpa whispered. "The moon's a-comin' up! And let's hurry, for somebody in that house might come to the outdoor privy. And he'd wonder what all the leaves and broomsage were doin' around the house! He might get the smell of oil but poured out in mountain air it loses its scent."

"We're rarin' to go, Pap," Uncle Cy said. I watched him fondlin' the trigger guard of his long rifle in the dim moonlight.

"Cy and Bill, you go to yan side of the house and watch t'other door," Grandpa said. "Soon as ye get back there, strike a match to our groundwork. When we see you light, we'll fire from this side. Rest of you stay with me. Here's the door they'll make fer and we'll pick 'em off like we do squirrels cutting in a hickory tree in August and September. We'll avenge your brothers on

The Hill and the white swelling in my leg. No ust to watch the winders since they have the shutters fastened."

"All right, Pap," Uncle Cy whispered. He and Uncle Bill hurried to the other side of the house.

When they walked away we heard great talkin' and laughter inside the house. We heard them cursin' the Gullets.

"They'll be a-cussin' more than the Gullets in a few minutes," Grandpa whispered to Uncle Kale. "We'll give somethin' to cuss about. We'll give 'em some of their own medicine! We'll give 'em a lot of what they give us a year ago! A year has been a long time to wait for us Gullets, who are slow to forget."

"There's the light of the match, Grandpa," I said. "Uncle Cy and Uncle Bill are settin' fire to the leaves!"

"But what's the matter?" Grandpa said. "The match went out! There's no flame!"

When Grandpa took a few steps forward he was followed by my uncles. I took steps backwards up the hill. I got behind an oak and then another as I made my way toward the ridgeroad.

"It won't burn," I heard Uncle Cy say. His voice was too loud. There was anger in his voice."

"You reckon Steve Bostick smelled a mouse when we bought all the ile?" Grandpa said above a whisper. "Ye reckon he put water in our cans! He's some a-kin to the Sizemores!"

Then a hound barked. And the little round lights from the auger holes bored through the logs went out.

"Reckon it could have been my grandson," Grandpa whispered hoarsely. "You wouldn't betray his Grandpa and our Gullet clan! He bears the name Gullet!"

I couldn't answer the charge. I was putting as much distance between my grandpa's and uncles' guns as I could. My breath was gettin' short, for I was running uphill in the dim moonlight. I had just got behind a tree when the guns begun to blaze out of the auger holes.

"Flat on the ground, my sons," Grandpa shouted in his natural voice. "Behind a tree if you can! Take kiver! We've been betrayed."

I stood behind the tree and heard bullets wheeze and sing past me, striking the timber with thuds like a hammer striking green oak bark on the winter trees.

I watched long streaks of flames coming from the north wall of the Sizemores' big log fortress house while I made it on a few steps more to the big oak between our cow pastures where I had met so many times with Subrina.

"Thank God she's safe" went through my mind. I dared not speak.

"Let them spend their ammunition," Grandpa said in a louder voice so all my uncles could hear.

"But it's hot here," Uncle Cy said. "I've been grazed by a bullet!"

"Careful, aim at the lighted auger holes," Grandpa ordered his sons and son-in-law.

"But Pap, we can only hit their rifle barrels," Uncle Seymour said. "Let's crawl on our bellies out of here!"

"Where are you, Felix?" Grandpa asked. "Are you safe?"

I didn't answer Grandpa. I was safe behind our love tree. Our big oak had sheltered Subrina and me when it leaked in spring from spring rains and summer sun. Now on this winter night it was sheltering me from a hail of bullets that was coming my way, for I was caught in the line of fire coming from the Sizemore clan. Grandpa had made his plans to get them and he would have too, if oil hadn't been poured from the cans and water put in. Grandpa would have burned the Sizemore house and he and my uncles would have shot all who tried to escape the burning house.

Now firing from the auger holes let up but I knew Sizemores' long hot rifles rested in these holes so a bullet from the Gullet rifles couldn't with a chance in a hundred hit one of these holes in the right. The Sizemores were fighters. Grandpa knowing this is why he'd make his plans to burn them out.

I heard noises on the ground. I heard the brown oak leaves rustling on the ground.

"It was too close," I heard Uncle Seymour whisper. "I got a hole through my right ear I can put my little finger through."

"Better your ear than your head," Uncle Bill whispered.

There had always been laughter among my uncles, aunts,

Grandpa and Grandma about Uncle Seymour's big ears. None of the others had big ears that stuck out like a mule's ears. My father used to tease his brother and tell him he was marked with a mule since he had such big ears.

"Betrayed," Grandpa said in his natural voice as they came crawling up the hill toward me. "We are lucky to get out alive—only one wounded in the ear! Who was the betrayer?"

"A Sizemore kin," Uncle Kale said in his mad booming voice. "Never would a Gullet betray the name!"

Now they were coming too close. I could see the outlines of their bodies in the dim moonlight as they squirmed on the ground like crawling snakes from tree to tree and behind trees as fast as they could.

I eased away from behind our love-oak tree, keeping the tree between them and me. I doubted they were looking up. But I knew what it meant to be safe, for all members of the Gullet clan could take true aim and fire their long rifles in a second. They could fire from the hip with their pistols and hit a target. I'd seen them do it.

But right now I was putting the distance between them and me on my young legs, running for home as I'd never run before.

Love in the Spring

IT was last April when I met Effie. It was over at the Put-Off Ford at the Baptis foot-washing. Effie is a Slab Baptis. She was there having her feet washed. And I can't forget that day in April. It is always work in the spring. Fence to fix. Plowing to do. Cattle to tend to. Seems like everything is to do in the spring on the place. Planting crops is the big job. We don't have no place to go only to church and we don't feel like going there only on Sunday. That is the day we have off and we don't have that day off until we've milked seven cows and slopped the hogs and got in wood and got up water for the day. I can't forget that Sunday in last spring when I met Effie. I just packed in the last load of wood and Mom says to me: "Elster, you are going to fall for a woman sometime so hard that it's going to hurt you. Run around and talk about Mort Anderson being in love and how silly he is. Wait till you fall in love once. The love bug is going to bite you right over the heart."

I went to the baptizing with a clean white starched shirt on and a blue necktie and blue serge pants and black slippers. I looked about as good in them as I can look. I felt good just to get off to the foot-washing. I remember that row of elms along Little Sandy River had just started to leaf out. The rest of the hills just had a few sycamores and poplars down along the creeks that had leafed a little. It was a pretty morning. And down by the ford I never saw as many people in my life gathered at that one place. And I've seen a lot of baptizings there. Horses hitched to the trees with ropes and bridle reins. Wagons here and there with washing-tubs of grub in them and chears where whole families rid miles in them to the foot-washing. And horses eating yaller corn out'n the wagon beds of a lot of the wagons. I just walked down where they's singing "Where the Healing Waters Flow." It was soft music and I wished I was a child of the Lord's then. Good people—the Baptis is—we live neighbors to them. Ain't no better people to help you out in a time of sickness or weedy crops in the spring. Come right in and help you out. Now on this bank and washing feet. I walked down along the edge of the river where the horseweeds had been tromped down. I just wanted to look the crowd over. A whole row up and a whole row down. The row standing up was a-washing the feet of them on the ground. Just setting there on the ground as unconcerned and washing feet. Then they would sing another verse of "Where the Healing Waters Flow."

I looked up in front of me. I couldn't believe my eyes. I saw the prettiest woman I ever saw in my life. She was prettier than a speckled pup. Honest I never saw anything like her. Eyes that just looked at you and melted like yellow butter on hot corn bread—blue kind of eyes—and a face that was smooth as silk and cheeks the color of the peeling on a roman beauty apple in September. Her hair was the color of golden corn silks in August hanging from the shooting corn. Hair pretty and curly waving in the wind. I never saw a woman so pretty in my life. Her hands didn't look to me like no hands that had held to the hoe handle like my mother's hands and my sisters'. Her hands were pretty and soft. Her teeth were white as a bubble of foam in the Sandy River. She was an angel among the sinners trying to come clean. My heart beat faster when I saw her. Some man had his back to me. He was washing her foot. He had an old chipped washpan and a big towel and a bar of home-made soap made from oaktree ashes. He'd put it on her foot like he was putting axle grease on a wagon hub. Then he would smear it with his hands and rub. Then he would take the towel and dry her foot till it would look pink as a wild crab-apple blossom. I just stood there and looked at her. She looked at me. He saw her looking and he looked around. Of all the big ugly devils I ever saw in my life it was this fellow, Jonas Pratt's boy, Tawa Pratt. Lived down on Little Sandy on that big farm in the bend by the grove of cedars. When he turned around and saw me looking he said: "Ain't you a Baptis?"

And I said: "No I ain't no Slab Baptis. I'm a Methodist and I go to Plum Grove to church."

"Go on about your business then," he said, "and leave us Baptis alone. This ain't no side show. We are here worshiping the Lord."

I could see he just didn't want me to see the girl. He didn't like me. I didn't like him. I don't care if he was worshiping the Lord. And I says to him: "If that's the way you feel about it, all right. But I want to know the name of the girl here with you and where she lives."

That burnt him up. His lips just spread out and he showed them big yaller horse-teeth in front. I just thinks to myself: "What woman could kiss that awful mouth behind them big horse-teeth?" He looked at me with them black polecat eyes and his hair was right down over his eyes. He was a sorry-looking devil.

The girl says to me: "I'm Effie Long. I live up on Duck Puddle." I never said a word. I'd go to Duck Puddle. That's just down on Little Sandy four miles and up a hollow that comes into Little Sandy not far from the riffles. I knowed right then and there I'd see that woman again. I said to myself as I walked back from the riverbank over through horseweeds: "That's my wife if I can get her. Pretty as a angel right out of Heaven."

I thought of what Mom told me. I would fall for a skirt. I did like the looks of that woman. I went home. I remember it like it was just one hour ago. The daisies looked good to me. First time flowers ever did look good to me. I pulled off the top of a sweet William and smelt it. It smelt sweet as sugar.

"The love bug's got me right over the heart," I said to Mom

soon as I got in at the door. "I saw my wife at the foot washing—over there among the Baptis today at the Put-Off Ford."

And Mom she says: "Elster, you ain't fell for no Slab Baptis, have you? No Slab Baptis woman can ever come under this Methodist roof until she's been converted into the Methodist faith. That bunch all running around and drinking licker. Won't see no licker in heaven nor no spittoons for that old terbacker."

That's how women are. Right half of the time. When a man is in love, what does he care for spittoons in heaven and bad licker or good licker? What does he care who a Methodist is or a Slab Baptis is? He wants his woman. That's the way I felt. Mom married Pop fifty years ago and she don't know what it is to be young and be in love. I just never said a word.

A week hadn't passed till I heard about church down on Duck Puddle. Slab Baptis holding a pertracted meeting down there. I put on a white starched shirt, a blue necktie and blue serge pants and my black slippers and I went down there. It was a awful walk through the brush and over them ridges. But I followed the fox hunters' paths for more than two miles across through the brush. I walked across the rocks at the riffle and hit the big wagon road up to the church. Meeting was a-going on when I got there. I had to stop and ask four or five times before I found the place. A pretty place after a body gets there but a devil of a time getting to it. I never went inside the house till I peeped in at the winders and looked over the house to see if I could see Effie. I looked and looked. And one time when I looked with my eyes up agin the winderpanes the Slab Baptis preacher said: "A lot of pilferers on the outside of the house tonight. The devil in sheep's clothing is out there. Methodists are snooping around." When I heard this I slipped back in the dark. I'm a Methodist and couldn't be nothing else. Methodist church is good enough for Pa and Mom and Grandpa and Grandma and it's good enough for me. Even if they don't want me, for I bet on chicken fights and play cards once in a while.

I slipped back to the winder. I had looked every place but the amen corner. I looked up there and saw the anger I had seen over at the ford. She was in a mighty good place to be. Me a Methodist and out in the dark. I picked up courage and just walked up and bolted in at the door. I found a empty seat and I saw Effie start looking at me. I started looking at her. And I looked up there and saw old Tawa too. He was in the amen corner. He started showing them teeth soon as he saw me. And I thinks to myself :"Old boy, one of these days I'm going to get me a rock and knock them ugly teeth down your throat. Running around here with a set of horse-teeth in your mouth."

The crowd looked at me. A lot of them had seen me at the Methodist church. A lot of them had seen me at the foot-washing. They all knowed I was a Methodist. They know the Harkreaders are all Methodist—every last devil of them!

I just waited till church was out. I was going to take Effie home. And I had my mind made up. If that horse-toothed thing of a Tawa should come around me and started anything, it would just be too bad. I was going to use my fists long as they would stand it. I got bad bones in my little fingers. And after my fists I was going to knife it with him and after that if he whopped me I was going to use the balance of power. I carried it right in my pocket. The prettiest little .22 you ever saw in your life—could put five balls between your eyes before you could say "Jack Robinson." I don't go into no strange territory unless I go prepared for the worst. That's the way we got to do here. I don't care if we are Baptis and Methodist.

The preacher was saying: "Men and women, since you got to work in your crops tomorrow and I got to work in mine, we'll call the meeting till tomorrow night at seven. All of you be here and bring your songbooks. Sing "Almost Persuaded," folks, and all who wants to come up and jine us just come right on." I never saw so many people fall at the altar.

Church was out and the people already saved—the young people went home and the old people stayed to pray with the people at the "mourner's bench." They was just a-going on something awful. A lot of them were sheep that had left the Methodist flock too. A bunch that wanted to stay in our church and drink licker and play cards and we just wouldn't have it in Plum Grove. Effie come right down the aisle and I said: "Honey, how about seeing you home tonight?" I know my face got red when she said: "All right." Here was old Tawa right behind her with that crazy grin showing that big set of yellow horse-teeth. I thought if he wanted anything he could get it on this night. I didn't speak to him. No use to hide it. He didn't like me and I didn't like him.

I got Effie by the arm, and I held it like a leech. We didn't speak. We just walked out of the house and past a bunch of boys at the door waiting for their girls and the other fellow's girl. People just looked at us. Boys lit up their cigarettes and pipes and the old men started spitting their ambeer. A lot of the women lit up their pipes too—old long-stemmed clay pipes. Something you don't see around our church at Plum Grove among them already saved. If they done it they went home or out behind the brush.

I hadn't got out from under the oak trees by the church house till I had Effie by the hand. And I said: "Honey, I can't eat, drink, work, nor sleep for thinking about you." And I reached down and got her by the little soft hand, and she looked up at me and said: "Ain't it funny? I feel the same way about you. I have felt that way ever since I saw you at the foot-washing. I can't forget you. I keep thinking about you. When I saw you tonight I was thinking about you." I just squeezed her hand a little harder and I said: "Was you, Honey?" Then we went on out the path without speaking.

We went out past the Duck Puddle graveyard. White tombstones gleaming there in the moonlight. Lord, it was a sad thing to think about. I wondered what had become of old Tawa. It was a little dark even if the moon was shining. I didn't care though. I had Effie. I didn't blame him for loving her, but I just didn't want him to get her.

I guess we went through twenty pairs of drawbars before we come to Effie's place. It was a little log house upon the side of the bank, pretty with flowers in the yard. I'd always thought flowers was for the womenfolks. I told Effie I'd never liked flowers till I met her. I told her everything like that. We just went up to her door. I said a lot about the crops. Before I started to leave we was standing out at the well-gum. The moon came down upon her old log house there among all them roses and flowers. It was a mighty pretty place. Effie said: "Guess I'd better get in the house and get to bed. Got to work tomorrow." And I said: "Where, Honey?" "In the terbacker field," she said. And then I said: "W'y, you don't work in no terbacker and stay as white as you are." She said: "That's all you know about it, Elster. I use stocking legs on my arms and a sunbonnet." And I says: "Honey, I love you. I want to marry you." I just pulled her up to me and kissed her there in the moonlight. Soon I left her there and run over the hill like a dog. Tears come into my eyes. Just to think about that. I used to laugh at such stuff. Now, I had six or seven miles to walk home and blue Monday and the plow before me the next day. But seeing Effie was worth a dozen trips like this. When a man is in love he just don't care.

I went to bed that night— must have been morning. It was after the roosters crowed for midnight. Lord, but I was tired. I just could see Effie. I could pull her up to me and kiss her. I could see her eyes, I could see her teeth. I could see her log house in the moonlight. I just couldn't forget it all.

I got up and et my breakfast. Drunk two cups of black coffee and went out to milk the cows. I'd just stop at the barn and look off into the wind. Pa come up to me and he said: "Elster, what in the devil and Tom Walker's got into you here lately—just go around with your head up in the air dreaming. W'y, you even stop when you are shaving your face. If I didn't see you the other day shave half of your face and put the razor up I'm a liar." I never said anything, for it was the truth. I just couldn't help it for thinking about Effie.

I went out to plow corn. I took the mule and the double-shovel plow and went down the path by the barn. I didn't pay any attention but I started the plow on the wrong side of the field and was plowing up the corn. I couldn't think about anything but Effie and how I run away and left that night with my eyes filled with tears. Then I thought: "W'y, I must be crazy to act like this. I'm forgetting everything. I'm not happy as I was. I can't laugh like I did. She didn't say she would marry me. That's it. That's what's the matter." I just couldn't get back to see Effie that week. I had too much to do. Too much corn to plow and seven cows to milk.

Well, I went out to work Tuesday morning. I couldn't work. I thought I'd go up and see Uncle Tid Porter. He lives right on the bank above us. He gives us boys a lot of advice. Uncle Tid was in the woodyard whacking off a few sticks of stovewood. I walked up and I said: "Uncle Tid, I'm in love with a girl. I can't sleep. I can't work. I can't do anything. I'm going crazy."

You ought to have seen Uncle Tid sling his ax agin the ground and laugh. You know Uncle Tid is a pretty good doctor when we can't get one from town. He uses the yarb remedies and he does pretty well. Used to be the only doctor in this section. Now, he gives us advice along with spring tonics of slipper-elm bark, shoemake bark and ginsang and snakeroot. "Well," said Uncle Tid, shaking his long thin chin whiskers stained with a little terbacker juice—his blue-walled eye squinted a little—"when did you meet this girl and where is she from?"

"I met her last month at the Slab Baptis foot-washing at the Put-Off Ford. She's from Duck Puddle. She's a beauty, too, Uncle Tid. W'y, Uncle Tid, to tell you the truth, I never loved a flower till I met her. Now I notice them. See the wild rose in bloom in the woods. I noticed them this morning. She is with me everywhere I go. I can't sleep. I can't eat."

"It's love in the spring," said Uncle Tid. "Love in the spring is so uncertain I wouldn't trust it. Don't be too sure of yourself and jump in and try to marry. Wait a while. Just go out and watch life in the spring. Go to the house and put the mule in the pasture. Take the afternoon off and go to the pond and watch the frogs. Go find some black snakes in love and watch them. Watch the terrapins and the turtles. Everything is in love now. Listen to the songs of the birds. Listen how they sing to each other. It is time to be in love. All the earth is in love now. And love is so uncertain in the spring."

I just got on the mule and went back home. I took the harness off old Barnie and put it on the stall in the barn and I slapped him with the bridle and made him skiddoo to the pasture. I laid up the drawbars and I made for the pond. There's a lot of bull-grass there and about a foot of water. It's a regular frog and water-snake hangout. Lord, of all the noise! I slipped up by the pond. They all hushed. I never heard another noise only I heard some plump-plumps into the water. I saw that I'd scared them. So I laid down on my belly behind a bunch of bull-grass out of sight from the frogs. It wasn't two minutes before they all started singing. The old frogs didn't do much singing. They'd been in love and out again or they'd just took on some other kind of love after so many springs. The little frogs made up for lost time. They'd get up on a log and jump off and chase each other. I crawled up to the edge of the pond and watched them. If you don't believe young frogs love in the spring when they are doing all of that hollering you just go around the pond and see for yourself.

When I got up to leave there, I heard the birds singing. They sung their love songs to each other and it seemed like I could understand some of the words. But the prettiest thing I saw was two snakes entwined upon the bank in the sun. They were black snakes and very much in love. If it had been before I met Effie I would have picked me up a rock and killed them because Pa says they kill all the birds and young rabbits. I saw two turtles out in the pond on a log. They were bathing in the sun. I just watched them a while. No wonder I fell in love with Effie, pretty a girl as she is. No wonder I dream of her at night and plan a house to take her to. My mother's bread don't taste as good to me as it used to taste. My bed at home don't look as good as it used to look and home and Mom and Pa don't seem the same. I just can't help feeling that way. I dream of the way Effie is going to bake my bread and fix my bed and clean my shirts and patch my pants. Life is great; and to be in love, love is so much greater. It's about one of the greatest things in the world—to be in love till you can cry. I just went to bed thinking about the house I had in mind and it was altogether different to the house here where we live. Just to see Effie with a blue dress and a little white apron on, lifting big white fluffy biscuits out of the pan—white biscuits with brown tops—and good hot gravy made out of milk—and butter yaller as a daisy eye—and steam off my coffee hot as hell and strong as love!

I just thought: "Well, I'm going to tell Pa and Ma that I am leaving them. That I am going to marry that little Slab Baptis and hunt me a home and help to replenish the earth with a good stock. A body can look at her and tell that she is of good stock and I ain't of such bad stock."

I went to the house. I never got the mule back out of the pasture. I was through. Of course I knowed Pa would hate to see me go and it would break Mom's heart when I told her. Mom is a shouting Methodist and it would kill her to see me marry one of them Slab Baptis that drink licker and bet on chicken fights and play cards. But no use to lie to Mom about it. I would go today and fix everything up. Frogs could fall in love and the birds and snakes and terrapins and lizards—well, why didn't I have the same right? And if Pa put his jib in I would tell him to stay out of my love affair and Uncle Tid Porter too. It may be love in the spring but I loved in the spring.

I'll never forget going into the house. Mom was making biscuit dough. I heard Pa telling her I put the mule up and knocked off for half day. Pa didn't like it and he was worried. "Well," I says to Mom, "I got news for you." And Mom says: "What kind of news, Elster?" And I says: "I am going to leave you. Going to get married."

"Who are you going to marry?" says Pa—his neck and face red as a hen's comb in the spring.

"I am going to marry Effie Long—that little girl I met over at the foot-washing last month," I said to Pa.

"One of them Slab Baptis?" said Pa.

"Yes, one of them Slab Baptis," I said.

"And you been raised under a roof like this one," Mom said, "under a Methodist roof—and then go and marry a Slab Baptis—one that has a religion that believes in drinking and playing poker and betting on rooster fights and spitting at cracks in the crib floor. Then you going to marry one of them kind. Remember, Elster, if you get burnt you got to set on the blister. You are brought up to believe a certain way it is hard to break away from. Elster, your people have been Methodist for nearly a hunderd years. And you go marry that infidel. Don't you ever let her darken my door. You can come back when you want to but you be sure you keep her away."

The tears come from Mom's eyes. Pa put his hands up over his eyes. And I said to Mom: "Home here ain't the same any more since I met Effie. Life ain't the same, I tell you. My bed ain't the same upstairs and the good biscuits ain't the same."

"Your Ma's bread is the same. Good as it was twenty years ago. Best cook in the country. Then you talk about the bread and even your bed upstairs. Son, I'm not going to stand for anything like that. You can get out of this house if that is the way you feel about things around here. Get your clothes and go." Pa said it and his voice kinda quivered.

I went upstairs and got my clothes. It didn't take me long, for I don't have many. Lord, it burned me up to think about the whole thing. Life with Effie and I'd never come home to see the boys and Mom and Pa. I'd stay away till they would be glad to see me. That's what I'd do. They'd have to send to Duck Puddle to get me.

I put my clothes into the newspaper and got my work clothes —my heavy shoes and my Sunday shoes and my .22 pistol. I thought it might come in handy about a home of my own. I went down through the front room. Mom was crying. "Ain't you going to eat a bite before you leave?" Mom said. And I said: "Nope, I don't believe I care for anything to eat."

"Take a piece of hot corn bread and butter it and eat a piece of smoked ham as you go."

I took it. Lord, but it tasted good. I had et Mom's cooking for eighteen years and it was good. But I went out of the house. I wasn't going to wait till fall. Couldn't plant any ground that late. I was going to marry early enough to rent some ground and get out a late crop and pray for a late fall so they would ripen. I could make it all right.

I walked out into the sunlight. It was a pretty day in May. I never felt so good in all my life. Had my clothes under my arm and going to get my sweet Effie—sweeter than the wild red rose. I went down past the barn and I said farewell to the milk cows, Boss, Fern, Star, Daisy, Little Bitty, Roan and Blacky. I waved my hands to them and to Pete and Barnie in the pasture—mules I'd worked many a day. Barnie nickered at me. He walked along the pasture fence far as he could follow me. I'd been his master ever since he was a colt. Now he would get another master. I said good-by to the trees, the barn, to everything. I was going to a new country.

Sky was pretty above me. The birds never sung any sweeter for me. The wind had music in it. Flowers bloomed so pretty by the road, whole hillsides covered with wild roses. Well, when I got to the riffles the sun was getting pretty low on tother hill. I knowed it would soon be time for them to come from the fields. I'd just get in there a little after suppertime. Lord, but I was hungry. I got across the rocks at the riffle all right, and I went right up the creek till I come to the church house. I was moving fast to get there before dark. A little moon in the sky already.

I crossed the ditch by the church and took out toward the first pair of bars. If I ever go over a road once I never forget it. I soon came to the second pair of bars. The moon was a little bigger in the sky. One of them quarter moons. And a dry moon at that. One edge kinda turned up. Darkness had come at last but here was the house. Light in the front room. So I goes up and looks in. There was old Tawa. He was setting on the couch beside of my Effie. I knocked on the door. Effie come to the door. I said: "How are you, Honey?" and I just closed her in my arms. Old Tawa showed them big horse-teeth with that funny grin—them polecat eyes just a-snapping.

"Come here, Mart Long," Tawa hollered.

"Come where?" said a voice from upstairs. I heard him getting out of the bed. Sounded like the whole loft was coming in. Must 'a' been a big feller. "What are you coming here for?" said Tawa.

"If it's any your business," I said, "I'm coming here to marry Effie. That's why I've come."

"You ain't getting Effie," said Tawa. "She belongs to me. I'm one of her kind. I am a Slab Baptis. I ain't no damned infidental."

I thought I'd take my .22 out and blow his lights out. Calling me a infidental. I never did like the Methodists so much as I did now. And I said: "Who in the hell are you calling a infidental? You polecat you. I'll clean this floor with you." I started to turn Effie loose and get him. Just then in stepped Sourwood Long, Effie's pap.

"There's that infidental Methodist," said Tawa to Sourwood.

And Sourwood said: "W'y, he just looks like the rest of us. Got eyes like us and a mouth and talks. W'y, he's like the rest of us only I don't want Effie marrying you until you repent and get into our church."

"I have come after Effie right now," I said. "Besides, I am a Methodist. I don't intend to repent neither. Why can't she get into the Methodist church? What's wrong with us?"

"And what's wrong with us?" said Sourwood. Black beard covering his face. His arms were big as fence posts and hairy as a brier thicket around a old fence row. He kept them folded upon his big hairy chest. He didn't have many teeth. Had a lot of snags in his mouth—a big nose and he was dark as a wet piece of chestnut bark.

"Nothing ain't wrong with us," said Tawa. "We are the only people right. You know we got a lot of them Methodists in our church when the pertracted meeting was going on. Left your church for ours."

"You got a lot that couldn't stay in our church," I said. I was ready to fight. I still had Effie in my arms. I hadn't turned her loose yet.

"You ain't going to marry Effie. I wouldn't have one of you fellers in my house for dinner let alone in my family to put up with you a lifetime. Get out of here right now."

Another voice from upstairs. "Sourwood, what's going on down there?"

"Malinda, what are you doing up there? A Methodist has come to get Effie. Come on down here."

"Better let a Methodist have her than that thing down there. That Tawa. Get 'em both out of here. Get 'em out quick."

I never saw Effie's mother. I don't know how it was done. It was done so quick. Old Tawa must 'a' come around the back side of the house and upon the front porch and hit me over the head with something. I remember I waked up out in the yard. My clothes were under my head for a piller. The moon was in the sky. It just seemed like I'd been asleep and had slept a little too long. Seemed like a dream. Lights all out of the house just like nothing had ever happened. They's all in bed, I guess. Don't know what ever become of Tawa. Have never seen him from that day to this. I can hardly tell you how I got home. I was about half crazy from that lick. I remember I was so hungry. I remember, too, the chickens were crowing for the daylight. I didn't have my .22 on me. It was gone.

Mom was getting breakfast. I went in and I said: "Mom, your biscuits are all right. Lord, I can eat twenty-two this morning. I'm so hungry."

"Where's your wife?" Mom said.

"I took another notion," I said. "I remembered what you said. I didn't want one of them infidentals after we've been Methodists so long. I thought it over and changed my mind."

"I thought you would," said Mom. "A boy with your raising and get into a mix-up like that. Couldn't bring her home. You'll do better marrying one of your own kind. I'm making you some good strong coffee."

"Good strong coffee is what I need. Strong as love but not love in the spring. Love in the fall. Coffee hot as hell too."

Lord, but Mom did look good to me in that apron. She just looked the best I ever saw her. And her biscuits tasted right too. "Mom, you are the best girl I've ever had," I said and I kinda give Mom a bear hug and she says to this day I cracked a couple of her ribs. She says she can hardly get her breath at times ever since I hugged her.

This has been a day in September. Uncle Tid Porter was down today. He said to me: "Now is the kind of weather to fall in love—now while the chill winds blow and the leaves fly—now while the frost has come. The spring is the time to marry and go on a gay carousal like the frog. Like the snakes and the flowers and all living things. Spring is the time to marry—not the time to fall in love. Love in the spring is fickle as the wind."

"I have often wondered what has become of Tawa," I said to Uncle Tid, "the fellow that loved the girl I loved last spring—w'y, he's the ugliest human being I ever saw for to love as pretty a woman as Effie——"

"She's married him, I guess," said Uncle Tid. "That's the way of a woman. They do the unexpected thing—not knowing which way the wind will blow and if there will be snow or rain tomorrow. That's what a man likes—he likes the unexpected thing."

The wind blows outside. The wind is cool. Pa is out at the barn putting a roof over the fattening hog pen. Mom is still complaining of her ribs: "I never heard of that but once before in my life. A teacher come to this deestrict to teach school and he hugged one of Mort Giggin's girls—it was Ester, I believe—and he broke three of her ribs. I tell you he never got another school in this deestrict."

The Water Penalty

"TELL us a bedtime story, Uncle Jeff," Sophia said.

"Yes do tell us one, Uncle Jeff," I said.

"Don't get Jeff started on his wild tales," Pa said. "I don't think it's good for you children to hear these wild tales Jeff tells. You can't go to bed and sleep after you hear them. You roll and toss and sometimes scream in your sleep! Sometimes you have nightmares after you hear a wild tale by your Uncle Jeff."

"Go on and tell a story, Jeff," Mom said. "Pay no attention to Mick. We like to hear something before we go to bed. A little screaming in the bed and a nightmare won't hurt the young'uns."

Mom always defended Uncle Jeff, her brother who had come for a visit and had been with us five years. He had been married and was the father of eight children who had married and left home. Aunt Sallie was dead and Uncle Jeff had lived alone for four years in his old home before he came to live with us. Now, Uncle Jeff and Pa argued over the size of a piece of land on our farm, which kind of tobacco would grow best on our land, and the breed of cattle, hogs, and sheep we ought to have on our farm. If Pa said an autumn leaf was red, Uncle Jeff would argue it was brown. If Pa said a big yellow poplar would saw eight hundred board feet of lumber, Uncle Jeff would argue it would saw a thousand feet and they'd cut the tree and have it sawed, even if we didn't need the lumber, just to see who was tight. And Pa was afraid to argue with Uncle Jeff any more on cattle, trees, and tobacco. Uncle Jeff was right more times than Pa. Now, Uncle Jeff could tell bigger stories than Pa and Pa had told Mom more times than one, and he had told Uncle Jeff to his face, that he was the windiest man he had ever heard talk. But my brother, Finn, and my sisters, Sophia, Mary, and Glenna, and I liked to hear Uncle Jeff tell a bedtime story.

"Mick, I'll tell them a story about sin," Uncle Jeff said.

"You ought to be an authority on sin, Jeff," Pa said.

"Mick, don't talk to Jeff like that," Mom said. "Let Jeff go on and tell his story on sin. Maybe it will be a lesson for our young'uns."

"Yes, tell them a story like that last one about copperheads and sin," Pa sighed. "Must be another one of them Elliott County stories."

"Yes, it is, Mick," Uncle Jeff said. "It's another Elliott County story all right, for I grew up there and I know the stories. And it's a story that might help the father of five young'uns in Greenwood County—a father who doesn't sit very far from me!"

We were sitting in a quarter-moon circle around our blazing fire. Outside, the December winds moaned. They rattled our window panes and we could hear the winds roaring through the barren branches of the oak grove between our house and the barn. Sometimes a puff of woodsmoke was shoved back down the big-throated chimney and fanned out into our living room but a little smoke didn't bother us. We'd smelled woodsmoke every spring when we burned the clearings for new corn crops. Inside our house it was warm and comfortable and Uncle Jeff sat all reared back, his three hundred and seven pounds on the big chair Pa had made especially for him to keep him from breaking down any more of Mom's chairs.

"Sallie, you remember the Timmins family in Elliott County, don't you?" Uncle Jeff asked Mom.

"I certainly do," Mom said. "One of the best families in Elliott County."

"I wouldn't say that, Sister Sall," Uncle Jeff said. "They thought they were the best people in Elliott County. And they norated it around that they were. Sall, you left Elliott County before this happened. You've never heard this story. Mark Timmins had talked so much about the good stock of the Timmins family, about the good blood that flowed in their veins, and about how much better they were than our people, the Sheltons, Penningtons, Leadinghams, Slusses, and everybody else in Elliott County that the Wise One, Old Clem Worthington, sent for Mark Timmins to come to see him at once."

"Mark Timmins must have trembled when he got the word that the Wise One wanted to see him," Uncle Jeff said.

"Yes, I spect he did," Pa said. Pa was sitting back in his chair on its two hind legs and he was looking into the fire. His face was red. Whether it was from the heat of the fire or from what Uncle Jeff was saying I don't know. Pa didn't like Uncle Jeff's big tales. "A Wise One," Pa sighed.

"Quit interrupting me, Mick," Uncle Jeff said. "There was a Wise One in Elliott County who warned the people. He told them of things to come. Old Clem had outlived his wife and he lived alone. I don't know how he made his prophecies but he studied the stars, read things in coffee grounds, and he studied nature and read the Prophet Hosea."

"Yes, I've heard you tell about Old Clem before," Pa said. "Go on and tell your story and get it over with. Let's have some peace before we go to bed."

"Mick, don't talk that way to Jeff," Mom said.

Uncle Jeff was silent now. He sat there looking into the fire. His big black eyes shone in the firelight like living embers.

"Go on, Uncle Jeff," Sophia said. "We want to hear your story."

"Yes, tell it, Uncle Jeff," I said.

"Don't just start and not finish," sister Mary said.

"I want to hear it," brother Finn said. "I can't go to sleep until I hear the rest of your story."

"I want to hear it too," sister Glenna said.

"Mick, there are some people in this world that appreciate

me," Uncle Jeff said. "I will go on with my story which is about sin of a father, Mick. You should want to hear this story."

"Then go on, Jeff," Pa said. "We might as well hear the wind blow on the inside of the house as on the outside. That wind out there tonight is kickin' up a rumpus. Maybe you can stir up a wind in here that will offset the noise of that wind out there."

Uncle Jeff gave Pa a hard look and then he continued. "Mark Timmins dared not go and stand before the Wise One. When the Wise One summoned anybody in Elliott County he heeded the call. He was afraid not to do it, Mick."

"I wouldn't have heeded his call," Pa said.

"When I get through telling my story tonight I think you would have harkened to the call, Mick," Uncle Jeff said. "Now, let me continue this story which will be good for my littly nephews and nieces. 'Mark, what is this you are norating over Elliott County about the Timminses being the best stock of people in this county?' Old Clem asked him. 'You are saying that the best blood of any family in this county flows in your veins. You say it is better than the blood that flows in the veins of the Sheltons, Penningtons, Leadinghams, and Slusses and in the veins of all other families in this county. Isn't it true you have had such talk?' And Mark Timmins was afraid not to tell the truth. He told Old Clem that he had had such talk. And he said, 'Wise One, this is the truth. We are the best stock of people in Elliott County.' 'All right, I will tell you something, Mark,' Old Clem said. 'Why do you take your young sons to the barn, unbeknownst to their mother, Lucinda Pennington Timmins, reach up in the hay and pull out a horse-quart of Highridge Moonshine and teach them to drink with you? Do you call this good blood in the veins? Have you ever heard of the "sins of the fathers" and the penalty for their sins?' "

" 'Wise One, how did you know this?' Mark asked Old Clem. 'I know these things!' he told Mark. 'Do not question how I know them. Is it the truth, or not?' And Mark told him that it was. And then Mark asked, 'What will the penalty be, Wise One?' 'It will be water,' Old Clem told him. 'Not fire, nor the sword, nor bullets, nor the knife. It will be water. You will see that it will be water. Your sons—Egbert, who is fifteen now; your Charlie, who is twelve now; and your John, who is six—will suffer the penalty of water. Yes, you gave little John, six years old, a taste from the horse-quart. And here you are telling me and everybody what wonderful people the Timminses are and running everybody else down. You have sinned, Mark, and you are still sinning. You will see, though I may not be here to know, that the water penalty will come to pass.' Mark Timmins left Old Clem's little shack in the woods. Old Peter Leadingham told me Mark laughed about what the Wise One had said. 'He's an old fossil waiting to die and the truth's not in him,' Mark told Old Peter. And Old Peter Leadingham was as truthful as man as ever lived in Elliott County."

"Now Mark and Lucinda's Egbert grew up to manhood and married Effie May Dillow. Their firstborn was a son who was named for Mark, his grandfather. He was Mark and Lucinda's first grandchild and always Mark's favorite since he was his namesake. Then, there was a family increase to seven children in this family. I've seen Egbert and Effie and their seven children, two years between each one, their blond heads tousled in the wind, as they played around their home. Mark and Lucinda went to visit them every week. They didn't have more than a mile to walk. The East Fork River separated their farms. And there was a bridge over the East Fork right in front of Egbert's house. And nearly a mile up the road was Mark and Lucinda's home, the largest white house in Elliott County. It stood like a palace upon the hill overlooking the East Fork River."

"Charlie, the second son, who wasn't as strong as Egbert, grew up and married Clara Middleton. Since Charlie wasn't strong enough to do farm work, Mark and Lucinda had to help him make a living. They had one son and then Clara left Charlie or Charlie left Clara; anyway, their marriage was dissolved and Clara took their son home to her parents. Charlie joined the Army to fight in World War I. When he returned, he was the strongest man in Elliott County. He was no taller than he was when he enlisted but he weighed twice as much and he was mostly muscle.

First thing he did was whip every man who had said an ill word to him when he was a weakling. He begged men to fight him. He was like a mad bull when a red flag is waved before him. Mark was afraid of his son Charlie. He begged Charlie to go back into the Army, where he could get all the fighting he wanted. But Charlie married again, this time Essie Bocock, and he re-enlisted in the Army and took his wife with him. She lived with Charlie a year and then this marriage was dissolved. Charlie remained in the Army for twenty years. Then he returned to live with his parents. Charlie had never forgotten the days when he drank from the horse-quart with his father. He was still drinking from the horse-quart."

"Now young John had grown up and he married Nadine Sluss. He hadn't forgotten the horse-quart either. But Nadine wouldn't leave him. He'd pass out and go to bed and she'd get old Brother McCormick to come and pray over him. 'I would like to quit but I can't,' John said. 'I do my drinking in the open and this is more than I can say about brother Egbert. He drinks more than I do and hides in the barn to do his drinking. The horse-quart has him but he doesn't want anybody to know it.' So they all had the habit which they couldn't control of imbibing Highridge from the horse-quart."

"Just like you had, Jeff, for forty years," Pa said.

"Mick, I know I had it forty years and this is the reason this story has been a lesson to me," Uncle Jeff said. "But my pap didn't take me to the barn when I was six years old and put the neck of a horse-quart in my mouth and tell me to drink. He didn't go around the county saying the Sheltons had the best blood in their veins of any family in Elliott County. I alone am responsible for my habit and I quit it, didn't I?"

"Not until you were knocked in the head and laid in the hospital a-talkin' crazy until they thought you'd lost your mind, Jeff, and it was there the habit left you," Pa told him.

"Mick, let Jeff finish his story about the penalty of water," Mom said.

"And I never let one of my six sons ever see me take a drink,"

Uncle Jeff told Pa. "Not one of my six sons is an imbiber of the Highridge. And just about everybody in Elliott County in them days, even to the preachers, imbibed."

"Go on with your story, Uncle Jeff,' I said.

"What about the penalty of water, Uncle Jeff?" Sophia asked. "Tell us what happened!"

"Old Clem, the Wise One, didn't live to see all this come about, did he, Uncle Jeff?" brother Finn asked.

"No, Old Clem had long gone to his reward and he sleeps in an unmarked grave on an Elliott County hill," Uncle Jeff said. "I know about where the people laid him but I can't mark the spot. I was there when he was buried in a homemade coffin. I saw the last dirt shoveled in over the old fellow who did so much for the Elliott County people. He gave them good counsel, and in a time of lawlessness many heeded to his call and his prophecies. And one of these who heeded to the call, even bore the penalty of water, was Mark Timmins. I know this to be a fact for the last time I ever saw Mark I went over on East Fork to buy a cow from him. He'd already sold the cow but he wanted to talk to me so we sat upon a rail fence and talked. And he said to me, 'Jeff, I was wrong about saying the best blood of any people in Elliott County flowed in the veins of my people! Look what has happened to my three sons! I was wrong to go to the barn and take a horse-quart of Highridge and pass it around to my boys. I am the only father on East Fork who has one-hundred-per-cent alcoholics in his sons. Jeff, you've been a drinking man, I want to talk to you. Do you know anything that I can do to stop them?' "

"What did you tell him, Jeff?" Pa asked. "Did you tell him how you were cured by that lick on the head in the White Spot Grill in Toniron, Ohio?"

"I am not listening to you, Mick," Uncle Jeff said. "And I am not telling you what I told him."

"This is some bedtime story," Pa said. "I never heard a bedtime story like this one. Do you like it, Shan?" Pa asked me.

"I want to know about the penalty of water," I said. "I want to know what happened."

"Yes, Pa, let Uncle Jeff finish his story," Sophia said.

"For my young nieces and nephews who appreciate my stories I will finish this story if it takes me until midnight, Mick," Uncle Jeff said. Uncle Jeff got up and stretched his six-foot-two and three-hundred-seven pound body. He laid his hands flat upon the ceiling above the fireplace and then he sat back down. "When Egbert and Effie May's son, Mark, disappeared, a posse of men searched the hills for him. Mark and Lucinda, his grandparents, were so upset they couldn't sleep. Young Mark was his grandfather's namesake and favorite among his grandchildren. It was in August when young Mark disappeared. They dragged the East Fork River above and below Egbert and Effie May's home. Old Mark had not forgot what the Wise One had told him about the penalty of water. And after they had dragged the river Old Mark said, 'Well, the Wise One missed on that one.' But there was one place they had forgot to look. Egbert and Effie May had a large barrel, a hogshead, set under their drainpipe to catch the water to wash their clothes. When Egbert looked in, there was his young son Mark, fourteen years old, who had climbed up and fallen into the water and couldn't climb out of the high hogshead. And when he had screamed for help down in that barrel, no one could hear him. No one had thought the tragedy could happen here. He had drowned at the corner of the house and no one had thought such a thing could happen here. So this was one for the water and Old Mark now remembered what the Wise One had said. He didn't call him an old fossil now. And he no longer laughed about the Wise One's reading his coffee cups, his study of the stars and nature, and his reading Hosea."

"John, Old Mark's third son, knew it was against the state law to dynamite the river to kill fish," Uncle Jeff said. "But that day he had had a party with his friends and they had had plenty of Highridge, warm from the still at the party. It was the same still where Old Mark used to get his Highridge—Old Flem Kinney's still not far from Bruin. And after the party had got wilder, John went to the barn to get his dynamite and caps and the crowd went whooping and hollering down to Little Fork. They walked along the river until they came to the Deep Hole where they thought the large fish were plentiful. Before John could get away from the fuse he had lighted, for it was said his foot slipped on the slick river bank, the charge went off and John lost his left hand and arm and his left eye and ear. He was taken to Gadsen Hospital in Gadsen where he lay for one month betwixt life and death. This was the second water penalty."

"And I saw Old Mark after this. He was a very upset man," Uncle Jeff continued. 'I'm so sorry about what I said about that good old man, Old Clem, the Wise One,' Old Mark said. 'My grandson Mark sleeps on the hill and my son John had just as well sleep. He's no more a man. Thank God he's got a wife that sticks to him. Lucinda and I help our sons until it's almost broken us up. Sins of the father is right, Jeff. It's my fault and I suffer. It's not the blood in the veins but it is what people help their children to make of themselves. When I drank Highridge with my sons I thought they had the stock in them to come around. I didn't think, due to the bloodlines and their breeding, that they would ever become slaves to Highridge. Oh, if I had only known to give other people credit for having some sense. Look at the men and women Lucinda and I wouldn't associate with, and what their sons and daughters have amounted to in life. Old Tim Wampler's son, Nathan, is a big doctor in Louisville today and they were so poor they lived on a dirt floor. And look at the schoolteachers, Jeff, who have come from the families I used to turn my nose up when one would pass. They've amounted to something in this world and look at my sons, one-hundred-per-cent alcoholics, and Lucinda and I have to help support their families. We've not got anything to crow about now. People we wouldn't consider, wouldn't look at, wouldn't help, because we felt we were so far above, as the stars are above the earth, today pity us. I tell you it is an awful feeling, Jeff, to grow old and have his happen before Lucinda and I pass from this world.' My little nephews and nieces, I know this isn't a good bedtime story because it is about the sin of the father, isn't it, Mick?"

"But, Jeff, I've imbibed some," Pa said. "My sons never saw me do it. If you think I ever offered my sons any rotgut Highridge, you just ask them. They're sitting here."

"I'm not saying you did, Mick," Uncle Jeff said. "I'm glad you didn't."

"Yes, but you act like I might have done such a thing," Pa told him.

"What about Charlie?" Sophia asked. "What happened to him?"

"Yes, tell us about the third water penalty, Uncle Jeff," Finn said.

"Well, about Charlie," Uncle Jeff said. "He'd retired from the Army and come home to live with Old Mark and Lucinda. He had a son by his first wife and a daughter by his second. He didn't know anything about his children for he was like the cowbird that lays its eggs in other birds' nests for them to hatch and raise the young cowbirds. And Charlie had bragged about begetting and leaving his bloodline, for he had been told by his father that his bloodline was so good he had left his offspring in other parts of the world where he had been stationed in the Army. He told about France, Belgium, and a place called Luxembourg. He said he'd left eggs in the nests for other birds to hatch and raise. And he spoke of California, New Mexico, Texas, Tennessee, and Florida. Of course everybody said behind his back, because they were afraid to say it to his face, that Charlie Timmins was as windy as the December winds among the oaks outside this house tonight."

"When Charlie retired from the Army on a pension and came home to Lucinda and Mark he might sleep all day and sit up all night. He was still a fighting bull of a man, with a head that looked like it set squarely on his broad shoulders, and he had small black beady eyes as mean as a bull's eyes. There wasn't a place on his face big enough to lay a penny that wasn't scarred from fighting. If Charlie wanted to sit up and sing all night Mark and Lucinda had no choice but to let him sing. If he wanted to go somewhere, as he often did, and get a man out of bed and whip him, they let him do it. Old Mark said to me, the last time I was in Elliott County, 'Jeff, what surprises me is that Charlie was lucky enough to get the water penalty instead of the fire, bullet, or knife. He had so many enemies who were afraid of him that we wonder how he lived as long as he did. He got the water penalty in the end. He got a soft death and an easy death!' Mark told me that he and Lucinda were glad he got a soft easy death since death had to come to him some way."

"How did he go, Uncle Jeff?" Glenna asked.

"He had a boat in the East Fork River," Uncle Jeff said. "No one knew when he went to fish but it wasn't in season. He didn't have a license, but he went in the night. Charlie, so Mark told me, stirred mostly at night and slept during the day. But when Charlie didn't come back to Lucinda and Mark one night, they didn't think anything about it. They had had a good night of sleep and some peace. When he didn't return the second day, they didn't think too much about it. When he didn't come the third day, they notified Big John Pennington and he norated to his neighbors that Charlie Timmins hadn't been seen for three days and that Lucinda and Mark were worried about him. And as it happened Little Lindsay Pennington had hidden behind a tree when he saw Charlie coming down the moonlit path with a fishing pole over his shoulder and a horse-quart of Highridge in his hand. 'I was afraid of him,' Little Lindsay said. 'That's why I got behind a tree for I would rather have met the devil on that moonlit path as to have met Charlie Timmins. I didn't want to be choken and beaten by him. I was ready to run if he found me behind the tree.' But Little Lindsay's seeing him that night was enough to know he'd gone to the Deep Hole in East Fork River where he kept his boat. Here a posse of searchers found his boat, and his cigars and lighter were still in his boat."

"There was an old saying when I was a boy in Elliott County that the East Fork River was slow to give up its dead," Uncle Jeff continued. "When they dragged the Deep Hole where no man was shedding a tear, they didn't find Charlie. The old men said they didn't see how he could get out of the Deep Hole. But Charlie had once been a sickly cowardly little boy. All of a sudden he had become a strong, tough man, a fighting man. And Hezzy Hall said when they were dragging the Deep Hole, 'Leave it to Charlie alive or dead to get out of this place. I'll bet he's on his way down the river.' And seven days later they found Charlie nine miles below the Deep Hole. He had gone over the Black Riffles, the East Fork Falls, and the Cedargrove Shoals. They had to carry him from the East Fork in a blanket. The fish he had sought to bite the bait he had for them were now biting him. They said he was the heaviest man ever carried in a coffin, he was so full of water, and they buried him in the morning and never opened his casket. This was the third one to suffer the water penalty. So it all goes back to the sin of the father and the warning the Wise One gave Old Mark. And now he knows since he is an old man who suffers much."

"I would think that he would," Pa said.

"It's a good story, Jeff," Mom said. "And I think the children will sleep all right after hearing that one."

"I liked the story, Uncle Jeff," I said. "I'll never forget it. I'll grow up and get an education and write it down some day."

"Well, come on everybody after that one and let's go to bed," Pa said. "Shan, if you grow up and write down some of these stories that your Uncle Jeff tells and if anybody ever reads them they will know what a liar Old Jeff was. The water penalty and the Wise One," Pa mumbled and then he laughed. "Yes, write them down when you grow up, Shan, so people will know about Jeff as I know about him now. I wouldn't be surprised these big tales he tells will live long after Jeff might have the fire, knife, or the water penalty."

Our Wiff and Daniel Boone

"I WAS born at the wrong time," Wiff Hendrix said in Pudd Bently's General Store and Post Office. "I wish I'd been born the same year Daniel Boone was born. Wish I could have come into the Kentucky wilderness with Boone, and with a long rifle, a powderhorn, and a bullet mold. But maybe I am Daniel Boone. You know, I could be."

When we gathered in Pudd's store on late afternoons after our work was done, Wiff would always be the first one there. All Wiff wanted to talk about was his hunting. He wanted us to believe he was the greatest hunter in Greenwood County, Kentucky, and the United States. We had heard him tell hunting stories we couldn't believe.

"Why would you want to be born when Daniel Boone was born?" Big Aaron Howard asked him. "If you'd been born then, you'd be dead now. Right now you are alive and talking to us!"

Wiff was sitting upon the counter with his long legs hanging over. He always liked to be the center of attraction and do the talking. He worked in the shops for Big Western Railway Company. He always wore pin-striped overalls, a jacket and a cap to match, and a red bandanna around his neck. When he took off the red bandanna, he wore a blue work shirt and a black bow tie. We wondered why he went dressed like one of Big Western's engineers who pulled the throttle of a long freighter. He might have fooled others but he didn't fool us. We knew he was a laborer at the shops. He had a sharp face, a long nose, and sharp black eyes that squinted like they were sighting over a gunbarrel.

"Well, I'd like to have been Daniel Boone who had plenty of game to hunt," he said. "There's not enough game left in this country to hold me, the Daniel Boone of today. I might be the greatest hunter in all America."

"Self-bragging is half scandal," Little Ed Howard said. Little Ed was Big Aaron's brother. "Who eats all the wild game you kill?"

"Of course, Effie and I can't," he said. "You know my wife works at the Deering Shoe Factory in Dartsmouth. She's had wild meat until she's tired of it. We give some of it away. Sometimes when I'm in the woods killing squirrels, I load my hunting coat until it's too heavy to carry. I enjoy hunting so much I go on killing and just leave the squirrels lay. I let the poor hunters who never get a shot when they hunt with me pick up the game I kill and claim the rabbits and the squirrels if they want them. They don't claim them in front of me but they go home and tell they've killed them. But old Wiff's the sure-shot Daniel Boone on the cottontail when one jumps up and starts bouncing over the field."

"No wonder we've not got any wild game left in these hills any more," Penny Shelton said. "No wonder everybody is posting his land. You've caused this, Wiff! You just work enough days in hunting season to hold your rights at the Big Western shops. So you kill game and leave it lay!"

Penny Shelton was my cousin, over six feet tall and weighed two hundred pounds, and with shoulders as broad as a pantry door. He cut and hauled timber to a sawmill. He was not afraid of Wiff Hendrix or anyone else. And when he spoke he looked Wiff straight in the eye.

"It's because of your hunting in and out of season that everybody around here is posting his land," Penny said. "That's why my father posted his five hundred acres!"

"And it's why my father posted our three hundred acres," I said.

"It's why Pa posted our two hundred fifty acres," Big Aaron Howard said.

Big Aaron and Little Ed Howard and I worked on our fathers' farms. The Howards raised strawberries and we raised corn and tobacco.

"There's not a groundhog left for miles around," Big Aaron said. "We hardly see a rabbit any more. We never hear squirrels barking where they used to den in the hollow beeches."

"You won't be bothered with old Wiff's hunting around here any more,"Wiff said. "I know you posted your land because of me. I don't feel bad about it. You can tell your fathers and mothers I don't. And you can tell them Wiff Hendrix won't fool with this little game here any longer! Tell them Wiff is going for bigger game!"

"Where are you going, Wiff?" I asked.

"Going to the Peninsula in Upper Michigan," he said. "I'm going after the deer!"

"You know there's a limit to what you kill up there," I said.

"Oh, yes, I know that," he said. "I'll bag my two bucks, bag a few for the other fellows too if they'll let me. I like to hunt and to kill. I like to see that rabbit tumble over after I shoot. I like to see that little squirrel tumble from the tree after the crack of my gun. And it will be the biggest thrill in my life to see that buck fall after the crack of my rifle! It's hard to stop Daniel Boone, Kentucky's long hunter."

"I've often wondered how it feels to be shot," Cousin Penny said. "And every time I pick up a rabbit or a squirrel, I can't keep from feeling how that rabbit or squirrel I hold in my hand felt when I shot it. I guess I'm a bit touchy about killing."

When Cousin Penny said this I never heard a man laugh like Wiff. He laughed louder than old man Martin White used to laugh when he got his afternoon *Dartsmouth Daily* and read the funnies. Pudd, who had been waiting on a few customers, stopped in his tracks while Wiff laughed. Wiff went up high with his laughter, then down to catch his breath, and then he went high again. It was like the waves on Big River rising and falling when winter storm winds blew up the river.

"You ever hear a man talk like that?" Wiff said at the end of a spasm of laughter. Then he laughed again. "A big man like Penny Shelton talking like that! What are we coming to in this county? Will we be a land of chickenhearted men? Daniel Boone thinks we are!"

"I'd think Daniel Boone killed game only when he needed food," I said.

"I don't care what Daniel Boone would think, or you either, Wiff," Penny spoke stoutly. "I'm no more chickenhearted with people than you are. I said I wondered how it felt to be shot because I've never been shot and you haven't either. And I don't go out hunting for the pleasure of killing. I hunt for food to go on our table!"

"Boys, you're getting a little loud," Pudd said.

Pudd didn't want to offend us, for we traded at his General Store. He never joined either side in an argument at his store. Pudd was about forty, short, fat, and balding, and he always had a half-moon smile on his jolly face. He even let Wiff sit on his counter so he could be above us while he told his stories. Wiff liked his high position where he could be noticed by everybody. We sat in chairs or we stood or leaned on the counter. The General Store was our meeting place in Kensington, a village of three hundred.

"We'd better be getting home," Big Aaron said to Little Ed. "I've heard the wind blow too often in here."

"Well, friends, I'm sorry I disturbed you," Wiff said. "When you see my next hunting story it will be in the paper. Old Wiff standing beside his car with a buck strapped on each side. I'll be standing right beside them with my trusty rifle. Game around here any more is peanuts to me. This Daniel Boone might even outshoot the old Daniel Boone."

When Big Aaron, Little Ed, Penny, and I left the store, Wiff was still sitting on the counter with his legs dangling down. He was waiting for another one of Pudd's customers to tell a hunting story. I don't know what was going through the others' minds as we walked silently away from the store but I know what went through mine. I was thinking about the lists of wild game Wiff had posted on the front of Pudd's General Store.

After squirrel season last year, this was before there was a limit, Wiff had posted five hundred thirteen squirrels killed. He had his name printed in block letters below this. According to his posters on the storefront, he had killed sixty-one groundhogs, five hundred ten rabbits, one hundred sixteen possums, twenty raccoons, four hundred eighty-two quails, seventy-three doves, thirty-five grouse, and sixteen pheasants. In December, just before Christmas, he posted his total, itemizing each animal and bird and adding the numbers to a total of eighteen hundred twenty-four. Below the figures in block letters he had printed: WILD GAME KILLED BY WIFF HENDRIX.

This was when everybody near Kensington began to post their land. Whether Wiff told the truth or not, everyone knew he stayed in the woods, in season and out, every day he didn't have to work at the shops for Big Western to hold his "rights." and this was the year Wiff had boasted that he would go over the two-thousand mark.

"I'm glad Wiff is going to the Upper Peninsula to hunt for big game," Big Aaron said, breaking our silence.

"Maybe there'll be something left for us to hunt," Little Ed said. "Pa said he was sure Wiff had been slipping past the signs and hunting on our posted land."

"You'd better never let me catch him hunting on us," Penny said. "He's not like he was at Walnut Grove when we went to school together. He just brags about killing all the time. Something has come over him. I believe he thinks he's Daniel Boone."

"I don't believe Daniel Boone would have cared for old Wiff," I said. "Daniel Boone didn't waste his powder and lead just going through the forest killing wild animals. He killed for food."

Now this was the end of squirrel season when Wiff sat on the counter and bragged to us about going for bigger game. He never made his two thousand animals and birds. At least we didn't see any posters. But we did read in the *Dartsmouth Daily* where Wiff Hendrix had gone to Michigan to hunt deer. Two weeks later we saw a picture in the *Dartsmouth Daily* of Wiff standing beside his car with a buck strapped on either side. There was a long write-up in the paper about him. I just saw his picture. I wouldn't read the article. I knew I'd hear all about his Michigan hunt and so would everybody else who would listen at Pudd Bently's store. We knew Wiff would be there, sitting on the counter high above everybody else, looking down and bragging about his hunting with his words coming faster than the wind blows up Big River in winter.

Wiff bought a hundred copies of the *Dartsmouth Daily*, so Pudd told Penny Shelton, who told Big Aaron, Little Ed, and me. He clipped the write-up and picture and sent the clippings to his friends. Pudd said he posted the letters at his General Store and Post Office. He said he sold Wiff one hundred stamps, the biggest stamp sale Pudd ever had from a customer. I went to the store once when Wiff was on the counter telling Mort Flannery and Elija Birdsong about his kill in Michigan on the first day.

"I could have killed fifty," he said. "I helped a dozen men get their bag limit on the second day."

I'd heard enough of this and I got out of the store as soon as I could.

It was just before Christmas when I was in the General Store and Post Office when old Wiff walked in where there were a lot of Christmas shoppers. He had known the right time to catch the crowd, the Saturday before Christmas. Wiff made everybody stop, even me, to take a look at him. He was carrying a rifle over his shoulder and he was wearing a buckskin outfit just like the kind Daniel Boone had worn in his picture in our old Kentucky history book. From his buckskin cap he had a coon's tail hanging down his back. There were little fringes on his buckskin jacket and up and down the seams of his buckskin pant legs just exactly like the clothes Daniel Boone wore in his portrait in the history book.

"Daniel Boone," a small boy said, looking up at Wiff Hendrix. "Mama, here's Daniel Boone!"

"Just how tall are you now, Wiff?" I asked. "You're over six feet four now! You're higher than the ceiling. But you do look like Daniel Boone in your buckskin suit. Say, who made that suit for you?"

"I had to get a tanner first to tan the hides," he said. "Then I got a tailor in Dartsmouth to make the suit. Think it becomes me?"

"You look like Daniel Boone," I said. "Only you're much taller than Daniel was."

What I said pleased Wiff Hendrix. With all the little boys looking up at him and following him as he paced up and down the store, their mothers and others looking on admiringly, Wiff Hendrix had his moment of glory. Some few had read the number of wild animals he had killed when he posted these after each season on Pudd's storefront and fewer had read his December totals posted there. Now they knew he was a great deer hunter and he was leaving their posted farms alone. And they were happy he was going to Michigan and hunt for bigger game.

Wiff went over the dirt walks in Kensington wearing his buckskin suit with its fringes and his buckskin cap with the raccoon's tail down his back. He went to visit his neighbors in his suit. He was the most talked-of man in Kensington, where there was a junction of four roads and people came in from over Greenwood County to trade. News of his new suit and his being a great deer hunter spread all over western Greenwood County. When he wore his buckskin suit, we never saw his wife, Little Effie, with him. But he had made his brags to Penny Shelton, to the Howard brothers, and to me that he and Effie would not have children but would both work and save their money until the day they had enough to move on to the North Woods of Canada where he would find a hunter's paradise. There they would settle in a cabin so he could hunt until the end of his days.

Since Wiff and I didn't go to the same church, I heard Wiff did go one Sunday to his church of Prophecy wearing his buckskin suit. I heard Effie wasn't with him that Sunday. This might have just been a rumor but it was talked all over Kensington. The Howard brothers heard it too. They went to the Free Will

Church, while Penny and I went to the Baptist. We heard this talk about Wiff at our Baptist church. There was always talk about Wiff Hendrix, what a great hunter he was and how old Wiff might be the new Daniel Boone of America. Here was this great man in our midst in Kensington. Some even called him the Second Coming of Daniel Boone. There were some people, the Tuttles, Sharps, and Birdsongs, who believed in reincarnation, and they believed old Wiff was Daniel Boone returned to earth again. And when Elija Birdsong told me in Pudd's store he was going to the Upper Peninsula with Wiff Hendrix who was the reincarnated Daniel Boone, I told him that Daniel Boone had grown six inches in his grave because the old Daniel was five ten and the new Daniel was six four. Well, that cooled old Elija off and silenced him.

Everybody on the farms in all directions from Kensington were happy not to see any more Wiff Hendrix posters on the store. Everybody was happy that he was a man of his word, that he had quit hunting the small game, and that he had gone to Michigan for bigger game. Wiff had become a better worker at Big Western's shops too. He never missed a day. And he boasted how he was saving money, putting it in two different banks so if one busted he'd have money in the other, saving for the day when he could retire with enough money to find a hunting paradise in Canada's North Woods. His wife, Little Effie, was still working every day in Deering's Shoe Factory over in Dartsmouth, where she left early in a small bus and crossed on the ferry over Big River. She was working for Wiff's later years in a cabin in the North Woods in his hunters' paradise.

The second autumn Elija Birdsong went with Wiff to the Upper Peninsula. When they returned they had their limit, all right. They had two bucks strapped on each side of the car. They must have made a pretty picture driving along the highway from the Upper Peninsula to Kensington. People meeting them must have stopped their cars to see Wiff's weighted car pass. This time it was Wiff and Elija in a picture together in the *Dartsmouth Daily*. Wiff was dressed in his buckskin suit and cap with his rifle across his shoulder. Elija Birdsong certainly looked less colorful standing there with Wiff in an ordinary hunting suit. Later we learned at Pudd's store that Wiff had hunted in his buckskin suit in Michigan.

One late afternoon when Penny and I went to Pudd's store to get groceries and ask for mail, Elija Birdsong was in the store telling about their hunt in Michigan. He was telling about all the wild woods up there and what a hunters' paradise it was and how Wiff was the Daniel Boone, the experienced hunter of the Kentucky wilderness.

"Well, if you believe old Wiff's really Daniel Boone reincarnated, who do you believe you are?" Penny asked.

There wasn't anybody in the store except Pudd and he stopped dead in his tracks with a big half-moon smile on his jolly fat face when Penny popped this question to Elija.

"Well, I know who I am," he shot the answer right at Cousin Penny. "You remember McGary at the Battle of Blue Licks, don't you? Remember when they tracked the Indians to the Licking River! I, Colonel McGary, took off my hat and waved it and I said, 'You who are not cowards follow me.' And that's when I didn't take warning, fell in the river with seventy comrades around me."

"That massacre was the greatest slaughter in our state's history," Penny said. Then he winked at Pudd. "You were brave, all right, McGary, but you got a lot of the best men in Kentucky killed! Do you remember how it felt to be shot?"

"No, after my long sleep I forgot the pangs of death," he said. "I don't know whether I was shot by a rifle or hit by an arrow."

Old Pudd walked away holding back his laughter. I had to laugh in Elija's face. Penny laughed louder than Wiff had laughed at him when he said he wondered how the rabbit or squirrel he had killed felt when he snuffed out its life for food for the Shelton table.

"I can't understand reincarnation," Penny said between spasms of laughter.

"Well I understand it," Elija said. "It's no laughing matter! You go on laughing like this at the truth and you might be resurrected into a laughing hyena in darkest Africa when you come back into this world again!"

"I'll take my chances on that," Penny said. He didn't like what Elija had said to him. "Come on, Shan," he said, "let's get out of here before we're turned into a bull, a fox, or a dog."

"Well, you could be," Elija said to Penny and me as we left the store.

"You ever hear such crazy talk," Penny said as we walked down the steps. "What's happened to people's minds?"

"I never heard anything like it," I said. "Say, there was a picture of Colonel McGary waving his cap at the massacre of Blue Licks in our Kentucky history book. He was standing at the edge of the Licking River waving his buckskin cap and he wore a buckskin suit just like Daniel Boone wore except it had longer fringes than Boone's suit!"

"Watch old Elija," Penny said. "He got two bucks and he'll have himself a suit made with the long fringes."

We didn't have long to wait. Before December, Elija Birdsong was out wearing his buckskin suit with the long fringes. He didn't have a coon's tail attached to his cap because McGary's picture in the Kentucky history book didn't have one. But there wasn't as much talk about Elija's suit this year as there had been last year when Wiff first wore his suit to Pudd's store. Everybody had seen a man in a buckskin suit and the newness had worn off.

"Never discourage their going to Michigan to hunt big game," Penny said. "You know wildlife is coming back here again. I've seen groundhogs again this year. I saw them playing with their young. I never saw any last year. I've heard squirrels barking in the tall timber the first time in two years. And I hear quails hollering 'bob-white' in the fields again. It's a sound good to hear. Little Ed said he heard a pheasant drumming in his father's woods near their strawberry patch the other day. And he said he'd seen his first grouse in two years. Said he saw a brace going up the hill. Never discourage reincarnated Daniel Boone and Colonel McGary from going to the Upper Peninsula for bigger game. If they go there we'll get some wildlife back here."

Time passed and autumn came again. This time when Wiff and Elija went to Michigan, it was a different story. Wiff was arrested for bagging four bucks, two more than his limit and Elija was arrested for bagging three. Their game was confiscated and they were fined two hundred dollars and costs. Little Effie and Pearlie Birdsong, Elija's wife, went over to Dartsmouth and wired them extra money to pay their fines and get home. This time they came without any deer and there was no write-up and no picture in the *Dartsmouth Daily*.

"But we promised to be good boys," Wiff told Little Ed, Big Aaron, Cousin Penny, and me in Pudd's store. "I made a mistake and I told them so. What we ought to have done was help the other fellow get their limits. But we took two cars this time We just got greedy. I guess if we'd got by we'd've come home with seven bucks. Say, big-time hunting up there is like the old paradise in the Kentucky wilderness. We'll go back next year!"

"What if you were turned into a deer, Wiff, when you leave this world, do you think it would be any fun to be shot at?" Penny asked with a laugh. "You believe you could be turned into a deer, don't you?"

"Yes, I know I could," he said seriously. "But if I came back as a deer I would expect to be shot at. And I'd run for my life. I would do all I could to miss bullets and live as long as I could. Don't think I've not thought a lot about being a deer in my next reincarnation."

This time Cousin Penny did the laughing. I thought such words coming from old Wiff were funny. I wondered why he went to any church. I thought he just went to accompany Little Effie.

Time passed and another season came. Wiff and Elija made preparations to go. Elija now had two buckskin suits. He had one with the long fringes like Colonel McGary's and one like Daniel Boone's. He had one buckskin cap made of hide not tanned. The other was made of tanned hide. Old Wiff had four buckskin suits now. I never knew how many buckskin caps he had, tanned and untanned. I know each one had the coon's tail. And when they went back to the Upper Peninsula for their big hunt, they dressed in their early pioneer Kentucky wilderness clothes, clothes they thought they had worn nearly two hundred years ago when they had fought the Indians together at Blue Licks on the Licking River. I wondered if they had followed their Kentucky history and remembered that Daniel Boone had advised Colonel McGary not to attempt to cross the Licking River. But I didn't know what the two hunters talked about in this modern world when they could drive a car over good highways to Michigan. There'd been a lot of changes in our Kentucky and our country since they had been reincarnated. Once I asked Penny if he believed they ever discussed the Battle of Blue Licks, when old Wiff, who thought he was Boone, advised Elija, who thought he was Colonel McGary, not to cross the Licking and McGary, who was now Elija, waved his hat and called hardy Kentucky pioneer Indian fighters cowards and they followed him and seventy were slaughtered from ambush in five minutes.

Well this was the trip to Upper Michigan that ended old Wiff's hunting. When the wire came to Little Effie to come as fast as she could get there, she drew money they were saving for later years in their Canadian North Woods paradise from one of the banks. She got young Sack Middaw, the fastest driver in Kensington, to take her to Wiff. He had been mistaken for a deer and shot by a nearsighted Michigan hunter. He had seen Wiff's buckskin cap when it was in motion and had cut down on him with an automatic. How many times he'd fired were not clear in the long telegram Elija had sent Little Effie. But he said Wiff was at the point of death and for her to get there as soon as she could.

Wiff wasn't as near dead as Elija's wire had said. But Wiff's being mistaken and shot for a deer was the talk of Kensington. No one could believe that Wiff had been shot. Well, Big Aaron, Little Ed, Cousin Penny, and I who had killed wild game in reasonable amounts for our tables could believe this. We were good hunters too who didn't really relish killing. And we certainly never bragged about it. We knew if Wiff had worn one of his buckskin caps made from a buck's hide that had been cured but not tanned that it was the same color of a deer and if old Wiff doddled his head and put his cap in motion some man at a distance could mistake him for a deer in woods where there were many hunters. We heard by the second wire Little Effie sent her mother that hunters had to pack Wiff ten miles to the little train that hauled him from the timber woods on a flat car for another forty miles to a little town and hospital. Now, Wiff was coming home in an ambulance.

Well, Wiff's classmates and friends who had once studied Kentucky history with him in one-room Walnut Grove School, where one teacher taught fifty classes in six hours, boyhood friends who used to hunt with him until he got on a wild killing spree and thought he was Daniel Boone, Cousin Penny, Big Aaron, Little Ed, and I were at Wiff and Little Effie's modest little frame house waiting when the ambulance with a Michigan license rolled up with Wiff on a soft bed closed in by glass. Little Effie was sitting there beside him with her hand on his head. Elija drove in behind the ambulance with Wiff's car. It was a pitiful sight. We weren't laughing at old Wiff now. We felt sorry for him. There he lay on that ambulance bed that looked like a hearse, a once big powerful man so full of life. We walked around behind the ambulance to carry Wiff on a stretcher into his home to transfer him to his own bed.

"I got two slugs in the back," he said softly when the ambulance driver released and rolled the stretcher up where we could take hold. "I'll never be able to use my right arm again. It's nearly shot off."

"We're sorry about this, Wiff," I said.

"We certainly are," Big Aaron said.

"Yeah, that nearsighted man shot me for a deer," he mumbled.

"And he never offered to pay any of Wiff's hospital and doctor bill," Little Effie said. "What's happened to us will end Wiff's dream of that happy hunters' paradise in the North Woods."

We carried Wiff into his own home. We lifted him into his own bed.

"Thank God, I'm home," he said. "No more hunting! I don't believe I'm the reincarnation of Daniel Boone either."

When he said this the young clean-shaven, well-dressed ambulance driver stood and stared at our Wiff Hendrix. Then Little Effie introduced him to us, William E. Westbrook.

"We're so glad to be back home," Little Effie said apologetically, "I forgot to introduce this kind young man to you. He's been wonderful to us."

I couldn't forget the way William Westbrook stared at old Wiff when he said he didn't believe he was the reincarnation of Daniel Boone. I thought he never knew who he had been transporting eight hundred miles in his ambulance.

"Yes, a close call, Penny," Wiff said. "And I'm not out of the woods yet. I have thought day and night about what you said about when you killed a little animal and picked it up how you wondered how it felt when its life had been snuffed out by gunshot. I remember how funny I thought it was then and how I laughed. Well, Penny, I know now. I couldn't count the times I was hit and how many slugs I heard sing past me, for it happened so fast. If I'd got all the slugs, I'd've been brought back in a coffin."

"Forget about that evening in Pudd's store," Penny said. "Try to get well and get back to your job!"

"I can't work any more unless Big Western gives me a snap job," he said. "I'll only have one arm. I'll never hunt again. I'll never shoot another wild animal or bird. I'm through!"

"Maybe you can hunt with one arm," Elija said. "Maybe you can go back to the little game around here."

"I said, Elija, I'd never kill again," Wiff spoke stoutly. "I know how it feels to be shot! I'm through playing Daniel Boone and you'd better stop playing Colonel McGary who got seventy men killed in five minutes. He was no hero. You are no hero. I am no hero."

William Westbrook had a puzzled look on his face.

"Fellows, we'd better be going," Big Aaron said. "Now when you need help, Little Effie, call on us."

"Yes, call on us for anything we can help you do," Penny said. "Yours and Wiff's folks are coming in."

"How did you know to meet us?" she asked.

"We heard you were coming and we've been here at your house all day waiting," Little Ed said.

"How wonderful to have friends," Wiff said. "When I get out of here I'll sit in a chair next time at Pudd's store and I'll have a different story to tell. And I won't be dressed like Daniel Boone either."

"We'll be back later, Wiff," I said. "I see plenty of company coming."

As we left the house Little Effie was writing a check to the young ambulance driver for bringing our Wiff back home.

Pa's a Man's Man All Right

OUR neighbors on Culp Creek called Pa "Old Windy," but when they got to know him better they called him "The Egg Man." Mom never liked these names and when a neighbor woman said to Mom: "Tell your Egg Man to fetch us a dozen eggs," Mom always replied, "When I get home, I'll tell Mister McMullen to bring you the eggs."

But my younger brother Puddie and I often had merchants who lived in Argill Village and in Woodstock say to us: "Tell Old Windy we are out of eggs. Tell him to hurry and fetch us some." Puddie and I never wanted to hurt Pa's business but our faces would get red and Puddie would speak up real fast and say: "Yep, we'll tell him so he can tell the hens to speed up production." But an answer like this from as quick a wit as Brother Puddie would never work. The merchant would say, bending over and laughing: "What about Old Windy's new kind of hens that lay two eggs a day?"

Once, after one-arm Joe, who ran a one-hoss grocery store in Argill, had asked Puddie to tell Old Windy to fetch him six dozen fresh eggs, Puddie grunted that he would and we left the store. "There's no use for us to get mad, Puddie," I said. "Pa is not as young as he used to be and you know he is windy. When a man gets a nickname there is more truth in it than in the name he was given when he was born." And Puddie got madder when I said every girl and man child born in these parts should be called X or Y or given some number until ten years old before he or she was named. Brother Puddie didn't think my suggestion a bit funny. And when I went home and told our sisters, Clara, Grace and Bunny about my suggestion, Bunny, as quick-witted as Brother Puddie, shouted: "No, Adger, no! Pa should never have gone into the chicken business. The way it is now, I'm Pullet Egg because I'm the youngest. You're Old Goose Egg, because you're the oldest and largest. And poor Puddie . . . well, he's Bad Egg—"

"Shut up, will 'ye?" Puddie shouted. "I'm tired of eggs!"

"Ah, take it easy, Puddie," Bunny said. "Grace is Guinea Egg because she's freckled. And Clara is Buck Egg because she's short and plump and always quacking. Mom . . ."

"Don't mention it," Puddie said, "She might hear you, and—"

"Well she does cluck to us all the time," Bunny interrupted, trying to keep from laughing.

"Yes, but just don't say it," Puddie said. "This egg business is doing something to her. She just sits and looks into space all the time!"

"But people call her that behind her back," Bunny said. Then she gave a wild little laugh.

"We've got the names all right," I said. "And you know why? Pa's to blame for it. I wouldn't be surprised if he didn't name us."

"Well, he sells his eggs, doesn't he?" Bunny said. "He couldn't make a living with all of us helping him on the farm on Culp Creek before he went into the chicken business. Now look what a thriving business he has! We live all right, don't we?"

"Yes, but with the names we have we had better have stayed on the farm," I said. "I'm a Senior and they still call me Big Goose Egg in Woodstock High School."

"His business got so big he had to move the chickens close to town instead of hauling eggs everyday, which cut down the profit," Bunny said real quick. "You're just ashamed of Pa's business here in Woodstock."

"Pa has worked things out mighty well," Bunny continued. "We don't live on Main Street. We live here in the edge of town with our yard fenced by hedge. Our big chickenhouse is up against the hill and it's kept as clean as a pin."

Well, there was no denying that Pa had found the right place for us to live and keep our chickens. And Sister Bunny was right about our keeping the henhouse clean, for Brother Puddie and I did the cleaning while Pa peddled the eggs in our little farm truck. Mom couldn't do too much talking because Pa had a nice family car for us to drive since he had been the most successful egg man in these parts. He had his old customers, those he got when we had only a hundred laying hens. Pa had started another business too from our chickens. He had arranged a new fancy henhouse from a plan he got from our State University where he trapped the roost's droppings, which Puddie and I sacked into small bags. Pa sold these bags to the women in Woodstock to fertilize their flowers. It was said of Pa that he marketed everything but the hen's cackle and the rooster's crow.

"Bunny, you've never gone with Pa when he sells eggs," I said "You ought to know how he talks to the merchants. I've been with him and I know they start laughing just as soon as he goes in with the eggs. Say a merchant wants five dozen eggs. Before Pa gets through telling the merchant about Goose Egg, Bad Egg, Guinea Egg, Pullet Egg, Duck Egg, and—"

"Don't say it, Adger," Bunny said. "She might hear."

"We ought to move back to Culp Creek," Brother Puddie said.

"And starve to death?" Bunny said real quick. "No, I'll take Woodstock and be called Pullet Egg! Well, now, the girls at school call me Pullet. They have left the egg off!"

"Good," Brother Puddie said. "But I still think we should move back to Culp Creek."

"Without a high school close and grow up in ignorance like the sassafras sprouts on them poor old hills' slopes?" I asked.

"The sassafras sprouts are happy," Brother Puddie said. "They're senseless but happy and don't know they're poor. I'm for going back. Who's happy around here?"

"Pa's happy," I said, "and. . . ."

"Sure, he goes on telling his big tales," Brother Puddie interrupted. "He tells the merchants how happy his Eggs are in The Little Love Nest he has provided for them in Woodstock. And now, they laugh and buy twice as many eggs as they ordered. They never call Pa Mister McMullin, as Mom wants him called. They still call him Old Windy or The Egg Man and Pa likes what they call him as long as he sells them the eggs, old fat hens and sacks of chicken fertilizer for their flowers. I've never seen anybody who can sell like he can. Now, he has another line he tells the merchants to make them laugh. He tells them how to control their wives. He tells them how he controls Mom. He tells them when their wives won't behave to use a switch like he does. You ought to hear them laugh!"

"He used to tell such tales to our neighbors on Culp Creek, but they knew better," I said. "That might not work here. Merchants might tell their wives about how he says he switches Mom and they might believe it."

"Oh, that won't happen," Sister Bunny said. "Don't be so suspicious about our father. He has a good sense of humor and it's paid off."

While we were doing this talking about the situation Pa walked into the kitchen with a big smile on his face. "What are my Eggs up to?" he asked. "Don't you think it's time you got under Mother's wings for the night? Then wake up in your nest in the morning feeling fine and refreshed?"

Pa laughed loudly as he puffed clouds of smoke from a half-dollar cigar. He had his thumbs behind his suspenders and he'd pull them out and let them fly back. Here he stood with a big grin on his face, dressed in his clean blue shirt and black bow tie. Pa would weigh over two hundred and forty pounds. He had broad shoulders and pink cheeks. And he always looked like he was ready to burst out laughing all over. His blue eyes laughed when he looked at one of us. We laughed at him like the merchants had, for we knew what a gentle man he was and how good he was to Mom. Pa was full of fun that radiated through his words as soft and crazy as a gentle lazy summer wind that blew through the henhouse and ruffled the feathers of five thousand hens.

When we went to bed, we laughed about getting under Mom's wing for the night. We knew we'd wake early in the morning and have fried eggs for breakfast. We just couldn't escape eggs.

Pa always got up early because Puddie, Clara, Grace and I were in Woodstock Senior High School and Bunny was in Woodstock Junior High. After breakfast Puddie and I had to clean the henhouse and sack the droppings while Pa got his truck-load of eggs ready to be on the road as soon as the merchants opened their stores. Then, Pa hadn't forgot how he started in business by peddling eggs from door to door among our neighbors. He had a short circuit he made late each afternoon in the area that surrounded us. I figured Pa told all these neighbors his big tales the same as he had told them to our neighbors on Culp Creek. Everywhere Pa went the men liked him. He was a man's man all right.

Next morning when we sat around the breakfast table, laughing and talking, Mom didn't join in our laughter and fun. She never talked very much but this morning she was too quiet.

"Silas, you know, I feel that something is going to happen," she said.

"Don't tell me that, Mother," he said. "You scare me!"

Well, I began to laugh. I thought Pa was being funny. Sister Bunny giggled and Brother Puddie grinned. Clara and Grace smiled.

"Yes, Silas, I feel that something is going to happen," Mom sighed softly.

"You never said this to me but once before in our life," Pa said. "And three days later the cholera struck my chickens, geese, ducks, guineas, and turkeys and I lost every one of them. I never went back into the guinea, turkey, goose and duck business. I stuck to the chickens!"

"Yes, but I didn't know."

"Well, she did," Pa said, before one of us had time to ask a question.

"Something is going to happen, Silas," Mom repeated. "Be careful as you drive the truck today."

"I will, Mother," he said, getting up from the table without finishing his eggs. Pa was a disturbed man.

When Brother Puddie and I went to the henhouse and switched on the lights to do our cleaning Puddie said: "Now you see how Pa whips Mom with a switch! She can say the least thing and it will upset him. I don't any more believe anything is going to happen to us than I can stand on my head on a roosting rail in this henhouse, do you?"

"I'm not so sure," I said. "Mom might be guided by a strange intuition."

Well, this day came and went. And Pa made his truck deliveries without accident. And he made his delivery route on foot to our neighbors. He carried a basket that held twenty-four dozen eggs. He got by all right for the day. And we got along all right at school. Then the second day came and went without trouble. Then, the third day came and had almost gone when something happened. We were all sitting around the supper table laughing and talking when Brother Puddie said: "Hush, everybody! Hear that?"

"Hear what?" Pa asked. "I didn't hear anything."

"A hen squalling," Puddie said.

"Yes, I heard it," I said.

"Be careful, Silas," Mom said.

When a hen squalled Pa got on his way. He jumped up from the table. We had seen him do this before. He went after his gun. He took off toward the henhouse. Brother Puddie and I were right behind him. Our chickens were in a terrible uproar.

"Careful, Pa," I whispered as he eased the door open and switched on the light.

"It's a weasel," Pa spoke softly. "I see it but I can't shoot without killing my hens. He's killed one hen and is after another."

Pa put the shotgun to his shoulder. But when the weasel heard

Pa whisper he ran out the door past us and I stomped at him but missed. Pa couldn't shoot when it ran past us through the door. Brother Puddie and I were in his way.

"Which way?" Pa shouted.

"Around the corner of the house," I said.

By this time Clara, Grace, and Bunny had run outside.

"It's a weasel," I told them. "It went around the house."

Pa was in front and we were behind him. We were hollering and carrying on something terrible. And then Mom came running out of the house. She was afraid Pa would shoot and hit one of us. So she began to follow and shout: "Silas, don't shoot! Have mercy, Silas, don't shoot!"

And here we went around and around the house after the weasel that kept running circles. Pa was in front, Puddie and I were right behind him, and Clara, Bunny and Grace were right behind us and Mom was behind them.

"Don't shoot, Silas!" Mom shouted.

There was much commotion around our house. The neighbors couldn't see us for the hedge but they could hear us. Around and around the house we went hollering and screaming about the weasel until there was so much noise people couldn't tell exactly what we were saying but they could hear Mom saying: "Don't shoot, Silas!" as she trailed us. I looked over the hedge and lights had come on in the second stories of all the buildings around and I could see faces against the windows.

"Don't do it here, Silas," Mom pleaded almost out of breath. "Please don't shoot, Silas!"

Well, maybe it was good the weasel got away and Pa never got a shot at it. And maybe it was good that our noise subsided and we went back into the house where we sat panting and mumbling with half breaths while Mom explained: "I told you something was going to happen. Maybe this is it. But I was afraid if you shot at the weasel you might shoot one of the children."

And then Pa said: "Well, I hope this is all there is to it. If this is what you thought would happen to us we have got by but I hate to let that weasel get away! Who would think a weasel would find my chickens in Woodstock?"

The next morning we were up as usual, had breakfast, and Pa got his load ready while Brother Puddie and I cleaned the henhouse. When we got through with out work and went back to the house to get ready for school the girls had already gone. Just as we were dressed and ready to go, the doorbell rang. I opened the door. There stood a woman with a wild look on her face.

"Is your mother all right?" she asked.

"Yes, why?" I asked.

"I'm Mrs. Melvin and I live across the street," she told me. "We've been buying eggs from your father! Where is your mother?"

"Mom, somebody here to see you," I said.

Mom came from the kitchen.

"Excuse us Mrs. Melvin," I said. "We have to hurry to school."

"That's all right boys," she said. "I just wanted to talk to your mother."

So we left Mom with Mrs. Melvin and hurried on to school.

We were running side by side down the street to get to school on time. "I heard her say she lived close," Puddie panted. "I've never seen her before."

"One of the women on Pa's afternoon egg route," I spoke with halfwords for my breath was coming a little hard. "See, people here in Woodstock aren't as neighborly as they used to be on Culp Creek."

"No one comes to see us unless he wants eggs, fat hens or fertilizer for the flowers," Puddie panted as we ran onto the schoolyard in time.

When Puddie and I hurried home from school ahead of Clara and Grace, for we had work to do in the henhouse, we passed two strange women on the walk just leaving our house. When we got to the door, Mom met us.

"We're having a lot of company, Mom," Puddie said.

Mom's dark eyes were bright and her face was alive. There was a strange little smile on her curved lips. She was dressed in a smart suit Clara and Grace had helped her select at Mylady's Shop in Woodstock. And I knew how come her to get that suit. I heard Pa whisper to Clara and Grace between puffs on his big cigar one evening in the kitchen. I walked in unbeknowns to them. I heard him say: "We're in Woodstock now. Mother has to go better dressed. See that she gets the smartest suit from the smartest shop in Woodstock. Don't say I told you. Help her. I want Mother to look like a queen. She's the prettiest forty-five-year-old in the United States."

"Mom, why are you all dressed up?" Brother Puddie asked her before I could.

"Oh, I was going to tell you," she said. "You just met two women going down the walk. They were the fifteenth and sixteenth women who have been here today to see me. I just had time after one left and another one came this morning to get out of my old clothes into my best. I've never seen the like."

"What's bringing them, Mom?" I asked.

"That weasel last night," she replied. Then she laughed and she really cackled like a hen out in the henhouse. "You know when I was hollering "Don't shoot, Silas," for I was afraid he'd hit one of the children? Well, everybody who lives close heard me. They thought Silas was trying to shoot me. They couldn't see what was going on over here for the hedge. They've been coming all day and asking if they can do something to help me. I think it's funny! See, I never told them what Silas was trying to shoot! I'm enjoying this! All this company! Women who would never have come to visit us! Honest, it reminds me of the days back on Culp Creek when the neighborhood women dropped in uninvited at all hours during the day. If I'd told them Silas was trying to shoot a weasel it would stop everything. And don't you tell them either! We'll have good neighbors from now on."

"Mom, you will," Brother Puddie said. "But what about Pa?"

"Yes, what about his business?" I said. "He'll lose all his afternoon delivery customers."

"Maybe the merchants too," Brother Puddie said. "You know how women control their husbands. You let it get out that Pa was really trying to shoot you and you had to beg him to spare your life, do you think merchants will buy his eggs?"

"He's due here about now," Mom said. "Let him take his egg

basket and start making his deliveries. We'll see what happens!"

Just then Bunny came running in with her face flushed. "Mom, there's a lot of talk about us down at Junior High," she said. "I heard them whispering and calling Pa an old beast, a brute, a devil and a lot of other names I couldn't figure out for they wouldn't talk to me about what they were discussing among themselves."

"All right, Pullet, you just keep quiet," Brother Puddie said. "I told you about all this egg business. And you laughed like a laughing owl in the trees at night. You thought Bad Egg was a good enough name for me."

"Now, Bunny, there's nothing wrong," Mom said laughing. Bunny was surprised because Pa had done the laughing in our home for all of us. Everything and everybody was funny to Pa. "Now, it's time for the rest of us to do some laughing."

Just then, Grace and Clara came in. They'd not run home. Their faces weren't flushed. But their faces were serious.

"All right, Guinea Egg, what's the matter with you?" Brother Puddie asked. "And you, Duck Egg, why are you so serious?"

"We heard whispers at school," Clara said. "Did you hear anything today?"

"Not a word," Brother Puddie replied.

"And Big Goose Egg didn't hear anything either," I added. "And I don't think Guinea Egg and Ducky heard anything either. I think they just imagined they did. What do you think, Mom?"

"Sure, you just thought you heard something," Mom said, with a broad smile.

"I don't understand all this, " Sister Clara sighed. "What's going on around here?"

"All right Ducky, now quack some more," Brother Puddie said.

"Shut up, Bad Egg," Sister Clara said. Then she turned to Mom and said: "I can't forget what you said at the supper table about something going to happen here. Something must have already happened but I don't know what it is."

Just then Pa walked in at the door.

"There comes my Darling Egg Man," Mom said, as she went

toward Pa with her arms open. She was smiling and cooing like a dove. Something none of us had ever seen her do before. And a crazy thought went through my mind that made me laugh. I thought a good name for Mom would be Dove Egg. I could just hear Pa calling her "My Little Dovie." And then I laughed louder than ever when I thought about Pa's taking his basket of eggs and starting on his delivery route in a few minutes. But all of us were tickled now as Pa held Mom up in his arms, real close against him and her feet were two feet off the floor and he billed and cooed like a rooster sidling up to a hen. And Pa was all smiles because he was greeted this way by Mom and he thought we were all laughing at their antics and this made Pa happier than I had seen him in a long time. This was saying a lot too, for Pa was always happy.

"Did you have a good day, My Darling Egg Man?" Mom asked when he set her back down on the floor.

"Well, this morning was wonderful," Pa said. "But in the afternoon eggs took a turn for the worse and no matter what I said I couldn't cheer my old customers up. Say, I believe the bottom has dropped out of the egg market. After I make my deliveries this afternoon I'm going to check the market in the paper and I'm goin' to listen over the radio to the Cincinnati Market."

"I'm sorry you had a bad afternoon, Darling," Mom cooed lovingly.

We could tell that Pa couldn't understand why Mom was all dressed up and why she was getting so affectionate all of a sudden. Pa had always been the aggressor before and now Mom was becoming one. When he went to get his basket of eggs she held onto his big hand with both of her little hands, and they went through the door together. We were still standing in the living room, while Puddie and I were listening to our sisters talking about the strange whispers among the students at school. Brother Puddie and I didn't let our sisters in on the secret. And when Mom came back Bunny said: "Mom, I don't understand what has come over you. I've never seen you act like this before!"

"Oh, My Nest of Eggs, I'm so much in love with your Egg Man father," Mom told her.

Puddie and I began to laugh and our sisters looked at us disgustedly. And they gave our mother a puzzled look. And just then Pa walked in with the big willow basket heaped with eggs. He had a load on his big woolly arm big enough for a pony to pack.

"I'm your Egg Man and I love our Eggs in Our Love Nest," Pa said to Mom.

"You'd better love us, Darling," Mom sighed as she went over to him again. He bent over and kissed Mom and said: "This will give me the luck. I'll have good sales on this trip."

"I hope so, Darling," she told him in her soft voice.

"You look so sweet all dressed up in that suit," Pa said.

"I put it on for you," Mom said. "Why not?"

Pa smiled, and then he said: "My little wifey that I beat up so often," and he gave a wild laugh and then put the big cigar back in his mouth. He opened the door. "Wish me luck."

"You might need it, Darling," Mom said. "So, I wish My Egg Man luck."

And then Pa was off with a cloud of smoke behind him.

Puddie and I went to the henhouse. We were late and had to work fast to get through by the time Pa had finished his delivery route. "We must be there to see how Pa made out," Brother Puddie said. So we worked fast and when we went over to the house Pa was sitting in his rocker like a big sad ox with his feet propped upon a footstool. His hair was wet and his shirt around the collar looked like it had been put in the washer but hadn't been run through the wringer. A cigar with a cold gray ash end lay on the ashtray beside him. Bunny, Clara and Grace were sitting on a divan facing him.

"Say, what's going on here?" I asked.

"You tell me," Pa said. "The bottom has dropped out of the egg market. It's dropped out of me too!"

Then, Mom came in from the kitchen.

"Boys, listen to what happened to your Pa," Mom said.

"Tell us, Pa," Brother Puddie said.

"Something has gone wrong," he said. "I never sold an egg."

"That can't be," Brother Puddie said.

"Well it has been," Pa grunted, staring at the wall. "One woman, Mrs. Melvin, spit at me but I dodged and she missed. Women slammed their doors in my face. And you know, over at Lathrops, a bucket of water was poured down on me from an upstairs window. A lot of the women wouldn't come to the door. What on earth have I done to cause this?"

"Nothing, Silas," Mom told him. "You're a loving husband."

"Well, of course I've kidded some of the merchants about how I control my wife, but I do it for fun and they laugh and buy more eggs," he explained. "But I have never said anything about you, Honey.," he looked up at Mom, "to any of the women on my delivery route. They always call me Their Egg Man in a friendly way and I like it. I like to sell them eggs too. So I didn't finish my delivery route, boys," Pa spoke in a grieved tone. "I was afraid one of them crazy women might throw hot water from a window. Cold water was enough."

"I've told him tomorrow might be different," Mom said.

"What have I done to cause this?" Pa asked.

"I can't think of anything," I said.

"Bad Egg, we told you we heard whispers at school," Bunny said.

"And you wouldn't listen to us," Clara said.

"I guess the eggs will pile up on us," Pa sighed.

It was a sad evening in our nest. All we talked about at the supper table was what had caused the drop in egg sales on Pa's delivery route, what had happened to sales to his merchants and why there had been whispering about us at school. Puddie and I pretended we believed our sisters after what had happened to Pa. "I couldn't get close enough to one of the women on the delivery route to ask her why she didn't want any eggs," Pa told us. "I'll tell you it was dangerous. Why should they fight their friendly old Egg Man?"

"We don't know, Pa," Puddie said. "You tell us."

"Well, tomorrow is Saturday," he said. "Adger, I want you to go with me. See, if you can help me figure this out."

On Saturday morning I helped load the truck with eggs laid on Friday and the cases of Thursday's eggs which Pa hadn't sold on Friday.

"I want to sell these first," Pa said. "Maybe Old Henry Gullett will take them. He's a big two-hoss merchant and he sells a lot of eggs. He's one of my best customers."

When we pulled up and parked, Henry had just opened his market. We had just got out of the truck when Henry come running outside.

"We won't need any eggs today, Mister Egg Man," he said.

"What?" Pa said. "I can't believe—"

"Peddle your eggs somewhere else," he shouted, waving Pa away.

Then, he ran back in and slammed the door behind him.

"He doesn't even want me in his store," Pa sighed. "I told you something was wrong. Your Ma said something would happen."

Pa got slowly back in the truck. Henry Gullett looked from the window. Pa didn't see him and I didn't tell Pa. When we drove away he shook his fist but I didn't tell Pa.

"Next stop will be Mutt Conley at The People's Store," Pa said. "Old Mutt's been a good friend. I've told him some big tales! He laughs at my foolishness and he buys my eggs!"

We pulled up before The People's Store. Pa knocked the gray ash from the end of his cigar and started puffing as he walked in.

"Hy'ya, Mutt," Pa shouted, as he pulled his suspenders back and let them fly back against his rib panels. "Need any eggs from your old Egg Man this morning?"

"I need for you to get out of here," Mutt said. "I don't want eggs from a man that pulls this rough stuff on his poor wife!"

"What are you talking about?" Pa said. "I've always kidded . . ."

"Kidded my foot," he shouted. "Get out!"

"But, I can explain," I said, "that Pa—"

"Get out with him, Goose Egg," Old Mutt shouted. "You're a chip off the old block."

"If that's the way you feel . . ."

"Get before I get the meat cleaver!"

"Oh, goodness," Pa said as we ran out the door. "Is everybody goin' crazy?"

Pa gunned the motor and we were off in a hurry.

"Where next, Pa?" I said.

"One more stop and if it turns out like these have, we're turning back," he said. "I can't take this. We'll move back to Culp Creek farm, and live with the sassafras sprouts on the old poor hills and listen to the wind in the broomsedge and the hootowls and the whippoorwills!"

"And the mockingbirds, cardinals and the quails!" I added.

"This hurts my pride, Adger," Pa told me. "We'll stop here at Wurts Brothers. Young Sammie always takes a case."

We stopped the truck and got out and walked in.

"Won't need any today," Sammie said politely. "I can't sell what you brought yesterday."

"Why, what's wrong?" Pa asked.

"Women won't buy 'em over the way you treat your wife," he told Pa.

"Your wife-beating, so close to murder, has got all the women against you, Windy!"

Pa looked at the floor. He never said a word, but walked out and I followed him.

"My trade is gone, Adger," he sighed. He knocked the ash from his unlit cigar. "I'm a ruint man. I'd as well sell my chickens! I've worked fourteen years to build a trade I've lost overnight. I guess a man can say too much. I couldn't give these eggs away."

"Let's try another store," I said. "We've got plenty of time. Let's got to Argill and see if One-Arm Joe," Pa said. "He's never bought more than ten dozen at a time but I'd like to know if he's against me too."

This was a nice ride over the old familiar road.

"Well, if it isn't Old Windy," One-Arm Joe snarled when Pa and I entered. "Goose, what do you think about your old wife-beating Pappie?"

"If you had two arms I'd mash your mouth," Pa said.

"No, you won't, Wife-beater," One-Arm Joe said. "I keep something handy to protect myself." He opened a drawer to his desk. He put his hand inside the drawer. "You start something with me, Old Windy!"

"You don't have to worry, One-Arm Joe," said a big beardy-faced man. "We've heard the story!"

I didn't know the big man dressed in overalls, jumper, brogan shoes and blue work shirt. He had his hand stuck down in his bulging pocket.

"Come on, Adger," Pa said. "Let's go. I'm finished."

"I say you're finished," Old One-Arm Joe said.

We walked out and I turned and looked back. One-Armed Joe and the strangers were in the door looking at us. Above the door was a sign TRADE WITH ONE-ARM JOE. And below this sign were these words: *Honest weights. Courteous Treatment.*

When we started back Pa detoured off the main road.

"Where are you going?" I asked.

"I'll show you," he said.

He drove the truck up so close the brink of the deep East Fork Canyon where people hauled their garbage, I thought we were going over. Pa got out and one by one he tossed the loaded egg cases over the thirty-foot wall into the deep hole.

"The eggs won't pile up on me," Pa said. "Your old father has pride, Adger! Did you ever see me beat your mother?"

"Never," I replied.

"Young Sammie Wurts even mentioned 'murder' to me!"

We drove home and Pa put the truck in the garage.

"Say, let's not disturb your mother," he told me. "When she asks if the eggs sold, I'll show her the empty truck."

"All right, Pa," I said. "I won't say anything."

"I don't want to worry her," he said. "She loves me and I love her!"

When we started down the walk, Pa relighted his cigar and he threw out his chest, reared back and smiled. "I'll go in happy," he said.

We stopped on the walk when two women came out our front door.

"I believe one of them was that Mrs. Melvin who tried to spit on me," Pa said. "The other one looked like Mrs. Lathrop who threw the bucket of water on me. What are they doing here?"

We didn't know who they were for when they saw Pa their steps got faster as they made it toward our front gate.

"They puzzle me," he said. "Wonder if they've had something to do with my trouble?"

"How could they?" I asked.

"Come to think about it, I don't see how they could," he said.

When we opened the door and walked in, Mom came to meet us. "Darling, how did you get along?" she asked. "You're home early."

"I had Adger's help this morning," he said as she lifted her arms and came toward Pa. Pa embraced her by lifting her up off the floor. "My Sweet Little Nest Egg, you just come out here to the garage and look at the truck for yourself!"

Arm in arm they went out while I stayed in the living room with Puddie, Clara, Grace and Bunny, who were happy and smiling.

"We know the secret now," Bunny giggled. "It's real funny."

"Has Mom told those women the real truth?" I asked.

"No, Mom hasn't told them anything," Clara said. "This is what makes it so funny. They've never been friendly neighbors. And now they're so friendly to Mom she doesn't know what to do. And she's so happy with good neighbors. This has what that's caused Mom's sadness. Now, she's a new woman. All of them are trying to help Mom."

"Will any be back while Pa is here?" I asked.

"No, they won't," Bunny said. "They're afraid of Pa. They think he tried to shoot Mom the other night."

"Shhhhh, here they come," Brother Puddie said.

Pa and Mom squeezed through the door and Pa was smiling big.

"No eggs on the truck, children," Mom said. Mom wasn't as pleased as I thought she might have been. "Your father is still an Egg Man."

"My bad reputation hasn't spread everywhere yet," Pa said.

"But they have accused me of being a wife-beater. One customer went so far as to mention 'murder,' but you know how it is with me. When I lose a customer, I usually get a couple to replace him. But what I can't understand is about the strange action of the women on my delivery route. Say, I believe I saw Mrs. Melvin and Mrs. Lathrop come out at the door and hurry down the walk ahead of us."

"You're right, my Darling," Mom said.

"They've never come before," Pa spoke in a surprised tone.

"They just come to see if I was all right," Mom said. "It is all over Woodstock that you've beaten me, Darling, you've joked and . . ."

"I'm not going to lie, Mother," Pa said. "I never sold an egg this morning."

"What? But the truck is empty."

"The eggs and cases all went over the East Fork Canyon," Pa said. "And I'm goin' to sell my chickens. My old friends threatened me! My kidding about you never caused this."

"My poor Darling," Mom said. She went over to Pa's chair and dropped into his arms. He was as tall sitting down as she was standing. "I love you, Silas. I'm sorry if I have caused this trouble!"

"Mother, I shouldn't have told you," Pa said. "Don't you worry. I'm not blaming you. But my business is gone. Fourteen years of hard work, vanished in a day and night."

"I'm going to stand by you, Silas," Mom said. "I'll cling to you and forsake all others just what I said on the day I married you."

"All the eggs in this nest will stand by you," Bunny said.

"Your Bad Egg will stand by you," Brother Puddie said.

"Goose Egg will too," I said. "You know that, Pa."

"Duck Egg will too," Sister Clara said.

"Guinea Egg will too," Sister Grace said.

"Then all my eggs are with their Egg Man," Pa spoke proudly.

"I've been thinking, Silas," Mom said. "Tomorrow is Sunday. There will be no sales and deliveries. We'll all go to church."

"No, I won't be going to church," Pa said. "A swarm of mad

human bees are after me. All of 'em queen bees that have got their drones all stirred up! I'm afraid to get out of this house."

Then Mom told him if he didn't go to church she wouldn't go either. Our sisters and Brother Puddie and I told him the same thing.

"We're sticking by you, Pa," I said. "There was never a better Egg Man than you to your hens in the henhouse and your family eggs in this nest."

"What a wonderful family I got," he said. Tears welled up in his big blue eyes but he smiled through his tears. "No mother, I won't be in church tomorrow. I won't be making any egg deliveries Monday. I'm finished."

"Give me time to do some thinking, Darling," Mom said. "Where there's a will there's a way."

The afternoon, evening and night were sad for Pa. But we agreed among ourselves not to tell him the secret. We'd let Mom handle this. We believed she had already thought of a plan to save Pa and his business. At the breakfast table Mom said: "Something good is going to happen. I had a good dream last night."

"I feel better already," Pa said.

"But you can't count the chickens before the eggs hatch," Mom said.

"I won't count them until you tell me, Mother," he said.

"I'll tell you by morning," she sighed. "But I think you had better get your eggs ready. You're my Egg Man and I love you."

"That's all I want to hear," he said. "I tell you Mother, something is wrong. I wonder if all the merchants in Woodstock haven't lost their minds overnight. I know I've not lost my mind. I've just lost my business."

We stayed in the house with Pa all day on Sunday. All Brother Puddie and I did was clean the henhouse and sack the fertilizer. And Mom went with Pa to help him gather and test the eggs and put them into cases. Pa had to pull out every reserve case he had in the storage room.

"You just can't give up, Darling," Mom said. "It's not like you. You are big and strong and full of fun and fire." Then Mom looked up into his blue eyes and whispered, "you're still full of love!"

"I'd try anything for you," Pa said. "Your last words would make me do it."

Monday morning we were up bright and early and Mom and Grace prepared breakfast. We gathered around our table to eat while there wasn't a light in another house in our section of Woodstock.

"My Darling, I'm going with you this morning," Mom said.

"Oh, no you're not," Pa said. "I won't have you insulted. The man who insults me can get by. He has. But one had better not insult you. If he does I will hurt him. I'm liable to crush him with these big hands." Pa held his hands up and they looked like shovels.

"No one will insult me," Mom said. "Wait until you see how I dress. I won't be looking like the Egg Woman I am. I'll stick with you to the end. If this won't work we'll sell the chickens and leave Woodstock."

"I agree," Pa said. "But nobody had better insult you."

"I'll straighten up some of these tales," Mom said. "I'll show them that little wife they accuse you of beating! We'll surprise them, won't we?"

"Sure will," he replied baffledly. "You never have gone with me to deliver. Many of my customers never saw you!"

"You've never asked me, Silas," Mom told him. "And I've stayed in this house so long with no friends comin' that it's got to be unbearable, Silas! I had another good dream last night. I feel everything will be all right."

"That makes me feel better and better," Pa said. "Another cup of coffee, please."

Before we left for school, Puddie and I helped Pa load his truck and while Mom dressed in her smart suit and slippers and her dainty little hat, our sisters had washed and dried the dishes, cleaned the kitchen, made the beds and put the house in order. When Mom climbed up beside big Pa in the little truck they were smiling and we waved to them and they waved back like they were flying away to Europe to spend the summer.

This was one day we could hardly wait for school to be over so we could hurry home. Brother Puddie and I got home first. Then, Bunny came running from Junior High. Clara and Grace, came last. We wanted to be home by the time Mom and Pa got there.

"They're still making the circuit," I told my brother and sisters. "If they'd got the treatment we got Saturday they would have been back."

"Do you suppose Mom will go with Pa on his walking delivery route?" Bunny asked.

"You girls ought to know more about that," Brother Puddie replied. "You've been here when the neighbor women came in and heard what they said about Pa!"

"Well, if Mom does go with him on that delivery circuit wonder what the women will think of her?" Clara said.

"They'll know she loves him," Bunny replied.

"Maybe Mom will explain to them," Grace said.

"Maybe she won't go," Bunny said. "Mom has enjoyed the friendship of those women. After the way Pa's been joking with customers how he controls Mom and her hollering the other night for him not to shoot caused our neighbors to think he was trying to shoot her."

"If Mom is forced to explain that incident to the women who have been coming here she will lose their friendship," Brother Puddie said. "Will she go with Pa to face them?"

"We'll soon see," Clara said. "Here comes the truck now."

When they came in the house, arm in arm, they were like a couple of teenage lovers.

"Things must have gone well, Pa," I said.

"That's not the half of it," he replied proudly. "You've always had an Egg Man Father now you've got an Egg Woman Mother. Ask your mother if we sold eggs! There's never been anything like it."

"All have sold," Mom said proudly.

"When your little mother, prettiest forty-five-year-old in America, walked in dressed up like she'd come out of a bandbox," Pa said with a smile, big cigar in the corner of his mouth, pulling his suspenders out and letting them fly, "the merchants wilted. They knew right then I had a wife. They knew I didn't beat her! I introduced her first as my wife and then I'd say: "What do you think of my pretty little Egg Woman? Boy, can she swing a rolling pin. Just ask her and see who runs our Little Love Nest and this was it. Merchants that insulted me called me off in the back room and apologized. Old One-Arm Joe in Argill almost got down on his knees he was so hurt over what he'd said to me after he saw my good-looking Egg Wife. "Why didn't you bring her with you before?' Young Sammie Wurts asked me. 'No one can tell me you beat your good-looking wife. She's a million-dollar woman if I ever saw one!' That's the way they talked. Wish you Eggs could have been along and heard the talk about your Mother. You'd have been proud."

"Goose Egg, you, and Bad Egg," Mom said, calling us eggs for the first time and laughing too, "go to the chickenhouse and gather us twenty-four dozen. Put eighteen in your Pa's big basket and six dozen in my fancy basket. You'll find my basket hanging in the storeroom beside your Pa's. Now, hurry! We don't have much time!"

"Mom, are you going to make the delivery with Pa?" Bunny asked.

"I sure am," she replied quickly.

"Do you reckon—"

"I don't reckon anything," she interrupted Clara. "I took your Pa to stand by him until death do us part. I'm his Egg Woman from now on. I've just found out I can sell eggs too. I have found out he needs me. We're going to double the business."

Brother Puddie and I had the eggs gathered and in their baskets in a jiffy. Mom had one of the fanciest baskets I'd ever seen. Her basket was of many colors. And you should have seen her and Pa when they left the house and went down the walk with their baskets on their arms. They went through the gate in the hedgerow and out into Pa's hostile world, our neighborhood in Woodstock.

"We'll get supper," Clara said.

"And we'll do the work at the chickenhouse," I said. "By that time Mom and Pa will be back."

"Do you reckon they can make it on that hostile delivery?" Brother Puddie asked. Then he laughed wildly. "I think this is funny!"

"Mom dressed like she is and out with Pa is enough to sell any woman eggs," I said.

When we got back to the house Mom and Pa had returned with empty baskets. Our sisters had supper ready and waiting.

"Did it work?" I asked.

"Look at these empty baskets," Pa spoke with pride. "We didn't take enough eggs. All my customers were out of eggs. And I heard women telling Mom there must have been some mistake. But I didn't inquire about what the mistake was. It didn't matter, did it, my Sweet Little Egg Woman, prettiest forty-five-year-old in America! Our trade was built back in a day and we have to double production in two weeks!"

Mad Davids and a Mechanical Goliath

THE two men stood at the foot of the steep bluff and watched the giant dozer turn from the unsurfaced rural highway onto the little meadow. The shorter man, with a heavy growth of black beard and a sun-tanned face, leaned on his long-handled shovel, never batting his wind-blue eyes. He watched this man-made monster tilt up and down as it moved awkwardly toward him. The taller man, whose shoulders were slightly stooped, leaned on his long-handled shovel, too, while he watched the dozer with a pair of beady black eyes. He puffed small clouds of smoke from the hand-rolled cigarette that stuck between his wind-dried lips and rested on his stubby beard. Neither man spoke until the sparrow-sized man drove the dozer to the creek that zigzagged down the meadow near the bluff's edge.

"Poodie, we'd better get outen the way of that thing, hadn't we?" said the short man as he slowly raised from the leaning position on his shovel handle.

But the tall, bean-pole man stood silently and watched the dozer and did not answer until the mountain of steel started climbing from the creek bed onto the narrow strip of meadow between the bluff and stream.

"We'd better get outen the way," the tall man said. He now stood up straight as a yellow pine beside his long-handled shovel. "Damned thing might run over us! It looks like a big animal, but it doesn't have any sense!"

Then Poodie stepped over to the edge of the creek and the short man followed him. They used their shovels as if they were canes to support them as they walked. The little driver, with a disgusted look, had to steer the dozer to his right upon the bluff to avoid hitting them. There he halted and let the engine idle while he climbed down.

'Good mornin'," he greeted the two men. "My name is Hal Burton."

"My name is Poodie Pitts," said the tall man. He spoke softly as he eyed the small driver suspiciously. "This is Shorty Pratt."

"Good mornin'," Shorty said. Shorty never took his eyes off the dozer. "That's a powerful lookin' machine you're a-drivin'. Don't believe anything could stop it."

"No, it will push tons of rocks before it," Hal told them. "It will push trees over. It will do the work of fifty men. I 'spect you fellows have been sent to help me?"

"That's right," Shorty said.

"You've brought the wrong tools," Hal told them. "You won't need a shovel around this dozer. You might have brought an ax along."

"Won't need a shovel?" Poodie said.

"Won't need a shovel?" Shorty repeated.

Hal Burton eyed the fringe of trees that grew from the meadow's edge upon the steep bluff and on up the mountain side. The trees leaned over the meadow toward the little stream and to the open space filled with light from the morning sun. There was a tangled mass of oak, sugar maple, beech, ash, sourwood, and poplar branches matted with wild grapevines. It was a green thick roof extending fifteen to twenty feet over the meadow in the path where the State Highway Department had surveyed for the new creek channel.

But when Hal told them they'd brought the wrong tools, Poodie looked at Shorty and Shorty looked at Poodie. They couldn't understand. They had used long-handled shovels on their jobs with the State Highway Department for years.

"See what I mean?" Hal said. He broke the silence as he pointed to the low green cloud of intermingled branches, vines, and leaves that might slow the dozer. "Now, if the trees were down off that bluff where I could get to 'em, I could root 'em up with the dozer without all that extra work."

But neither Poodie nor Shorty made any effort to go after the axes. They looked at each other, then at Hal. Hal didn't waste much time. He started knocking out wedges with a short-handled sledge hammer to change the blade. Shorty and Poodie watched him climb up the dozer, pull a lever and lift the blade, then jump down and do more pounding on the first steel monster they had ever seen in this mountain county. They watched Hal go bobbing slowly toward the bluff while he angled the blade into position. They watched Hal jump down from the dozer again and hammer the giant pistons into position and drop big steel pins into holes and hammer them down.

"I'll bet that blade'll weigh six or seven hundred pounds, won't it?" Shorty said.

"Yes, and then some," Hal said disgustedly. He pulled a blue bandanna from his hip pocket and wiped sweat from his flushed face. "That blade weighs three tons!"

"How much does the whole thing weigh?" Poodie asked.

"Fourteen tons," Hal replied.

Poodie leaned on his shovel handle again and squinted his black, beady eyes as he looked at the well-worn blade that was shining like polished silver in the sun. But neither Shorty nor Poodie offered to help Hal drive the wedges as he angled the big blade and got ready to change the creek from the meadow over to the bluff. For the county turnpike was on the other side of the creek, and in three places the swift current was turned directly toward the highway. This was causing the roadbed to crumble and slip. But Poodie and Shorty didn't bother to go after axes to cut the overhanging branches. They watched little Hal Burton work furiously to angle the big blade. They watched him sweat.

"Where you from, Mr. Burton?" Shorty asked while Hal wiped sweat from his eyes.

"From Ohio," he said. "What made you ask me that?"

"I could tell from the way you talked you didn't come from these parts," Shorty said.

"But I was born in this state," Hal said. "I left here when I was two years old."

"Where did you learn to drive that big dozer?" Poodie asked.

"In Michigan," he replied. He put the sweat-soaked bandanna back into his hip pocket.

"How long have you been a-runnin' one?" Shorty asked as Hall started to climb back onto the dozer.

"Fourteen years for contractors," he said. "Two years in the Seabees."

Poodie looked at Shorty and Shorty looked at Poodie. Then they both turned toward the dozer. Hal had dropped the blade and the big dozer started rolling along at the bluff's edge. The blade bit deep into the earth and a small mountain of dirt came up. Poodie and Shorty watched the bright blade turn the dirt aside similar to the moldboards on hillside turning plows they had used on their steep hillside farms. The dozer crept along while the engine roared and the dirt hooved so high in front of the blade that Hal had to get a new start to hit it again. Poodie and Shorty followed the dozer, using their shovels for walking sticks. For they saw the wild cherry standing in the path of the dozer only a few feet ahead. It was big enough for a saw log. And when the dozer came up to it, they looked like a horsefly on the back of a broad draft horse.

They watched Hal pull up to the wild cherry gently. Then, they watched the big blade bite deep and nudge at the cherry roots. They watched Hal back the dozer, drop the blade deeper, and push the tree over this time.

"That's what I call grubbin' saw-timber," Poodie said. "It would take a powerful man a day to grub that tree with a mattock and shovel."

"That thing's a mountain on wheels," Shorty said. "Crawls like a big turtle! Watch it!"

Then the dozer stopped. Hal sat up high on his little seat and broke branches from the tree that swiped him across the face. He looked over toward Poodie and Shorty, who leaned on their shovels watching him.

"Fellows, I'm goin' to have to have some help," he said.

But Shorty and Poodie didn't answer Hal. They stood as silent as the big uprooted wild cherry that lay sprawled across the meadow, its roots withering and its leaves wilting in the morning sun. When Hal didn't get any response from his helpers, he seated himself again and bent low so his head and shoulders wouldn't be up among the tree branches and vines. Then he put the dozer in gear and dropped the blade into the dirt. He went fifteen or twenty feet farther and a wild grapevine caught under his chin and lifted him from his seat.

"He almost hung himself that time," Shorty said to Poodie in a humorous tone. "Guess the only way to stop that dozer is not to have any driver!"

Poodie reached mechanically into his hip pocket with one hand and pulled out a tin of tobacco. With the end of his long-handled shovel resting securely under his armpit, he lifted the other hand to his unsoiled work shirt pocket and got a package of cigarette paper and rolled a cigarette. Then he put the cigarette to his lips where it stuck as if glued though it dropped like a chicken's bill down on his bearded chin. He lifted a match from his hatband, struck it on his shovel handle and lit his cigarette without taking his eyes off Hal, who was still fighting to free himself from the grapevines.

"Fellows, I need an ax here and need it bad," Hal shouted. He finally got himself untangled from the vines. "Have you even got a pocket knife? This channel has to be cut. I'll have to cut it, whether these branches are cut or not."

He put the dozer into gear and pushed the dirt ahead. When the blade struck rocks that dropped from the bluff's edge, smoke quickly ascended into the bright morning air. Poodie and Shorty didn't blink an eye as they watched Hal stop the dozer and break limbs out of his way with his hands so he could get through. When the limbs were too big to break with his hands, he lay almost flat on the dozer and went under. Once he was thrown from the dozer by a beech limb but he climbed back on in less than a minute. Poodie and Shorty looked at each other when Hal climbed back on the moving dozer. But neither of them said a word. They stood like two statues until Hal had gone the entire length of the bluff. They watched him back down the ditch he had made. Every few feet he had to stop and break brush and vines. And once a stub of a limb that he had broken jabbed him in the face and drew blood. Hal wiped blood and sweat from his face with his bandanna and then went on about his work with determination.

When Hal started up the ditch-line, dropping the big blade and cutting the ditch deeper, if he tangled with the brush, he stopped and untangled himself. He didn't ask Poodie or Shorty to help him again. He took his dozer to the far end of the bluff again, cutting the channel deeper and piling up a wall of dirt that looked like a narrow-ridged hill. Shorty and Poodie watched him as eagerly as they had when he first dropped the dozer blade. And the third time he started through with the dozer, it looked like the dozer was sitting up on its side and might turn over at any time. But Hal drove it through to the far end of the bluff. There he turned and drove down over the backbone of dirt and flattened and spread it into a thick, solid, dirt wall to hold back the stream when the heavy rains came.

"Will he try to go through again?" Poodie asked Shorty. He looked at him with a couple of winks and then turned to watch the dozer as Hal turned on such little space. "Trees, rocks, and dirt won't stop him. The devil in hell couldn't stop it! That monster is a dangerous thing!"

"Wouldn't want to ride it," Shorty said. "Not even if I could drive that big thing! I wouldn't want it to run over me and mash me flat as a biscuit."

"But he's a-goin' up there again," Poodie spoke excitedly. "Look at 'im! I'll bet it feels to him like he's a-ridin' on a mountain!"

Both men leaned forward on their shovel handles while their faces sparkled with excitement as little Hal hugged the driver's seat and dropped the three-ton blade into the earth. Smoke ascended in little clouds, for the blade had reached the slate bottom of the valley. The dozer stood on its side, but the dirt rolled up from the channel into a heap like it was trying to reach the sky. After the heap of loose dirt reached a pinnacle, it spilled loose round clods down its slopes in all directions.

"That's something to see," Poodie said. "Think of that!"

"In about four hours he's turned that creek into a new channel for a quarter of a mile," Shorty said, shaking his head with excitement. "Hal lied about this dozer's doin' the work of fifty men. I don't believe five hundred men could do that much in a day with picks and shovels! There's not anything to stop that mountain-monster of a machine!"

Far beneath the vines and tree branches that canopied the new channel, Poodie and Shorty watched the dozer move along like a big turtle crawling on its side about to turn over on his back. They watched it crawl to the other end of the channel, turn and come back toward them, flattening the dirt and spreading that which had been thrown from the ditch. Then Hal brought the dozer where he had first dropped the blade and where Poodie and Shorty were still standing. He stopped the engine and got down.

"Well, I got the channel changed," Hal said. "I've got to adjust my blade and do some filling-in and this job will be done."

"We've not been any help to you, Hal," Poodie said, grinning. "We can't think about workin' ourselves for watchin' that powerful monster work!"

"It's the most powerful thing I've ever seen," Shorty said. "Not anything in the world could stop it. Do you believe there is, Poodie?"

"No, I don't believe there is, Shorty," Poodie said.

"Yes, a mountain of solid rock will stop the big boy," Hal told them. "But if the rock is blasted, it will shove the big rocks over the mountain."

"Do you reckon this dozer will take our jobs away from us?"

Poodie asked Hal. "I've been workin' with my shovel on this road gang for years!"

"No, there will always be things for you to do," Hal said. "You could have cut brush for me this mornin'."

"Not this mornin'," Poddie said.

"Not this mornin'," Shorty echoed.

Hal had knocked the large steel pins out with the short-handled sledge hammer. Now he climbed upon the dozer, pulled a lever, and lifted the blade into a new position. Then he jumped down, put pins back and started driving it to hold the heavy blade into its new position. Poodie and Shorty watched him do this in their customary silence. Then, they watched little Hal climb back into the driver's seat to finish the job.

His giant blade, polished silver in the sun, began to push the ridge line of dirt that lay parallel to the stream's new channel. The blade took a big bite onto the silver tongue in its gaping mouth. With a little strain on its motor the big man-made prehistoric-shaped monster pushed the bite into the old channel, leveling it across from bank to bank as if there had never been a stream here.

"Ain't that something!" Poodie exclaimed.

"Never saw anything like that, Poodie," Shorty said. "That bobtailed thing will change the face of the earth. There will never be a place in this world now for our picks and shovels."

"You're right, Shorty," Poodie said, shaking his head sadly. "I'm thinkin' the same thing. We're goners! We'll never be able to lean on our shovels any more!"

Then Poodie and Shorty stopped talking and looked at Hal when he raised his small hand and struck at something on the wind.

"Damn you!" they heard Hal say, but they couldn't see anything as they looked up into the blue summer air. They saw his little hand come up again, slicing the thin-blue summer air like a sand-colored oar dips in and out of colorless water. "Damn you! Damn you!"

But the sagging beech branches that extended over the old

channel were two feet above Hal's head. He had plenty of room to roll along undisturbed under this green canopy of rustling leaves. The polished-silver tongue cut another bite into the big open steel-jawed mouth to deposit into the old channel.

"Something's atter that big monster and little Hal," Poodie said. "See him a-strikin' at somethin' on the machine?"

"Boys, it's bees," Hal shouted back to Poodie and Shorty. "They don't like a big machine! I don't know where they're comin' from! They're a-flyin' in from some place! Can you help me?"

"Must be a bee tree close," Poodie said to Shorty. "Hope there is. I'd like to have some long-sweetening from the shoemake and sourwood blossoms!"

When Shorty and Poodie took off trotting toward Hal with their shovels in their hands, Hal was letting the engine idle while he sat there striking at the honeybees.

"Ouch! You little devil!"

Then before Poodie and Shorty could reach Hal, he stopped the engine and leaped from the dozer. He was running as fast as his pipestem legs would carry him. And he was striking at something with both hands at the same time. Bees were following him, trying to get to his face. Little Hal was running beside the old channel while a hundred or more gold-dotted honeybees dove as furiously at their target as jet fighters after a big jet bomber.

"Look at the ten thousand little Davids on that mighty machine," Poodie screamed. "They've swarmed on it! A hive of bees have—"

"They stopped the Goliath, didn't they?" Shorty interrupted him. "Look, won't you, at little Hal! Watch 'im run!"

Hal had his hat in his hand now striking at something on the wind. Each time he lurched forward with a long step.

"He's a-runnin' on the wind," Poodie said, raising his voice. "His feet's not touchin' the ground. Bees all around me, but I'm not afraid. They're not a-botherin' me!"

"Buzzin' around me, too," Shorty laughed. "But they ain't botherin' me! Look on that dozer, won't you! They're crawlin' alive. They're a-strikin' that thing!"

Then Poodie laughed as he had never laughed before when Hal rounded the bend and was out of sight. He was still striking at the wind with his cap.

"I didn't think anything could stop that monster!" Poodie screamed with laughter. "I thought our jobs were gone and there'd never be any more need for shovels, but the little Davids . . ."

"They stopped the mechanical Goliath, didn't they?" Shorty interrupted as he joined in the wild laughter. "Yep, they stopped him! Look how lonesome he is there by himself and his work not finished."

Poodie and Shorty leaned on their long-handled shovels and looked at the dozer and laughed until they mocked the rising wind. Then they lifted their faithful shovels into the air and clanked them together and laughed louder than the wind and the roaring of the maddened bees now crawling over and stinging the senseless dozer.

The Last Round Up

I UST to be ashamed of Pa and Ma when we went to dances together. I wasn't ashamed of the way Pa and Ma went dressed to the dance. Ma would wear the best dress she had. Ma would look better than any woman at the dance. But it took Pa to dress. He allus looked trim as a rooster redbird in the spring. Pa would allus wear his double-breasted blue serge suit. He'd wear a wild red rose in his coat lapel. If the roses wasn't in season, he allus wore the bouquet of wild roses Ma made 'im out'n paper. I can see him and Ma as they walked over the mountain paths together goin to a square dance, Pa dressed in his blue serge suit with a bouquet of red roses in his coat lapel and his fiddle under his arm. Ma would be holdin onto his right arm with her left hand and liftin her long, sweepin dress with her right hand so it wouldn't get caught on the briars as we went over the mountain paths to the square dance.

I'll tell you what got Pa. It was licker. Pa wouldn't start sawin the fiddle until he'd downed a pint. He'd be just gettin normal when he'd downed a quart. He'd just be gettin right when he'd killed three pints. Then you'd hear some fiddlin. And when Pa got a couple of quarts under his belt, then Pa would want to fight. Ma would have a time with 'im. Ma could hold her licker better than Pa. She would never drink more than two pints all night long. She'd drink a pint with Pa before the dance and then she'd drink another pint during the dance. Ma said a pint made her step lively on the floor. Ma was a good dancer and the boys and the old men allus wanted to dance with Ma.

I remember the big all-night dances we had. I remember the big times. I remember how the men gurgled moonshine down their long bull necks. I remember how the fights would start and somebody would shoot the lights out and two or three men would be stabbed layin on the floor bleedin when we got the lamps lit again. I remember how men would get into a fight and pull their guns and the wimmen would run between 'em to keep 'em from shootin it out right on the dance floor. Just somehow Pa allus managed to come out'n the fracases unscathed by bullet or knife. He'd come out lookin fresh as a mountain daisy in the mornin dew. Pa would never fight with men. Pa and Ma would allus get into a fight. Then is when I'd get ashamed. I'd get so ashamed of 'em I'd hold my head. There wasn't anything I could do about it. I'd just haf to say "a fair fight atween you two" and let 'em fight.

If Pa had too much licker under his belt, Ma would allus get the best of him. She'd knock 'im down faster than he could get up. Men and wimmen at the dance would laugh at Pa and Ma fightin. They would think it was great fun to watch Ma knock Pa down. If Pa got the best of Ma, the crowd wouldn't laugh as much. They'd feel sorry for Ma because she was a woman. Ma was a tall woman and she could use her fist like a man. She come from a fist-cuffin stock. She was a Gullet from Rocky Branch. They fit all their lives. That's all Ma ever knowed was to fight. She didn't mind fightin and she loved to watch any kind of a fight, rooster fight, man fight or dog fight. Just so it was a fight, Ma loved it. I can hear her hollerin yet at the fights we had at the square dances. I can see her clappin her hands and I can hear her laughin at the top of her voice.

Ma would dance with so many men while Pa sat in the corner and led the musicians with his fiddle. Pa was one of the best fiddlers in the mountains. When Pa got all lickered up, he would make his fiddle talk, laugh and cry. It all depended on the way Pa felt. The fiddle played the same way Pa felt. I can see him bending over his fiddle with his hair fallin over his fard on the fiddle strings and gettin tangled up in his fiddle bow. I can see Pa pullin on his fiddle bow when it was tangled in his raven-black locks. The music would stop until some of the men untangled Pa's hair from his fiddle bow. That was when Pa was gettin too much licker. I've seen him throw the fiddle bow on the floor and take a whop-stalk and run over the fiddle strings and play the fiddle. That was when Pa was happy. He was showin the dancers how he could play the fiddle.

Sometimes atter dancin all night when we'd start home around the mountain path and the mornin stars would be fadin from the sky, Ma and Pa would get into another fight and I'd haf to separate 'em. They'd try to fight with clubs. I'd get betwixt 'em and they wouldn't fight over me with clubs. I was their only livin child. I had seven brothers and two sisters planted on the Three Mile Hill. Pa called it "That Lonesome Hill." Atter I'd get them to throw down their clubs, Ma would edge around me and ground Pa with her fist. Pa would get jealous of Ma and Ma would get jealous of Pa. They loved one another so that's the reason they fit so much. Pa was a gay man. Ma was a gay woman. They loved their licker and they wanted a good time. They never missed a dance in the mountains. A dance wasn't a dance unless Pa and Ma were there and they wouldn't go unless I went with 'em. I know now why they wanted me to go along. I didn't like licker and I didn't like to dance. Pa and Ma wanted me to go with 'em and take care of 'em. That's all they wanted with me. They knew I wouldn't let 'em fight with clubs and maim each other. They knew if they fit with me around it would haf to be a fair fight. I've kept Pa from ruinin his good fiddle many a night. I've run in just as he started to come over Ma's head with a fiddle.

I'll tell you what hurt me most. It was when Pa was all lickered up with more than two quarts under his belt and Ma had only two pints under her belt, Ma would ground Pa somewhere on the mountain path. Pa'd just lay on the path in the moonlight and the starlight and he'd look up at Ma, and say, "Totem, you will remember me in 'The Last Round Up,' won't you Baby? We've had sicha wonderful times together!"

"I'll remember you, Dennie," Ma'd say. Ma would look at Pa layin there on the ground afraid to get up; then Ma'd go to weepin.

"Remember me just like I'm layin here on the ground when I'm in that oak-board box, Totem," Pa'd say.

"Yes Darlin," Ma'd say. And Ma'd weep harder.

"See that old music-box is under my arm, Baby."

"Yes, Dennie," Ma'd say. "Please don't say any more, Dennie!"

"Remember to have the wild roses on my coat lapel, Baby," Pa'd say.

"I won't forget," Ma'd say. "It won't be you, Dennie, unless you have the wild roses in your coat lapel and that blue serge suit that you've worn to all these dances."

"You're right, Baby," Pa'd say.

Ma would go to weepin until you could hear her at the foot of the mountain.

"Just remember 'The Last Round Up' and 'That Lonesome Hill.' "

"Don't talk like that, Dennie," Ma'd say. "You're killin me, Dennie. I can't stand it! You know you have a bad heart."

"My ticker will last me a while yet," Pa'd say. "Long as it lasts, Baby, old Totem and old Dennie 're goin to have their fun! Right up to the day of 'The Last Round Up' Baby! Right up to 'The Last Round Up' on 'That Lonesome Hill.' "

Ma would begin weepin like her heart would break. When Ma went to weepin like this, Pa wasn't afraid to get up. Pa'd get up and brush the leaves and the dirt from his good suit of clothes. He'd pat his fiddle with his hand and pet it. "You ain't hurt, are you, Jolly?" Pa'd say. "You stick with me through thick and thin and you come out unscathed. You come out without a scratch."

Pa'd lay his fiddle on the ground or give it to me to hold while he held Ma close in his arms and loved her. Pa'd stand and kiss Ma five minutes at a time atter they'd had a fight. I'd have a time sometimes breakin 'em apart atter they'd fit all over the mountain top.

"I do love you, Dennie," Ma'd say.

"I love you too, Baby," Pa'd say. "Totem, you're the only Pal I've got in the world besides my old music-box. I love you, Baby." Pa'd grab Ma again and hold her close and kiss her. Ma'd kiss Pa until finally I'd haf to say, "If we're goin to get home in time to feed and milk the cows you'll haf to stop so much lovin." Pa and Ma'd listen to me. They'd break apart and move along. It would be breakfast time and I'd be gettin hungry. Pa and Ma would walk in front of me. Ma would have her left arm around Pa and he'd have his right arm around her. He'd have his fiddle under his left arm and Ma'd be holdin her skirt with her right hand so it wouldn't drag on the briars along the mountain path. We'd move toward the house.

I can say this much for Pa. He was a good father. Ma was a good mother, too, but she didn't give me the advice that Pa did. Ma'd never tell me not to drink licker like she had. Pa'd say, "Son, look at me. I've had the best time of any man on this earth. But you can overdo the thing. I've overdone it. The old body can only stand so much. It is the old ticker that ticks the time. It don't take much to get 'im out'n gear. Your Ma has handled her licker better than I have. You can do as you please but I'd advise you to take it easier than I have. When I climb a little bank now I can hear my old ticker thumpin my time away like the tickin of a clock. I know it ain't goin to tick but a little more time for me. How I wish it would tick the time forever. I hate 'That Lonesome Hill.' I've been there too many times with your brothers and sisters. When my ticker sends me to 'That Lonesome Hill,' I hope it will be a wonderful day for you and Totem. I hope there is a lot of excitement."

Pa and Ma couldn't go to any more dances. Pa's ticker would just let him get out as far as the barn and the woodshed. Winter had come again and the snow kivered the hills. There was a white quilt of snow spread over the land. The land was the color of the stones on 'That Lonesome Hill.' Ma was watchin over Pa. She'd track him around the barn to see that Pa wasn't gettin any licker. She was afraid it would stop his ticker. Once Ma tracked Pa where he had left the barn and walked over the sandrock gap by the poplar trees. Ma tracked Pa up among the bushes. She found his jug by a leant-over blackjack saplin. Ma poured the licker from the jug. "Much as I like licker," says Ma, "I got rid of that. I hated to see it sink down in the snow. But since your Pa can't drink, I can't drink it before 'im and tanalize him with the smell. I kept smellin licker on his breath. That's why I tracked 'im to where he kept it hid. I want Dennie to live as long as he can. Dennie has lived too fast. He's the greatest Pal a woman ever had."

Pa kept gettin licker that winter. Ma didn't know where he was gettin it. I was standin behind the woodshed one cold January morning and I watched Pa as he went to the barn. He turned and looked all around like a pullet goin to her nest. Then Pa made a bee-line for the barn. I thought somethin was up. I watched Pa until he went around the upperside of the barn. I just stepped around on the furside of the woodshed where I could look around at Pa. I saw him slowly climb up the barn logs. He took it easy, a step at a time. Atter he made each step, he'd look around to see if anybody was near. Then Pa would make another step. He clim up to the barn loft. I saw Pa pull a plug out'n what looked like a knothole. I saw the moonshine spurt from the knothole until Pa put his mouth over it and drunk. I didn't think he's ever goin to turn it loose. Pa took his mouth away and the moonshine spurted from the hole but Pa wasn't long gettin the plug back. He didn't fool me. I knew he had his keg in the barnloft hay and a hollow limb runnin back through a auger held into the keg. Bill Blevins sold Pa the moonshine and he'd fixed the contraption for Pa. Pa looked so happy as he come down the barn logs like a cat comin down a tree backwards. When he got on the ground he looked all around. He wiped his mouth with his coat sleeve and said, "Ahem, fellars she's good as ever. Chickens crowin in the sourwood mountains, Hum dum diddle 'm a' day." I couldn't tell Ma. I thought I'd let her find out where Pa was gettin his licker.

I didn't haf to tell Ma. She found Pa's tracks up the logs. Ma found the plug in the knothole. She went up in the barnloft and got the keg. She threw it out on the ground and split it up with the ax. She didn't tell Pa and when he clim the logs again he found that his knothole was dry. I could tell from the way Pa acted. He didn't say anything to Ma. He just didn't have any life in 'im. I remember that mornin Pa got lively again. He was singin "Sourwood Mountains." He put the bouquet of wild roses in his coat lapel that Ma had made for him. Pa was wadin around the snow around the barn. I know Ma wondered where he got his licker. I was wonderin where he got it too.

Ma hollered for me to come to the barn. I started to the barn and I saw Pa down in the snow on his all-fours. He had the corn-cuttin knife in his hand. He was tryin to get up. Ma had him around the waist with her long arms. She was bent over him tryin to lift him up on his feet. "Leave me alone, Totem," Pa said. Pa was laughin as he talked. "Leave me alone, Baby," he said. "I'm all right. You remember Totem the roses in my coat lapel and the music-box under my arm the way I ust to carry it. You remember the blue-serge suit that I wore to the dances with you, Baby —and whatever you do, you drink an extra quart for me."

"I can't stand it Dennie," Ma said. "Don't tell me, Honey—I remember."

I just stood there and looked on. It looked like one of the old fights Ma and Pa used to have. I'd have to pull Ma off'n Pa when she'd ground 'im with her fist. Ma was tryin to help Pa up from the snow.

"It's "The Last Round Up,' Baby," Pa said. "I can feel my old ticker flutterin like a rooster with his head chopped off. It ain't tickin the time right, Baby. I can see black spots in front of my eyes. I've got a few things to tell you, Totem. I've been up on 'That Lonesome Hill.' There's a stump that's goin to haf to be blowed out with black-powder. It's right by John's grave. I want to sleep by our baby, John. Our family row has been pushed right out in the woods. It looks like tater ridges up there, Baby. We've planted so many up there. Have the boys to blow that big black stump out and plant me there."

Pa got his breath hard. He held the corn-cuttin knife with a death grip when I tried to take it from his hand. Ma was screamin to the top of her voice.

"Hush, Baby," Pa muttered. "Ain't no use of that. Take the furniture out'n the room and have a good old time square dance. Have Abe Billings to play 'Sourwood Mountains, 'Little Grain of Corn,' 'Hell among the Yearlings' and 'Little Birdie,' on my old music-box before you plant it with me. Have a good time at the wake. It's 'The Last Round Up,' Totem. I'm goin. Meet me in the skies. I'll be waitin for you, Baby. We'll dance again. My old ticker is tickin his last—"

Pa strove for his breath. he fell limp on the snow with the corn cuttin knife in his hand. Ma fell beside of Pa. She held him in her arms and wept like her heart would break. "No use of that, Ma," I said. "Pa is dead. Let's do what he said. We'll haf to get 'im to the house."

"Wonder what he planned to do with that corn-cuttin knife," Ma screamed.

"God only knows," I said. "I'll get it out'n his hand."

I had a time pullin each one of Pa's fingers loose from the death grip. He held that corn-cuttin knife like he held a fiddle bow. I finally got his hand loose and stuck the corn-cuttin knife in the butt of a barn-log. Then I helped Ma carry Pa to the house. She carried his legs and walked toward the house. I carried the heaviest part of Pa—his head and shoulders and I had to walk backwards all the way to the house. We got Pa to the house and put him on the bed. I went out that atternoon on the mule and norated that Pa was dead to the people of the deestrict.

I was on my way home when I stopped at Grandma's little log cabin at the foot of the Myer's Hill. I hated to tell Grandma that Pa was dead. Grandma lived alone and just went around doctorin people and deliverin babies. Pa was the only boy that Grandma had left. Now Pa was dead and I was afraid she would take it powerfully hard. I hollered first. No one answered. Then I got down off'n the mule and knocked on the door. I found there wasn't anybody at home. I looked around the house and I saw Grandma's track. She had gone in the direction of our house. I saw where she'd pulled up the snow-kivered bank by sprouts and grapevines. I got on my mule and I hurried for home.

Grandma was there. She was settin in the big rockin chear in the middle of the front room smokin her pipe. The room was filled with people. They had just poured into our house from all over the deestrict. People liked Pa. All the dancin crowd had come in to pay Pa their last respects. Many of the religious people had come too. They hadn't approved of the way Pa and Ma had lived but all was forgotten in the time of death.

"Grandma, I went to your cabin," I said. "I hollered from the mule's back for you first and you didn't answer. Then I got off'n the mule's back and knocked on your door. You didn't answer and I started lookin and found your tracks in the snow. I knowed you'd come this way. Did anybody tell you Pa was dead?"

"Guess I knowed Dennie was dead afore anybody knowed it," Grandma said. She held her longstem pipe in her hand. "I knowed the minute Dennie started dyin. I had an awful dream last night. I dreamt Dennie died. I could see Dennie down on the snow plain as I ever saw 'im in my life. I could see somethin in his hand but I couldn't tell what it was. Dennie lived too fast. I warned Dennie and told them both about the way they's livin but they didn't heed my warnin."

Grandma put her pipe back in her mouth. She wheezed on the long pipe stem and puffed the big clouds of smoke from her toothless mouth. Men and women talked to each other about the weather, crops, and death.

Men worked at the barn makin a coffin for Pa. They worked all atternoon and made Pa's coffin out'n black-oak boards. They brought the coffin to the house before supper time and set each end on a chear in the middle of the floor. The wimmen all went in the kitchen while the men put Pa in his double-breasted, powder-blue-serge suit. We found a pint of whiskey tied around Pa. He had a straw through the stopper. That's the reason Ma couldn't find where he got his last licker. Pa was strawin it. Ma put Pa's bouquet of wild roses in his coat lapel just as Pa had allus told Ma to do. She put his fiddle under his arm and put his hand on the fiddle neck—just the way Pa allus carried it. Pa just looked like he's goin to a dance. He didn't look like a dead man. Pa looked like he was pleased. He looked like he used to look when he was walkin over the mountain paths with Ma to a dance. I just wondered where Pa was now. I just wondered about his 'Last Round Up.'

That night we cleared the furniture out'n the room. We had one of the finest wakes the people ever saw among the hills. The wimmen cooked in the kitchen and made coffee, pie and cake for us. We had a big dance. Abe Billings took Pa's fiddle out'n his coffin and fiddled the tunes Pa asked us to play at his wake. The young people of the deestrict danced and loved all night. People et until their stummicks were tight as banjer heads made of groundhog skins. We had a wonderful time. Ma tried to get Grandma to go to bed but she wouldn't do it. Grandma just sit in the big rockin chear and smoked her pipe and looked on. The young people sorty laughed at Grandma settin there with her bonnet straps tied under her chin and her big checked apron with her pocket in the upper right hand corner that held her pipe and burley terbacker crumbs.

"I ain't goin to bed," Grandma said. "I am here fer a purpose. Anything might happen here. I just want to be here."

Grandma had brought nearly everybody at Pa's wake into the world. She ust to ride muleback and doctor. Atter Grandpa died, she ust to go to a house and stay two weeks before a baby was born. Atter the baby was born Grandma would move on and stay with another woman. Sometimes Grandma wouldn't get to stay long until she'd be called to another place. Grandma was a Grannie Woman and a charm Doctor. She was used all the time. She didn't get much rest until she begin to get old; then, Grandma settled down in her cabin again.

Atter we danced all night, Eif Walters and Charlie Preston walked up to the house. They had the diggin tools to dig the grave. Flossie Bryan and Minerva Brown were in the house. Eif was sparkin Flossie and Charlie was sparkin Minerva. They looked at Grandma sittin in the middle of the front room in her big rockin chear smoking her pipe. They looked at one another and the girls started gigglin.

"Foot o' mercy," Grandma snapped, "Eif, if it hadn't been fer me, your Ma would have been a dead woman today. You ain't got no right to laugh. Your Ma was about to bleed to death when they sent fer me. I saved your Ma."

Grandma pulled another cloud of smoke from her long pipestem and funneled it from her toothless mouth. Eif looked funny when Grandma told him about his mother. Ma looked plagued for Ma hadn't been able to get Grandma to go to bed. She'd sat in the rockin chear all night and smoked her pipe.

"And you ain't got no right to laugh, young man," Grandma said to Charlie Preston, "I saved you too. I was right there when you was born, young man. Just because you are sparkin the young gals today don't mean nothin to me. You're the same picked chicken that I brought into this world."

Charlie looked funny out'n his eyes. Grandma looked hard at Charlie and Eif. They said goodby to Minerva and Flossie and picked up their tools. "You might need me again," Grandma said. "I ain't so shore but what you will. The Lord needs me a long time yet. What would you people among these hills adone if it hadn't been fer me?" Grandma puffed hard on her pipe. Flossie and Minerva acted like they's afraid of Grandma. They ran out'n the front room to the kitchen.

It was atter dinner when Pa's old friends started toatin his black-oak box up the long Three Mile Hill. There was an awful crowd following the coffin. Ma said to Grandma, "Grannie, you're goin to stay here, ain't you?"

"No I ain't goin to stay here," Grandma shouted. "Why should I stay here?"

"I thought the hill would be too slick fer you to climb," Ma said.

"Ain't no more fer me to climb," said Grandma, "than it is fer you to climb. I can climb a bigger hill right now than you can climb."

"Grannie, I just thought it would be better if you stayed down here at the house and rested," Ma said.

"Shucks, I ain't goin to do it," Grandma snapped. "I feel like I'll be needed at that graveyard. I'm goin with Dennie every step of the way to 'That Lonesome Hill.' I've seen 'em all go the same way. I've followed the other seven there and I aim to follow my baby, Dennie."

Grandma followed the funeral crowd up the hill. She kept along with the crowd. Grandma would smoke one pipe of terbacker and empty the ashes out'n her pipe. She would refill her pipe and light it with a match from her apron pocket. She just kept smokin her pipe. When we got to the top of the Three Mile Hill, we met Horace Stubblefield runnin hard as he could run from the graveyard.

"They air blowed up," Horace shouted. "They air blowed up."

The pallbearers set Pa's corpse down with each end of the coffin on a newground stump. Horace turned back wavin his hands for everybody to follow. The crowd made a wild run toward a pile of dead tree-tops. There laid Charlie Preston and Eif Walters pinned against the winter earth with splinters from a stump. Blood was streaming from them and makin little red branches on the snow.

"I just popped up on the hill in time to hear the blast like thunder," Horace said, "and I saw two men go up with their legs and arms spread out like they were trying to fly and a big stump was under them pushin them higher into the air. I didn't know what to do when they fell bleedin and full of splinters."

"Stand back," Grandma shouted. "Stand back. They will stop bleedin in less than a minute." The funeral crowd pushed aside for Grandma. She held her hands over her heart. Her wrinkled lips worked when she whispered somethin to herself.

Minerva and Flossie tried to throw themselves down on the snow beside of Charlie and Eif. All the clothes that Eif and Charlie had on their bodies were patches of their clothes the splinters had pinned to them. Grandma pulled her apron off and spread it over Charlie. Lucretia Holmes pulled her apron off and spread it over Eif. They didn't more than get the aprons over 'em until the blood stopped flowin. Part of the funeral crowd followed the men down the hill as they carried Charlie and Eif away. Minerva and Flossie put their arms around Grandma's neck atter she stopped the blood. They tried to kiss Grandma but she wouldn't let 'em.

"You gals go on with your Sweeties," Grandma said. "They won't bleed to death now. I'll be down to the house soon as Dennie is planted here. I knowed somethin was goin to happen. That's the reason Dennie was allus so gay. He was born in August under the sign of Leo the Lion. Things had to happen to Dennie from the cradle to the grave."

Atter one crowd went over the hill with Charlie and Eif we still had a big funeral. All the men had to do was to square the hole a little bit where Charlie and Eif blowed the stump out. The hole was too deep fer the grave. They had to fill it in some before they lowered Pa.

"This is Totem, Dennie," Ma said when she looked at Pa before they lowered him in the stump hole. "You look good, Dennie. You look just like you ust to look when we went to the dances together over the mountain paths. Your suit is clean and pressed and the wild-rose bouquet looks fresh in your coat lapel. You have our old music-box. I can tell from that look on your face, you're goin on 'The Last Round Up,' Dennie. Your Baby, Totem, will drink a quart for you. Goodbye, Dennie—good luck."

A Land Beyond the River

MY Pop was the best water-dog that ever rode a raft of logs from the Levisa Fork down the Big-Sandy. He was the Captain of a crew of water-dogs. He got the job because he could holler the loudest, and shoot the straightest. Pop was a big man with iron jaws and mullein-leaf gray eyes. His hair was the color of a yellow-clay clod. His arms were big and where the sleeves were torn out of his shirt his big muscles rippled up like where wind bends down the grass in the yard and when the wind passes over it the grass comes up again. Pop was the strongest man on the Big-Sandy. People called him Big-Sandy Bill. Nobody along the Big-Sandy wouldn't call him a water-dog and get by with it either. He shot at them till they got out of sight. If they shot back at him from the woods he'd just stretch out on the raft of logs and answer them long as he had a shell. And Pop always kept plenty of them.

I can see Pop now going down the Big-Sandy on a raft of logs—a long train of rafts—I can see Pop standing there waving his hand from the front raft showing the boys the way to dodge the shoals and follow the current—great trains of logs—pine, poplars, oaks, beech, ash, maple, chestnut—great mountains of timber in them days on the Big-Sandy and God knows it was the roughest place in Kentucky. Everybody carried a gun. Pop made all his men on the river carry a gun. They couldn't get a job unless they had a gun and a pole with a spike in the end of it. They had to be men who could jump from log to log like squirrels—good swimmers too or they'd better stay off the Big-Sandy. It's filled with swirlholes and shoals and mean currents that twist log trains into the banks and then you have to wait forever to get a flood to clean the log-jams up—a flood in March or April—sometime in the spring. No man that worked on the Big-Sandy that had any raising would ride a raft of logs and let a fellow call him a water-dog. Pop give his men orders to shoot the first man down in cold blood that called them water-dogs.

God but them was awful days on the Big-Sandy. A lot of people didn't like Pop. One day when Pop and his crowd was passing through Evans—a little town on the Big-Sandy—some fellow called Pop a water-dog and he swum to the bank—went up in the town and run the fellow around the square pouring the hot lead at him. Pop would a killed him but the Law come down and told Pop to get back on the Big-Sandy where he belonged.

I remember how we used to hear about Uncle John Hampton and them old men that lived on the river till their hair got white. I remember how we used to hear how they'd shoot a man every now and then and they wouldn't try them for the killings. These fellers would come out and mess with the river men. They didn't like the "water-dogs." Pop was a water-dog and Pop wasn't afraid of the Devil. He'd come home and take his guns off his belt and have Mom to fix him a bite to eat and then he'd go right back to the river. Pop loved the Big-Sandy as every man that lives on that river loves it. Pop was known from the Levisa Fork to the Gate City down on the Ohio River where the Big-Sandy gives up her logs to a bigger river. Everybody called Pop "Big-Sandy Bill who'd never died and never will."

Every spring Pop would stay away from Mom. It would be in the rainy season when the logs would have to be floated down the Big-Sandy. Pop would never get to come home and stay with us. We'd watch the river day and night for Pop. He had a fox horn he'd blow when he's coming down the Big-Sandy and Mom would have a basket of fine grub waiting for Pop about the time he'd come down the Big-Sandy. We'd run down to the river and Hilton would take it out to Pop in a john-boat. And Mom would write Pop a letter and have it in the basket. That's all she'd get to say to Pop was what she could say in that letter. Pop would take the basket and grab the letter before he would the cake and fried chicken. His big hand would grab the little letter. He would read it and tears would come to his eyes. Then he would turn and start cussing at the men and tell them to watch the train of rafts—for a mile up the river or more. Pop would read the letter. Then he and his men would eat the chicken and cake. They would walk the raft of logs up to Pop—one at a time while the others watched the rafts. They were afraid to leave the rafts. It was easy to ground a raft of logs on the Big-Sandy—river so crooked flowing around the mountains like a black-snake in a briar-patch.

I remember when my sisters, Clara, Grace and I—we used to stand out on the bank of the Big-Sandy and watch the big rafts go down. We'd watch to see if the raft belonged to Pop—if it was Pop or any of Pop's men. We could see the blue water from the house for we lived right upon the bank on the Kentucky side—we lived under a patch of Big Oaks and my brother Hilton kept his fishing poles hooked under the oak roots right in the yard. He kept his nets further down on the river. He fished from a split-bottom chair in the front yard. We'd lived in this house all of our lives and Pop said his Pop had lived here all his life and raised him and his sisters and brothers here and his Pop's Pop on before his own Pop had come from old Virginia and raised his family here. Our house sagged a little in the middle—but it wasn't the house so much we loved as it was the Big-Sandy! We fished in its waters. Pop rafted logs on its back. We went riding on it in our john-boats. To us the Big-Sandy was a brother and he was a bad brother at times, especially in the spring after the mountain rains. I used to read in my old primary geography about the Don River in a far-off land called Russia and I always thought the Big-Sandy in my country was something like the Don River in Russia. The Don River had its Cossacks that rode horses and fought—the Big-Sandy had its mountaineers that rafted the logs and fought one another. Big men and tall men with sun-tanned, hard, iron faces and heads of shaggy hair that never was covered with a hat. And I saw mountains in a far-off land in Italy that come down to the blue waters—high rugged hills covered with trees—that looked something like the mountains that come down to the Big-Sandy on the West Virginia side—on the Kentucky side there were fields of corn back on the mountain slopes and in the narrow valley. It was a pretty country. We loved the mountains and the Big-Sandy.

Jim Hailey ran the next biggest raft train on the Big-Sandy—the next biggest to Pop's. He worked as many men as Pop. He had nine men. Pop and Pop's men didn't like Big-Sandy Jim and his water-dogs. They would pass Pop and his men when they was coming down Big-Sandy with a raft of logs and Pop and his water-dogs would be going back. They wouldn't call Pop anything but they didn't speak. Big-Sandy Jim would just grin at Pop. All Big-Sandy Jim's men would just grin at Pop and Pop's men and keep their hands on their pistols. Big-Sandy Jim's horses always beat Pop's horses at the Evans races every spring too. Pop bet last spring and lost all he'd made on the river. Pop's not afraid to bet even on a horse he's not sure of. He would say: "I'll take his damn bet. It's a good one even if I lose from that low-down river rat. The Big-Sandy River is disgraced to have a thing riding its back like Big Jim Hailey—if ever I get the chance—something he's got agin me—" Then Pop would cool down and smoke his pipe and twist his hands on his knees.

One night in April I saw a light hanging out in our yard. Mom slept in the room next to the river downstairs. She slept there alone. Hilton and I slept in the north-room across the hall from the girls upstairs and they slept in the south-room just across the upper-dogtrot. I got out of the bed and run down and told Mom there was a light on our back porch. I run down the stairs and I broke into Mom's room. She was up in bed. She was wide awake. I said: "Mom, there is a light on the porch. What's it doing there?"

Mom said: "Go on back upstairs and tend to your own business. I had to draw a bucket of water from the well. I lit the lantern and I forgot to blow it out." Mom got out of the bed and walked out on the porch. Mom hooked the bale from off the nail, lifted the half-smoked globe and blew out the quivering blaze. She walked back in the house—and it was light enough until I could see her. She went back to bed—pulled up the cover—I could not understand. There was light enough in a quarter moon for Mom to go to the well and get a bucket of water. The girls and Brother Hilton never did wake up. I told them about it the next morning and Hilton said: "W'y you've been dreaming Don. Never was a light on that porch. I was awake a long time last night. I looked out at the West Virginia mountains—I saw them in moonlight. I looked at the river and thought of all the times I'd swum it and of all the pike I've caught from it and the jack salmon. I just laid there last night and listened to that old river flowing—the moan of the water and the wind in its willow banks. I thought of Pop—wondered where he was on this old river with a raft train of big logs—that's what I want to do some day—I want to follow the river like Pop only I want to run a boat on the Big-Sandy and let the whistle do my hollering—Don, I was awake far into the night last night—dreaming—dreaming—but with my eyes open—that's a fact, Don. I never saw a light."

And then I thought: "I could not be dreaming. I went downstairs. I remember stepping on the steps. I remember the broken step with the knot hole in it. I remember it sagged with my weight. I remember hearing the wind out there in the oak tops. I remember how the light scared me. And I remember going in Mom's room. I remember the words she said to me. That she had used the lantern going to the well and forgot to blow it out. And how she told me to get back to bed. I remember Mom getting up in her night gown. I remember how pretty Mom looked to me when I went back up the stairs. When she went out and got the lantern—she looked so tall and straight—her hair—pretty and golden as cornsilks in an August wind—was loose down her back —her eyes big and blue flashed in the lantern light—I remember —I surely was not dreaming."

And the next night—I thought I saw the light again and I was too sleepy to go downstairs and see. I just don't remember. I thought I was going, maybe, I went to sleep dreaming I was going down to see about the light. And, maybe, I just dreamed about the lantern the night before. No one can remember a dream not knowing it was a dream. But I remember the night and the stars—night around the house and the stars over the Big-Sandy. I thought about Pop and wondered where he was on the river. Pop traveled nearly two hundred miles on the Big-Sandy with the log rafts.

Grace and I were out in the swing on the oak tree in the front yard that day when we saw Pop and his men pulling up Big-Sandy in a john-boat. They had gone down the river to Gate City with a raft train of logs. I would swing Grace awhile and she would swing me from a split-pole swing that was fastened with a horseshoe to a limb in the oak tree. We could swing out over the river and look down on the Big-Sandy. Our house faces the Big-Sandy River. All the houses face the river instead of the road. All the houses on the West Virginia side of the Big-Sandy face the river instead of the road. We face one another. And when I swung out over the river and saw Pop coming up the river I told Grace to catch the swing and hold it. She held the swing and I run into the house and told Mom: "Mom, Pop is coming. Pop and his men are coming up the river."

Mom run out in the yard. Pop was the first to get out of the big john-boat and tie it to a willow. He said: "Get out, you fellars, and we'll shade awhile and eat before we mosey on up the river." Pop led the way up the bank. His beard was out long on his cheeks and chin. His hair fell down on his shoulder—hair the color of a dry yellow-clay clod in August. I wouldn't tell Mom but I thought Big-Sandy Jim Hailey looked better than Pop. He did go shaved. He had a clean face. He wasn't a big man like Pop and he wasn't near as hairy as Pop and didn't look as mean as Pop. Pop's men all looked mean. All had hairy faces like Pop—just a hole in the hair on their face for their mouths that worked when they talked and their eyes flashed blue, black and gray under heavy ledges of hair—They had big pistols belted around them and they walked up our bank to the house like they owned the Big-Sandy.

Pop grabbed Mom and kissed her. Mom said: "Ah, them old beards, Bill. They don't become you one bit. You look awful in them." And Pop said: "Honey, they ain't no razors out there on the Big-Sandy when a fellar has to live for three and four days on a log train. Has to sleep on a raft—catch a wink when he can and when the Big Boy's mad can't catch a wink of sleep. That's what's happened now. Had rain on the head o' Big-Sandy and the river is just a foaming like a mad bull." And Mom said: "I didn't get the basket to you as you went down. Didn't hear the horn and I'm so sorry, Bill—I had chicken a plenty for you and the men." And Pop said: "And we missed the chicken too. I thought I saw a light on the porch. That was Thursday night. And I wondered what it was doing there. I thought maybe it might be Hilton that had come from his nets and then I knowed he's got eyes good as a crow's eyes—and I just wondered about that light." And Mom said: "I don't know anything about a light on that night." And then I thought: "Well, maybe, I was not dreaming. Maybe, I did see the light. I dreamed it or I saw it one of the two." And Pop said: "We saw a light here didn't we boys?" And the men—all nine of them squatted around over the green grassy yard said: "Yep—we saw a light." Mom never said another word and Pop said: "Honey, fix us a bit to eat and we'll be getting on up the river. Another big train of logs waiting to be rolled in—got to get them to the Ohio by Sunday."

I can see Mom, Clara, and Grace yet. They went into the kitchen—put a fire in the stove. They put on every pot. It took grub for ten river men where they'd been eating cold grub on the river. The table looked like it would feed twenty-five men. I remember the steam from the chicken and dumplings. I remember the white chicken dumplings going in at their hairy mouths. I remember how they'd never ask for anything but just reach over the table and if they couldn't reach a thing one would say: "Dam it Zack, can't you give a body a lift to the dumplings? Can you hand over the beans there—what the hell do you think this is—your birthday?" And they just went on like this and Pop would say: "By-God boys, not so Goddam much cussing around over my grub." And Mom and Grace would just get out of the dining room and let them have it. They'd clean every plate and sop them out. They'd come out with eggs in their whiskers and gravy all over their vests—picking their teeth with goose quills they carried for that purpose and they'd light up a long green cigar apiece and pat their stomachs and stretch and make it back for the boat. And we'd see them far up the river—we'd see Pop wave goodby to Mom. It seemed like Pop just come and went and Mom went about the place hunting for Pop. And the days just come and went—spring on the Big-Sandy when the trees leafed along its rippling blue waters—and then the rains and the muddy waters and then blue waters again with mountains that come down—mountains of quivering green clouds of leaves. Then would come a dry season when white clouds would float in the West Virginia and Kentucky skies and the water would get low and a raft of logs would run on a shoal—water would get low and the river bottoms would look white in the sun—mare-tails would float in the sky. Pop would wipe his sweating brow and say: "Mare-tails in the sky. Sign of rain in three days." Butterflies would flit along the Big-Sandy and water moccasins would sleep along the banks on a log and just plump in the water when they saw the raft coming. Turtles wouldn't move—there were so many of them. And they had been in the Big-Sandy so long and knew as much about the river as the men and the snakes.

Another night and I dreamed I saw, or went to sleep dreaming I saw, a light downstairs and a man get out and come up the bank. I dreamed that it was Pop. I just don't remember. But I thought this or I dreamed this: "Now the other time I didn't go down. I don't know whether it was a light or whether I just dreamed it. Tonight I'm going down and see." But I didn't go down and see. I must have just dreamed it was Pop back to see Mom but he hadn't been gone up the river but three days. He didn't have time to be back. I told Hilton about it and Hilton told Mom the next day. And Hilton said: "Don, you must be having nightmares. I never saw a thing and I just sleep right across the room from you." But it seemed to me like there was something. I just felt it. Something bothered me. It was something very strange. I thought of Pop on the water. I wondered where Pop was and if he'd shot at anybody for calling him a water-dog. I just know

Pop would kill a man and do it quick. We don't know but we heard once Pop and a fellar quarreled over a bottle of licker and they agreed to shoot it out. So they turned their backs—each one holding a pistol of the same kind with the same number of cartridges in it—and they walked so many steps apiece—ten I believe, and turned and started shooting. Pop got the fellar. That was when Pop was a young man though. Pop's got a big scar on his wrist. We heard there was where he got it. He never told us. We don't know.

When Pop come down the river with the next train of logs and blew his horn it was on a pretty day—sun high in the sky—and Mom just piled in all the grub she had cooked in a basket that she always kept waiting for Pop and the men about the time for them to get back. And Hilton took the basket out in the john-boat. He brought a letter back to Mom. And Pop said in the letter: "Elizabeth when I was going up the river old Jim Hailey was coming down with a train of logs. He was on the front raft with a white shirt on. He was all dressed up and on the river. And when he passed me he just looked at me and laughed and laughed and the men all laughed and looked at me. I'm not for taking such foolishness. I thought once I'd tell my men to fire on them after I'd bumped Jim off for the signal to start. I thought I'd redden this river to the mouth with their blood. I don't know why he's got the laugh on me. You know the only laugh us river men have on one another is when we get the other man's money playing poker, out shoot or out holler the other fellar, or take the other man's wife. This is something Big Jim ain't done to me, can't do to me, and never will do to me long as my pistol will bark." I found the letter in Mom's room. I read it.

Pop and Big Jim both were down the river now. Big Jim had been down the river five days. He'd had time to get to Gate City with his log train. Pop had just passed. He would be down the river at least a week. The next day we saw Big Jim at the head of his big john-boat with a white shirt on and he looked toward the house. Mom was not in the yard. We didn't wave at him. We had been taught to hate Jim Hailey from the day Pop could tell us a word about him. He's getting mightly friendly to us. Pop ought to have been here when he waved. Pop would have killed him like he would shoot a rabbit. It was five days before Pop got back up the river and we told him Jim Hailey passed and waved at us. Pop said: "He's getting too smart of his pants. That low-down vile water rat!"

Pop said to Mom: "Fix us a basket of grub and we'll take it to the boat. We'll mosey on up the river. We don't have time to stop long. A train of logs is waiting us up on the Levisa Fork." Mom and Grace fixed a big basket of grub. Two of Pop's big hairy men took it down to the boat. The rest of the crowd followed. I remember seeing them grabbing into the basket as they pulled away up the Big-Sandy—I remember seeing the boat dip and swerve as they hogged into the basket.

Eleven more days and I remember. It was night and a full moon was up. Was I dreaming when I heard a shot fired? I heard a scream! It was not the wind among the oaks this time—the wind that blows from the Big-Sandy. It was gunpowder. I smelled it. Hilton and I jumped out of our beds. The girls rolled out on the other side the dogtrot. I heard them "Who was that that shot?" hollered Hilton and we run downstairs. "You low-down vile skunk of a water-rat, may God send your soul to hell—trying to break up my home," said Pop, and he kicked a man lying on the floor bleeding and he held to Mom's hand. "Goddam you and your kind—roast in hell, damn you—and you, Elizabeth, what do you mean! That's what the lantern's been hanging out for and what this son of a bitch has been doing wearing a white shirt on the river! Stopping to see my wife—you children get back up them stairs—every last one of you! No man that is a true river man on the Big-Sandy can wear a white shirt and go clean-shaved on a log-train—that's why you done it, you lousy river rat. I'd throw you in the river but you are not worthy to pollute the water with blood of your kind!"

Pop was standing over a man on the floor. I could see from the stairs the gun Pop was holding and the blue smoke leaving the barrel. "Don't shoot Mom!" said Clara screaming. "Oh, I fooled you," said Pop to Mom, "I've been smelling this rat ever since he laughed at me when we passed on the river. I just went up to

Evans with the boys. I sent them on, I slipped back and waited for the lantern. I saw the boat let a man out—I saw them anchor a boat that they run in from the log-train—oh, yes—And that's why the lantern has been out—a signal that I am not here. I happened to be here tonight! And you, damn you—" and Pop kicked the man on the floor—kicked him over and he kind of drew up one of his legs like a swimming frog—moaned and his head fell over on the floor—his breath sizzled and he lay there perfectly still. We could see the white shirt and the blood down the front. We didn't go all the way up the stairs. Mom there holding to Pop and crying—just bawling on his shoulder and all us children crying like we'd take fits. All scared to death too. Lord, that smell of gunpowder and smoke! And Pop there—the big bearded iron-faced man that he was—his shirt torn—his hairy body in the light of the lantern and the moon that hung above the river! Lord, what an awful time it was. Hilton got on the mule and rode for Sheriff Lakin to come and get the dead man out of the house. Pop told him to. He held Mom in his arms. "For one cent," Pop said, "I ought to blow out your brains for being with Jim Hailey. Jim Hailey! My God, Jim Hailey with my wife—Well, he'll never be any more."

We went upstairs and went to bed. Mom and Pop stood together by the dead man on the floor. Blood had run a big stream and dripped through a knot-hole in the floor. Mom was holding to Pop and crying: "Bill, spare my life for my children. I'll never do this again. I didn't love Jim Hailey—I love you—you was gone so much. You was always on that river. You never stay with me. You leave me. A woman can't be left so long as you leave me." And Mom sagged to the floor crying—almost into spasms.

Sheriff Lakin came. He put Big-Sandy Jim Hailey in the express, took Pop to Evans and Uncle Jake went Pop's bond. Pop had to appear in one of the biggest murder trials that there ever was on Big-Sandy. People talked about us. They talked about my mother. When I would go to school the children would say: "Don's mother had a man killed over her. She ain't no good for my Mommie said Don's mother wasn't no good." And the children wouldn't play with Clara, and Grace either. The big boys would say things to Hilton at school and he would fight. They would talk about Mom. Mom never left the house. She never went to see a neighbor. She would sit out under the oaks and smoke her pipe—her blue eyes gazing steadily at the waters that flowed forever past our door—through drought and freeze, summer, winter, autumn and spring. The waters of the Big-Sandy kept flowing on and on and boats passed and big rafts of logs in the spring and corn in the fall went down by barge loads to the mills at Gate City. Mom would talk to herself and look at the river. Pop went back to work on the river. Pop went back to the log-trains. He kept two guns on him now. Once Pop was shot at from the bushes and the bullet hit Tim Zorns in the arm after it had gone through a bunch of men and just glanced off Pop's spike pole. It left its mark right in front of Pop's heart. And word was sent to Mom: "We are going to kill old Big-Sandy Bill—he ain't died yet but we guess he will."

They took us to the trial for witnesses. They asked to tell about the light. And I told them I didn't know whether I'd dreamed it or whether I saw a light. But it was one of the two. The whole house was crowded with people and Pop's men that worked on the log train with him was right there with their hands on their guns waiting for Big Jim's men to start something. They were all there and the Law was there but the Law would a had a time if one shot had been fired. Mom told that she didn't love Big Jim and he didn't love her—that she had told him to get away and stay away and he wouldn't do it. And that he come there that night with a gun and said if Pop ever come while he's around there he'd kill Pop. So Pop beat him to the draw. And somebody said in the back of the house: "That woman ought to go to a limb. Having men killed over her." And the tears come into Mom's eyes. She just sat there and waited for the lawyers to ask her questions. And they asked her a God's plenty. They asked her how many times Big Jim had come to see her. And a lot of stuff like that. And Pop just sat there mad as a hornet. He looked like the very devil was in him. The jury was out awhile—about an hour I guess, and when they come in the foreman of the jury said: "Murder in self-defense." Pop come clean of the charge. There was all kinds of cussing around the court house. And one fellow says to Pop: "See that sign up there on the court house. Reads 'God is not mocked. Whatsoever a man soweth that shall he also reap.' And you, Big-Sandy Bill, will reap a bullet in your own heart. Kill a man over your vile wife. Oh, we are going to get you. I am a Hailey. I have not washed my hands with you yet. I am a second cousin to the man you murdered. There are many of us left yet." And Pop said: "Bring on all your damned Haileys. There are many Fraziers yet in these mountains. Bring 'em on and shut up—bring 'em on and be damned. I love my wife. Or I would have killed her right there! I would kill another man over her." Pop walked out down the road to the wagon. Mom never lifted her head out in the crowd. They were all looking at her.

When I would go to school the children would not play with me. They would whisper to each other about me. I would go home and go upstairs to my room and cry and cry. I couldn't help it. They would talk about my mother. And I would hear them say at school. "I'll bet Charlie Hailey gets Big-Sandy Bill. He's a laying for him. He's going to kill him. He's gone longer now on Big-Sandy than any other man has ever gone to kill a good man over a woman. Big Jim Hailey's men must not have anything to them to let him be killed like this and them not do anything about it." I would hear all this. And to think Pop was back on the Big-Sandy! I would think this: "I can see Pop. He is on the floor. He, too, has on a white shirt. He is bleeding at the heart. A stream of blood runs from his heart to a knothole in the floor. It runs down the knothole. Pop works his leg like a frog that's swimming. He turns on his back. He moans. His last breath sizzles. He is dead. Pop is dead. Pop, a mountain of a man—one unafraid of men and the river—but Pop is dead. A bullet went into Pop's heart from the dark. His heart was easy for a bullet as any man's heart. Now Pop is no more than a dry clod of yellow clay in August. Pop is dead."

Mom would turn the coffee cup in the morning after she had drunk her coffee. She would say: "I see the river—I always see the river. I can see a dead man floating down the river." Then

Mom would scream. She would get up and go out in the yard. She would sit down in the chair where Hilton sits and fishes. She would sit there and look at the river. It was the valley where we had lived for more than a hundred years—ever since the first white settlers had come to the valley. Now we would have to leave the valley—not that we were afraid to die—we would have to leave. Mom would have to leave. When a woman in the hills meets another man—she and her girls for generations are doomed. We would have to go to a new river.

Pop stopped the john-boat at the willows. He got out and threw the chain around a willow root. He walked up the bank holding to the oak roots to pull his heavy body up the bank—Mom was out in the chair under the oak trees. Pop said: "Timber is growing scarcer in these mountains than ever before. Things just don't work like they used to. I got the whole river to myself now and I don't want it. Big Jim is gone and God be thanked for the riddance. But we are going to have to leave this river for a new river. Hilton cannot do any good on this river because he is your son. No one will ride his boat. Grace and Clara will have a hard time marrying a respectable man because they are your daughters. We'll have to go to a new river. Let's pack on a barge all the things we have and pass through Gate City and go down the big Ohio and land where there are hills on the Kentucky side. We must have hills coming down to the edge of the blue waters. We will be lost without the hills."

I remember packing things that afternoon and putting them on the barge. We took all we had and put on the barge—Pop's men helped us load. Big hairy men would carry big loads down the bank. They would sweat and work—their guns in their belts. We got all our belongings and left down the Big-Sandy—not anything to pull the barge—it floated down the river that we had known all our lives—the river that had carried Pop so much up and down on its blue bosom—sheltered by the tall mountains and the green timbered slopes—the high jagged cliffs near the tops of the mountains where the mountains shouldered to the skies——

We looked back to our house on the bank. The sun was on the

other side of it. We could see the oak trees and the swing between us and the sun. We could see the willows and the well-gum and the barn. We could see the sun moving down over the green hills we had seen so many times. And Pop looked back and said: "Well, old river, it's goodby." Pop steered the boat—it floated along. And Pop would say "I know this river like a scholar knows a book. I know every shoal in it and almost every snag. It is like a person to me. I know even how its heart beats. I've been over it since I was seven years old. And I've started down the other side of the hill." Mom would say: 'I hate to leave this river. I've loved it all my days. Lived on it since I was a little girl. All my people lived on it in these mountains. I was born here, raised here and I've never been any place else in my life. I learned to swim in this river. I first dived in this water. Lost a comb from my hair and I jumped down after it. I got it too. But now we leave." And Mom looked at the water—blue rippling in the sunlight—water pretty and flecked with little whitecaps. We moved down the river—night came and a pretty moon and we kept floating—floating to the new river. The next morning we passed through Gate City and onto a broad river of blue rippling water. One man stood on the bank at Gate City and I heard him say to another man: "Look at them Big-Sandians, won't you, on that barge. Going down the river like a lot of them here lately to find a pot of gold."

We floated down the Ohio all that day and till a moon came up that night. The moon was up in the sky. And Pop said: "Must twist her in to the bank and wait for morning. Here is where we stop. I have been here and found this place. I come on down here after I brought the last log-train down the Big-Sandy. See these mountains on the Kentucky side. Over there is a town in Ohio. It is Radnor. We can boat between Lowder, Kentucky, and Radnor, Ohio. A lot of Kentuckians work over there in town and they must cross the river."

We moved from the barge to a house overlooking the Ohio. It was a pretty house with maple trees in the yard. There are no mountains in Ohio. We could see the town. Pop started to build a boat. He called it the *Hilton Frazier* for my brother Hilton. He would start it to making trips across the river. My brother Hilton would pilot the *Hilton Frazier.* He was learning to be a pilot now at a boat down the river between Anderson, Ohio, and Vanlear, Kentucky. He was working without pay. He didn't get to fish in the river and swim like he used to when he was free as the wind on the Big-Sandy. Now he was a water-dog. He had followed our people, the Fraziers.

Mom would turn the coffee cup and she would say: "No women here to talk. I cannot see the Big-Sandy in this coffee cup. I see a wider river. I see more money. I see my daughters married to steamboat captains and boat owners. Life looks so much better now." And then she would go out under the maple tree and watch the boats pass with barges on the Ohio. Great loads of coal and sand and steel. But Mom would look for logs. We never saw the log trains on the Ohio we saw on the Big-Sandy and we never saw the men with guns around their belts we'd seen back in the mountains. And the man that got to run a crew of men didn't get his job by being able to holler the loudest either. He got it when the old got too old to do the job if he was of blood kin and next in line. That's the way it works on the Ohio.

Pop built the boat. Pop saved some money on the Big-Sandy. "A Frazier is never without money," people would say on Big-Sandy, "them Scotchmen can live on a rock." Pop said: "Now this boat will break us or make us. It just depends on how the town on the other side of the Ohio grows. If it does much growing we'll not be able to handle this business in a few years."

First the steel mills came to Radnor, Ohio. Then the shoe factories came. Kentuckians went over the river to work. The days passed and the gold poured into our hands. When a man paid his fare in pennies to brother Hilton, he would throw the pennies in the Ohio right in front of their eyes. Brother Hilton grew to be big like Pop and he was a pilot first and then captain of the *Hilton Frazier.* Pop made a new and bigger boat and we ran two boats across the river. The years passed. The days passed into months and the months into years. We grew to be men and women. We learned to love the Ohio as Pop loved the Big-Sandy. Pop never went back to the Big-Sandy. He would say:

"Elizabeth, we'll live here together until we die on this river. They can take us back to the Big-Sandy and bury us in the old churchyard where we was borned and raised."

When Pop got on the Ohio River he shaved the whiskers off his face. Pop didn't look like he used to look upon Big-Sandy. We remember how he worked there. He worked yet. He would swim to the middle of the Ohio River and catch a boat that had broken loose somewhere upon the river. Pop was still a water-dog. Gray hair on his head didn't matter. He worked and told the men what to do. Money come in and plenty of it. Pop built another boat with a dance hall on it—a fancy boat and called it the *Elizabeth Frazier*. And Brother Hilton piloted it up the Big-Sandy with the calliope playing. He stopped at Gate City and gave a big dance. Had his old-time band right on the boat. No one remembered Elizabeth Frazier. They remembered Big-Sandy Bill Frazier that shot Big Jim Hailey. But a young man in a blue suit with a cap, white cuffs, a black tie and bright buttons on his suit took the boat up Big-Sandy. He went right up Big-Sandy with the music—stopping at every town for a dance. He went right in with the music playing, "My Old Kentucky Home." People shed tears to see the big boat and to know this nice looking captain was old Big-Sandy Bill's boy that left the river years ago over killing a man over his wife. People danced on the boat and had a good time. Horses scared at it and broke the tongues out of the wagons. And children ran from the banks of the river afraid of the big boat. People would say: "Big-Sandy Bill's boy, Hilton Frazier, captain of that boat. They say Big-Sandy Bill's made money like dirt since he left here. Made barrels of money and got rich down on the Ohio. Had a bad wife though. Remember that trial? It's been about twelve years ago—you remember don't you?"

While Brother Hilton was up to the Levisa Fork—the only man to ever put a boat that far up the Big-Sandy and the biggest boat that ever plowed the waters of the Big-Sandy—a big rain fell and the water raised. It got so high the smoke-stack on the boat couldn't go under the new bridge that spanned the river right above Evans, Kentucky. Brother Hilton had to lay up twenty-four hours. The Government paid him $300. He told the people that spread over the Big-Sandy River valley: "W'y Hilton Frazier is a big enough man that when his big boat is delayed the Government pays him." And the Big-Sandians went on the boat and talked to Hilton and asked about old Big-Sandy Bill Frazier—when the boat stopped at the town and the calliope played "Old Kentucky Home."

At home Mom turned the coffee cup after she finished drinking her cup of coffee. And she said: "I can see Hilton. Hilton is dead. Hilton married. Hilton, dead. My first son! I can see the gun. I can see it spitting smoke." And Mom screamed. She said: "I tell you when you sow the seeds of life you reap the seeds of life. When you sow the seeds of death, you reap the seeds of death. Things come home to you on this earth. There is not any getting around it. I'll reap what I sowed on Big-Sandy. There is not any escape. I can see it here. I know it is coming regardless of the money we have and the three boats we have."

Hilton told Mom: "Mom, I am going to marry Hilda Thombs. Her people are river people. They've been on the Ohio for three generations. Her Grandpa used to run the old Grey Steamer here fifty years ago. I love her. I make the money. I am going to marry her.

Hilton did marry Hilda Thombs. She was a pretty girl. She looked like Mom used to look. She was every bit as pretty as Mom. And when Hilton married her, he started running a boat from Hardin, West Virginia, to Cincinnati, Ohio. It was bigger money for Brother Hilton. He ran the *Elizabeth Frazier*—one of the big passenger and freight boats—on the Ohio. We would be out and wave when he passed. He would always whistle and whistle for home. Mom was proud of her boat and Hilton running it on the Ohio. Old Jink Hammonds tipped Brother Hilton off: "Hilton, do you leave a light hanging on your porch on every Thursday night? Is that a signal you leave?" One night—I remember—Mom had read the coffee cup that night and she said: "I see a dead man. I see him bleeding. It is Hilton." And Grace said: "Mom, you think too much of Big-Sandy. That is over. Forget about it. Coffee grounds are coffee grounds. They don't mean a thing."

Hilda and Hilton just lived a stone-throw from us. Mom said: "The other night I saw a lantern swinging at Hilton's house. If I did not I was dreaming. It looked to me like a lantern."

The boat whistle never moaned this night on the river. It always whistled before. Hilton slipped to the house.

There was a lantern on the porch. Lester Shy, captain of the *Little Ann,* beat Brother Hilton to the draw. Mom heard the shot. She screamed. She jumped out of the bed. "I told you," said Mom, "Hilton is dead. Hilton has been killed."

We jumped out of our beds. We ran over to Hilton's house. Hilton was on the floor. Blood was spurting from his heart onto the floor. Pop was along, "Oh, my God," said Pop. "Oh, God—I remember." Mom was screaming. "You will reap what you sow," said Mom, "I was twenty-eight when this happened on Big-Sandy. Hilton is twenty-eight." Mom fell to the floor screaming. She had her hand in the little stream of blood running from Hilton's heart. Lester Shy had gone. "He'll be brought to justice," said Pop, "Big-Sandy justice where each man is his own law. I'll bring him to justice. I still can shoot."

"No you won't," said Mom, "we have just reaped what we sowed. I've thought this was coming all the time. I have expected it. You'll lay your gun down. You'll not shoot any more. Enough has been done already without any more killings and heart-aches in a world where you and I are growing old. We are growing out of the world. It is not leaving us. We are leaving it."

Hilda was down beside of Hilton. She was screaming: "I have caused it all. It has been my fault. Hilton has been away so much. God knows a man on the river is never with his wife. If I'd been on the boat with Hilton." And she would scream. And Mom took her by the shoulder and said: "Take it easier than that, Hilda. No use to cry now. It is all over. I believe I understand."

I could smell the gunpowder. It smelled like it did that night on Big-Sandy—the night I was a lot younger than I am now. I remember the stream of blood that night and how Big Jim moved his leg up like a frog. I saw Brother Hilton do the same thing. I wonder why a man shot through the heart always does it. Grace and Clara just having one fit after another over the death of Hilton—they, too, heard his last breath go like a sizzle of wind and he fell limp. His whole huge body relaxed and would be relaxed forever—Hilton, so much like Pop—his big arms—his hairy chest—his hairy arms—his color of a clay-clod hair—his big body stretched on his own floor in death and the killer gone free to kill again.

The *Elizabeth Frazier* did not make its regular trip on the river. It hauled the clay of its young Captain Hilton Frazier up the Ohio and through Gate City—Pop was piloting the boat. Pop can take a boat any place. A flag was floating at half-mast from the boat. We passed through Gate City and onto the waters of the Big-Sandy: "I used to know every snag in this river," said Pop, "but I guess it's changed as my hair has changed in the years I have been away. It seems like home to me—this little river where it takes more work to make money—more skill to pilot a boat." Mom never spoke. Her eyes were swollen. We stopped at the little house we left—the oak tree in the yard—where we had played—we anchored to one of the oak trees. We carried the casket up the steep bank to the house where the funeral would be preached that night. The old men that used to work for Pop—that used to river-rat with him—would come back. They would be there. They would come from the mountains.

Mom walked into the house. She saw the old stains of blood upon the floor. Mom screamed and started to sink to the floor. Clara caught her.

That night, mountain men, huge men—tall and bony with steel bearded faces, filed up the path from the river. Women came with them—women lean and tall—dressed in long flowing loose dresses and with shawls around their shoulders—came up the bank with their men. I slipped into the room where Hilton was in his coffin. I had played on the river with Hilton—the river whose water washed him to cleanse him for burial—I had talked to him. I knew him as intimately as I know a stalk of corn in the garden. I went in the room while the crowd was gathering in to hear Brother Ike Strickland preach the funeral. I went up to where Brother Hilton was laying a-corpse. And I said: "Speak to me Brother Hilton. Speak to me about the river. Tell me about the Big-Sandy—did you know you was back at the old house on the

Big-Sandy. Speak to me—oh, speak to me, Brother Hilton—" The wind came through the window and moved his hair and ruffled the window curtain. "Uncle Jake lives here now. Do you know it—you remember him don't you, Hilton?" But not a sound came. I could see the moon and the white clouds in the sky. I could see the Big-Sandy up between the two mountains—a ribbon of silver fading away between two rows of willows—far up between the mountains.

I could hear them in the other room crying. I could hear them singing, "*There's a land beyond the river, that they call the sweet Forever.*" The moon was high above the Big-Sandy and the wind was blowing through the window. Hilton lay there with his lips curved like Pop's—just like he wanted to say something. I could see the tombstones around the church where we used to go to Sunday school and church—the place where all of Pop's people are laid after they left the Big-Sandy. Tomorrow we'll take Hilton there. He'll be laid there among his kin that have followed the river—have been shot and shot others—those who have cut the timber from the mountain slopes and cleared the valley. That is where Hilton will sleep. The Big-Sandy will flow not far away—one can hear it murmuring from the church where Hilton sleeps for it is not a stone's throw away. It knows the dreams and holds the dreams of three generations of Fraziers now sleeping in this Big-Sandy earth.

Powderday's Red Hen

SATURDAY afternoon at three, Finn and I just finished cutting sprouts on our pasture field. We had cut over forty acres of persimmon, pawpaw, and sassafras sprouts with our mattocks and sprouting hoes. We had scythed blackberry-brier thickets and the low saw-brier stools with our heavy brier scythes. The weather had been so hot in July and August we had taken off all our clothes but our shorts and shoes. The only part of the pasture that was cool was on the hilltop where winds never ceased to blow. We were sunburned as brown as ripe hickory nuts, ripened and falling from trees after frost.

"I'll banner you walkin' five miles to the Little Tavern to get a mug of beer," Finn said.

"No you won't banner me," I said.

We put our clothes on in the sprout field. We hung our scythes over an oak limb at the end of the pasture field so they wouldn't rust if it rained. We set our mattocks and hoes up against the side of an oak shade at the end of the pasture. Then we started walking around the ridge for town. We had five miles to walk to reach the Little Tavern.

We hurried around the ridge. When we left the ridge we went down the hill past the Gus Murray home. Then we passed the town graveyard and cut across the railroad tracks to the Little Tavern. Our faces were brown. Our shirts were unbuttoned at the collars and our sleeves were rolled up.

"Hello there, boys," Wid Coldiron said. "How's the work among the sprouts today?"

"All finished," I replied.

"What about it Finn, old boy," Wid asked Finn. "What do you say?"

"Wid, if I'd tell you something truthful would you believe me?" Finn said.

"Maybe I would," Wid said. His tiny black eyes looked Finn over. Wid's mop of brown hair nearly reached his eyes. His blue shirt was unbuttoned at the collar.

We walked in th' Little Tavern. Wid followed us.

"Wid, we got a hen out home that says bad words," Finn said. "She can blackguard. She can crow like a rooster too."

"I'd love to see and hear her," Wid said. "Do you really mean you've got a hen like this? You're not trying to spoof me, are you?"

"Sure, I mean it," Finn said.

"How did you ever get a hen like her?" Wid asked.

"I don't know whether she's been this way since she was hatched from the egg or from the time she first stepped up on the porch and crowed. Pa let the screen door catch her neck when he was trying to shoo her from the house. Pa's goin' to have her killed. She's too vulgar for our women folks to hear around the house."

"Oh, don't do it," Wid said. "Come over here, Jamsey, you and Laff! Listen to this!"

"Another mug of beer," Finn said. "I'm thirsty and this beer's good. Won't you have one, Wid?"

"Don't care for it," Wid said. "I want you to hear these Powderday boys to tell you about their hen."

"There's nothin' more to tell," Finn said. "She's got something the matter with her neck 'r something. When she opens her bill to make a noise she says bad words. I don't want to quote anything she says in here. She's so vulgar Pa's going to have her killed."

"Don't do it," Jamsey Griffin said. "I'd like to see that hen."

"We'll come out and see her," says Laff Litteral. "Goodness, I'd like to see and hear a hen like her. She's worth a fortune. Don't let your Pa kill her."

"You can hear her if you'll walk out home," Finn said. "Everybody in the country is talkin' about her. People call her Powderday's old red hen! Haven't you heard about her?"

"Have you heard about her, boys?" Wid asked his friends.

"First time I ever heard about 'er," Laff said. "First time I've ever heard of a hen like her in my life."

"We've got that kind of a hen," Finn said. He took the last drink from his mug of beer. "Our hen is the talk of everybody out where we live."

"Another beer, Little Doc," Finn said. "I'm thirsty. Won't you have one on me, boys?"

"No, tell us more about th' hen," Laff said.

"I've told you all I know," Finn said. "She's just a blackguardin' hen that will have to be killed. Pa says she's not fit to run with the other chickens."

"If that doesn't beat me," Jamsey sighed. "Never heard of a chicken like her."

"I feel better now," I said. "I'm ready to go if you are, Finn!"

"I'm ready too," he said.

Finn laid a five-dollar bill on the wet table. Little Doc picked it up. Finn waited for his change. I got up and walked out. Finn came out of Little Tavern behind me. Jamsey, Wid and Laff came out with Finn. They were asking him more about our hen. Laff was about six feet four, nearly as tall as Finn. His face was red, his hair was brown. Jamsey was big around the middle and little on each end. His face was pale and his eyes were blue. He smoked a pipe.

"How far is it out to your house?" Jamsey asked Finn.

"About five miles if you go up the Murray Hill and down the ridge path," Finn told him. "It's much farther if you go around and up the valley."

"Think I'd be able to walk it?"

"Don't see why," Finn said. "What are you a bag of sugar? Are you afraid you might get wet and disappear?"

"No, but I got a lame leg and a lot of weight to carry on it," he told Finn. "I weigh two hundred and twenty pounds and I'm not but five feet and six inches tall."

"Walk some that weight off," Finn said. "Come out and see and hear our hen!"

"We'll be out Sunday," Laff said. "Expect us about three o'clock in the afternoon."

"Okay, we'll be lookin' for you," Finn said.

Finn and I walked up the street, then we crossed the railroad tracks. We followed the road to the hills. Soon we were high upon the Murray Hill looking down on the town and the valley below us.

"Reckon the boys will come to see our hen?" I asked Finn.

"Sure they'll come," he replied.

"Where'll Pa be Sunday?" I asked.

"He'll be goin' with Mom to the Baptist Association down on Smith Branch."

"Oh, yes, I remember now there is a Baptist Association on Smith Branch," I said.

We reached the ridge. We walked along the ridge until we came to our pasture. We crossed th' sheep pasture to the house.

The September sun shone on the dry pasture fields. The sheep were huddled under the shade of the black oaks above our house. The yellow jackets worked in and out of a hole under a stump near our house. The hornets came in one by one and caught flies from our sheep's backs. Finn and I lay down in the dry grass under the shade of our poplar tree in the front yard and watched the hornets work. Bob, our shepherd dog, lay down beside us and cuffed the fleas from his ears with his stubby toenails.

Next morning Pa and Mom went to Baptist Association on Smith Branch. Finn and I milked the cows, fed the hogs and mules. Then, we waited for Laff, Jamsey and Wid.

"The boys are not comin'," I said.

"They'll be here," said Finn. "Jamsey's a little fat. He'll be slow walking five miles on his lame leg."

"Where is our hen?" I asked.

"Oh, she's around here someplace," Finn said. "She's somewhere with the other chickens."

Just then, old Bob jumped up, pricked his ears to the wind. He let out a yelp and took over the hill running.

"He either winds or hears them," Finn said.

"He hears them for he didn't sniff," I said. "He doesn't smell very well any more."

We looked and beyond the house where we saw three boys coming down through the orchard toward the sheep pasture. We watched them crawl under the fence into the pasture. Jamsey was limping slowly behind. Long, lanky Laff was in front and Wid was walking between. They were pointing toward our flock of sheep. Bob was the first to greet them with a whine and wags of his bushy tail. He sniffed each pantleg, then ran down the path ahead. He came back to tell us that strangers were coming.

We greeted our friends with a cold bucket of water from our well in the back yard. They were wet with sweat and thirsty. Their wet clothes were covered with needle-burrs.

"I'm about winded and my boiler is dry," Jamsey said.

"This will give you more steam," Finn said. He gave Jamsey the first dipper of cold well water.

"It's great stuff," Jamsey said after he gurgled the water down. He caught his breath and wiped his lips with his sleeve. Laff followed with two dippers and Wid took one.

"Now, where's that hen?" Jamsey asked.

"All right, we'll look 'er up," Finn said.

When we walked toward th' barn, I called the chickens. They came running from the pasture and the woods beyond the barn where we kept our mules. They came running from the tomato patch in the garden.

"She's a red hen, isn't she?" Laff asked.

"She sure is," Finn replied. "Look for her."

"How can you tell her from the rest of the hens?" Wid asked.

"She'll crow in the minute," Finn said. "Then she'll start using her foul words. She's easy to tell from the rest of the hens. When she starts crowing the other hens scatter out!"

"She's some hen!" Jamsey said.

"She certainly is," Finn agreed with Jamsey.

"I'm afraid she's not here," I said. "I heard her crowing a while ago. Then I heard her say a few bad words."

"Wonder where she is?" Laff asked.

"I don't know," Finn said. "Maybe Pa killed her."

"I hope not," Jamsey said. "I wanted to see and hear her."

"Then let's scout the hills to find her," Finn said. "She runs out in the far pasture field. She follows the cattle around out there."

"All right, I'm ready," Laff said. "Are you too tired, Jamsey?"

"No, I can make it all right," he replied.

We walked out the path by the barn. We crossed the hill by the pine trees and circled the north side of the pasture field. We didn't see a sign of the hen. We scared up two coveys of quails. We came upon six very gentle cows Finn and I milked morning and evening. We crossed the far end of the pasture. Then we circled back through the oak woods on the south side of the pasture. We never saw a chicken of any kind. The sun was going down and we saw two gray squirrels chasing each other through the limbs of the oaks. We walked back to the barn. We called the chickens again. I fed them cane seed. Our red hen wasn't there.

"She's not here," Finn said. "I'll bet a hawk has caught her."

"There's not anything I want to see more than that red hen," Jamsey said. "I'll bet we've walked twenty miles to see her. And now we've missed seeing her and hearing her crow and say bad words. I'd like to hear a chicken talk."

"When Pa and Mom get back I'll find out if they've killed 'er," Finn said. "If they didn't, I'll let you know. I'll let you know if I have to write you a letter to tell you if she's living or dead. If she's alive you must come again to see her."

"We'll do it, won't we, Griffin?" Laff said.

"You bet your life we will," Jamsey replied. "I'll tell other boys in town about her. They'll be wantin' to come too. The whole town is talking about that hen."

"Looks like it'd be better if you brought the hen to town," Laff said.

"No, Pa wouldn't let us take her off the place," Finn said. "He's ashamed we've got a hen like her."

We watched our friends walk back across the sheep pasture.

We watched Laff and Wid help Jamsey under the fence. They walked up the path through the orchard. They stopped and looked back at the house from the ridge. They waved good-by to us. We waved good-by to them.

"Sorry we couldn't find that hen," Finn said. "Old Jamsey just can't take it. I doubt if he'll get back to town. He's walked over twenty miles to see a hen. Then we couldn't find her."

When Pa and Mom walked back up the path, Finn walked down the hill to meet them.

"Pa, did you kill our red hen that crows and says bad words?" Finn asked.

"What are you talking about, Finn?" our father asked.

"I was asking you a question," Finn said.

"What hen are you talking about, Finn?" our mother asked.

"The one that cusses and crows," Finn said.

"No, I didn't kill her," Pa said. He began laughing.

Monday morning Finn fed the chickens. He called them to the barn and fed them cane seed and shelled corn. He walked out the path to the house. He came to the smokehouse where I was feeding our Irish setter.

"Shan, that old hen's still out at the barn," he said. "I'll tell the boys when I go to town next Saturday Pa didn't kill her."

Two weeks passed. The September rains had begun to fall. The roads were as slick as a soapy washboard. The water stood in the deep ruts in the road and a wind as cool as frost was raining the dying leaves down from the trees. Finn and I stayed at home all Sunday. We heard the straining of a car engine that we first thought was a plane flying over. We couldn't believe anybody would try to drive over a country road like ours in dry weather, let alone a time like this.

"That car can't be coming here!" I said.

The seats were filled and they were hanging on the running boards. We walked down from the poplar tree in our front yard to meet the boys. They couldn't drive up the slick bank to the house. We didn't think about such a crowd coming back to see our red hen.

"It's Jamsey, Wid, and Laff, all right!" Finn said."They've brought a crowd with them! That's Jamsey at the wheel."

"We're here, and if we didn't have a old-time car built high enough to straddle the rocks, chug-holes, and ruts we'd have never made it," Jamsey said.

"Jamsey had to stop for me to put water in the radiator three times," Laff said. "She got awful hot coming through the mud."

"She didn't straddle all the mud," Finn said. "You're pushing a barrel of yaller mud in front of the car now."

"But we've come to see the hen," Wid said. "We brought our friends Toad Kinner, Boogie Greene, Bill Thompson, Bill Ashworth, Clarence Hailey and Tod Crum with us."

"Do you reckon we'll find the hen?" Jamsey asked.

"I think so," Finn said. "But when we go to look for her she might be hard to find."

"We brought a gun with us too," Jamsey said. "The barrel is forty-two inches long and she's a ten-gauge. She's just half-choked and shoots one hundred and fifty yards. The shots don't scatter over a place bigger than the bottom of a dishpan. She's loaded with Super-x shells."

"You're not killing the hen," Finn said. "I'll tell you that right now."

"We can see her though, can't we?" Wid asked.

"Yes, if we can find her," Finn said. "But I don't want her killed."

"Well, let's go and find her," Jamsey said. "Let's go listen to her crow and say bad words!"

Then all eleven of us went to the barn. Finn called the chickens to the corn-crib door. He scattered cane-seed on the ground. They came running from the pasture fields and the woods. They came from the barn and the garden.

"No red hen here," Jamsey said.

"Don't believe she's gone," Wid said.

"If you don't believe we've got this hen, I'll ask you to go over the hill and ask Bill Hillman," Finn said. "You'll believe 'im, won't you? No, my father never killed her!"

"Sure, I'll believe old Bill any time," Jamsey said. "Bill Hillman won't lie."

"Bill will tell you how he was over here walking to the barn once when this hen followed him, crowed and said bad words until he thought some foul-mouth person was behind him," Finn said. "When Bill turned around our old red hen was behind him. He didn't know whether he was asleep or awake. He thought he might be asleep and dreaming."

"Let's scout the woods again," Wid Coldiron said. "Let's go to the hills. Let's hunt all over the pastures and the orchard until we find her."

All eleven of us walked over the mule pasture back of the barn. Then we went to the far pasture field. We hunted over the same pasture we had hunted over before. We went to the sheep pasture. We looked behind the cliffs. Then we hunted the cornfields and the stubble-fields where the wheat had been cut. We hunted over forty acres of woods. Jamsey was the last one on the tail end of the line. He limped, but he was on his lame leg. He kept up with us as we covered our farm looking for the hen. We looked over three hundred acres hunting for our hen.

"Sorry as we can be, fellows," Finn said as we walked back to the car. "I know just as well as I know that you are here with us the hen is around here someplace. Pa's thrown so many rocks she's getting wild and might be hiding."

"We'll come again," Jamsey said. "We'll come until we find her. There'll be more with us the next time. We had to knock them off the car when we left town. They're all wanting to come out here!"

"Walk out here and bring them next time," Finn said.

"We'll do it," Laff said. He wiped sweat from his face with his shirtsleeve. Then he took the gun from his shoulder and laid it down in the car.

"It's getting late, Jamsey," Wid said. "We'd better turn and go back before dark. If we hadn't had enough with us to push us out the mud four times we'd have a big expense paying farmers to use their mule teams to pull us from the mudholes. Let's get out of here before dark."

"I'm sorry you've had all this trouble for nothing," Finn said.

"It's okay; we'll be out again," Wid said.

Jamsey got in the car. He was so tired he dropped on the car seat. He switched on the engine and backed away from the pile of mud. He turned the car. Wid got in beside Jamsey.

Laff got in beside Wid and held the gun on his lap. Toadie, Boog, Bill and Ash got in the back seat. Clarence stood on one running board and Todd stood on the other. Th' engine clattered like a mowing machine in tall grass. The car moved slowly down the holler pushing the mud in front.

Two more weeks passed before the frosts came. Then a blanket of snow covered the fields. The winds had swept the trees bare of leaves. The wind was cold and biting on a Sunday afternoon. Finn and I were sawing logs for firewood to keep our fire going. We didn't have anything else to do. Bill Hillman was holding the log steady on the sawhorse.

Bill was sitting straddle of the log and smoking his pipe. We heard men talking. Bob ran from under the smokehouse and began to bark. He run toward the peach orchard. When we looked up that way we saw a crowd of boys coming over the hill.

"They're coming from Blakesburg again to see our hen," Finn said. "You know Powderday's red hen, Bill! Everytime she opened her bill she'd crow and say bad words!"

"Sure, I know about her," Bill said.

Then Bill Hillman let out a wild laugh as loud as the hoarse winds blowing among the barren oak branches in the grove above the woodyard.

We stopped to watch them go one by one between the barbed-wire fence on the side of the pasture. The tall ones straddled the fence to come over. Some climbed up the wire on the posts like they were going up the steps on a ladder. After they crossed the fence they ran down the pasture hill, crossed the holler and walked up the bank below our house to the woodyard. Jamsey walked behind.

"Howdy, fellars," Wid said. "We've come to see the hen. We're bringing all our friends with us! Your hen is the talk of the town."

"Too bad, Wid, the hen has been killed," Finn said. "You can see her feathers down there by the smokehouse."

"Yes, go down thare and see fer yourselves," Bill Hillman said.

"Why did you kill her?" Laff asked.

"You'd have killed her too, if you'd had company and she'd acted at your house like she did here," Finn said.

"Tell us about it," Toadie said.

There stood John Campbell, Erf Bishop, Dod Young, Woody Gilbert, Troy Holbrook, Ron Ellis and Ennis Martin. This was their first time to come to see our hen. They had come with Jamsey, Laff, Wid, Toadie, Boogie, Bill, Ash, Clarence and Todd.

"Brother Baggs, his wife and two daughters come over here for dinner last Sunday," Finn said. "We were all sittin' around the table when it happened. The hen came up and stuck her head in at the door, crowed like a rooster. Pa got up from the table to scare her away. Then she said bad words in front of everybody."

"Then what happened?" Toadie asked.

Everybody listened silently to hear the story. There was disappointment written over all their faces.

"You might have known what happened," Finn said. "Pa's face got as red as a sliced beet to have our hen blackguarding before Brother Baggs, his wife and daughters. Our mother and three sisters heard her too. Pa was so embarrassed he ran to the fireplace and got the poker."

"Did he kill her with the poker?" Laff asked.

"No, Reverend Baggs was up from the table in seconds," Finn said. "He ran for his hat. He beat Pa through the door and he hit her with his big stiff hat. This finished our hen. After Reverend Baggs and his family left, we scalded our red hen, plucked the feathers, cleaned and cooked her. Reverend Baggs said he'd never eat a hen like her. But we didn't mind."

"All this trip again for nothing," Jamsey said. "I'm about pooped out! I can't get back to town."

"Sorry about the hen," Finn said. "I wish you could have seen that hen and heard her just one time!"

"So do we," Wid said. "We've got to walk all the way to

Blakesburg through this mud. It's a stiff mud that sticks to your feet like glue. It's as heavy as lead. We're all so tired."

"It's more like ten miles out here than it is five," Wid said. "We've come through mud, briers, cockleburrs, brush and water to get here. We've crossed creeks and fences. We've climbed banks and one mountain to get here. The cold wind was so sharp it cut our faces like a cold-bladed knife."

"Well, we'd better start back," Jamsey said. "I don't know whether I can make it or not."

They were a disappointed crowd because Reverend Baggs had killed our hen with his hat. They left without saying good-by to us.

We watched them follow the pasture path in single file with Jamsey limping behind. They looked like a small army of men wading through the mud with their faces rubbed raw by the winter wind. Laff and Wid helped Jamsey through the fence. They walked up through the orchard, a long, line of tired men.

"They've walked a hundred miles, searched over a thousand acres, then never got to hear the old red hen, hear her crow and say bad words," Bill Hillman said. Then he laughed as loudly as the wind among the barren oak branches above our house.

"That's too bad," Finn said as he began laughing too.

Bill Hillman was too lazy to help us pull the crosscut saw. But he didn't mind sitting on top the log to keep it steady on the sawhorse while Finn and I pulled the saw.

Fast-Train Ike

"OOOOOOO—OOOUH—UH," the whistle screams. The black smoke rolls in great puffs—clouds with their sides puffing out and bursting into ash-colored and cream-colored swirls. "Oooooooooo—ooouh," and the smoke falls in a stream back across the engine top like a rabbit laying its ears back and taking through the brush—back from the tall stack like smoke sucking groundward from the rock chimney at home when there's going to be fallen-weather. See the engine coming like a bench-legged bull—stout as a bull, mad as a bull, and charging against the wind—right down the track—two streaks of rust—red in the sunlight of August among the ragweeds and the rotted crossties. "Oooooo—ooouh," and huffety-huffety-puffety-puffety and the bench-legged bull slows down for Fast-Train Ike's red handkerchief. Any bull will stop for red. People stick their heads out the window and look—look at the hills on each side the track—the old worn-out Kentucky hills and the sprouts and briars and the cinders along the track—the piles of rotted crossties—the dewberry briars among them—vining and crawling and running around over the company's premises without their permission.

"Ah," says Conductor Harry. (Everybody knows Conductor

Harry on the O. L. S., The Old Line Special. He's been on this train for forty-nine years.) "I thought you wasn't going to ride this train any more. The way you've been acting ever since I've been on this road—w'y you've given us more trouble than any man that's ever gone to town with us. Keep the passengers scared to death the way you go on—" And Conductor Harry helps Fast-Train Ike on the train—a tall man with a long nose—with curly locks of uncut hair—hair that is going to seed—a man with a slow walk—a take-your-time walk—a man with big hands that dangle from pipe-stem arms. A mouth that is always about to say something and seldom ever does. Fast-Train walks into the last coach and takes his seat. People on the train draw their heads in at the window and quit looking at the old worn-out Kentucky hills, the saw-briars, the dewberries—and the sassafras sprouts on the hills. Women sitting by their men whisper in their ears and point to Fast-Train Ike. He is something for them all to look at—not a man in forty miles dressed like him. "Got the old time dress that man has. Big high stiff collars and the necktie outside. Tie pin big as a goose egg. That hat was the kind Grandpa wore—look at that suit won't you—wrinkled and old-fashioned—" And the train starts just as Fast-Train Ike sits down and picks up the paper. It leaves the station like a bench-legged bull. Mad because it had to stop for old Fast-Train Ike. Goes out huffety-puffety-huffety-puffety—mad, pawing and scraping—scraping and pawing—and belching hot cinders from his belly—mad as a bull right down the two streaks of rust. "Oooooooo—oooooooo—woooo—wooooooooouh—uh—woooooo—uh—uh." And the clouds of smoke boil from the long stack—the big bull's-eye right up in front looks through the long dark tunnel ahead—one tunnel and then another—right down two streaks of rust over the rotted oak ties and the burnt-top ragweeds—down, down, down—down the grade. People on the train going somewhere. Going from the hills to the town—laughing, laughing—talking and looking out at the windows at the worn-out hills with sulphur blood streaming from their pierced sides where the railroad gets its coal—stumps on the hills where the railroad hauls its logs.

"W'y," says Conductor Harry, "we got that crazy old bachelor Fast-Train Ike back there on the train. Never was a man in this country like him. Have trouble every time he gets on the train. Raises cain and gets all the women scared. Says the train is going to wreck and kill him. Yet he's rid this train ever since I have been here—forty-nine years last April—seems to me like he's never changed his suit—I know he's always wore that big tie pin and read the paper. People know him for miles around. That's why they call him Fast-Train Ike. Just because he's afraid of the train. Brakeman Charlie, keep your eye on him. Watch for him to take one of his tantrums. When he does—warn me. He'll have one when the sun goes down and it starts getting dark."

"Mama, will that old Fast-Train Ike hurt you? I heard he would, Mama—he's so ugly. Mama, I'm afraid of him—" "Honey, Fast-Train Ike won't hurt you. He's been riding this train ever since I have. That's been thirty years. He's never hurt anybody yet." And the train moves on—a little bench-legged, one-eyed bull, with its square eye in the top of its head—right down the track a charging over the ragweeds—over the rotted crossties and the two streaks of rust—charging against the wind —going to town down the grade—down the grade to town. Sunset, but the one-eyed engine looks straight ahead for a tunnel—a dark hole in the earth and under—under the big rocks and the hills—one eye to see the bridges and there are so many of them across the rivers—bridges and trestles where the sawbriars climb all over the company's premises.

Ah, babies crying on the train. Men talking about coal in these hills, gold in the hills that the Indians left and silver among these hills—men talking about women—and women taking care of their babies and their men—women talking to each other about other women—getting acquainted on the train—laughing—laughing—talking as the wind blows past the coaches outside—the three passenger coaches and the mail car. Over the hills to a destiny—and the wind zooms in the rusty telephone wires and through the sawbriars along the right-of-way—along the track—coaches lumbering, lumbering, lumbering over the two streaks of rust—train going into the night following two streaks of rust—into holes under the hills and across rivers. See the sunset against an August Kentucky hill—a great blotch of blood above the trees. A blotch of blood that is growing darker—and the night is coming—night in Kentucky and the whippoorwills in the oaks—the zoom of the night winds among the rusted wires and the sawbriars—the people talking to each other—the laugh, the cry, the endless chatter—and all going to some destiny and some end.

"W'y they tell me that old Fast-Train Ike's got a whole pot full of money. W'y I've heard he wasn't crazy only on some things. Just afraid of a train. You know you've seen people crazy in some ways. There's a lot of ways to be crazy now—you know that. He can't be crazy and make all the money he's made. W'y the man has to be smart—" "Sssssssssss—he'll hear you talking about him. Leave him alone," says Conductor Harry, "long as he's contented with the paper. About the time he finishes reading the paper and sees dark against the window—and feels the train plunging into the darkness—then he takes his spell—God, and a lot of people on this train won't know about him. It takes too much time to go around and whisper it to people about him. It takes too long to explain to people. And when he starts hollering it'll scare all the women to death. They'll be lunging and plunging through these coaches like rabbits in front of a ferret in a hole. Maybe we'll have to stop the train. I'll run for representative next time myself and get to Frankfort to pass a law that no nut can ride a train. We need more laws about fools and nuts. I'll tell you the world is crazy or that man is one. We need more laws against men like him. I can't tell him to stay off the train. If I could have he'd not have been on this train in the past forty-nine years. So, sssssssshhhhhhhhh—don't bother him. For God's sake. Let him read the paper."

Fast-Train Ike turns the pages slowly and scans the gray pages —up and down and his eyes peep over the big-rimmed spectacles that cover his eyes. His Adam's apple moves in and out as he works his head. He reads the paper—and the train still huffety-puffety-huffety-puffety like a bench-legged bull a running over to the other side of the pasture to fight another bull—right down the two streaks of rust now—plunging and lunging into the night. Kentucky's night winds try to follow the train. Hear them zoom among the rusted wires and the sawbriars—Hear them sweep across the hills—Hear them sweep into the night—mocking the voices inside the coaches—voices of women talking to each other and about their children, their loved ones, their homes, husbands and the women about them. Men meeting on the train and drinking—smoking together the fragrant weed—getting to be friends the first night. "I tell you if you never saw a fellow and you take a drink together—or a good smoke on a train—you'll wake up friends the next day. That's why Kentucky is one of the best states in this United States. We furnish the good whiskey to drink—Government booze—or mountain white mule. Just about anything you want. And it brings friendship between men and tides men over sorrows, trials and tribulations. It's a tonic—a medicine. And the fragrant weed is good to partake of—good to see the swirls of clouds go away from your lips when you are riding over the hills on a train—sitting on a good seat—riding a train into the night. And Kentucky grows the fragrant weed—great fields of it under the Kentucky sun—great fields of burley—great broad leaves flapping for men on the train to partake of in their pipes of peace—riding, riding, riding over two streaks of rust to some certain destiny with a nut on the train and only a few people knowing he is a nut when it comes to riding a train. And if you could hear the endless chatter here—if you could see the red moon on the low hills and hear the rumble and the tumble of the coaches in the night—the zoom of the wind in the rusted wires and the briars—and the moan of the engine's whistle—ah, if you were only here as we speed over the rough earth on a one-eyed train to some destiny—over the rivers, under the hills, over the hills and around the hills and up the valleys—speeding, speeding behind a mad bench-legged bull that stops for a red handkerchief and to get a drink of water—a bull mad and hot and blowing cinders from his belly into the night—red hot lumps into the night—when over our heads the red moon rides and the stars twinkle over the Kentucky earth.

"I told you," says Fast-Train Ike—"I told you didn't I—what the world is the matter you put me on this tail-end coach—Didn't I walk back there on the little porch—didn't I walk back there—

come nigh as a pea walking off the train—and what do you think would have happened to me the way this train is going—tearing out down over these hills. Didn't I tell you once I didn't want to ride on the last coach. I want to be safer—ah, if I had any other way to get out of these hills—I'd never ride your train—ah, you low-down scamp of a conductor. You ought to be fired—think no more of your passengers than you do. Put me on the last coach—W'y this train is going to kill me. I am going to die on a train. How many times have I told you—how many times have you listened? Have you ever once believed me? Listen, you will believe me—when I die you'll see that I die in a train wreck. Take my suitcase in another car. Get it—don't wait for someone else—carry it yourself. It's not going to hurt your hands."

"Stay off'n this train from now on," says Conductor Harry. "You have been more trouble to me than all the other passengers on this road. I've had them to get too much licker—want the winder raised—and I couldn't raise it quick enough—they've pulled their pistols and shot them out—vomited out the winders—paid me like gentlemen for the glass and said they's sorry but they were in a hurry and had to act—but you—you are the worst I ever saw—You stay off this train—I'd have this train stopped for a minute and put you off into the night—" "What's the matter Conductor—what's the matter—something wrong with the train—" "Oh, no, my good woman—just this nut here—He's afraid of a train. Says he's going to die on a train—" "Yes, but I had a dream last night—a bad dream about a train. I dreamed it wrecked—yes I did—honest—and it all comes back—a train wreck—God, but I can see it all now—I can see it—a train wreck." And she screams. "Oh, it's going to happen," says Fast-Train Ike, "it's going to happen. I've been forewarned fifty years ago. People think I'm crazy but it's going to happen. You all get prepared for we've got several more rivers to cross before we get to town—" "What did you say?" says the big red-faced woman with the little girl on her lap—" "I said," says Fast-Train Ike, "that this train is going to wreck. Get prepared for we've just a few more rivers to cross before we get to town. That is what I said, Lady." "Why don't you get prepared yourself if you know the train is going to wreck?" "Lady, I've been prepared for fifty years. Ever since I've had the dream—ever since I got the vision—ever since I've been forewarned. I've always taken my time about things. That's why I never married. I knew it was a matter of time when I'd have to leave my sweet little wife and my children—So, I just didn't bother about marrrying. I knew I'd have to ride this train if I stayed among my hills—and I knew I was going to stay—for I've drunk water from the same well for fifty-eight years. Pap drunk it from the same well his lifetime. Why should I quit drinking it because I'm to die in a train wreck. Why should I leave my happy home—ah, why should I—got to go one time. Just as well be in a train wreck as any other way—only I want to hit on the dirt or a soft cushion—I don't want to be ground to sausage or squeezed between the walls of one of these coaches. I want to get out of it with my natural body not changed a particle. That's me, Lady—I know the train is going to wreck. That's why I come from the other coach in here—"

"Train's a going to wreck—ah, train is going to wreck—"

"Who said the train was going to wreck—ah, ah,—that fellow huh—well that fellar's not all there—now who knows the appinted time like that—who knows—w'y that fellar is a nut. He oughtn't be allowed to ride a train with respectable people. Look how he's dressed with that high collar—it's fifty years behind time—" "Well, you old Big-Belly you—you—you can talk about his collar if you please—but it's better than what you got on—a homemade shirt without a sign of a collar—He looks a devil of a sight better than you—And there can be a train wreck. Guess I had a dream last night. Guess I dreamed of a train wreck. I know I would rather believe what I dreamed and what he said as to believe the things you say—you old Big-Belly fun-maker you. Keep your tongue inside your toothless gums and you'll have enough to do—" "Quiet, quiet please—quiet—quiet—please—I've a few words to say. Who said this train would wreck?" says Conductor Harry—"who says it will wreck?" "I," says Fast-Train Ike, "I say it will wreck—" "W'y this fellow," says Conductor Harry, "ought to be in the asylum. He's not all there. You people can see that. Had me to move him from the last coach up here. I tell you this fellow is not all there. You've seen 'em like that. I've been moving him from the back coach and giving him a newspaper to read or to look at the pictures for the past forty-nine years to keep him quiet on this train. Wish the Kentucky Legislature would make a law to keep nuts off'n the passenger trains. Sight what a conductor has to go through with —got my coat tail cut off two or three times and a gallon jug busted over my head—three or four bottles busted around my temples—and have been vomited over a half dozen times—yet, can't get any help from the Kentucky Legislature. The man is a nut—that's all—a nut—you all can see that—now this train is not going to wreck. Set in your seats and keep quiet. You are running me crazy—"

"I told you," says the Big-Bellied man to the woman with the red face. "I told you the man was a nut. He's not all there. How does he know so much about the train's business—the Lord's business. You know if it is the Lord's will to wreck this train he's not going to tell a lot of people about his business and let them know as much as the Lord knows himself. That's a evident fact. It wouldn't do for the Lord to let everybody know when they were going to die. It would be giving them a chance they already ought to have taken. Warn them like a rabbit before you shoot it—w'y have the whole bunch a screaming—w'y they wouldn't even be patronizing the train. The Lord would be interfering with Business too. It don't make sense—" And the red-faced woman says: "I'll just show you how to make sense—talking about the Lord and that poor ran over there and all—making me out of a liar about the dream I had—I'll let you have this umberell right between the eyes—"

"Ah," days Conductor Harry, "no fighting on this train. I'll stop the train and have you both put off. That's what I'll do. I'll have that old codger put off over there for starting all of this fracas on the train too. That nut over there started it all. Wish we'd a never stopped back there at that flagstation and got him—"

"You can't have me put off," says Fast-Train Ike, "for I know the Law. You say I'm a nut. I can prove to you after this night I am a smart man. This train is going to wreck. I have come up here in this coach so I can have it easier. You can just say what you please. I haven't lived all these years for nothing. Guess I got a little sense—You can't even stop the train now. The train is running away—It's going I tell you—I can see it—something the matter with the pistons and the brakes won't hold —going, going, going, going—down—down—down—all of you not right with the Lord had better pray. I know I'm a goner. I'm ready—Don't need to pray—I'm ready—I know I'm a goner—I've been looking for this since I was a child. I'm getting cold right now as a beef hung out in the October wind to cool—I know it's not long off—"

And the scream of the whistle—under the red moon on the low hills—the gray smoke in long streamers in the wind—running, running, running—lunging, plunging through the night. The wind zooms among the rusty telephone wires—the wind follows the train—the wind can't catch the train—a train running downgrade on two streaks of rust—running, running—rolling—and the whistle screaming—"Boys, something wrong with the O. L. S.—something wrong with the Old Line Special—never stopped for a station—went right past—Jim Henly out there at Salt Center to flag her and she come batting it right out'n the tunnel and right down the track—Jim just did clear the track as she passed with the whistle down and the people with their heads out the winders screaming like a bunch of wild geese lost at night—something is wrong I tell you—something bad the matter—smoke just streamed back like a rabbit's ears laid back when it's running from buckshot. You'll hear about all this tomorrow—maybe tonight. That track can't hold a train running that fast—people just tumbling over one another in the coaches—could get a snake's eye full of them when they passed—and of all the hollering—hollering—"

And the red moon in the Kentucky sky—red moon over the low August hills and the wheat and corn thereon—the ripe wheat—the growing corn—over the scars on the hills where the sulphur blood runs from the bowels of the Kentucky earth. If you could see the O. L. S. running away like a mad bull down the beaten path of a century with both ears laid back—mad because it's had to work overhours—It's had to work too long—it ought to be retired and a new bull—bench-legged, take its place—and throw up new white hot cinders from its belly into the night. Work an old bull to death—no wonder it wants to run away—gets something wrong with the pistons and has all the people screaming to the moon with their heads out'n the windows—out into the night air—under a million cold stars twinkling in the August heavens—no wonder—no wonder. You might think I'm crazy but the old bench-legged engine ought to be retired—one-eyed and that big tall stack—w'y it's as old-fashioned as Fast-Train Ike's collar—and the track needs a rest—rails that have held up loads for a century—"Just take a rail out when it breaks. That's all." And the great night—nothing we can do about it—and the wind—following the train and humming a song—very nice of the wind—nothing really we can do about that—nor the wheat on the hills—nor the red moon in the sky—nothing, nothing we can do about the whole affair.

"I told you you couldn't stop this train. I told you it was running away. I could tell it would happen soon as I got on the train. Pull your cord fifty times and you can't stop this train. It's gone—gone down the two streaks of rust. That's the reason I read the paper so long tonight—went over the pictures and all the print—even to the funnies—something not funny to me. But I read them tonight and shed tears. Saddest part of the paper anymore—pull one hundred times on the cord. I know what you are trying to do—stop the train—you can't stop the train—it's running away. I knew after I got on the train it was my last ride. I'm taking my last look at my hills—it's in the night too—in the moonlight. Wish I could see them in the daytime. Lord have mercy on these hills when I am gone and keep the coal picks out'n their bellies and the axes out'n the trees. Wish I could see the trees again—and the sawbriars and the old piles of crossties along the tracks. W'y if I'd a stepped off'n that train when I got on—w'y I'd a broken my neck—I know it just as same as I know this train is going to wreck—pull you old Conductor—pull two hundred times on that cord for it to stop—it won't stop until it wrecks—can't you feel the speed coming on? I can just feel it. Hear the engine whistle past these cars. Hear the wheels clashing on the weasly rails—hear it—rush, rush-rushing into the night—I'm getting cold as a cucumber—I'd be all right if I could just see the hills one more time. Pull your cord a thousand times and the train won't stop—swing on the cord like a squirrel in the grapevines. Swing on it you polecat you—we are going down, down, down—down the grade through a tunnel—Oh—I've been over this road so much I can feel the curves on every mile—I know just about where the train will wreck—just about at the next river. Don't know whether you all will come out alive or not—but know I'm a goner. I'll tell you that right now—pull you polecat—pull ten thousand times on that cord and the train won't stop—"

People are tumbling through the coaches—running and praying—babies are screaming—"Oh, you Big-Belly—pray—you—yes, you—pray. Now you see don't you—You'll believe in dreams won't you—You'll believe in prayer won't you. Oh, you old Big-Belly you—look how you treated that poor man. He'll never get off this train alive either—and you—a thing like you will be alive—you'll get off—you ought to die—" says the red-faced woman with the little girl in her arms—and the mingling of curses and prayer from the lips of the women—all, all, all, and laughter from the lips of youth—from the fun-loving youth—just another adventure—all going some place—down the two streaks of rust and the moon in the sky—down through the night—down, down, down—to where and to what destiny? To the city at the end of the road? To what city—yes—and the runaway bull keeps snorting across the pasture of hills and through the holes in the ground like a rabbit—people on the train—a living mass of creatures with minds flashing with excitement and life like lightning on a storm-clouded night when the greyhound sky is filled with leaping dog-clouds—gaunt and trim across the sky—ah, this night and the screams and the prayer—and the night—all across Kentucky—under a Kentucky moon—all something people won't believe—that old man—shivering in the cold—and it is not cold—it is an August night on the train—and the moon can see it—the wind can feel it—a night in old Kentucky and a train load of people headed for a destiny—maybe a hole in the hill—just some place—some afraid and some glad of excitement—some laughing—some crying with excitement—some crying with fear—rock-rock—screech—screech—whistle-screaming, screaming, screaming—"Ooooooooooooooowwoooo-oooooooooo — woooooooo — woooooooouh — uh — uh — uh wooooooooooooooooowouh — woooooooooooooooooo-uh-uh-uh-uh oooooo — wooooooooooouh-uh — Screech — rickety-pickety-nickety — splutter — flutter — mutter — apple-butter — Wo-oooooooooooooo-uh-uh-uh — woooooooooooooooooo — uh-uh-uh — woooooooooooooooo (Hold her, Newt—she's headed for the barn. Let her rare. Let her rip. Let her tear. Let her splutter. Let her splash. Let her derail—let her crash. Let her jar. Let her scold. Let her crash in a dark hole. Let her ride the rails. Let her never. Make it across a river. Whooppee! Hold her, Newt—she's headed for the barn. Hold her, Pappie, by the old crumpled horn. She's got some life as sure as you're born. Woooooooooooooo-Wooooooooooooooooooooooouh-uh — wooooooooooooooooo — uh, uh — woooooooooooo — Shut up children and hush up your crying. Get you a new Pappie on the Old Special Line. Wooooo-ooooooooooooooooooo — uhhhhhhhhhhhhhhh — woooooo."

"Oh you old Big-Belly—you old thing—you'll wake up in hell with your back broke. I hope you do. That poor man. He told us what would happen. Why don't they stop the train—?" "W'y Lady—hold your tongue and take it easy—They can't hold the train—w'y it's running away. It's mad as a bull—it is a bull or a hornet and it's selling out—the first opportunity in one hundred years to run away—and all life has changed upside down and why hasn't the train got a right to run away—let her rip. Let her tear. Don't give a damn. For I don't care."

"Stay quiet, you people. Get your seats. Set down. You are going to wreck the train by first piling on one side and then t'other. Set down before we do wreck. Is this a dream? Am I crazy? What is the matter? Am I in the clouds? Am I floating through space? Is old Fast-Train Ike on this train? Have I lost my mind? Am I dreaming—hit me somebody? Wake me up—" "Hit you hell—you never had any mind—You'll find out about this train—can't you feel it leaping through the air—it's a matter of minutes—maybe seconds until you'll be cold as a piece of icicle or dead as a mackerel. Just stand up there and holler and let 'em run wild on your train. You are some conductor—you are—You ought to have been fired off this road forty-nine years ago—are you dreaming? Yes, you've always been dreaming—never any other way. Wish I could see my hills in the sunlight. A matter of minutes now—take it easy you all. Maybe it will be a quiet wreck —Just the same it's going to wreck."

"Wooooooooooooooooooooooooo — Wooooooooooooooooooooo — uh — uh — uh — woooooooooooo!" "Be ready—felt it jump then—too much speed for the train on these rails. The river is close. I feel it is close—prepare to meet the wreck and the eternity. Get my suitcase up there Big-Boy—I'm standing between the coaches so I can get a soft ride into eternity." Big-Boy hands Fast-Train Ike his suitcase. He is shaking like a man with the first chills of the 1917 influenza. "Rickety-pickety-jickety-mickety—wickety-split—whooppee—whooppee—let her wreck, by-heck—down in the gravel up to her neck—whooppee—Wooooooooooo —Wooooooooooooooooooooooooo."

"By-by boys. If I'm all that's gone don't break this great O. L. S. by suing for a lot of money. Let 'em keep it and fix the track with it and dig out the tunnels. I've had a good stay with you and the rest of my stay wouldn't be worth all the money you'd sue for. To the O. L. S. with the compliments of Fast-Train Ike—the smartest man that ever rode these rails by-hell. Sleep tight and don't let the bedbugs bite—" And Fast-Train Ike walks out between the coaches. "Woooooooooooooooooooooooooooo — uh, uh — uh — wooooooooooooooo — woooooooooooooooooooooooooo — rip—rip—uppety-fluffy—muffety—tuffety—over and over—and roll and roll—people together—on the floor—what of the weather forevermore—a dream it seems—uppety—cuppety—juppety—duppety—whooppee! Hold her, Newt—she's headed for the barn. Didn't I say get her by the old crumpled horn—over the river and through the woods to Grandpa's wedding day—snow on the ground is white instead of gray—and have you a word to say—

whow-pow-let her rip. Let her tear. Don't give a damn. For, I don't care. Rickety too-toot she shot right through that hardwood door. W'y he's my man—but he done me W—R—O—N—G. She's my train—but she's done me W—R—O—N—G. Whow—brick-bats—snakes and cats—whow and my friend—the end—lumber, number—spinter—Hot-as-hell-cinder comes up from the belly. Like a bowl of jelly—red as a coal. God bless our soul—Like the old cucumber—maybe he's cold."

Train crumpled on the trestle—the big bull—bench-legged with legs broken—Derailed on the trestle and the people pouring out of the windows. Walking the trestle to the land—right over the river—cars just a hanging and not a one over. "Lucky wreck," says Conductor Harry—"a wonder we hadn't all been killed. Get 'em all safe to the bank—all off the train and the trestle. Run through the cars boys and see that they are all out. I can't find anymore—maybe it is a dream and I am fooled. Maybe it's the Lord's will that we got out safe—ah, let me see where's old Fast-Train Ike—ah, let me see—go see if you can find him—He's not in the crowd is he boys—?" "I told you," says the red-faced woman, "guess you'll believe in dreams from now on. I believe in dreams. Had a dream last night about this wreck. Looked it up in the dream book and it said I'd be in a wreck. Now I guess you see, old Fat-Belly—You ought to be in hell with your back broke. But you are the kind that would get out of a wreck—"

Steam flying from the engine— Engineer out all right—limping a little—out standing by the fire kicked out of his firebox—out in the moonlight—and the brakeman's lantern waving to and fro—over the wrecked rails—bent up among the ragweeds like big rusted wires. Steam in the air—white mist going to the red Kentucky moon over the low hills in August—what a night—what a night—what a ride. What a ride—people screaming in the moonlight. Children lost from their mothers—people crawled out of the cars like ants out of a dead stump. Like ants crawling out of a dead black snake the carrion crows killed and just ate his pecked-in skull and left the rest for the ants. Train looks like a snake in the moonlight—only a blunt-tailed copperhead instead of a long pretty-tailed black-snake. And the ants come out from the ribs—ants alive—cursing, praying, screaming—laughing, splashing, dashing—screaming for their children. All alive and all safe? Ah, no—where is Fast-Train Ike? Gone—where is he—Crushed under the train—squeezed between the sides of a coach—? Ah, no—Where is he then—who knows? "Why he's dead," says the red-faced woman. "I know he is dead for he said he'd not get out alive. That was one man I've met in my life—met only for a matter of hours—that told the truth. That man is dead. W'y didn't he say the train would wreck at the river—wrecked right on the trestle. Didn't he try to tell that Conductor what was going to happen? And he said he was a nut—He'll pay for the words he said to that man. That man—Fast-Train Ike—is in a different world by now."

"One man gone—Fast-Train Ike is not with us." says the Conductor—"we've checked everyplace for him. Can see under the cars—they're just derailed—He's not there. He's not hiding in the coaches and pretending he's dead I don't guess—might be in one of the toilets. Didn't look there. Go back and look, Brakeman Charlie, and see if he's hiding in the toilet on one of the coaches if the doors aren't sprung and you can get them open." All night—and the people, shook with excitement, were hauled away. Men came to straighten up the wreck. Men came to lay new rails and put in new crossties and do something with the engine and the coaches. People talked and laughed and shouted—prayed, cried—ran through the fields like wild rabbits—proud to be away from the train. What a night there at the river—what a wreck—people will tell it down for a hundred years to generations unborn about the man with the high collar—they'll speak about old Fast-Train Ike. But where is he now and the people hunting for him—hunting for his bones—his ground-up dust! Where is he now? Will we have to wait until daylight to find him? Did he go through the thin air like some spirit—run out and take wings and fly through the skies to Heaven? Just where is he? W'y he took his suitcase—it can't be found. Went through all the toilets. He's not hiding there. Just where is he? Do you reckon he jumped off before the train hit and took across the field? Or, just what has happened to him? "You are a bunch of fools," says the red-faced woman—"all of you—a bunch of fools—a bunch of stinking polecats. Didn't he say he'd be a goner if all the rest come out alive? What did he tell you? Didn't he say that he'd rather go through space and have an easy seat than to be ground up in sausage meat for the ants—or be squeezed to death between the sides of a coach—Why can't you believe him? His prophecy has all come true so far—and why isn't the rest of it true—you bunch of hypocrite-polecats. Stand there—will you—look for him. He's here some place. Is there any water in that river or has it gone dry enough so the fish won't have drinking water like a lot of other Kentucky rivers do every summer—if there's water down there he's in it. He wanted a soft ride and a soft seat in eternity, you know. That's where he is—down there in that water."

"There's a deep hole right under the trestle. Water for the fish. Rest of the river above the trestle and below the trestle is dry. It's a deep hole below. You know Kentucky is not Kentucky any more without we have nine-tenths of our rivers dry in the summer during crop-time." The winds hum lonesome through the wires—And the winds sweep off the cries of the babies, the prayers of the women and the curses of the men—the moans and groans of them all. It is the wind—and the flutter of the leaves—and the red-moon in the sky. It's going down through—See it going down, down, down—morning will soon be here—what a night, what a night in old Kentucky—ah, huh—the barking of the dog—the four-o'clock crowing of the cock—and the streaks of light in the east. The smell of cinder smoke—and the ooze of piston steam—the tired bull has been stabbed. Good for him when he tries running away once every hundred years. See the big black monster humped up there stabbed—throat cut and his back broken. Can't run away on two streaks of rust—that's it. Just can't do it when the odds are five to one with the wind—and ten to one with the night—fifty to one with destiny.

Morning and the people gone and new faces coming to the wreck. New people come and kick scrap iron a hundred years old—scrap iron that has been serviceable—sides and flanks of the precious bull—why should they do it after all the years of service? Ought to give a medal—make it a Colonel instead of kicking the thighs and the ribs—the elbows and the shins. Ought to be hunting for Fast-Train Ike instead of pranking around the fire—around the cinder bed and the last breaths of steam.

"Come down to the deep hole under the trestle," says Section Foreman Press Kelley—he won the turkey last Thanksgiving for having the best section on the O. L. S. Devilish nigh worked the water out'n his men to get it. But he got the turkey. "W'y," says he, his red face showing in the morning August sun—his flat nose that looked like it was battered with a slab of steel and burned to a red crisp by the heat from the tee rails—"W'y the way to find a man in that hole is to take a pole and split the end of it—a hickory will do—and put it down in the hole and twist it around—if he's in there you'll more than likely twist his coattail or the pants' legs—or the seat of the pants—maybe the sleeve—maybe the hair. So cut me one, Dave."

Dave cuts the pole—poor little Dave runs around like a cricket. He trims the hickory pole—splits the tip of it in tiny withes to twist with.

He puts it in the water and twists—and the people watch from the bank. "Not quite. Thought that was him. Must a been a mud turtle or a stump." "Found something. Feels like a coattail—" Twist—twist—twist—a heave—"Help me Dave—Help me—pull—Get holt there." And they pull—and again they pull—up to the muddy surface—it is a man—it is Fast-Train Ike—His color just like it was before he left the train—His face about the same—on up and he holds the suitcase with a death grip like he's traveling someplace. Taking his old suit—his suitcase and his tiepin.

"What did I tell you," says the red-faced woman on the bank. "Didn't I tell you that you'd find him here in this water? He wanted a soft seat—a quick ride and he got it—Ah, that crazy Conductor that you call Harry—He's a nut. Think of this man. He prophesied it all—and it's come true—wouldn't even sue the railroad. Said his compliments to them. Take the money and build a better track. Poor old Fast-Train Ike—he's riding on a different train now." And she shouts and screams as they pull him from the water—his long gangly frame with the wet suit sticking close to his flanks and his ribs.

"One thing about this wreck," says Conductor Harry, "we won't have that Fast-Train Ike on any more trains scaring everybody to death about a wreck. The wreck is over—it's worth it to get rid of him. Seems like the Lord just takes 'em out like that. He's had old Fast-Train Ike spotted ever since I been on this road and He just got his work caught up last night. He got him. It'll save me a lot of worry—it'll give me joy to know he's riding on some other man's train and not one where I'm conductor. Just to tell you the truth I'm glad to get rid of him. I won't have to run for a member of the Kentucky Legislature and be up to have my rep probed and my character peeled with rocks. That's what I was going to do until the Lord interfered and took Fast-Train Ike home. It's strange the way things come out in the end. But they do. You just wait and see—but that night—ah, last night—what a night—what a time—in all my life that was the worst I ever put over my head."

Dave gets between the tall man's legs. He gets a leg under each arm. Hiram Pratt gets him by an arm. Judd Sluss gets him by an arm. They start around the deep hole—around among the poison vines—his clothes wet and dripping—the suitcase still in his hand. The crowd follows—the red-faced woman, Conductor Harry, Brakeman Charlie—a whole crowd of children and nearby people who have come to see the train wreck. They whisper to each other about the long dead man. "W'y the glass in the door is out," says Conductor Harry, "he went right through the door." "Don't know whether he tried to jump off, or whether the train just bumped him through the door. Guess he could tell you if he could speak." Right up the railroad bank they carry him. "Lord," says Judd Sluss, "he's heavy as any old soggy crosstie I ever took from under the tee rails. Honest, his arm's a load for me." "What about me back here with both legs," says Dave, "a trying to get up this bank." "W'y we're a pulling you up the hill with your load," says Hiram Pratt, "heavier than a switch tie." Up the bank a past the rotted crossties, past the sawbriars. The sun is hot and the sunrays dance on the old rusted rails and the wrecked train—all heaped up on the spread out, bent up rails. The big black horses hitched to the dead-wagon chomp the bits and the foam flies from their thick, gummy rubber lips.

"Heave on him, boys," says Section Foreman Press Kelley, "heave-oh—heave-oh," and they heave the wet-stiff body holding to the suitcase up in the dead wagon. "Got a death grip on that suitcase," says Section Foreman Press Kelley. "They tell me a death grip is harder to come undone than a hangman's knot. Just like he's holding to that suitcase and traveling on." "Glad he's on some other road than the O. L. S.," says Conductor Harry. "Hope he don't give the new conductor as much trouble as he's give me. Worried me for forty-nine years. Every time he got on the train. My worries are over, for the rest of my years on this road will be spent in peace."

Uncle Fonse Laughed

HE wasn't no akin to us. He was just a good friend to Pa. I remember when Pa would say to Ma: "Get every big pot on today, every little pot, every dirty pot—every clean pot. Fonse and Effie's coming over and bringing all the youngins." Then I'd see Pa just tickled to death—a smile on his thin brown lips from ear to ear. He would grab the ax and start to the woodyard. He would get a pole of wood and put it on a block. He would whack off a stick at a lick. He would cut two arm loads of dry stovewood. Mom would take a chair with her apron full of soupbeans. She would lift them from her apron and blow the chaff from them as she let them fall from her hand into a crock. It took plenty of beans when Uncle Fonse brought the family over to see us.

I can remember seeing the mule straining at the Tillman family express right down at the yellow bank below our house. He would stop, pant, wiggle his ears—then try again. He would pull the express about two cornrows wide at a time coming up the bank slonchways. Uncle Fonse would holler at Pa ("Good a mule, Mick, as ever was hooked in the harness. Never have to touch this mule with the withe." Pa would say: "Fonse, you old lazy devil you—why don't you get out and walk up the bank?"

Then Fonse would laugh and Pa would laugh and slap his knees. And the mule would pull again up the bank—the yellow clods of dirt a-flying from the hoofs—the foam spattering from the nostrils—white breaths of air going from the nostrils and spreading out thin on the blue air.

When the mule would make it with his heavy load to our yard, Fonse would get out and he'd slap Pa on the back and Pa would slap Fonse. They would go around and around: Pa would say: "How are you, you old turkey buzzard you?" And Fonse would slap Pa on the back hard enough to scare us children for Fonse was so much bigger than Pa. Fonse would say: "How are you—you little game rooster you?" And they would laugh—Uncle Fonse's red face beaming in the sun—his blue eyes twinkling—his heavy jaws bobbing up and down on his wattled neck. Pa would say: "You're getting dough-bellied, Fonse. You ain't doing enough running up and down the hills. Maybe you're getting more to eat than I'm getting. My old woman won't feed me only when I got company. That's why I wanted you over here today." Then Uncle Fonse would hit Pa on the shoulder and Pa would laugh.

Aunt Effie would start in the house with all seven of the children. Pa would say: "Finn, you take your Uncle Fonse's mule out to the barn and give him seven ears of that good white corn and some of the clover hay." Well, I would unhook the traces, and do up the lines on the hames—take the mule from between the shafts and feed him hay and corn that our mules couldn't get. We were saving it for tougher plowing days. But Pa didn't have anything that was too good for Uncle Fonse's mule. Finn and me we had fists that made his boys stand around. Pa said once: "Why don't you call his boys Cousin Bill, Cousin Charlie, Cousin Henry and the girls Cousin Effie, Cousin Martha, Cousin Grace and Cousin Fleece."

We never said anything to Pa but we thought he was better to Uncle Fonse's boys than he was to us. We didn't like it. We put the rocks to Bill a couple o' times out in the cowpasture. Brother Finn peeled a pine tree right above Bill's head when he was running toward the house. Uncle Fonse's boys were afraid of us.

We couldn't get 'em into the woods to play with us. Finn would say: "Them boys ain't no kin to me. I don't like 'em. Pa can't make me like 'em. I'll peel the bark off'n one's head with a rock when I get a chance."

Aunt Effie would go in the kitchen where Mom was. She would say: "Now let me help you right along with the dinner Mrs. Powderday. Let me blow the chaff out'n the beans. Let me peel the taters. Let me do something." Mom would let her peel the taters. She was so fat and to stir around in the kitchen between the stove, the safe and the kitchen table and the woodbox, she'd get to wheezing a getting her breath. Mom would tell Pop when she left: "I just can't stand that wheezing. It is like catching a young mouse in a trap. It run all through me. I can't stand a mouse screak in the kitchen. So, I put Effie to peeling taters. She's so fat. She can't hardly get around in her fat. I don't see how she can cook for seven brats that eat as much as hers eat. Pon my words—I thought mine could eat. But it's just a drop in the bucket the way her youngins eat."

We would get Uncle Fonse's boys out as far as the smokehouse to play with us. We would play fox and dog. We kindly liked the little girls—they wasn't our cousins and we didn't want them to be. We helped them make playhouses behind the smokehouse. Sister Clara, Belle, and Sophie wouldn't like to see us play with Uncle Fonse's girls all the time—carry them the biggest arm loads of moss and broken dishes—but we did. We were the men and we watched over the house and kept away the Indians that were hiding behind the trees out in the pasture—out there among the pines.

Before dinner was ready—Pa and Uncle Fonse would sprawl down in the floor. They would wallow on the floor and talk. Pa would say: "Fonse what makes me and you such big fools? We ain't no kin are we?" Uncle Fonse would say: "We got good fences between our farms, Mick. We pay our debts. We take time off to go and see one another like them old folks used to do when we was boys back in Flint County . . . We ain't no akin unless Pa's fox hound run a fox across the creek back yander on Gimpson creek in Flint County and your Pa drunk of the waters below." Then Pa would laugh and laugh. He would say: "Drunk of the waters below," and slap Uncle Fonse on the shoulder.

Pa would say: "Something I'm forgetting, Fonse . . ." He would get up and bring a couple of tastebud cigars rolled out'n homemade tobacco by Pa's own hands. Uncle Fonse would lay there in the floor and look to the ceiling and laugh. He would say: "W'y you'd forget your head, Mick, if it was loose." And he would laugh. He would lay there in the floor with Pa. They would smoke their long cigars and look to the loft and blow smoke at a spider on a web. "Make that sucker sick up there, Fonse. A dime you can't do it." Uncle Fonse would blow smoke toward the spider on the low loft. It would fidget around on the little white strands of the web. It looked like it was looking over the edges of its mountain at the deep canyon below—at the big devils on the floor where the clouds of strong smoke were coming from.

Pa and Uncle Fonse would talk about farming. Pa would say: "I'll raise the best corn in the country over there in that new ground. Awful freeze we had this winter will make the ground meller as meal. I'll get some good taters out'n that ground too. You watch me this year. I'll raise more corn than you—you old pup. You beat me last year. But I'm going to lower the boom on you this year." Uncle Fonse would say: "You ain't going to beat nobody. Your wife might." And he would laugh and Pa would laugh. Uncle Fonse's neck wattles would shake like a turkey gobbler's red wattles.

Mom would come to the door. She would say: "Dinner is ready, Mick. Call the youngins." Pa and Uncle Fonse would jump up from the floor and Pa would go out and holler like he was blowing a foxhorn: "Dinner youngins—come to it. Yaho! Yaho! Dinner is ready! Come to it youngins if you want any." Well, we'd come running from behind the smokehouse and from the woods like chickens coming to the corncrib of a morning for corn. We would run in to get dinner. It would be late on Sunday when Mom and Aunt Effie would get dinner.

We didn't have to wait for a second table. Mom would say:

"Put two tables together so everybody can eat." And we'd all eat together.

Uncle Fonse would say: "Pass me a little sugar for my coffee, please." Pa would hand him the salt. Uncle Fonse would be busy. He wouldn't notice. Uncle Fonse would say: "Three spoonsful of sugar to my coffee and if it ain't sweet enough I have Effie to dip her little finger in it." Pa would be trying to hold back a laugh so Uncle Fonse wouldn't catch on. And when Uncle Fonse would take the drink of coffee, Pa would stand up at the table and laugh at Uncle Fonse running to the door. All of us children would laugh at Pa and Uncle Fonse. Mom would say: "Pon my soul, Effie, I do believe there is two of the craziest men in this country. I believe we got 'em." Mom would laugh. Aunt Effie would shake in her fat and laugh. Then Uncle Fonse would say: "I take better care of my woman than you do though, Mick. I feed her better. Your woman is poor as a snake. She don't get nothing to eat only when I come over." Then Uncle Fonse and Pa would start laughing again.

"We got the two craziest men in the world," Aunt Effie would say to Mom. "Fonse just plagues me to death. When we go down the road in the express to town, Fonse hollers something at everybody. They stop and look at us in that old express setting upon that little hug-me-tight seat till we get out of sight." Aunt Effie would shake in her fat laughing at Pa and Uncle Fonse. Pa would say: "Want so-more sugar for your coffee, Fonse? You'd better let Effie stick her little finger in it the next time." Then Mom would start laughing.

After dinner Pa and Uncle Fonse would light their tastebud cigars. Mom and Aunt Effie would get their long-stemmed clay pipes. They would get homemade tobacco out'n the oatbox where Mom always kept her tobacco. They would fill their pipes —shove the tobacco down with a forefinger—light their pipes with a piece of rich pine kindling. I'd take it to the stove and light the kindling from the kitchen stove fire. And big clouds of smoke would go up from our table. It would be hard for us to get our breath around the table. I would say: "Bet I never smoke when I grow up. I hate the old stinking stuff." Pa would say: "Got the bluff on our youngins, ain't we Fonse?" And Fonse would say: "That boy ain't no Powderday if he don't smoke the blessed weed when he grows up. Comes by it honest you know—his Ma, his Pa and all his Uncles and Aunts on both sides used the fragrant weed—a blessing to all mankind."

After Pa and Uncle Fonse would smoke, they would walk out in the pasture. Mom and Aunt Effie would put my sisters and Uncle Fonse's pretty little girls in the kitchen to washing the dishes. I would come in and offer to dry the dishes. Mom would try to get me to help my sisters. But I never would do it. I'd say: "I ain't going to do no girl's work. I'm going to work outside with Pa. Ain't getting me in no kitchen." Mom and Aunt Effie would take their chairs out in the yard and put them under the peach tree. They would smoke their pipes and blow the blue smoke into the pretty spring wind. I can see it going to the sky in tiny swirls. I can see Pa and Uncle Fonse—Pa, little and spry—Uncle Fonse, big, square-shouldered and fat—walking slowly out the pasture path—talking, laughing, whittling.

We would play fox and dog over the hills. We would forget about Uncle Fonse's boys liking Pa and him liking them. We would forget all our troubles and play. We would quit throwing rocks at each other. Uncle Fonse's boys liked my sisters and I liked their sisters and Finn did too. We got along all right—running in the sunlight—jumping over the creeks—laughing, playing, shouting, screaming under the sun. It just seemed like the time was too short. Uncle Fonse and Pa would come back around through the pasture—around the path under the pines by the hog-pen. Pa so little and thin—Uncle Fonse so short and heavy. They would come whittling, laughing, talking. I could see Pa slap Uncle Fonse on the shoulder. Pa would say: "Fine day this has been, Fonse. Come again and see me." And Uncle Fonse would say: "I ain't never coming to see you again till you bring Sall and all the kids and come to see me, Mick. Now this has been twice on the straight I have been to see you. You got to come to see me next time."

Well, Brother Finn and Uncle Fonse's boy Bill would have the mule out and hooked to the express. I can see the mule standing in the blue wind by the hollyhocks—switching his tail in the bright blue wind at the flies. I can see the sun the way it went down over Lonesome ridge dragging a patch of red clouds behind it. I can see Pa and Uncle Fonse and Mom helping Aunt Effie into the express. They would put a chair by the express stirrup. Aunt Effie would step on a rock—from that up in the chair—from the chair to the stirrup and from the stirrup to the express bed. And when she got up to the chair, Pa, Uncle Fonse and Mom would all be ahold of her to keep her from falling. "I don't want to break a bone at my age," Aunt Effie would say. "And if my wife gets any more pounds," Uncle Fonse would say, "she going to break a seat. I'm going to put a good hickory chair up there in the front for myself." And Uncle Fonse would laugh again and say: "I feed my wife. Now look at your wife there, Mick—thin as a beanpole." Uncle Fonse would slap the mule's back lightly with the lines and say: "Get up! Get up there, boy! Guess I got all the youngins."

"Come back again," Pa would say.

After they would leave Pa would say: "I tell you Sall, they don't make a better neighbor than old Fonse. Of course, he don't belong to my Party nor my church. I can't help that. He can't help it. He's just what he is and I am just what I am. But he's a good neighbor as a body ever lived by. It's good fences that we got between our places that make us good neighbors. You remember we couldn't get along with that hirm-skirm piece of a man that used to live over there. I built my part of the line fence and couldn't get him to build his. He would just brush it—keep throwing more brush on it. Cattle is smart these days on them brush fences after they've been used to barbwire. So his cattle kept getting in and eating up devilish nigh everything I had planted in the ground. Since Fonse has moved over there and bought that place we don't have any more trouble."

"But you all are the craziest-acting men I ever saw get together," Mom would say. "I don't care if he does belong to the Forty Gallon Baptis and you are a Slab Baptis and you belong to one Party and he belongs to the other. You all just plague women folks to death the way you lay around in the floor and go on about this and that."

Pa would say: "I popped it to him out there in the pasture when we's out there a looking at my cattle. I ast him some questions he couldn't answer about Resurrection. They've got some funny beliefs in his church. Them Forty Gallon Baptis is a funny church. And I sure did get him about his Party. Then he popped it to me about my Party and the Slab Baptis. Even jumped on me about my fox hound. He said the night out there when old Gun Powder led that pack of hounds that I put moonshine in sweet milk and give it to him. He'll have that going all over the country. Devil can't uptrip that man."

"You beat all men I ever saw," Mom would say.

"Something heavy in my coat pocket."

And when Pop pulled it out it was a tack hammer Uncle Fonse had made for Pop and slipped it in his pocket. "What do you know about that, Sall! Look here what old Fonse has made for me. He heard me say I needed a tack hammer and he made me one. He can make anything in the world he wants to make in a blacksmith shop and just to think what I used to slip in old Fonse's pocket. I used to slip a dead bird in his pocket every week. I'd do it and he'd come to me and he'd say: 'Funny thing, Mick. I find a dead bird in my left coat pocket every week. It is some kind of a token.' I would laugh and say: 'You are just a dreaming. You don't find no bird in your pocket.' He would say: 'Oh, yes, I do. I know I ain't that crazy. I remember what happens to me. I remember too, that I don't put the bird in my own pocket. I reach down in my pocket. It is there—a dead bird. There's something strange about a dead bird. It is a strange token of some kind.' Yes, I put the birds in his pocket—and he gives me this fine tack hammer—big enough to draw nails with from the old planks."

Time will go on as time will. New people will be born into the world. The old people go from the world and give place to the new. Children grow up and babies are born. And the world goes on. There is not any turning back the hand on the clock. Time is in a swift race—it keeps running and running and it never gets anyplace. I could see the gray hairs come to Pop's head. He was getting older. Uncle Fonse was getting older. I remember when we made the blackberry wine and had it in a churn in the smokehouse, how Pop and Uncle Fonse went into the smokehouse. They walked in straight as sourwood saplings. They come out bent over and swaying like windblown willows by the creek. Uncle Fonse wasn't laughing when he said to Pa: "Mick, we ain't young as we used to be. But this old heart is young, Mick, even if the old body is getting old." Uncle Fonse was holding to the corner logs for the smokehouse and helping Pa around by the shoulder. . . . No, time is a thief that comes in the daylight, the moonlight—sunlight. He steals what that can never be brought back. He is a thief that cannot be jailed. There is not a jail big enough to hold him, nor money enough in the world to bribe him. But not a thief of time could keep Pa and Uncle Fonse from bringing the families together for a big dinner once and twice sometimes each week. Not even a thief of time could stop them from laughing and argying—They were against time. It didn't matter. They went laughing freely with the wind. Growing older had made them younger in a world where one sees joy, sorrow, has music, life, love, tears—where life is before one—life so big, so great—high as the skies are high—deep as the earth is deep.

I remember how Pa laughed at the table that morning. He said to Mom: "Pour me another cup of coffee, Sall. You remember how I got the salt in old Fonse's coffee that day for dinner here. Well, he tried to get a good one on me yesterday. I went over there to see him about my boy Finn and his boy Bill—You know how they are since they got to running together. He can't get no work out'n Bill and I can't get no work out'n Finn. I heard they'd been plum up there at that bad dance hall where them Perkins boys got cut the other night. So I says to Fonse: 'Fonse, ain't they something we can do about our boys running around together the way they do?' Fonse was getting in the express then. Had the mule all trigged up. Had red tassels on the bridle. Had brass rings on the hames for the check lines to run through and snap into brass rings on the bristle bitts. So, Fonse says to me:

'You take care of the boys, Mick. I won't be here to take care of them after tomorrow night.' And I says: 'Why, Fonse—you're not skipping the country, are you? Ain't stole no sheep—broke no bank—shot no man have you?' And Fonse says: 'No, I ain't done nothing I'm ashamed of. I am just going to die. It's my heart. The whole thing was pictured to me in bed last night. I saw the whole thing.' And Fonse, he just laughed and laughed. He thinks he's got a good 'n on me. And when he started driving off, I says: 'Where are you going, Fonse?' 'Going to town to have the James boys to make my coffin tomorrow.' And he drove off down the road. He was laughing. And I was laughing. You know how Fonse acts. I can see old Fonse going yet—the mule trotting down that piece of sandy road by the pear trees. I can hear the creaking of the buggy wheels. And it all just kindly went through my mind that I'd have to slip another bird in the old boy's pocket. But instead of a bird this time I got a ground mole with baby hands. I'm going to slip it in his pocket. I'll pull a rich 'n on old Fonse. . . ."

Finn went to town the next day. I remember when he came in he said to Pa: "You know I believe Uncle Fonse is going crazy. I was over to see Bill awhile ago and Uncle Fonse was up on the hill cutting briers and sprouts off a little knoll. He said he was going to die tonight. Had the James boys to make him a coffin out 'n planks he's had seasoning in the barn for ten years. He's said he didn't want no undertaker's fancy-coffin. Said he wanted a coffin made out'n them oaks back of the barn. That's where he got them planks from ten years ago when Ben Ulling had that mill back there in the head of the hollow. He had a couple of trees cut and sawed into heavy planks. He had his coffin made out'n them very boards. While I was over there he got down in his coffin and tried it out. 'It is just a fit,' he said. Bill is a laughing at his Pa. Aunt Effie is a crying. The girls are crying. Aunt Effie said: 'He is either telling the truth or he is going crazy. And they ain't never been a Tillman gone crazy to the extent of my knowings yet.' He don't act to me like a man that is going to die. He won't tell how he knows."

I remember how Pa laughed. He said: "He's pulling a good

one this time. He's got it up his sleeve to have some fun. If he's going to die, old Fonse would make his own coffin. He can make a hammer, make nails, wagon wheels, guns, smoothing irons. He can make anything he wants to make. He surely can make a coffin."

Pa went to bed that night. The wind howled through the green hickories at the end of the porch by Pa's bed. I remember seeing Pa get out of the bed in a night shirt. He looked at the moon and the stars in the heavens. He walked across the dewy grass barefooted. That was strange for Pa. Pa is a solid man. He is hard to move to tears. But Pa was in trouble. I heard him come to the bed. He got Mom up from sleep. He said: "Sall, I am troubled about Fonse. I can't sleep. I hear the death-bells ringing in my ears. I have tried to sleep. But I can see a wooden box in front of me. Get out of the bed and make a biler of strong coffee."

Pa put on his clothes. He walked to the barn and to the pigpen while Mom was making the coffee. I knew he went to the pigpen for the shoats squealed when Pa went past. The cows mooed when he passed them sleeping in the dewy grass by the barn-gate. Pa was in trouble. I never saw him act like this only once before in my life. That was the night Brother Finn got cut at the square dance and they brought him home all slashed up with a hawk-billed barlow knife. I heard Mom call him to get his coffee. And I heard Pa lumber through the house. I heard him pull his chair up to the table. I heard him say to Mom: "I am going over to Fonse's place just as soon as I've got light to travel by. I know something has happened. I have seen Fonse. I have heard him laugh. I know what I am saying is true. You know he said to me once when we's out in the pasture: 'Mick, you ought to be in my church. To prove to you we are right, if I die first you'll hear me laugh out there in the little pine grove where we always went on Sundays to talk and whittle by that salt-trough. If you die first I'll go out there and see if I can hear you laugh or speak to me first. And we'll see who's right—the Slabs or the Forty Gallons—' And I says to Fonse: 'It's a go, Fonse. You laugh to me. I'll know that old crow laugh you got.' And I would know it in Halifax too if I was to hear it there. So, I went out to the pine grove this morning. I've just come from there. I heard old Fonse laugh. I know it was his voice. Lord, I know his voice. I know that laugh. I know it was his laugh. It wasn't the wind. It wasn't the rustle of the green leaves. It was his laugh. I am trembling like a leaf in the wind."

I saw Pa cross the hill. It wasn't a good day. He told me to feed the hogs and not harness the mules till he come back. I saw him going up the path to the top of the hill. He walked beside of the good barbwire fence Uncle Fonse and Pa built. I saw him go between the wires and disappear among the green sassafras sprouts—wet with dew. They would soak Pa but he didn't care. Mom said: "It is a funny thing the way them men act. Maybe they're both going crazy. Your Pa is about crazy this morning. He drunk six cups of strong coffee. He says that something has happened to your Uncle Fonse. He says he knows that something has happened. Said he heard Fonse speak to him from the pine grove out there where they go on Sundays to talk and whittle. He said it wasn't the wind. He said it was Fonse. But wonder if it wasn't the wind in the pine needles? Wonder if it wasn't something besides Fonse? How could it be Fonse there so soon?" And Mom went to looking off into space. It kindly scared me. And I said: "Mom, there is something funny about the whole thing. I know I am right. I saw Uncle Fonse cutting the sprouts off a place to bury him on yesterday. He was having the James boys to make his coffin. He got down in it and tried it out. He said: 'It's just a fit.' I remember it well. I know that I am not dreaming. I come on up the road. I met Ben Ulling and told him about it. Ben said: 'He's either got a communication with the sperit or he's losing his mind, I-jacks, one.' I come on up there at that sweet apple tree below Aimes' barnlot and frailed me some sweet apples with a crooked limb. I remember it as if it had just happened. I was not dreaming."

When Pa walked down the hill, Mom run out to meet him: "What has happened to Fonse?" Mom said. Pa just walked right down to the porch. He almost fell on the edge of the porch. He was quivering like a leaf in the wind. "Fonse is dead as a piece of dirt," said Pa. "He died last night sometime. I was there just a few minutes ago. I took the mole along to slip in his pocket. But he was dead. The family is all crying and going on something awful. I didn't stay. I couldn't stay. Fonse, there so quiet—not laughing! W'y he laughed when he was going to have the James boys to make his coffin. I thought he was joking. He didn't care to die. He laughed quietly into the arms of Death. I've always thought God would want a man that could laugh no matter what church he belonged to . . . Fonse there so quiet, so silent. He didn't speak to me. I couldn't stand it."

Mom shed tears. "What will Effie do now," Mom said, "with all that family of children? She can't keep 'em in grub the way they eat. Place not paid for with all them good fences around it. One thing Fonse believed in was a good fence between him and his neighbors. . . . Poor Effie. No way to turn back time. It just keeps slipping up on a body like it slips up on the flower and a stalk of corn. Everything has a season—even to man. God wanted Fonse to do something else—maybe to make fences in Heaven. Maybe, God wanted to hear him laugh."

Pa went about silently all day. He would walk to the pine-grove, then to the house. He would watch a crow fly over. He would look at the growing corn. He would watch the white clouds float over. Pa would not turn his hand to work. He would not let us work. He did not go back to Tillman's house. Pa stayed at home all day. He was nervous as a shoemake leaf in the wind.

"Just to think about it all is a funny thing," said Pa, "life is so strange. To think about it all the time would make a man lose his mind. Fonse has left the earth. He was a good man—tended to his own business. He owned his land. He took care of his family and sent his children to school. He went to church. He believed in God's workings through the sperits. He didn't belong to the right Party but he belonged to the one he thought was right. Fonse Tillman was the kind of a man the country is built on. Yet, God called him out of this life. He left men in it not worth powder and lead to kill 'em. I just don't understand it. And tomorrow!"

"Yes, tomorrow, at two o'clock," said Mom, "right back of the house on that old poor point up there where the blackberry briers and the saw-briers take the place. That is where they will plant Fonse. That is where he wanted to be planted—up there where he used to tend corn. I remember seeing him go around that hill behind the mules. I can't forget it."

I remember the day at two o'clock. Yesterday never caught up with tomorrow. We were there. The crowd was there. The hill was lined with people. Pa said to Mom: "See what the people think of Fonse. Respected in life. Respected in death. Look at this crowd here. It's the biggest funeral I've ever seen among these hills. I have to help carry him up the hill to the grave. I don't know whether I can make it or not." I remember seeing Pa. He walked over the old corn rows—puffing and blowing under the corner of the heavy box. The crowd followed up the hill. We passed under Fonse's heavy fruited apple trees.

The crowd stood there with heads bowed and heads bare. The check lines were slipped under the box—the heavy box was lowered into the earth and the check lines slipped from beneath it. I remember the tears that flowed down Pa's brown cheeks. I remember the cries of Uncle Fonse's children and Aunt Effie. I remembered they were not my real aunt and uncle but Pop and Mom taught us to call them uncle and aunt and they taught their children to call Pop and Mom uncle and aunt.

I remember the farm that Uncle Fonse owned. I remember the roses in bloom in the woods not far from where Uncle Fonse was buried. I remember how they waved in the wind—how the mountain daisy gently swayed on the hill where Uncle Fonse would sleep—the old furrows where he had plowed that time would soon blot out and leave the land level as a yard. I remember the silent crowd that left the hill—the wind overhead in the apple tree leaves.

Before my eyes were the eternal Kentucky hills. The crow flew over them. The buzzard sailed high above them. Among them men and women worked for their bread—knew the change of season. They saw life ripen sweetly and sourly with the years. They saw the flowers bloom in their season—die in their season. But even among these hills eternal in their great beauty of lilting green leaves in the wind—no one could stop time. No one could deny Uncle Fonse knew he was going to die. He had his coffin made himself. He cleared off his ground to sleep upon. Now he rests in that vast silence—under the sighing of the wind—the passing of the white cloud in the heavens—under the bloom of the rose and the mountain daisy and the swift wing of the crow. He lies in eternal Kentucky hills that if they were alive and could speak they could tell greater stories than any man of life, love, death, darkness, gloom, despair, the communion of the spirits. They could tell stories of many a carcass that does not sleep in a grave. They could tell unbelievable stories to make a book stalwart as a mountain.

Does the Army Always Get Its Man?

"LOOK, Shan," my father said, pointing toward the road. "There goes Tim! He's AWOL again!"

"You don't mean Tim's on that bicycle?" I said. "That's a woman!"

"A woman my eye!" Pa said. "That's Tim Stacy! Can't you tell by the way he rides? And look what he's got fastened behind him!"

"Looks like a rifle to me!"

"That's what it is," Pa said. "And somewhere under that dress he's carrying a pistol. He might have two pistols under that dress!"

"It's hard to believe that's Tim," I said, watching his white skirt balloon in the wind as the rider stood on the pedals, pulling the bicycle at great speed down the dry August road leaving clouds of dust to settle on the wilted roadside weeds.

"He's going down the road to see his brother Ben," Pa said.

"But how could he get back again, Pa?" I asked.

"He's got out someway," Pa said. "Remember how he used to break jail!"

I remembered the first time Tim came back. He wore his uniform and told everybody he was back on furlough. He hadn't been drafted into the Army then but a couple of months. John Pratt and Enoch Stevens talked about Tim's getting back so soon when their sons didn't get a furlough. Tim stayed at home a month and rabbit-hunted every day, including Sundays. Everybody talked about how long the furlough lasted. And then we heard Sheriff Bill Cremeans came to Ben Stacy's home and arrested Tim and turned 'im over to the "authorities."

After he'd gone back this time, it wasn't two months until Tim was back again. He wore his uniform and said he'd come home on a furlough. That was in December, for Tim got home for Christmas. I remembered how he went among the snow-covered Seaton hills and tracked foxes, minks, and possums to their rock-cliff dens and set traps for them. Once I looked inside Ben Stacy's smokehouse, where I saw pelts stretched over boards and stuck in the cracks between the logs where the winter winds would cure the pelts. And this time we knew Sheriff Bill arrested Tim, for he brought three deputies and we heard there was a lot of shooting before he arrested Tim. This was in February.

In August Tim came home again. He didn't wear a uniform this time. He wore overalls and a blue work shirt. Tom Glenn had seen Tim jump from a fast-moving freight train in Greenwood and take toward the hills running. It was during August that I would hear Tim's gun barking among the tall hickory trees in our woods where squirrels were plentiful. Pa would run to the woods with his gun to chase Tim from our squirrels. But he would never find Tim. And then Pa would come home disgusted because Tim was out of service again while three of my brothers were in the military service.

"He's no better than my sons," Pa would say. "They ought to have a place to hold that man!"

In September, when Sheriff Bill Cremeans and four deputies arrested Tim, he put a bullet through Sheriff Cremeans' foot. And one bullet hit Deputy John Greenslate in the leg. Another bullet nicked Deputy Eif Compton's ear. But they arrested Tim again and turned him over to the military authorities.

"What are you dreaming about?" Pa asked as I stood watching

the last cloud of dust settle at the bend of the road the way the bicycle had gone.

"I was thinking about the times Tim has escaped," I said. "This makes four times!"

"He's made it back for squirrel season," Pa said. "He'll be in my squirrels again since squirrels are feasting on hickory nuts now!"

"If that's Tim I'd like to see and talk to him," I said.

"Don't let me ever catch you around that fellow," Pa said, his lips trembling. "If I do, I'll cut a withe and stripe your back even if you are seventeen years old!"

Pa's face was as red as a turkey's snout and his whole body trembled as he talked.

"That Tim Stacy is a dangerous man," Pa continued. "You stay away from him. There's going to be a gun battle down at Ben Stacy's or up at Mart Stacy's before long. They'll take Tim dead or alive. The law here won't fool with him any longer. Tim ought to know that!"

After Pa had finished saying these words he started down the yellow clay bank for home. I wanted to go down to Ben Stacy's to see if Tim was there but I was afraid. Pa went home and oiled his single-barrel shotgun and hunted his high-powered shells he had used for shooting at sheep-killing dogs.

"If I catch Tim in my woods killing my squirrels I aim to sprinkle him," Pa said.

Next morning Pa took his gun to the squirrel woods to wait for Tim while I went down the hollow to sucker tobacco. As soon as I had reached the tobacco patch I looked across the hollow on the other hill slope where Ben Stacy had his tobacco and I saw two men suckering tobacco. It was Ben and Tim.

"Hello there, Shan," Tim yelled across the hollow to me. "Come over and see me!"

"Can't do it, Tim," I said. "I've got all this tobacco to worm and sucker myself!"

"Where's your old man?" Tim yelled back.

"I don't know," I said. "He went someplace."

"Then if you won't come over to see me," he yelled, "I'll be over in a few minutes to see you!"

I wanted to tell Tim not to come. I was afraid Pa would come to the field and catch Tim there. But I saw him leave Ben's tobacco patch. I watched Tim hurry across the hollow, stopping every five seconds to look up and down the hollow to see if anybody was coming.

"How are you, Shan?" Tim said, reaching me his hand.

"All right, Tim," I said, looking up at his sun-tanned face. "How are you?"

"I'm lucky to be alive," he said. "They shot at me seven times. But it was a little dark and they couldn't see well enough to hit me. I felt the wind from two bullets!"

"But they'll get you, Tim," I said.

"Not this time," Tim said, patting a bulge on each hip beneath his overalls. "I've got the difference on each hip and I got something over there in the tobacco patch that'll send a bullet a long distance! Just let them try."

"But, Tim—"

"I've been here a week already," Tim broke in before I had time to finish my words. "And I've had a lot of fun a-wearing my dress at night. I wait for the crowds coming from church and I slip from the bushes and take one of the bashful boys by the arm. I'm walking with him before he knows it. When he turns around and sees me, he's scared to death. But I hold on until I get ready to dart back among the bushes. Haven't you heard about the Plum Grove Ghost yet?"

"No, I haven't," I replied.

"If you haven't heard, you will," Tim said laughing. "I'm that ghost. I got old George Mennix by the arm the other night and held onto his arm when he tried to squirm loose. When I did let him loose he ran like a rabbit!"

And then Tim laughed and laughed.

"Where'd you get your dress, Tim?" I asked.

"One of Ma's old dresses," he said. "I shave my face close and then I put on a lot of powder. I wear one of Ma's old hats. I don't look too bad in Ma's clothes. No one knows me after dark!"

"Aren't you afraid to be over there working in the tobacco?" I asked.

"Not a bit," Tim replied. "See all the woods and cliffs up there. Anybody would have to come up or down this hollow after me and I could see him. And as soon as I would see him I would take to the cliffs!"

As Tim talked to me I walked along my tobacco row pulling the suckers from behind the broad leaves and pulling worms from the leaves. I wanted Tim to know I was busy and take the hint to leave. He followed me an hour and talked before he left.

"Did you see Tim this morning?" Pa asked me when I went home to dinner.

"He helped Ben in his tobacco all morning," I replied.

"Didn't I tell you yesterday that was Tim?" Pa said. "He's the Plum Grove Ghost who is going out in that dress at night and scaring the wits out of the young boys and the old men! It's a good thing he didn't come to my squirrel timber this morning. I was waiting for him."

"You'd better put that gun up, Mick," Mom said. "Let the sheriff get Tim. You're going to get into trouble!"

That afternoon when Pa and I worked in our tobacco, we saw a car come up the narrow winding hollow road and stop just below Ben's tobacco patch.

"That's them," Pa said, his face beaming with joy. "They have come to get Tim!"

"But look, Pa!" I said pointing toward the tobacco patch.

We saw Tim grab his rifle and take toward the cliffs. Sheriff Bill Cremeans and five deputies got out of the car with Winchesters and rifles. Sheriff Cremeans limped along behind his deputies with a pistol in each hand. They hurried up the slope toward the tobacco patch.

"They mean business this time," Pa said. "When a man shoots Bill Cremeans, he'll get him if he has to follow him to Jericho!"

We stood in our tobacco rows when they stopped to talk to Ben Stacy. We couldn't hear what they were saying but we saw

Sheriff Bill Cremeans shake his hand in Ben's face while he talked.

"He's warning Ben not to harbor a deserter," Pa said.

We watched the sheriff and his deputies go into the woods the way Tim had gone. We worked all afternoon and at sundown we saw them come from the woods into the open field, but they didn't have Tim.

"They've scared Tim away from here," Pa said. "And I'm glad of that!"

It was a week before Sheriff Cremeans came back. This time he brought three deputies and two soldiers with him. Pa and I stood in our tobacco rows and watched them climb the slope to the tobacco patch where Ben was working. The soldiers were big men wearing bands around their arms. They didn't carry guns but each carried a small billy club in his hand. We saw them stand in the tobacco patch where they talked to Ben. And then they came back down the hill, got into the car and drove up the road toward our house.

"They're going up to Mart Stacy's now," Pa said. "They're going to search the place! I can't understand why Mart puts up with it. I guess it's Madge. A mother will hang onto her son no matter what he does!"

Pa and I had been back home and had finished supper when the sheriff and his deputies and the two soldiers walked down the hollow and got in the car in front of our house. They couldn't drive their car any farther than our house since only a path went on up the hollow to where Mart Stacy lived. We watched them get into the car without Tim.

"He's hiding out someplace," Pa said. "They'll get him yet!"

Then we heard Tim was hiding among the Seaton hills. George Mennix told us he was sleeping in a rock cliff and eating the wild game he killed. He said Tim was killing foxes too and that fox hunters had banded together and had gone up each finger onto the main ridge to catch Tim since they thought if he tried to escape he'd have to come down one of the finger-paths. They found where he had lived, saw his fresh tracks in the sand but he had escaped them. George said the hunters reasoned he had slipped down one of the deep hollows between the cliffs.

In late September a little car drove up and four soldiers got out. They were big men with bands around their arms and on these bands were the letters MP. They carried small billy clubs in their hands as they walked quietly up the hollow toward Mart Stacy's shack. It was nearly dark when they came back to the car. I asked one what kind of a car they were driving and he told me it was a jeep. Then one big soldier with a brown mustache asked me if I'd seen Tim Stacy.

"I haven't seen him for a month," I told him.

"He's a hard man to get," a short heavy soldier said. "But we'll get him."

The next day Madge Stacy told Mom how the soldiers had come, surrounded the house, and searched it.

"They even looked up the chimney," Madge told Mom. "They looked under beds and under my feather-bed ticks, on the roof, in the barn loft, in the cellar, and in the smokehouse!"

"They ought to have burned the house," Mom said. "Remember, I've got three sons in service!"

Madge left our house without saying another word to Mom.

"Serves her right," Mom said as Madge slammed our gate. "Her boy is no better than my boys! If Tim was a son of mine I'd turn him over to the authorities."

In early October the jeep came back. This time four men dressed in green uniforms got out.

"They'll get Tim Stacy," Uncle Jason Hinton said. "They are Marines!"

"Brother Jason, you say this because you've been a Marine," Mom said.

"Four years a Marine," Uncle Jason said. "If it wasn't for my age I'd be with them now! But I've got three sons who are taking my place in the Marines."

"Sheriff Cremeans will get Tim," Pa said.

In the middle of October the jeep came back and this time four men dressed in white uniforms got out. They wore bands around their arms with the letters SP on them and in their hands they carried billy clubs.

"They look good to me," I said to Pa as I looked at their clean white uniforms, their tan boots that looked like hunting leggings, their flowing big black ties and the little white hats perched upon their heads.

"Sailors from the Navy and they belong at sea," Pa said. "What can they do here among the hills! They'll never get Tim!"

We watched them go up the path toward Mart Stacy's shack.

"It's strange to me that neither soldier, sailor nor Marine has brought a gun," Pa said. "Don't they know Tim Stacy is a dangerous man? Don't they know he'll shoot to kill? I'll bet the sailors don't bring Tim back! I'll bet he's hiding not more than a hundred yards from the house!"

While we waited for the sailors to come back to the jeep, Uncle Jason walked in. And we told him the sailors had now gone after Tim.

"They'll never get him," Uncle Jason said. "I'll wager any man a bet they won't. You'll see that the Marines will get him."

"I believe the soldiers will get him," Mom said.

I knew that Mom leaned toward the Army because Bert and Walt, my oldest brothers, were soldiers.

"I say Sheriff Cremeans will beat all the branches of the military service," Pa said. "He understands his ways better than the men in service. Sheriff Cremeans is still limpin' over that bullet Tim put in his foot!"

"What about the sailors?" I said. I thought of my brother Finn, who was a sailor.

"No good on land," Uncle Jason said. "Their home is the sea!"

While we waited for the sailors to return we argued who would get Tim. Uncle Jason wanted to bet Pa five dollars the Marines would get Tim. Pa wanted to bet Uncle Jason five dollars Sheriff Cremeans would get Tim. Mom wouldn't bet money on anybody but she made an agreement with Uncle Jason that she would cook him a Christmas turkey dinner if the Army didn't get Tim.

"Pa, since you, Mom, and Uncle Jason haven't said anything for the Navy, I would like to make an agreement with you," I said. "If the Navy gets Tim, you sign my papers so I can enlist. If the Navy doesn't get Tim, I won't beg you again!"

"I'll take you up on that," Pa said. "I'm getting tired of hearing you beg us to join the Navy."

"I told you about the Navy," Uncle Jason said as he pointed to the sailors getting into the jeep. "They're not for land service."

I don't know how it happened, but everybody was watching the soldiers, sailors, and Marines when they started racing to see who would be the first to get Tim. Once, twice, and often three times a week each group came and went back without him. I don't know how many trips they made. It seemed to me that one of the groups went to Mart Stacy's shack every day. But the roads got muddy in early December and they couldn't drive the jeep. They didn't come as often when they had to walk.

George Mennix came to our place one day and he said Tim was back. He said he met him on the Seaton Ridge.

"That fellow's never been away from here," Pa said. "Sheriff Cremeans ought to be put wise so Tim Stacy can get what he deserves! Tim has always defied the law! Now he defies Uncle Sam!"

But when Sheriff Cremeans and six deputies walked over the hills to Mart Stacy's shack and surrounded the place, they didn't find Tim. They searched everything and even found the place where they thought he had been sleeping on top of a potato heap in the cellar. They found blankets that were still warm. But they also found a hole in the top of the cellar where he could have escaped into the night.

Two days before Christmas Mom, Uncle Jason, Pa, and I were sitting before the fire when we saw George Mennix hurrying up the flagstone walk.

"George only comes when he hears news," Pa said, getting up to open the door.

"They got Tim," George said as soon as Pa opened the door. "They played a trick on him!"

"You'll be cooking me a turkey dinner day after tomorrow, Sallie," Uncle Jason said to Mom.

"Tell us about it, George," Pa said, his face beaming.

"Tim went to Dartmouth, Ohio, to get married," George said.

"Who was the girl?" Mom asked.

"The way I heard it," George said, "some strange woman with an order book went to Mart Stacy's to get an order. Since it was late, they offered to let her spend the night and that's how she met Tim. She fell in love with Tim at first sight and Tim fell in love with her. She told Tim she would make the living and she'd hide him where Sheriff Cremeans, his deputies, and the military authorities would never find him. She told Tim they'd get married in Ohio and she helped him plan his way there to dodge the authorities. And when Tim went inside the church with her, four men went in behind them. 'I'm sorry about this, Tim' was all she said. Then Tim noticed that the blue dress she was wearing was the uniform of a WAVE."

"Did Bill Cremeans and his deputies go in behind 'em?" Pa asked, jumping from his chair.

"No," said George laughing.

"The soldiers followed them in?" Mom said.

"Not the soldiers," George said.

"It must have been Marines," Uncle Jason said.

"You missed it too," George said.

"Were they sailors?" I asked.

"Right," George said.

Uncle Jason sat looking at the flames leaping from the dry forestick. Mom looked at Pa and Pa looked at Mom. I didn't say anything, but I knew what they were thinking.

Seventy-Six Days

PA was always a frolicsome devil, full of banter and good fun. And when old Rudolph Anderson came into the store with a willow basket of fresh eggs on that Saturday morning, it was October thirteenth, two days before quail season opened.

And he said to Pa, "John, I'll tell you what I'll do. I'll bet you can't eat one quail a day from now to the end of quail season. That means a quail a day for seventy-six days."

Well, each season Rudolph had been selling Pa quails. He hadn't sold him all the quails we had eaten, for Pa liked to hunt birds and he was an excellent shot. But as Pa said, when a man got older he took on responsibilities and he didn't have the time to hunt like he had when he was a young man living beside the Tiber River where the cornfields and wheatfields were full of birds. He'd told me how when he was a boy of sixteen, younger than I was now, that he had taken his father's single-barrel and shot into a covey and killed as many as fifteen birds. Now he said a man wouldn't flush fifteen coveys in a day and just a few years ago when he was a boy a man could flush fifty to a hundred coveys if he started hunting early in the morning and didn't stop shooting until night fell.

When Rudolph put this bet up to Pa you could hear him laughing all over the store. He laughed until he let an egg fall from his hand and splash on the floor. Since I was handyman around our store, for Pa liked to meet the customers, I had to get a mop and bucket of water and clean up the egg. Pa shook all over with laughter. He laughed until he jerked and if he hadn't been put together well he would have gone to pieces.

"What do you want to bet me, Rudolph?" he asked.

"A big bet this time," he said. "I want to bet you a thousand pound, white-faced, corn-fed, two-year-old beef, one that's better than quail, against a hundred pounds of colored soup beans, two barrels of flour, two barrels of meal, a barrel of salt, and a hundred pounds of sugar."

"Your staple winter groceries, huh?" Pa said. "Sure, Rudolph, I'll take you up on that. You know how well I like quails, don't you?"

"Yes, I ought to know how well you like 'em," Rudolph said. "I've been killing birds for you for the last sixteen years."

"You think I might get to liking beef as well as my birds?" Pa asked him.

"Yes, I think you might," Rudolph said.

"And then you'd sell me a lot of beef," he said.

"I shore would," Rudolph told him.

"Rudolph, you have a hard time making a living on that farm," Pa said as he took the last eggs from the basket. "I hate to take that big fine beef from you. I want to keep you for my friend and my customer. If I win I'm afraid it will hurt your feelings and I'll lose you for a friend and customer. For I'm as sure to win as my name is John Sewall."

"It takes a good man, strong and with a good appetite, to eat a quail a day for seventy-six days," Rudolph said. "You must remember sickness does not count. I win the bet if you get sick and can't eat your bird."

"Yes, I understand all that," Pa said. "I never get sick. I've got the health and appetite of a big boar hog."

Well, the store was full of people and they got interested and gathered around Pa and Rudolph and listened to the bet.

"Now, this is a gentleman's bet," Rudolph said. "I know you will do what you say. There won't be anybody but your wife and son to check on you."

"I won't need anybody," Pa said. "How do you think I've built my fine business up here? Best grocery store in this town. Even the other merchants will admit this. I've never lied knowingly to a customer in my life. And I won't lie to you, Rudolph. My conscience wouldn't let me lie to a stranger, let alone an old friend like yourself. We grew up together, Rudolph. The Andersons and Sewalls lived on adjoinin' farms for over fifty years, went to the same little church, and voted the same party ticket on election days. My bet with you is my bond. Now you bring me the birds. I furnish you the shells and I pay you a quarter for each bird. And we start Monday."

"Right," Rudolph said. "I've been studying this bet up for the last week or two."

Well, everybody gathered around thought this was a funny bet. And they got to betting among themselves who would win, Pa or Rudolph. Old Jake Cremeans said he could eat a quail a day for three hundred and sixty-five days. Said the only thing that kept him from it was he just couldn't get quails the year around for they had a mating and a nesting time and that was no time to kill quails. And ol Aunt Effie Crump said she believed she could eat one a day for six months if she could get the quails and if she hadn't lost her teeth. This bet caused a lot of confusion in our store.

Pa said, "I lost count of the eggs, Rudolph. How many did you count before you brought them?"

"I didn't count them at all," he said. "But Murtie said there were fifteen dozen."

"Fifteen dozen it will be," Pa said. Then he began to laugh until I thought he'd come apart. He jerked all over again. "When the quail season is over, I'll have me a juicy white-faced, cornfed, two-year-old for beef. A thousand pounds of him on foot. Enough beef to do me until quail season starts again and I'll get me another bet with Rudolph. If I win, Ruddie, will you bet me again next year?"

"That's too far away," he told Pa. "I'm not so sure."

"Well you might bet me on two quails a day for the whole season," he said.

"Yes, I might do that."

"A quail for dinner and a quail for supper wouldn't go bad."

"And a quail too for breakfast wouldn't go bad," Old Jake Cremeans said. "Quail is better than chicken, guinea meat, grouse any old time! Better than fish and frog legs too."

Well, Pa and Rudolph's bet flashed all over Blakesburg. Say there were twenty customers that heard it on this Saturday morning. Before sundown each customer had told twenty more people and this made four hundred people. And there were only eleven hundred people in Blakesburg. Well, say each one of the four hundred told twenty more by sundown on the second day, this would be eight thousand. And these eight thousand wouldn't have enough people in Greenwood County for each of them to tell his twenty by sundown on the third day. There were nineteen thousand people in our whole county. It was a mighty big place for this many people. But this was the way news was norated in our county. We had a newspaper, *The Blakesburg Gazette*, but we didn't need it. Our paper couldn't get the news to the people as quickly as the people could get the news to one another. So Pa and Rudolph's bet went all over Greenwood County.

On Monday morning Rudolph came with a dozen dressed birds for Pa.

"Take them over home, Timmie, tell your ma to have one cooked for my supper," Pa said. "Of course put the others in the icebox."

Pa paid Rudolph three dollars for the quails. Then he gave him another box of shells.

"What if I eat all twelve in less than twelve days?" Pa said.

"Eat all the extras you want," Rudolph said.

"Now and then my wife will eat part of a bird," Pa said. "She's kindly douncy like city women. And my son Timmie doesn't care too much about quail. I tell him the reason is he never come up on good grub a-livin' in the city like we had a-livin' in the country. A lot of people here in Blakesburg don't know good country living like you have now, Rudolph, and like I used to have at home with Ma and Pa. Raccoon, groundhog, squirrel, rabbit, quail, grouse, wild honey from the trees, all the wild fruit and jellies made from them, sorghum molasses! Talk about good grub, we had it. No such things to eat in the stores and cities, Rudolph! Gee, I'm proud to start on my quails today."

I'll never forget how fast Pa put the little quail away. Here he sat at the head of the table, a big man eating that little bird and a few trimmings Ma had cooked with it.

"Not much more than a bite," he said. "Since I'm a much better off man in this world than poor Rudolph, and since we came up as boys together, played together, went to Red Hot School together, after I win his beef I might not take it. Irma, I'm a successful man in the store business," Pa talked on. "I don't like to take a big fine beef free from an old friend."

"There could be some reason why you don't win the bet," she said. "I am not certain of anything."

"But I don't know what in the world will keep me from it," Pa said. "Only thing about a little bird is a fellow has to watch about injuring his teeth on buckshot. I got into some in that bird I've just et. I don't want no broken teeth. I've got all my teeth and they're hard as flintstones. Ah, maybe a chip or two on 'em where I've bit down on buckshot when I've eaten birds in the seasons gone by. But there's only a few bites in a little bird."

"Yes, but to have a quail every day is a different matter," Ma told him. "Your boyhood friend, Rudolph Anderson, might be smarter than you think, John. Why in the world would he think of such a bet? You suppose he's heard of one before where some man didn't win it? I can't understand such workings in a country man's mind."

"But a country man thinks as same as a city man," Pa said. Pa always held up for his people living out on the land, and since my mother was from the city and Pa was from the country, I had a divided mind. "I'd say the country man is a damn sight smarter than the city man. You look at me! I'm from out there in the country. And I figure myself to be a damn sight smarter than a lot of these ambitionless men in Blakesburg. Look how successful I am! We own our store, our home and other properties, stock in the railroad, pipeline, and I'm not a director of the Blakesburg Citizens' Bank for nothing."

"Let's don't get into an argument, John," Ma said. "I know you're successful and you're a good provider. But I just can't get over this bet. It's the talk of Blakesburg."

"People have to have something to talk about," Pa said. "It's better than an ad in the paper—better than a whole page ad. People get to know my name better. It will bring more people to the store."

"But you got the trade of the country and town now, John," Ma said.

"More money, more success, and more birds," Pa said. And then he let out a wild laugh at his own joke. I didn't see any fun in it. And I know Ma didn't for she didn't even smile. She'd often pretend to smile when Pa told us a joke at the supper table. But Ma, so Pa said, never had the sense of humor that the country women had.

"I love my family even if they can't eat quails and can't laugh big robust laughs like I can."

Well, Pa kept up his laughter through October after he had eaten a quail for his supper. Pa was a big hearty man and he could eat like a hungry hound every time he sat down at the table, morning, noon, and night. A little quail was just a few bites for him. Rudolph Anderson brought him birds every Saturday and Pa gave him shells and the customers gathered around to hear them talk about the bet. And Pa was right about this news being better than a one-page ad in *The Blakesburg Gazette*. Strange people were now coming to our store. They would come in and before they bought anything they'd take a big long look at Pa. They seemed to wonder if Pa was made of something not exactly quite mortal man. Pa's name had gone to every crossroads store, every village, and about every farm home in Greenwood County. He was the most talked-of man in Greenwood County. And his friends came and tried to get him to run for County Judge, Sheriff, and Clerk. Many wanted him to run for Representative to represent the people in Greenwood County in the State Legislature.

"Too busy feeding my friends to run for a county office," Pa told some of them. And he often turned the subject by telling his customers, "I have to eat my quails and win my bet before I can think this matter over."

Then they would laugh. Pa, even if he was my father, was the most popular man in Greenwood County. There wasn't a man in our Party who would dare run against him in the primary. And he could beat any man the other Party could nominate to run against him. And Pa used to sit at the table and brag to Ma and me how he had Greenwood County in his pocket, in his mind, and in his heart just because he could eat a quail a day.

About the middle of November, Pa stopped his eatin' an extra quail two and three days a week. He said he believed a fellow could get too much quail. He explained it at the supper table one evening to Ma and me.

"Now say you like apple pie," he said. "And you just get one piece at a meal for dessert. Then you keep on wantin' apple pie. But say you act a pig and you eat six pieces, a whole pie, for dessert. Next day you might not want to look at a piece of apple pie."

Then he said to Ma, "Don't fix me another quail and send to me for my dinner."

We'd never heard Pa talk like this before. Ma got to wondering if something was goin' wrong with his stummick. By the early days in December, when snow covered the country and the town, Pa would sit and look at the quail on his plate before he'd stick a fork in it. Then he'd mince around and he'd finally eat the quail and he wouldn't eat much else.

"I'm gettin' douncy," Pa said to Ma one evening. "I can't figure out what is wrong with me. But I believe something is wrong. My appetite has never failed me in my life. And I believe it's failing me now. I might even have to see a doctor for I'm worried about myself. I might not even win this bet. And when I began it last October I would have bet my life, my store, my wealth, everything but my lovely wife and fine son, that I would have won it."

"Then see Doc Torris," Ma said. "Good old reliable Henry Torris. He can tell you what is wrong. He can cure a body, Darling, like you can make friends and more friends and money and more money!"

Ma's voice was soft and sweet. She loved my Pa. And she had never heard him complain, so she told me, about his appetite since they were married twenty years ago.

"I hate for the news to be norated that I'm ailing and might not win my bet," Pa said. "It might even hurt my business."

"Well there comes the time in a strong man's life when afflictions come," Ma said. "Go see Doctor Torris, old reliable Henry. He might make you as good as new and bring your appetite back."

"That's what I'll do but I won't let anybody see me do it," he said. "I'll walk the streets at night until I see the light on in his office. When no one is around I'll dive in there to see him. I might mosey down that way tonight. I might have luck and see him. I know something is wrong, Irma, for my stummick ain't nigh right. Not when a big man like me can't eat a little quail a day. I don't want this to get out," Pa continued talking as he got up from head of the table. He had his napkin stuck down in his shirt collar to cover the front of his shirt. Ma got onto him about his being mussy at the table for a gentleman of his standing in Blakesburg.

"Yes, I had trouble gettin' that quail down tonight," he said.

Well, Pa walked out of the house onto the street. And he walked up and down the street in front of our house at first. And then he made a beeline down the main street toward Doc Torris' office.

"Follow your pa, Timmie," Ma said. "See if he goes in to see Doc Torris. If he does, he might be a sick man. He's never had no serious sickness before, just childhood diseases, colds, and he had the flu once. He's strong as men come in this world. He's a durable man. When he complains it frightens me. I know something is wrong with him!"

I did as Ma told me. I was about a hundred feet behind Pa. He walked straight as a ramrod down the street, his head high, speaking to everybody he met. And I know he was smiling because he couldn't speak to a man, woman, or child when he didn't smile. The light was on at Doc Torris' office. No one was on the street near the office and Pa raced from the street over to the door and went in. I turned and walked back up the street and back home and told Ma that Pa was right now in Doc Torris' office.

"You can bet your pa is a sick man," she said.

Pa was staying longer than we had expected.

"He won't come out as long as he sees someone on the street," Ma said. "Maybe this is what's keeping him."

Of course we sat up and waited for him to come home. It was two hours before he got back.

"Doc Torris said I might be a sick man," Pa said. Pa's face was a little pale. "He asked me about this bet I had. And he said to me, 'John, don't be a fool and try to eat a quail a day. See your friend Rudolph Anderson and call this bet off. And I says, 'Doc, I can't do it. It would ruin my reputation.' Then Doc says to me, 'It's your stummick, John. It's tired of quail. You've got to change fuels. It might even rebel on you. Something is wrong, John, something I can't put my hand on right now.' Then he says, 'What you need is to get on another diet and take some of my medicine to whet your appetite and make you have the old vim and vigor again.' Well he fixed me this bottle of medicine. He told me to take a spoonful after each meal. I took my first spoonful in the office and I thought I'd sink to the floor. It gagged me, Irma. It's bitter as gall. And he said, 'Come back to see me on the twelfth if you're not better'."

"Listen to him, John," Ma warned. "Do as Doc tells you."

Well this was the evening of December ninth. On December tenth Pa ate his quail. Then he took his medicine. Ma and I thought he was going into a faint. He had to hold to the table to stand up.

"Just dizzy, Darling," he said to Ma. "Don't you worry. Everything is going to be all right."

Next morning Pa didn't eat much breakfast. But he went to the store as usual. And at the store I did most of the work while Pa sat behind the counter all reared back smoking his cigar. And he smiled and nodded to the customers and bragged about my learning the store business. He said I could really do the work, and I could too. But Pa had never bragged on me like this before. He didn't want to tell the customers that he didn't feel up to meeting them and this was the reason I was doing all the work. If Pa had felt like it he'd have been right in there pitching.

Pa managed December eleventh and twelfth. I did most of the work in the store and he ate his birds and took his medicine. But as he told Ma, if he got through December eating his quail a day he was a lucky man. Pa was beginning to have his doubts.

Pa had always laughed about people who wouldn't go around the opposite sides of the tree from each other. But Friday, December thirteenth, he didn't eat but a few bites at the breakfast table.

"Food gags me, Irma," he said. "Can you believe it? And this is not quail. I believe it's something in the medicine Doctor Torris is giving me."

"But he's a reliable doctor," Ma said. "You'd better take it, John. If you get sick your public is going to find it out."

That day at the store I did all the work. Pa never got up to wait on a customer. And I had a day of it. When Ma came over and brought his lunch, he opened the basket, looked at the food, and since there was no one in the store at this minute he let out a sigh.

"It gags me, Darling. I can't go it. I might not eat my quail tonight."

Well, Pa was right. Mom had his quail fixed for she thought it was a delicacy he might eat. Pa put his fork in it, cut with his knife and took a bite, and then he tumbled from his chair.

"Go for Doctor Torris," Ma said. "Go in a run!"

I ran down the street as fast as my legs would carry me. I was lucky to find Doctor Torris in his office. Somebody was in the office, a person I didn't know. So I whispered in Doctor Torris' ear what was wrong.

"I'll be right up as soon as I give this man his medicine," he said.

Doctor Torris came in just after I got there. Pa was still down on the floor moaning and going on. He didn't have any power in his strong body. So I got him by the legs and Doctor Torris and Ma got his shoulders and we put him on the bed. He was as heavy as lead. It was all three of us could do to put him there. If Doctor Torris hadn't been a strong man for a doctor and taken most of the weight of his shoulders and head off Ma we couldn't have done it.

"It's my stummick, Doc," he said.

"I told you to quit eatin' a quail a day," Doctor Torris said. "You wouldn't do it."

"Just eighteen more days to go, Doc, and the beef would have been mine," Pa said. "My reputation would have spread far. It has already spread all around me."

"Well you're goin' to lose your bet," Doctor Torris said. "Let's hope you don't lose your life. I know what is the matter with you. I've had another case almost like yours. You've got lead poisoning."

"How did I get lead poisoning, Doc?" Pa asked.

"From the shots in the quails," he said. "I'll bet you've got enough shots in you to rattle. If you weren't so thick on all sides we could hear them rattling now when you walk."

"Is lead poisoning dangerous, Doctor Torris?" Ma asked.

"You know any kind of poisoning is dangerous," he replied. "Lead poisoning might be the most dangerous of all poisoning. It gets through your system in a hell of a hurry. You've really got a dose of it, John. I'm changing your medicine. And stay in this bed."

"What happened to your other patient that had lead poisoning, Doctor Torris?" I asked.

"Don't ask me that, Timmie," he said.

Well of course if he had lived Doctor Torris would have told me. When he gave me this kind of an answer I thought Ma would sink in a faint. She got very pale and Pa's eyes looked up at the ceiling. Pa had lost his old smile after he fell from the table and couldn't eat his bird.

News flashed over Blakesburg next morning that Pa had lost his bet, that he fell at the table when he had faltered on his fifty-ninth bird. Word had spread that Pa was bedfast and in a bad way. And word norated over the town and to the county that he had lead poisoning. Well, I tried to take care of the store. I thought Pa had missed when he lost the bet. I thought he had lost his reputation. So many customers came in, I had to have help. I phoned Ma to send me two or three helpers, experienced clerks if she could find them. And it surprised me when two of Pa's competitors each sent an experienced clerk to help me. What was it in the Bible that I remembered hearing the preacher quote for a text for his sermon, something about you win your life by losing your life! Well, I never could understand that. And now by losing a bet that Pa thought would make him more friends if he won, he had made more friends. Even the merchants, Tom Harrison, a rival competitor to Pa who had talked a lot about him, sent his clerk Willie Jarvis over to help me; Tobbie Dravenstot, another rival competitor who'd talked awful about Pa, even said once he watered the kerosene and put sawdust in the meal he sold, sent Jack Harrell over to help me. They were young and experienced clerks. With their help I managed to answer the questions customers asked about Pa. When Rudolph Anderson came with the quails, he'd not heard of Pa's collapse until he reached Blakesburg, I told him to sell the quail somewhere else for we couldn't use them. He wanted me to ice them at the store and sell them for him and I told him I would. But he had won the bet and I told him Pa would take care of honoring his bet, if and when he was able to get back to the store.

Somehow I made a statement like this, "If he doesn't ever get back to the store, Mr. Anderson, I heard that bet and I'll honor it for him."

I didn't know that my words to Mr. Anderson might be prophetic. Pa lingered from December thirteenth to December twenty-fourth. It was on Christmas Eve when the streets were decorated and there were many wreaths and various colored lights shining from windows that Pa went to meet his Maker. The lead poisoning from the birdshot he'd got by eating so many quails had poisoned his strong body. And we never questioned what old reliable Doctor Torris had told us. This was the verdict of his death. We didn't open our Christmas presents on Christmas Day.

We buried Pa on The Hill among Ma's people on the day after Christmas. We buried him on the plot where her people were buried. And her people had the highest stone markers of any plot on The Hill. There was never a funeral as big, not even when they buried the old Civil War or World War I soldiers, as there was at Pa's funeral. All the people in Blakesburg went and it seemed all the people from Greenwood County came. They carried Pa's casket from our house across the town and up on The Hill. There were three shifts of pallbearers, two resting while a shift carried him, for he was a big heavy man. And I knew by this great crowd that Pa up to his time and since was the most famous man ever to live and die in Blakesburg. The crowd was so big the preacher preached his funeral on this moderate December day out on The Hill where we laid him to rest.

When Ma and I got back to our lonesome home, lonesome without Pa, she said, "I'll see to it he has the highest stone on The Hill. I'll have one so big a truck can't take it up there. There's still enough cattle pullin' sawlogs in the lumber woods to take the one I'll get up there. It will be all in one piece too."

Well, I went back to the store. I had to wear Pa's shoes now. I had to take over his business. The first thing I did was to honor his bet with Rudolph Anderson. And Rudolph, who had taken it so hard at Pa's funeral, was happy now to have his winter's supply of the solid staples that he had always bought early each fall. He hadn't bought them this fall for I thought he might have had the feeling he'd win his bet.

Ma ordered a marker for Pa that was shipped to Blakesburg on a flatcar. There was no truck big enough to take it up onto The Hill. But the old teamsters, the few of them still left, came with their ox teams to Blakesburg. And they lined their log carts up and chained them together. They had loaded heavy sawlogs on the carts. They knew how to use skids and load the marker. Twenty yoke of oxen moved it across the town and up on The Hill. They made a big scaffold and inched it up and up until they fit the stone onto the base which they had made of concrete.

"We've got the money and I won't spare anything to perpetuate John's memory," Ma said. And she didn't spare money to buy his marker and to have it erected.

People who drive along the highway below can see this tall stone for miles. And now a hard road goes up on The Hill. There are no more working oxen left to handle such a stone. And people come from everywhere to see Pa's tall stone. On the stone there sits a little quail. A lot of people who come to admire the stone wonder what a quail is doing up there, for all it says is:

In Memory of John Sewall
A loving husband and a fine father
April 22, 1880   December 24, 1922

The Rainy Day at Big Lost Creek

WHEN the news got out that Cousin Penny Shelton was going to tear down the old log shack where we'd lived when I was a boy, I jumped in my car and drove in a hurry to his sawmill. I couldn't stand the idea of seeing that old shack torn down. It wasn't just sentimental reasons. I had another reason. I owned the land on the right side of Middle Fork of Big Lost Creek and Cousin Penny owned the land on the left side, and the old shack was in the middle under a big white oak tree that shaded it like a giant green umbrella in spring and summer. The clear blue Little Fork water trickled over the rocks beside the shack and used to lull us to sleep at night when we lived there. I wanted to buy this shack and annex it to my farm. My wife liked this old shack too. Said she'd just love to get hold of it and fix it up. This was my idea when I pulled my car up at Cousin Penny's sawmill.

"Penny, I understand you're goin' to tear down my old home place," I said. "I've come to buy that place from you!"

"Who in the world told you that?" Cousin Penny said, looking strangely at me with black eyes that shone like embers in the dark. "I wouldn't sell that shack at all. Shan, I've got a renter for that shack. Not exactly a renter," he laughed. "I don't expect to get anything in the way of money for it. But I'm letting an old friend move in!"

This stunned me into silence. I wondered who on earth would move into that shack the way it was, with sagging floors, a leaky roof, mud fallen from between the logs, window panes gone from the windows in the four rooms where the early April winds whistled in. I couldn't believe Cousin Penny was telling me the truth. He always liked a good joke and he looked at me and grinned, showing four front upper teeth and three front lower teeth. The rest were gone. I started laughing too. It was a joke, all right.

"I'm not jokin' you, Shan," Cousin Penny said, slapping his thighs with his leather-gloved hands, bending over and laughing until tears came into his eyes. "I'm movin' Old Hawgie Cawhorn in that shack! Old Hawgie, his wife, two children and eleven hounds!"

As soon as Penny mentioned Hawgie Cawhorn's name I quit laughing. Just the mentioning of his name ended the best laugh I'd had in months.

"Cousin Penny, do you mean that?" I said.

"I'm not jokin' you, Shan," he said. "Hawgie Cawhorn, his family and his hounds will be in that shack this afternoon. I've sent one of my trucks with two of my men to move him. You know they put him out of the cottage where he was living in Wurtsville. Couldn't pay his rent and his things are out in the yard up there right now."

"I'm not surprised," I said. "Everybody on Big Lost Creek works to make a living. Why on earth would you move in a fellow like Hawgie Cawhorn!"

"We need 'im on Big Lost Creek, Shan," Cousin Penny said. "Every community in this country needs a man like Hawgie. You need to know Hawgie better," Cousin Penny twittered like a bird. "If you did you'd laugh more and you'd be a happy man. This is a sad country. Not many people laugh any more. Old Hawgie makes 'em laugh and he doesn't try to make anybody laugh. I can just look at Hawgie and start laughing. Never was a man like him."

I gave up. I thought Cousin Penny must have tipped the jug before he talked to me but I knew that was against his rule while working at the sawmill around the buzzing circlesaw. I turned on the switch and started my car. Cousin Penny took his arm off my car window.

"Don't worry about Hawgie! He has the right philosophy of life. He'll make a different man of you," Cousin Penny shouted as I drove away. "There are not any sourpusses laying-up-for-a rainy-day in Hawgie Cawhorn's company."

The whole thing is hard for me to believe, I thought, as I drove up Shacklerun to the Shannon River Turnpike. What has come over Cousin Penny? Under what kind of a spell is he? All that talk about a rainy day. He's not moving Hawgie Cawhorn on Big Lost Creek and in his shack free of rent. That's not Cousin Penny. He's joking. He'll laugh about the big joke he's tried to make me believe. A big joke to keep from selling me his shack.

I had driven about a mile when I came up behind Cousin Penny's truck on the narrow Big Lost Creek road. On the back of that truck, I saw some house plunder roped to the truck cab. But it didn't cover half the truck bed and it was covered with old quilts and blankets. Under the quilts and blankets I could see bed legs, table legs, chair legs, with dog chains fastened to 'em. I counted not eleven but fourteen hounds, besides a box filled with hound pups. They were rearing up trying to get out. Old Hawgie was sitting upon the furniture, clapping his hands and laughing. He was telling Beany-Eye Smith, one of Cousin Penny's sawmill hands, something and Beany-Eye was laughing fit to die.

When the truck slowed to turn up Middle Fork, I dashed past and glanced in at the cab window where I saw Eif Blevins, another fox hunter who worked for Cousin Penny, under the wheel. Beside Eif sat a very pretty woman with a child of about three on her lap. Down between Eif and Hawgie's wife I saw a towheaded boy of six or seven. That was Hawgie's family, all right. They were moving up the little winding mule road with the big truck. I stopped my car and switched off the engine. Hawgie was clapping his big hands and talking to Beany-Eye

Smith. When Hawgie stopped talking, I heard laughter hit a rocky cliff, and echo across the narrow-gauged valley. I had never heard any laughing on Lost Creek like Hawgie Cawhorn's laughter.

I wanted to follow the truck up to the shack. I wanted to listen to more of Hawgie's laughter that got fainter in its echoes as the truck turned the bend and was out of sight. A lonesome feeling came over me, though I did hate to see a man like Old Hawgie move in on us. I started my car again and drove up where Check Batson was sitting on his front porch watching his garden grow. I stopped in front of the porch and said to Check: "We got new neighbors. Hawgie Cawhorn is moving up on Middle Fork in Cousin Penny's shack!"

"Oh, my heavens," Check shouted. "How did that thing get in here? Has Penny Shelton lost his mind? I heard he was about to. Won't hire a man to work for 'im unless he's a fox hunter. I guess Old Hawgie Cawhorn will about suit 'im. Only Old Hawgie won't work in a pie factory!"

"I'd love to know 'im better," I said. "I followed the truck and he was riding on the back with his hounds and house plunder and I never heard a man who could laugh like Hawgie."

"He can do that all right," Check said. "But I'll be his closest neighbor and he's got young uns and I can't stand to see little young uns go hungry."

Well, I knew what poor old Check was thinking as I drove up and stopped at Winston Gore's shack. Old Gore was out in the yard working with a pair of pruners.

"Got new neighbors, Gore," I said. "Hawgie Cawhorn has just moved in Cousin Penny's shack on Middle Fork."

"Fasten the henhouse door," Old Gore laughed, showing his tobacco-stained front teeth. "I've knowed Hawgie since he was a little boy. Had a fine pappie and mammie and he's the only one that won't work. His pappie, long dead and gone, used to be a old-time schoolteacher who teached me my ABC's. I owe all my larnin' to 'im and I shouldn't be talkin' about Hawgie, but he ain't worth the salt that goes in his bread. I'm real sorry he got on Big Lost Creek."

"I thought I'd stop and tell you," I said, as I started to drive on.

"Thank you, Shan," Gore laughed again, "I'll know to put the lock on my henhouse door from now on."

When I told my wife Deanems about what had happened, that I was too late to buy the shack and I followed the truck bringing Hawgie, his family and his hounds, she laughed as I had never heard her laugh before. "Let 'im have the shack, Shan," she said. "We don't need it anyway. We got plenty of land. Maybe enough for Hawgie Cawhorn to foxhunt on. Sounds like he's a wonderful man," she laughed again. "Maybe the hounds will bring us some music on Big Lost Creek where everybody works like he's mad trying to lay up for a rainy day. I think this Hawgie Cawhorn might have the right philosophy of life after all. You said Cousin Penny Shelton had changed his way of living until you thought he talked crazy."

Well on that very day, at about six o'clock, I saw coming up the Big Lost Creek road a tall man leading a pack of hounds. It was Old Hawgie. He was holding a big chain in each hand. He had seven hounds fastened to each chain. Little chains ran from the big chains and snapped into beautiful collars around his hounds' necks. Collars on each dog with nice brass platings and their names engraved and the name of the owner, who was Hawgie Cawhorn. I wondered how he could afford all of this.

"Shan, I thought I'd have me a chase tonight while The Lady got the shack fixed up," Hawgie said. "Which is the nigh-cut to Seven White Oaks?"

"Seven White Oaks?" I said. "I never heard of that place!"

"Ah, shucks," Hawgie roared, his big laugh booming against the rock cliffs on the other side of my henhouse and echoing back to us, "It's on your farm. It's just the other side of yer terbacker barn!"

"Oh, yes, I know what you're talking about now," I said. "Go up Big Lost Creek to the first gate on your left and go up Coon Den Hollow and hit the ridge. You know your way from there!"

"I know more about men's farms all over this county than they know themselves," Hawgie laughed again. "But see I'm down in this hollow. You know I love the ridges and the mountain tops right up there under the stars where I can hear my hounds take the fox clear around the circle. And you got the best place in the county right up here. I've been thinkin' about askin' you to have the State Fox Hunting Association's field meet up there on that mountain!"

"They wouldn't come here," I said. "How'd they get up there?"

"Build a road," Hawgie shouted. "I'll help 'em do that!"

"Build a road up there for a field meet?" I couldn't see that.

"Sure," Hawgie said. "It's worth it. You attend one of them things once. I've never missed for twenty years except the war years! Greatest thing in the world."

"You've got some nice dog collars there," I said to change the subject.

"Yeah, my fox-hunting buddies donated them," Hawgie said proudly.

The restless, long, lean, hungry hounds pulled on the chains and whined. They moved six-feet-four, two-hundred-forty-pound Hawgie from his tracks.

"They're telling me to come on when they whine like that," Hawgie explained. "I understand their talk. I talk back to them and they talk back to me. I've got to get goin'. You'll hear us in a few minutes."

One hour had passed. The thin sickle April moon, hung above the deep valley of Big Lost Creek. When we heard the barking hounds, Deanems and I ran to the porch just in time to see the fox, big as a small shepherd dog, run under the plum tree white with blossom at the edge of our yard. The fox streaked across the little bottom by the henhouse with his bushy tail floating on the wind. We watched him climb the rocky bluff, just as fourteen hounds reached the plum tree, their noses in the air sniffling his hot scent on the wind.

"Gee, Shan, this is wonderful," Deanems said. "Why haven't you ever fox hunted?"

"Never had the time to spend out on cold ridges at night with a fire that burns you on one side and freezes you on the other," I answered.

"You've missed something."

"Never missed a thing," I told her.

"But you stand here and watch the fox and the hounds and you listen and love it," she said. "You're deceiving yourself, Shan. This Hawgie Cawhorn might get in a henhouse but he's got something."

"There's no record of his getting in a henhouse," I explained. "Everybody's just afraid he will. That's why we're locking up against him."

"Let's go fox hunting with him some night," Deanems pleaded. "I'd love to go. Let all the men on Lost Creek go and take their wives and let us cook supper on Seaton Ridge. Up there against the stars. I heard Hawgie talking to you about loving to be up on high ground and not down in the valley—up against the stars. Said that was his world."

"All right," I said. "I'll do it just to please you and if you get a cold not I but Hawgie Cawhorn caused it."

We stood on our porch and listened to Hawgie's hounds for two hours. Our feet got tired and then we brought chairs and sat and listened and counted the times that fox circled down into Big Lost Creek valley over the mountain and back again. Thirty-one times. We waited for the thirty-second time at two o'clock in the morning. But the hounds didn't come back. They ran the fox into a hole under a cliff on my farm.

Check Batson told me how it had been arranged for Hawgie to make a living. Cousin Penny had rented the shack to him free. He had also rented the land to him free and Hawgie had become a farmer. He was attending a farming school and drawing a monthly check for around ninety dollars a month from the Government. Check Batson said his wife, Lottie, had paid the new neighbors a visit and that Hawgie's wife, Gracie, had made a new place of the old shack. Said she had put in the new windowpanes with tacks and putty into the decaying sashes—windowpanes that Cousin Penny furnished—said she had daubed the big cracks between the logs and patched the leaky roof and cut the weeds and cleaned off the yard and raked it clean as a pin. Said she'd scrubbed the floors clean as a table top. Said it was a pretty place now. Said there wasn't any hams of meat hanging in the smokehouse but Old Hawgie had taken it over for his hounds. Said they slept on the floor and in shelves upon the side of the wall while the puppies ran over the floor below. Said each hound knew his own quarters and wouldn't allow another to take them. Said she never saw anything like the way Hawgie had his hounds trained and the way his wife baked corn pone to feed 'em.

Then Check started laughing. He said when Lottie got ready to leave, Hawgie and Gracie came part of the way over the hill with her and there was a nice pole of dry wood across the path. Said here they stopped and Hawgie picked up the pole and said: "Ah, shucks—that's too heavy to carry home." So Gracie, without saying a word, shouldered the pole of wood and she and Hawgie turned back toward home. Check laughed about it like it was funny and said he was going to get better acquainted with Hawgie Cawhorn.

Then Check told me Cousin Penny had helped Hawgie burn his tobacco bed and sow it and that he had helped him clear some land, that he had brought his sawmill crew in and they had plowed for Hawgie and helped him with his farming according to "Government specifications," raise so much of this and that, before he could go to the farming school and get his ninety bucks a month. Said they were goin' to help Old Hawgie measure up to specifications.

Hawgie farmed all right. All through April, May, June and July. Cousin Penny and his crew helped Hawgie. Once I stopped my car at the mouth of Middle Fork and I thought from the sound of their voices and laughter there were a hundred men working up in Little Fork instead of nine—ten including Cousin Penny. They had tobacco, corn and sweet potatoes and, according to specifications, Hawgie had to have a couple of hogs or more and a cow or two and a span of mules or horses. He got a span of horses but didn't have feed for them or anything else and he let all the animals have the freedom of the unfenced hills where there was plenty of green. Where there was freedom for the fox, freedom for the hounds and freedom for Old Hawgie.

But on every other night, moonlight, darkness or rain, through April, May, June into July, I heard Hawgie's hounds on the mountain. I got to know each one's bark and we lost more sleep over those hounds than anything that had come into our lives in the sixteen years we had been married. We stood on the porch and sat on the porch and listened. When Hawgie's hogs, searching for food, visited about every house on Big Lost Creek and rooted up yards, people shooed them off to the next one, kept them running from place to place, but never said anything to Hawgie. Not until they planted their gardens, and Hawgie's hogs found more and better food, did they persuade him to put them up. Cousin Penny built a hog lot for him.

And when his horses got into the young corn in unfenced fields, we had to ask him to put them up. It was my old-fashioned father that grumbled most. He told Hawgie he didn't like livestock running helter-skelter, that he had never seen such farming, and for him to keep his horses out of his meadow. So we saw to it that Hawgie had a fence for his horses. Hawgie saw two stacks of old hay in my meadow that he took a liking to. Said it would be good horse feed and I let him haul them out so I could use the old foundations for the new hay that would soon be ready to mow.

Then came July Fourth and the great celebration of our Country's Independence in Whetstone. Platforms were not big enough to hold the dancers. They roped off the streets under Hawgie Cawhorn's supervision and had as many as twenty dancing sets, eight dancers to the set, all going to the same old-time music and it was here that people admired old Hawgie for his dancing and for his endurance.

Hawgie Cawhorn called all night July third. All day July Fourth and all night of July Fourth. The only times he rested was when he danced with his Gracie. Then Hawgie would jump up and crack his heels together three times, something not any other dancer could do. Not one of the dancers in their teens and twenties could do it and Hawgie was thirty-nine years old. Hawgie did take a little time out when they changed the old-time bands, for musicians got tired but the dancers didn't. Then Hawgie made for drink and refreshments. It was here that everybody in Whetstone County knew Hawgie Cawhorn. I wondered how he could dance and call like that when he couldn't carry a pole of wood, set tobacco or hoe corn. Dave Whitten said he saw the sparks fly from Hawgie's big hands when he clapped time with the music.

It was after this big dance, sometime in August, when every man and his wife on Lost Creek took chicken to fry, plenty to eat, climbed to Seaton Ridge for the big fox hunt. Hawgie led his fourteen hounds, and six half-grown hound pups trailed behind while Gracie carried a few skillets but not any grub. This was a night up against the stars where we could look out over Big Lost Creek and the ridges and ranges below. There were about forty of us men and more women, for we'd brought our wives and children. Cousin Penny and his sawmill men were there. They were the men who brought the majority of long, lean hungry hounds.

Cousin Penny, Beany-Eye Smith, Red Brooks, Check Batson and I built three big fires so all the women could get around and cook. And while we did this, Hawgie and the other fox hunters walked out on the ridge and turned two starters loose. The fox must have crossed the ridge, for the two starters chased it by sight, then all the hunters turned their hounds loose and the chase was on. I never heard a chase like that one. Hawgie walked back where the women were cooking and they let the chicken burn in the skillets while he hollered, laughed and clapped his hands and called out his hounds by name and said: "Listen, they're leadin' that chase. I've got the secret about hounds. I've worked my secret on 'em tonight."

Cousin Penny laughed, too, while Hawgie bragged on his hounds. When his Crowder lost the lead, Hawgie stopped bragging. But when Crowder regained the lead, Hawgie jumped up and cracked his heels together three times. Not until the hounds chased the fox so far we couldn't hear their barking, did we eat. It was a good meal even if the fried chicken was burned a little. We ate and talked and laughed up on Seaton Ridge against the stars. I didn't know there was so much fun in the world as when farmers, timber cutters and neighbors got together for a big meal and listened to the hounds. I could see what had changed Cousin Penny's philosophy from that of hard work to that of fun and frolic. Putting the fun before the work. It was all right. I wondered where my wife Deanems and I had been all our sixteen years of married life! This life that Hawgie Cawhorn lived and loved was intoxicating. One got drunk until he reeled on it up where the air was light and thin, where the pine tops bowed to the wind.

When the hounds were bringing back the fox, the music of their barking was sweet in my ears. Old Hawgie stood beside me with a drumstick in each hand. He said: "Come with me, Shan. I want to show you something you've never seen or heard before."

I followed Hawgie to Seven White Oaks just in time to see Hot Foot, that I'd seen many times before when he came under the plum tree at the edge of my yard. His tail wasn't floating on the wind now. It was almost dragging the ground, for a hundred or more hounds were not two hundred yards behind him and I saw them too, every kind, color and description of hound, with all different-sounding barks, come pouring from the tall timber after Hot Foot.

"Ain't it wonderful," Hawgie said as he pulled a bottle from his pocket and held it to his lips. Then he handed the bottle to me. "Take a swig of that and it will lift you up to heaven and make the barking sweeter than you've ever heard."

If anybody had ever told me the night I was locking my henhouse door against Hawgie Cawhorn that I would be on Seaton Ridge fox hunting and tipping the bottle with him, I would have called that person crazy. I found myself going the way of Cousin Penny Shelton and all his lumberjacks and all our neighbors on Big Lost Creek. I was getting under the spell of the hound-dog music, the highlands and the stars. Every time we passed the long horse-quart it seemed that I got up nearer the sky and the hound-dog music was closer and sweeter and I didn't think Cousin Penny was wrong at all. I thought he had changed things for the better and this was the life.

"You're my friend, Shan, I know it," Hawgie said. "When men tip the horse-quart together nothin' ever will come between 'em. And since you don't fox hunt, I'll tell you my secret. You don't have hounds, see, to run against my hounds. Not even Penny Shelton, best friend I ever had and one of the best fellers on earth knows my secret. Hear that old Crowder leading that pack, don't you!"

"Yes," I said, listening to a hound with a booming voice.

"That old hound used to follow us around in the woods," Hawgie explained. "Wasn't worth powder and lead to kill him. Couldn't run a fox one circle and not a hunter here would look at 'im. Well I tried my secret on him. I knowed if it worked on him, it would work on any dog. And he, and all my other thirteen hounds, have the secret, tonight. You see what old Crowder's adoin' too!

"I feed my hounds gunpowder just before a chase," Hawgie laughed with his booming voice, slapped me on the back with his big hand, "and, brother, how it works; I give old Crowder three tablespoons full. That's why he's running so. I give the others less. See I give a different one the biggest dose every night. He's the lad that brings home the bacon! Hell's fire, when I give old Crowder that powder the first night, he come around the fire like he'd allus done and all of a sudden he got hot and took off up the hill and jumped a 'leven-rail fence and was off into the chase and outran every dog. Gunpowder, boy," Hawgie laughed again, "that's the secret. That's what it takes to make a hound get up and go. And here's what it takes to make me get up and go!"

Hawgie tipped and I tipped and the music got sweeter.

"Hope, Shan, you have a lovin' wife, so if you get hounds all will be well with you," Hawgie said. "My first two wives were as good to work and as nice a wimmen as you ever saw, but neither one wanted me to bring a hound on the place. Think they were jealous of my hounds, and see where they are today. They don't have Old Hawgie. Boy, right out there at that fire, and I can't help it if she is an outland woman—got her in Iowa when I was in service—is as fine a little woman as she is pretty and good to work. She loves my hounds same as I do! Boy, I've settled down for life!"

We stayed on Seaton Ridge until the chickens started crowing for four o'clock. That was the time the hounds put old Hot Foot in the cliff. What a night! We ate, laughed, talked and walked the ridge and listened to the hounds and the wind and reached up for the stars and grabbed for the great puffs of good-to-breathe pine-scented August wind. That was the night of all nights and just the beginning of what was to come.

When Hawgie moved to Big Lost Creek it was April 1947. This was the year we got to know Hawgie and his wife and hounds and we got to know each other better. We and our wives and children got to know our farms better, especially the high-land parts, up where the foxes lived in the cliffs. We got to know the fox paths and the foxhounds' barks, even the tone of each hunter's horn. We let the fertile valley take care of itself. Weeds often got high in the corn and the tobacco. Worms feasted on the broad burley leaves.

In 1948, Old Hawgie was still a Government farmer. And not only Cousin Penny and his sawmill crew helped Hawgie when he needed help, but Check Batson, Old Gore and I helped him in the wet season set his tobacco. We let our work go to help him. This man who had changed our lives from one of lay-up-for-the-rainy-day to one of fun and frolic. We didn't know where it was going to end and we didn't care. Why should we care? was the way we felt about it. We lived only once somewhere on this upheavaled earth and why not live it to the fullest? Why not reach up for a star? Or, out for a good clean puff of pine-scented wind in August?

So we went through 1948 trying to get the stiffness out of our knees that we'd accumulated over the years when we stooped to set tobacco in the long rows. We got that out dancing. And our hearing was much improved too. We listened more carefully to the music of the fiddle, guitar and the barking hounds than to a dinner bell or the clank of the plow against the rocks and roots or the ting-ting of a little hoe against the weeds and dirt. And our way of life started spreading to other hilltops and hollows on beyond us. Hard telling how far it would have gone if it hadn't been for a little man, Government man he was, that come up to Hawgie's shack with some kind of a funny report. Something about "specifications." Hawgie had failed to produce enough of something. Maybe enough eggs from the chickens, for the foxes feasted from our hens but we didn't care.

Hawgie wasn't any longer a Government farmer and getting his ninety a month. But what Hawgie didn't have, we had for him. Every farmer but my old-fashioned father had something for Hawgie too. We didn't lock our henhouses. We were sorry we'd ever been so foolish as to think of doing that, and we never let Hawgie know these thoughts we'd once had.

"They can have the school," Hawgie said as he drove his team into my field to get another haystack. "I don't like this Government way of doing things nohow. Too much paper stuff. I've got a idear that will make that farming school look sick. Let me tell you!"

"All right," I said.

"Old boy, I thought this one up," Hawgie told me. "You ask your Cousin Penny. You know where Middle Fork divides into right and left forks above my shack! Right there could be made one of the prettiest little lakes in these mountains. Could dam the water up there for two miles and cover this thirty acres of ground and have boats on it and charge people to come and fish. And that's just what Penny is agoin' to do!"

"Will Cousin Penny do that?"

"Will he do it?" Hawgie shouted. "He's sawing his last lumber with that mill now. It's poplar lumber for boats and ash lumber for oars. Oak lumber fer little houses around the lake. Going to sell his mill. Already contracted for it. Going to put his crew up in Left Fork and cut down every tree that will be in the way of the boats. Going to make a paradise up there and I'm goin' to run that paradise. That will beat this Government farming."

I was old-fashioned enough to wonder how Cousin Penny was

going to do it. All he had ever done was run a sawmill. What would he do after he sold his mill? I thought it might just be another one of Cousin Penny's dreams.

But it wasn't a dream. Two big bulldozers moved in and they hewed down the sides of the mountain and built a dam. Not ten or fifteen feet high—that was not enough to back the water to the springs in the upper end of Left Fork—it had to go twenty-five feet high and Cousin Penny's sawmill and all his equipment were sold to pay for the lake. Then Cousin Penny and his sawmill crew made boats while the lake filled with water as blue as the sky.

Cawhorn Lake, they called it. It was something to see. Cousin Penny got the State's Fish and Game Commission to stock it with fish. This was in the spring of 1949, while Penny and his sawmill crew made boats and a dozen little summer houses.

Whether there were fish big enough to bite or not, Hawgie and Cousin Penny, through the Fox Hunters Association, spread the news about the paradise for fishing on the Left Fork of Middle Fork of Big Lost Creek and the people came in multitudes. There were not houses enough to accommodate them and Cousin Penny and his sawmill crew built more. They rented them for good prices and Hawgie rowed over the lake that bore his name during the day and fox hunted at night. When Deanems and I went with him and Gracie to the far end of the lake one Sunday, Hawgie told us that he had reached the apex of happiness.

Cawhorn Lake was a beautiful body of water. It was something to see the bright blue water splash over the spillway. Hawgie would laugh and tell the lake guests about his once being a Government farmer as he rowed them over the blue placid water, wearing a big bow tie on his long neck beneath his Adam's apple and cracking together his fine set of natural-looking false teeth, a present from Uncle Sam when he was overseas in service. Hundreds of us rode on moonlit nights over this lake. After we heard the soft strumming of a guitar and the magic of the mountain fiddle.

The summer passed and September came bringing the showers of leaves that fell like drops of golden rain onto the twenty-three little houses where tired fox hunters had come to spend their summers.

On an afternoon in mid-September, the sky darkened and jagged streaks of lightning knifed the muddy-colored clouds. All the boats went in for mooring and the lake dwellers went into their little summer abodes. Old Hawgie went home to Gracie, his boys and his hounds. Cousin Penny went home in his truck. He lived at Centerville, just a mile across the lowest hill from Big Lost Creek.

Just as I got home the downpour started. We'd had them on Big Lost Creek before. One had once covered Big Lost Creek from hill to hill. This one was that sort of rain, for I saw big yellow streams of water coming down the steep slopes into the narrow valley. Soon the water was up under our floor. I watched the stream rise between the quick lightning flashes. By midnight it had subsided and the sky was clear but Lost Creek was wilder than I'd ever seen it. It was out-of-banks, running wildly over my meadows from hill to hill.

The following morning the sky was clear and bright. The mild September wind rustled the brown leaves on the tough-butted white oaks along the cliffs. Big Lost Creek was running within its banks. I was standing on the porch, inhaling the fresh morning wind when I saw Check Batson come around the bend as fast as his legs would carry him. He ran up the walk to the porch. There was a wild look on his face.

"The dam went out last night," he grunted for he was short of breath. "Got poor Old Hawgie, his family and his hounds."

I was stunned. Deanems came running to the porch.

"Hawgie, his family and hounds are lost," Check repeated, wiping tears from his eyes with a red bandanna. "Penny Shelton and Red Brooks have organized a searching party. They're huntin' for 'em now. Dam must've broken loose all at once, for there's not a foundation rock left of that shack. Swept Middle Fork clean as a pawpaw whistle. Swept Big Lost Creek below Middle Fork clean too."

"Let's go, Deanems, and hunt for Hawgie and his family," I said.

Deanems said softly as we followed Check down the walk, "This place won't be the same without Hawgie!"

As we waded through the mud down the Big Lost Creek road behind Check, splashing it high on our legs, we talked about Hawgie Cawhorn. We wondered if the lake had swept them on to Big River. If it had, we knew that they would be hard to find. Might find Hawgie miles down the river after seven days floating with his eyes open to the sun and a big smile on his lips. We talked about why a man like Hawgie should have to go, one who had brought new life and joy to us, when the few others, the work-hard-and-lay-up-for-a-rainy-day people, unnoticed and unknown in our community, had gone unscathed in this great catastrophe. It wasn't fair!

We talked until we got out of breath, for our fast walking had increased into running. We were running to join the searching party and to find Hawgie and his family if we could. Even find his hounds.

Byrne's Point is a rocky finger extending from Seaton Ridge into Big Lost Creek valley. Here, the road makes a sharp turn around the cliffs. I was watching Check, running through the mud, slinging it from his heels and splattering over his back as he started around this turn. All at once he threw up both hands, made some sort of a funny noise and stopped suddenly. When I reached Check standing there still as a tree, I saw what had happened to him.

Hawgie Cawhorn was scaling down the bank into the road with his seven hounds fastened to each big chain. Check had heard his children up in the brush and had looked up and had seen Hawgie coming. For his wife and children and the pups were behind in the brush and briers as they were making their way down from the cliffs. The boys were crying and the puppies were whining as the briers stuck them.

"Where are you goin', boys?" Hawgie asked.

"Don't you know Cousin Penny and Red Brooks have a searching party hunting for you and your family," I said, my voice trembling. "Gee, it's great to see you alive! Dam broke last night, not a foundation rock left of your shack!"

"Hear that, Gracie," Hawgie shouted up the hill. "You didn't want to go with me last night. Said it looked too much like rain! Now you see who was right. You can't go wrong by fox huntin'."

Then Hawgie laughed like he did when he rode on Cousin Penny's truck up Middle Fork that day when he was talking to Beany-Eye Smith.

"Oh, Hawgie, I can't believe it," Deanems grunted when she came running up, with her legs mud-splattered to her knees. Gracie came down the bank into the road holding her son's hands.

"How lucky we are, Hawgie," Gracie said. "But where will we go now?"

Twenty-three shacks up there above where the lake used to be," Hawgie told her. "We'll have our choice. Don't worry just so we're alive and have our hounds!"

"Fox huntin' up on the high places among the stars is the safest thing in the world," he told us while we calmed ourselves by looking at Hawgie Cawhorn and his family. "Go tell Penny and Red and their searching party to look in the best shack up there and they'll find the Cawhorns."

Then Hawgie laughed until his laughter hit the cliffs and came back to us.

The War and Cousin Lum

"IT'S about time," says Pa, "for Lum to be rolling in here. Rabbits getting ripe. Hills turning brown. You know that's the time Lum gets in here. Gets here about the time corn is cut, taters dug, and the lassies made. The time when wood is cut for the winter and ricked to dry. All Lum wants to do is hunt, you know." Pa is sitting on the chop-block. He is whittling a stick of rich pine kindling with a barlow knife. Pa looks to the brown hills as he whittles. He sees the hills where the saw-brier leaves are turning from green to brown, red, yellow and light yellow. He sees the hills where the poplar is turning, the red oak, the chestnut oak, the pawpaw, sassafras, hickory and the beech. It's time for rabbits to be getting ripe after the little bit of frost we've had on the Kentucky hills. It is time for Lum to round in for a rabbit hunt.

"Your cousin Lum," says Pa, "is a rounder. I guess he gets it from the Saddlers—that going places on freight trains. Never rides a passenger train when he's got the money. That's Lum."

"Takes it after the Powderdays," says Mom, picking up chips and putting them in her apron. "That's who he takes it after. Look at his daddy before him. Rode freight trains over the country. Went off and left his family on sufferance. If he hadn't been in the war and got a little pension I don't know what the family would a done. Lum takes after his own Pa—Jake Powderday. He don't take his running around from the Saddlers. He takes it from the Powderdays." Mom picks up the hickory and oak chips and puts them in her apron. A blue smoke—thin as the air—swirls from the kitchen flue. The martins chatter from the doors of their box.

"It's time for Lum," says Pa, "when the martins start getting ready to go south. It's time for Lum to pop in. Rabbits ripe. And the leaves turned brown." Pa looks at the brown Kentucky hills where the rabbits hide under the tufts of broomsage and fresh new heaps of fallen leaves.

Cousin Lum is a tall man with eyes blue as an April Kentucky sky. His hair is a dirty brown, the color of dying broomsage. His legs—there was never another pair like them in Kentucky—long and straight as two broomsticks. His feet big as two fire shovels—plenty big enough to hold his body on the ground. His hips are about as big as your hands spread out and you can nearly span him with your hands at the waist. "Always looks like he's never had enough to eat," says Pa, "when you look at Lum's waist." But it's a sight to watch that man put away grub. But his shoulders—his big broad shoulders—looked like a one-horse road-scraper. And his eyes that looked steadily at one—stout enough to look a hole through you! His gray eyes that looked like a hawk's eyes and his long nose on his face looked like a hawk's bill.

"Come here, Sall," says Pa, "look coming yander. It's Lum shore as God made little green apples. I just felt like he's coming. Shore enough he's coming." And Mom looks over on the pasture hill at Cousin Lum. He's coming down the path carrying a little bundle under his arm wrapped in a newspaper. "Come as usual," says Pa, "come from Cincinnati on a freight train."

"Only way he ever comes," says Mom, "that's the way the Powderdays go places. Ride freight trains. W'y Lum never did come to this house any other way. He's been come every year to rabbit hunt since he was fourteen years old. Come here and got a taste of it that time with Jake. He's been back every year. You know he run off from school and come here to hunt for two years while he was in the school-law and got poor old Jake fined."

"Funny," says Pa, "comes back to us here among the hills after he's been raised up in town. Raised in Cincinnati. Got a taste of the gun and dog and he comes back every fall to hunt with us soon as the leaves turn and rabbits get right. God, he's a shot too. Kills rabbits a setting. Shoots 'em right there. He's got a eye like a hawk or a buzzard." Lum walks down the hill on the longest pair of legs in Kentucky—his overalls twisting around them. Too much bluedrillings wrapped around his pipe-stem legs. His shoulders are swinging as he walks and his arms dangle at the hip-seams of his overalls. "Lord, that's Lum all right," says Pa. "I just begin to wonder if my eyes fooled me."

"Yes," says Mom, "it will be rabbits now. Rabbits and birds, possums, coons, groundhogs and squirrels. That's all you'll do now and the corn will be left to stand in the shock and the taters left dug in the field. Won't be another thing done after Lum gets here but hunt, cook and eat. I'll even have to pick up chips to use in the cookstove. You won't have time to cut a stick of stovewood."

"Howdy, Lum," says Pa, reaching his brown hand to my tall Cousin Lum. "W'y howdy, Uncle Mick," says Lum. "You little rascal, how are you any way?" says Lum, swinging Pa around and around over the chips.

"Ain't doing much good," says Pa. "Never do any good until I get me a bait of rabbits in my craw." And Pa laughs and Lum laughs and they go around and around.

"How are you Aunt Sall?" says Lum to Mom, stopping long enough to reach Mom his hand.

"Oh pretty good," says Mom, handing him her right hand, using her left to hold her apron filled with chips.

"We're needing rabbits around here," says Pa. "Glad you've come, Lum. You know I don't get any fun going out and killing them by myself. I like to hunt with somebody."

"That's right," says Lum, I like to hunt with somebody too. I like to hunt with you, Uncle Mick. You know I like my Pa's people. Since I got to coming back among them—w'y I've had a fine time. I don't like Cincinnati—only her freight trains that takes me places and bring me back to these hills. The hills are home to me. I've never lived among them but Pa did. Like a rabbit, blood is. Wherever you jump a rabbit it circles back there. Wherever you stir up blood—it will go back there." And Cousin Lum takes Pa by the arm. They go in the house talking.

Mom says to me: "Son, I hope you don't take to the woods like the rest of the Powderdays with a old gun and dog. It's just in their blood to hunt and kill and drink licker. I've never seen a family like 'em. I've wished a thousand times I'd never got mixed up in it. Here I am now with a nest of little youngins mixed up with a den of Republicans, boozers and hunters. W'y your Pa just acts like a wild man ever time Lum comes. Knows just when he's going to round in. Fools around out there in that wood yard and waits for him on the very day he comes. He won't do another thing all the time Lum is here but eat and hunt." Mom walks down the path, under the poplar tree in our kitchen-yard that has a dead top. She walks with her apron filled with chips till it is big as a pillow. Pa and Lum have gone into the house. We can hear them laughing in the house. "W'y Lum," says Pa, "I never tried to get that rabbit. I give you a chance to get it. You was a strip of a boy then. W'y don't you know I could have knocked its trotters easy as eating a piece of pie."

And Lum bends to his knees laughing. He says: "W'y Uncle Mick, you know I always thought I just beat you to that shot—and you got scared and shot too soon." And Cousin Lum bends over and laughs again. When he bends over Pa slaps him on the seat of the pants.

"Guess they're drinking a little aready," says Mom. "If they're not now they soon will be; you can mark my word."

"Now," says Pa, "we'll just go right out this evening and I'll show you how to bring down cottontails. I'll show you who gets the rabbits, young man, and who don't. We'll let Shan go along and pack the rabbits in a coffee sack. Gives us a better chance to shoot. We don't want a lot of rabbits hung to us—will be in our way shooting."

"Suits me just fine," says Cousin Lum. "I believe I can put the cat on you, Uncle Mick. I believe I got that rabbit first that time that you said you let me kill it because I was just a boy. Ah, Uncle, I know you!" And Cousin Lum laughs and laughs and Pa laughs too.

"Oh, Shan, come here!" says Pa. "Bring a coffee sack and come here."

I go get the coffee sack from the smokehouse. And I think to myself: "It's not fair Pa won't let me take a gun out to the woods and hunt. I am nearly ten years old. He makes me carry the rabbits. He gets to do all the shooting. Cousin Lum is just twenty. He's been hunting with Pa for six years. I have to go and carry the rabbits and birds." I wipe the tears from my eyes as I go to the smokehouse.

Mom says: "Young man, you are another chip off the old block. You quit that snubbing right now. You're not going out there with a gun and shoot somebody or get shot. That's Powderday in you. Love a gun from the time you can crawl." I go on to the smokehouse and get the coffee sack. It is a sack I used gathering dry dead leaves for the fattening-hog pen.

"Wait till I get old hulda," says Pa. And he reaches up on the joist in our front room and takes down our single-barrel Columbia shotgun that does not have a sight—the barrel is battered and worn thin. Three generations have hunted with this old family single-barrel. Pa lifts the trigger guard from over the nail where it is hooked and the barrel-tip from over another nail where it rests. "This is the old hulda that has brought 'em down among the rocks, the brush and the cliffs," says Pa. "You got it on me with that double-barrel there. You get two shots to my one."

"That's the worst-looking old gun I ever saw," says Cousin Lum. And he laughs and Pa laughs.

"I strained my gun once, Lum," says Pa.

"How'd you do that, Uncle Mick?" says Lum.

And Pa says: "I shot it up hill at a rabbit and it went out of its way to get it." And Pa bends over, laughing and slapping his knees with his small brown hard hands. And Cousin Lum laughs and laughs and slaps Pa on the seat of the pants.

We walk out of the house. The October sun is golden as a rain-washed sandrock in the sky. The leaves are mellow on the trees as ripe pumpkins and there is the smell of goldenrod and wild grapes in the wind—the smell of ripe corn and dying flowers—the sweet smells of autumn in the wind. Pa has his battered single-barrel across his shoulder. I have a coffee sack across my shoulder. Cousin Lum has the prettiest little twelve-gauge double-barrel across his shoulder. "How'd you bring that double-barrel?" says Pa. "Did you bring it wrapped in that newspaper?"

"Yes," says Cousin Lum, "brought it along wrapped in my duds." We walk out into the yard.

Pa says: "Heh Rags. Heh Scout. Heh boys! Heh! Heh! Heh!"

Rags is a red hound-dog with ears that come down and lap over the tip of his long nose. He has black patches on his sides the shape of a cucumber. He comes running up to us barking his "wow-wow-wow" and snuffing when he sees our guns. He knows Pa and Cousin Lum are going hunting. Rags is pleased. He smells of Cousin Lum's legs and whines. He leaps upon Pa and barks and flaps his long thin ears. "Good blood in that hound-dog," says Cousin Lum. He rubs Rags' head and feels the little knot on the back of his head. "He's got that knot on his head too, Uncle Mick," says Cousin Lum.

"W'y," says Pa, "do you think I'd ever take a hound-pup along to raise that didn't have that on the back of his head? Never any account unless they have that knot. That's the hunting stock of hound-dogs that have that knot back there. Wait till you see Scout." And Pa calls again: "Heh Scout! Heh Scout! Heh boy! Heh! Heh!"

Scout comes from behind the smokehouse barking. He is a tall long-legged hound, white with blue specks on his flanks. "Now you talk about your dogs," says Pa, "right here he is, Lum. He was the little pup that trailed us last year when we took that hunt. You ought to watch him drive a rabbit now. He can really bring them around."

Scout and Rags start barking as we walk toward the barn. They know we are going rabbit hunting. They are glad to go. "Two dogs," says Pa, "that you don't have to call and coax along.

Have to chain them to get them out of the woods." Pa takes a chew of tobacco. He takes a chew of Honest-Scrap and says: "Have some, Lum."

"Don't chew," says Lum.

"Take a chew," says Pa, "and spit a little ambear in my eyes so I can see clear. Can't see clear as I ought to." Lum takes a chew of scrap with his thumb and index finger. He puts it in his mouth —munches the fine black shavings of scrap tobacco. Then he says: "Ready, Uncle Mick." He squirts a bright sluice in Pa's eye. Pa flinches and looks down at the ground. "Wait a minute," says Lum, "you're like a blooded horse prancing around. I got to get the other eye." Pa holds still. A bright sluice into Pa's other eye. Pa wipes the ambear from around his eyes with his dirty leaf-colored handkerchief. "Now," says Pa, "I can see a bug on a black oak at fifty yards."

"Do you want the bottom side of the hill or the top side?" says Pa.

"Makes no difference to me," says Cousin Lum. "I can drop them anyplace." "If I jump them at the bottom of the hill you need not worry—you'll never get a shot at them," says Pa. "I'll have them before they top the hill. I tell you, Uncle Mick, I never miss. Now we kill them setting too, don't we?"

"Suits me," says Pa, "just anyway to kill them. W'y they are skinning my fruit trees. It always looks like we're going to have to move out and let the rabbits move in until you come around." Pa laughs and laughs and Cousin Lum laughs. The October wind laughs too in the old corn stubbles and the sourwood sprouts. The wind laughs in the dewberry briars and the blackberry vines. It laughs and wheezes like it's got the asthma. "Pow," and Pa walks up and picks up a kicking rabbit. "One for the sack," says Pa. "You said kill 'em a setting, didn't you?"

"Yes," says Cousin Lum.

"Not my way a hunting," says Pa, "but I'll hunt that way with you, Lum. I used to beat your Pap for pastime. Oh it would nearly kill old Jake when I got more rabbits and birds than he did."

"Pow," and Cousin Lum walks up and gets the rabbit—kicking

by a tuft of broomsage. Its brown wool fluffy to the October wind and the brown hairs on its back the color of oak leaf now drifting to the ground. Blood running from its ribs the color of the frostbitten sourwood leaves. "One apiece," says Cousin Lum.

I do hate to walk along and carry the sack. I say to Pa: "Looks like you and Cousin Lum could carry your own rabbits."

"That used to be my job," says Pa, "before I got big enough to hunt with a gun. That is your job before you get big enough to hunt with a gun. Son, the old man used to make me step with a coffee sack filled with rabbits. He used to didn't hunt so much but when he did hunt he went into it right. Never let the sun set on him on a short winter day that he didn't have a two-bushel sack filled to the drawstring with rabbits. Now you come along with that sack."

The sun above us in the high October sky. Red around the sun and the leaves floating to the earth. A lazy wind searching the dead weeds—maybe telling the rabbits to get up and move. Mick Powderday and his nephew Lum Powderday, a long-legged city-dude from Cincinnati, was right after them. Cousin Lum from Cincinnati with Kentucky hill blood in his veins—the love of the Powderdays to hunt in his blood—their love to kill, to fight, to drink—their love of life, the beauty of the hills in autumn and the great silent rocks, the leafless trees and the music of the barking hound-dogs and the pow-pows of the guns. That is the music that a Powderday loves—a Powderday of the old breed—and he loves, if there is love in his blood for anything—he loves the great hills that shoulder to his autumn skies that float above his fields and his woods.

"Pow," and Pa walks over and picks up a cottontail. "Another one for the sack," says Pa. "Come and get it, Son." I put the kicking rabbit in the sack. I see the flow of red blood from its flank. I see it bend its pretty neck and its bullet-torn ears drop down—it kicks its leg. It is silent. It is dead. It is with two more rabbits that once ran over this hill—found the green sprigs of clover after frost has fallen—found the scattered grains of corn the crow didn't find. Now these rabbits are dead—dead to the earth, the great fields they loved and the fields we love—the hills, the brier patches, the timber and the skies. They cannot rove over these hills at night or day—play with their mates. They are dead—silent as their big clay silent hills.

"Pow," and the rabbit runs upon the bank and falls. "I told you," says Cousin Lum "that no rabbit will ever get up the hill to you, Uncle Mick." And I go up on the hill and pick up the kicking rabbit and put it in the sack. I do not feel as sorry for it as I did the first one I saw die. "They are to be killed," I make myself think.

"And," says Pa, " never will a rabbit get down the hill to you if I see him first." And Pa eyes every little sprig of broomsage and every little nest of briers.

"Wow-wow-wow," barks Scout. He leaps out of the brush.

"Got him a going," says Pa. "Watch for it. It'll run out the hill there, turn over on the pint and then come back." Rags joins in the chase. "Listen to that music," says Pa, "don't make any sweeter music do they? W'y it's prettier than fiddle music." And it is wow-wow—yow-yow—one in the lead and then the other—following the track and never a lose of the track.

"Pow," and Lum walks up the hill. "Pow,"and Lum walks over by a stump. "Well, Uncle," says Cousin Lum, "got two that time. Got one here by the stump. Got the one the dogs was bringing around. Got it on you now."

"Luck," says Pa as the dogs run up to where Cousin Lum shot the rabbit. They whiff the blood and lick the leaves where the rabbit has bled on them—they curl their tails and walk on into the brush, whiffing as they go. Lum reaches me two rabbits and I put them in the sack. Lum reloads his double-barrel—He breaks down the barrel, blows out the smoke and puts in two nice brass-butted shells and mashes the barrel down with a click. Zoom-zoom-zoom. Out of the brush the covey flies—wings spread like gray sails and they wheeze like bullets out of the brush. "Pow-pow." Two birds flutter down to the earth. "Pow," and Pa's gun speaks as the covey flies over Pa's head. "Three of 'em" says Pa. "Not bad for one shot do you think?"

"He's a hard old boy to beat," says Cousin Lum to me. "I tell you your Pa hates to let me beat him. I'm going to put the cat on him today. He's got that old single-barrel. You watch me put it on him before the day is over. He'll be wanting more ambear spit in his eyes."

I hear the guns like thunder. It is all afternoon. When a gun "pows" something falls. It is first Pa's gun and then it is Cousin Lum's. And I put the game in the sack. Pa is first ahead and then Cousin Lum. The wind blows through the brush and whistles lonesome like. The scattered quails call to one another. The rabbits do not call at all—they do not make a noise. They run for life before the powerful hounds and the truthful hounds. It is hard for a rabbit to get away. The sun is going down in the sky now. The day is nearly over and night will soon come with darkness and the hunters cannot shoot the rabbits. They will get out on the hill and play in the moonlight—just mindful of the fox, the mink, the polecat and the possum—it is the hunters' guns by day and war of their neighbors at night.

"Pow," and Pa walks up the hill. "Pow," and Cousin Lum walks up the hill. "I got him," says Lum.

"Say," says Pa, "take a chew of this Honest-Scrap and put a little ambear in my eyes."

"Say, Uncle Mick," says cousin Lum, "you know that tobacco made me about half sick. You'll just have to hunt the rest of the day without it in your eyes. Day is nearly gone anyway."

And Pa says: "My luck is going. I can't see as clear as I ought to see." And I can barely walk with the sack of thirty-one rabbits and eleven birds.

"Pa," I says, "I can't carry this load any farther. You'll just have to take it."

"What do you say," says Cousin Lum, "that we go in? Aunt Sall won't know what to do with all these rabbits anyway and the dogs will be too tired to possum hunt tonight. Let's quit for today."

"Yes," says Pa, "since you got a rabbit and a bird on me—then you want to quit. Well, I put it on you the first five years. I guess you can beat me once." And Pa looks at the brown hills before him, the sinking sun. Pa puts his hand up and wipes the sweat from his high brown brow.

"To tell you the truth," says Cousin Lum to Pa, "I wanted to come and take this hunt with you. It might be a long time before I get to come back and take another hunt with you, Uncle Mick."

"Why," says Pa, "Lum, are you talking like that? I ain't made you mad, have I? Just tried my damndest to beat you is all that I have done. You know that has always been a old game in this family, Lum, and you mustn't get mad because I come nigh as a pea putting the cat on you. Just a little more ambear and I would. You know my eyes ain't clear as they used to be."

"No," says Cousin Lum, "Uncle Mick—it ain't that. I am going to take a bigger hunt. You see that hawk up there in the sky, don't you?"

And Pa says, "Yes, I do, Lum."

"Well," says Cousin Lum, "I'm going to be flying around like that hawk in a short time. I am going to join the Army and get in the air service."

"Fly a airship?" says Pa.

"Yes," says Cousin Lum. "War is coming to this country and I am going to join. We are going to be in it. I am going to enlist."

"I'll be dogged," says Pa, "but I guess if I was a young man I'd be right in it." We walk out the ridge—past the old cornfields, the saw-brier clusters that have caught great armloads of leaves, the black-berry briers and the thickets of sourwood sprouts.

I carry the heavy sack of rabbits back of the smokehouse. Blood has seeped through the sack and stained it in big dark reddish circles. There is a nail on the back of the smokehouse where we hook the leader of a rabbit's hind leg and then we start jerking his fur down toward his head—jerking off pieces of his brittle hide. Jerk the fur off down to his head and then we cut off the head and take out the entrails and fling them on the ground. The hound-dogs come around and eat the best parts we throw away of the rabbits. They lap up the blood with the long clean tongues. "Sall," says Pa, "Lum is going to leave us. He's going to jine Uncle Sam. Going to fly a airship and get in the war."

"What makes you want to do that?" says Mom. And then she

says, "Guess I'd be doing the same thing if I was a man and was a young man."

And Lum says: "I've done joined. Just waiting for them to call me. No backing out now. I am in the Army. I think I'll like it better than I do living in town. It's nearly killed Pa living down there. But you know Ma—she likes it and won't live any place else."

"That's the way of a woman," says Pa.

We skin the rabbits. Pa and Cousin Lum skin them and I help. We put them in crocks of salt water to soak overnight. Mom picks the feathers from the birds. She has a teakettle of hot water she scalds them in and then she peels off their feathers and throws the naked birds into a crock. "We'll have plenty of rabbits and birds and possums while you are here," says Pa. "I believe you like possum baked with sweet-taters. We got plenty of sweet-taters and just whatever you say you want to eat we'll have it—even to groundhogs," says Pa and Pa laughs and laughs. The wind laughs in the hickory leaves back of the porch and the red-brownish leaves fall to the earth.

In the morning Pa goes to the bed to wake Lum. He says: "Lum, you'd better roll out'n that bed. Don't you know it's gettin-up time at this man's house? It's four o'clock, and breakfast will soon be put on the table." Pa hollers and hollers at Cousin Lum. Cousin Lum does not answer. Pa says: "Get me some cold water and I'll bring that Jasper out'n the bed." He gets a cup of cold water and walks in Cousin Lum's room.

"He's gone," says Pa, "slipped out at night. Just like Brother Jake used to be for the world. He's gone—slipped out last night. W'y he never stayed to eat any rabbits or birds. Got the Army on his mind. Flying like a hawk or a buzzard. Got fighting on his mind. Just slipped out of here like he come in. He's left on a freight train."

"He's been here six times," says Mom, "and we never have knowed when he's a going to leave. I don't see any use making a big to-do over it. He's just caught a freight train back to Cincinnati. That's the way he always goes. Just blows in like a leaf—a short time here—and he blows out like a leaf. We never know when the wind is going to blow neither."

Uncle Mel come to our house. He says: "Mick, you know I saw the funniest thing the other day in Gate City. Guess you wouldn't think of who I saw in a thousand years?"

"No," says Pa.

"W'y," says Uncle Mel, "I saw Brother Jake's boy Lum."

"You did?" says Pa.

"Yes, I did," says Uncle Mel. "I thought I saw the back-of-a-head and some dirty-colored hair that looked familiar. I saw him on the train. I went up and shook his arm. He was on a train eating a biled tater. He was taking the bark off it. I says: 'Where you going, Lum?' And he turned to me and says: 'W'y it's Uncle Mel!' And then he told me he was going to Berlin to get the Kaiser. He said he was going to France to fly a warship. God, I thought first I was dreaming but it was Jake's boy Lum shore as the world and he left on that train."

Pa comes in and he says to Mom: "Lum was right. We are in the war. We have to fight in France. God, I'd like to take that trip. I'd like to jine up."

And Mom says: "That's in your blood, Mick Powderday. It's in your blood to fight and kill. Look at your father before you. Look at the men he killed. Look at you how you want to go to France and leave me with all these little children. W'y you just can't do it."

And Pa says: "Look at Joe's boys. They've gone, ain't they? Look at sister Belle's boy, Harrison? He's gone, ain't he? All the boys are going—and here I'm at home hunting and plowing."

"They are your brother's boys, too," says Mom, "not your brothers." "I know," says Pa, "but I'm just about their ages. You know I'm the eleventh child—the youngest of eleven. I'm not too old to fight in France."

We never hear from Cousin Lum. The days pass into weeks, the weeks into months and the months into years. The clouds of autumn—the great red skies of October float above woods where the rabbits play and the foxes hunt the rabbits and no man hunts the foxes. Men from America that used to hunt these woods are hunting men in France and not rabbits. The rabbits go free to play now—Pa does not hunt like he did. "Wish Lum was here," Pa says, "to take another hunt with me. Would like to know what he's got to say about the war. I'd like to put the cat on him too. I believe I could do it now." And Pa looks at the great brown autumn hills where the boys who left the hills do not return to hunt the rabbits, groundhogs, birds and possums and coons on their slopes. The winds of autumn blow over these hills so desolate and forlorn. Cousin Lum does not return to shoot the rabbits and the birds. Pa does not hunt any more. There is so much work to do—wages are so high. Manpower is so scarce. Pa does not have time to hunt. He clears more land and plants bigger crops. Pa is working at home while men are killing one another under different skies.

"I'd love to be on the other side of the pond," says Pa, "as to be here tending these hills where everything is so quiet. That's what the years bring a man and—time brings gray hairs to his head. And he can't do the things he used to do when he was a young man. Look at me now—couldn't get in the war. Couldn't get in the war because I was too old and had a family. I could outshoot half the men they have in there. Yet time will not allow me to go." And Mom says: "You are driving me crazy, Mick. You talk about the war all the time—wishing you was single. Wishing you was in the war. I wish you was in it. I wish you was right over there with Lum and Joe's boy and your sister Belle's Harrison. I wish you was all right together."

"You don't wish it any more than I do," says Pa, "just to have to stay here and see the boys all go. Have to stay here and hunt by myself. It's a dead world without the boys."

The paper says: "Lum Powderday killed in action in France." It went on and said he was shot down by an enemy plane in France. That Lum was killed in action "bravely defending his country" and so on. And then it said: "He soars with the eagles." And Pa didn't wipe a tear when he heard it read. He says: "W'y Lum'll be back here. He don't soar with no damned eagles nor hawks nor buzzards. He'll be right back here to take a hunt soon as that war is over. You can't kill old Lum. He'll be back across the seas if he has to fly his airship across them."

The wind blew across white fields and a million rabbit tracks and bird tracks on the white sheets of snow. The winter sun, a weak yellow sun, would cross the heavens and settle in the west—not molesting the deep snow that laid on the winter long and the shaggy cattle walked out in the barnlot, munched at corn-stalks and drank water where the ice was chopped through with a broadax. They slept in their stalls at night and heard the wind rattle in the barnloft of hay above their heads and through the bare chest-oak twigs on the rocks above the barn. Pa walks out to the barn. He says to himself as he forks out hay to the cattle: "I believe old Lum will get back. He'd soon die as to live. That's why I believe he'll be back."

I remember 1919. It was autumn again. The crops of 1919 were good crops on the hills—but in the valleys between the high hills, the craw-dads come out of swamp holes and pinched off the corn. We couldn't get a stand of corn. It just wormed up spinly stuff through the swamp grass and the corn on the slopes was a green heavy cloud that summer and it turned like the color of the rabbit's back—to a brown autumn wave in autumn. It was a heavy crop. I remember the great hills—autumn colored in the sun and the winds blowing the leaves from the hickory back of our smokehouse. I remember the way the saw-brier leaves turned that year, the sassafras sprouts turned on the slopes. I remember the calls of the wild geese going over the great wastes of deserted acres the old men couldn't farm while the boys were in France.

"I just feel like," says Pa, "it's not going to be long until old Lum rounds in here for a rabbit hunt. It just seems to me like it's time for him. Leaves turning and the war over. Rabbits getting ripe in the Kentucky hills. Wherever old Lum is he'll think of these hills if he can think at all."

Mom saw Lum first. She thought it was Lum. She says: "Mick, ain't that Lum coming down through the orchard there?" And Pa says: "Yes, not another man in Kentucky's got the legs Lum's got. That's Lum all right. That's Jake's boy Lum. I told you he didn't soar with no damned eagles, hawks, nor buzzards. I told you Lum would be back. He's the kind of fellow that don't give a damn and he ain't afraid of death nor anything that looks like it. That's why I said Lum will get back. That's Lum shore as the world. He's just not walking as fast as he used to walk. Guess he's been used to wings and not legs." And Pa laughs. "Lum, is it your ghost?" says Pa. "Is it your sperit or is it you?"

"It's what's left," says Lum and he reaches his hand to Mom and to me.

"Where is your uniform," says Pa, "what are you wearing that old blue-drilling for when your name has been in all the papers about the things you was doing in France?"

"I'm just tired of a uniform," says Lum, "tired of seeing so many of them. Want to feel the good old clothes again." And Lum and Pa sit down on the chop-block and begin to talk.

"How did you like the war?" says Pa. "I've just been doing everything I could to get in it. But my wife and children and the years on top of me kept me out of the war."

"You ought to have been proud of that," says Lum. "It was a poor hunt. The men I hunted—well, I liked them better than the men I hunted with. I had an old crate for a plane. It was a real old dangerous buzzard—but I brought down a few with it—waved to them good-by as they zigzagged down to the earth and went up in flames. I just didn't give a damn. Would as soon died as to have lived. I escaped some way. I am here to tell the tale—much as I want to tell. How's the rabbits—let's don't talk about the war." And Cousin Lum looked into the bright blue October air—at the brown stretch of hills.

"Rabbits are plentiful," says Pa, "I've just said if you didn't get back w'y I was going to move out and let the rabbits move in. But Rags and Scout have gone to the happy hunting ground. Somebody pizened them on fried Irish taters. Spread them all over the hills here for the hounds after somebody's killed a couple of Mort Hawkin's sheep."

Cousin Lum wipes the tears from his eyes. "And the dogs are dead," says Cousin Lum. "I hate to hear that. Funny me shedding tears for dogs and I never shed them for a man in France. When a man was killed we looked at him and said: 'You lucky son-of-a-bitch.' That's the way I felt about the whole war. Didn't know who you was killing—and you just didn't give a damn."

"What do you say," says Pa, "we go out and get a mess of rabbits? Are you too tired?"

"No," says Cousin Lum, "I brought my double-barrel along. I am ready to hunt with you. But you won't need any ambear in your eyes to beat me now."

"Why," says Pa, "ain't you the shot you used to be, Lum?"

"No," says Cousin Lum. "I'm getting tired of shooting and killing, Uncle Mick. I have been hunted like a rabbit. I have hunted man closer than I hunt the ground for rabbits."

"Get the sack, Shan," says Pa to me. "No need to bring a sack this time," says Cousin Lum. I leave the sack and walk along behind them. Lum does not walk like he used to walk with his giant road-scraper shoulders weaving with his body. His great arms hanging loose—his dirty broomsage colored hair loose to the wind.

We walk over the gap out by the barn and over the rocks into the sprout pasture where there is always a crop of rabbits. "This is the very way we went the last time," says Pa.

"Yes," says Lum, "I remember old Rags hunting out that brier patch there. I remember old Scout jumping that first rabbit the dogs brought around and I got—jumped it right over there by that stump."

"Pow," and Cousin Lum walks up the hill. "Pow," and Pa walks up the hill.

"I got him this time," says Pa. "Why do you shoot from your left shoulder instead of your right? You used to shoot from your right."

"Look at my eye," says Cousin Lum. And Pa looks at his eye. He does not speak. We didn't notice it when he walked into the woodyard. He does not have an eye that furnishes sight. It is a man-made eye of glass. "Glad I got one," says Cousin Lum. "I'm not cussing about it. Lucky to get out with one good eye to get to see these old hills again. A lot luckier than a lot of poor devils who don't have any."

We walk around the hill. The wind laughs again in the briers after these few years. Maybe it laughs at the rabbits that play and man has gone. Man is not here to kill the rabbits and to hunt for sport as man has been. Man has gone this time farther away for bigger game in bigger hunting grounds. Man has gone to hunt man and so many have not returned. Cousin Lum is back but he can't hunt like he used to hunt. The wind laughs through the dead leaves—the saw-brier leaves in old October hanging to the briers—still clinging to the stem of life that nourished them. Maybe the wind laughs for the dead dogs, Rags and Scout, that used to hunt these hills—maybe the wind laughs for the hundreds of dead rabbits that have been shot on these hills.

The wind laughs and laughs—maybe the wind laughs about the crazy war where Lum has been—who knows why the wind laughs. It just laughs and laughs.

Autumn is here—October again and the wind blows and the land is lonely. The dogs are dead and Pa has been lonely. "I tell you," says Cousin Lum, "war is not what it used to be when Grandpa fought at Cold Harbor and Gettysburg. He could see the men he was shooting at. We couldn't see the men we were shooting at. We just figured out on a piece of paper about where they were and started feeding them the hot lead. We fought in the air like a bunch of buzzards—shot each other to the earth. You wouldn't have liked that war, Uncle Mick. I'm telling you you wouldn't." And Cousin Lum pitches over the hill tangled in briers. He lies there beneath the sun of October and the wind that laughs. "Lend me a helping hand, will you, Uncle?" says Cousin Lum. "I'm afraid I can't get back unless you give me a lift."

"W'y," says Pa, "what's the matter, Lum? Any bones broke?" And Pa looks down and sees one of Lum's feet has come off. "Oh, I see," says Pa, "yes I see."

"I just lost that one," says Cousin Lum, "honest I did, Uncle Mick. Just lost that foot. Lost the toes off the other one but not my whole foot. I am so tall you know it's hard for me to hold my balance on one-half of one foot where I've been used to two good feet when I hunted over this hill before with you—with two good dogs that have gone where one of my feet and half of one of my feet have gone." Cousin Lum tries to laugh and him lying down among the briers—the sun beaming down on him from the October sky.

The wind laughing in the briers above his ears. Maybe he cannot hear as well as he used to hear after the thunder of guns. He wouldn't tell us if he could not. Pa sheds tears. He lifts Cousin Lum from the briers. Pa is a little man and he has a big load to lift big Cousin Lum back up the hill.

"Wait till I get my foot back on," says Cousin Lum, "then I'll be ready. We got to take it a little slower, Uncle Mick. I can't get around like I used to get around, remember." And we walk through the dead grass, the briers, the autumn sprouts on a Kentucky hill where the frosts of autumn have changed the color from the green of summer to the brown, gold, yellow, light-yellow and the rabbit-blood red sourwood leaves of old October.

"To tell you the truth," says Cousin Lum, "I've never been discharged from the army yet. I walked out too soon. Guess they'll get me. I don't care. When I got to this side—I thought of the ripe rabbits and October here—I thought of you, Uncle Mick, and I wanted to come back to these hills and hunt. So, I just walked out like I walked out and left you the last time without saying good-by. If they want me they can have me—all that is left of the real me. I just left six days too soon. Don't think they are going to raise much stink about that. They have my war record. Never deserted in time of battle. They'll tell you that. And I never was shot in the heel." And Cousin Lum smiles a little. He does not laugh now and Pa does not laugh.

"You can stay here with us," says Pa, "until they find you. I'll harbor you Lum. You know I'm glad to see you back even with just one eye and a half of one foot. Better than not having any eye or no foot at all."

The sun of October burns red on the sassafras sprouts and on the dust of the Powderday dead and the Powderday living. There is Powderday dust at Cold Harbor, Gettysburg, Bull Run—and there is Powderday dust sleeping in old Virginia, North Carolina and plenty of it in the hills of Kentucky where the Big Sandy River winds between the high Kentucky hills and the West Virginia hills like a pied cow-snake. There is the dead and living Powderday dust in the West Virginia hills. There is the Powderday dust in France—dust sleeping now that the wars they have known are done. That the hills now have taken back their blood for rest—a long rest. "I'm not going back and serve that six days," says Cousin Lum, "unless we have another war." And we walk around the hill among the dead weeds and the blood-tipped sourwood sprouts. We hear the wind laugh—maybe it laughs because we have returned after these few years to hunt rabbits on the rugged slope without old Rags and Scout.

King of the Hills

"POOR Black Boy," Finn said as he stood beneath the pine tree in our front yard and watched Black Boy wallowin on the pine needles. "His short hair is not black as a crow's wing like it used to be. Black Boy is gettin old. He's gettin too old to hunt.'"

The October harvest moon like a big wagon wheel rolled above the autumn-colored hills. It was one of the prettiest nights I had ever seen for the moonlight on the hills and fields was bright as day.

"Most dogs are in their graves when they get as old as Black Boy," I said. "He'll be nineteen years old tomorrow. Black Boy is older than you are."

"I know it," Finn said. "That's why I hate to see him get so old he can't get up when he lays down."

"That dog taught me to hunt," I said. "I didn't teach him."

"He taught me to hunt too," Finn said. "We ought to try somethin to make him live longer. Try somethin that will put pep in him and make him happy."

"You're right, Finn," I said as I watched Black Boy make several tries before he was able to get up from the pine needle bed and stand on his feet.

"After he gets on his feet, he's all right," Finn said. "It's just hard for him to get back on his feet after he lays down."

Now Black Boy came up to us and smelled of our pants legs. He put his nose against my hand. The soft tip of his nose rubbed against my arm as he sniffled the familiar scent of me—a scent that he had tracked in the huntin woods—a scent that he had known all his life. I rubbed Black Boy's head and petted him. After I had petted him, he walked lazily over to Finn and sniffled the scent of his hand—sniffled another old familiar scent that he had known most of his lifetime. Finn patted his head and rubbed his nose. Black Boy was so pleased that he barked to Finn.

"Watch Black Boy strut after he gets up on his feet," Finn said. "You couldn't tell that he was an old dog only by the gray hair around his mouth and on his head. And he's lost all his teeth."

There Black Boy stood between us. He was kickin the pine needles high in the air with his hind feet. As he kicked the pine needles he growled as if he were still master of the place. He looked like a small black lion except for his gray toothless mouth and his gray head. Black Boy had a big mouth, big neck and his barrel chest rested on strong forelegs that were set wide apart. His hips were narrow like a lion's hips; his tail was long but he shortened it by carryin it over his back in two bristlin curls. Black Boy had been for many years, and was still, the king of the hills. But now age was showin its marks upon him; still he had never been whipped by any dog.

Now Black Boy stopped kickin the pine needles high into the air. He just stood and growled. There wasn't anythin near for him to growl at. Maybe he wanted to hear the importance of his own growl—maybe he growled at the wind.

"You're still king of the hills, Black Boy," Finn said. "But you won't be long. Too stiff to get up after you lay down. You can't last much longer. But you need pep today. You need to have one more glorious huntin night, Black Boy."

"He needs a spring-herb tonic," I said.

"Say, that makes me think," Finn said. "Pa's got a pint of Honorable Herbs that he keeps in the barnloft for his 'cold remedy.' That ought to be good for Black Boy."

"I'm not givin Black Boy that moonshine," I said.

"It will be good for him," Finn said. "A hangover won't bother Black Boy."

Finn hurried to the barn fast as his long legs could step. He climbed up the wall of barn logs, placin his feet and hands in the cracks until he reached the place where hard-pressed hay bulged through a wide crack between the logs. There was a little hole in the hay where Finn ran his hand back and pulled out a bottle. He scurried back down the low-walk and hurried back where Black Boy stood growlin at the wind hissin through the pine needles.

"This is the tonic that will make him young again," Finn said.

"It might kill him," I said.

"Wonder if he'll drink it raw," Finn said.

"Finn, let's don't give Black Boy that whiskey," I said.

"Why not?" Finn asked.

"It will be mean of us to give him whiskey."

"Ah, hell," Finn said as he poured the pint of whiskey in a trough where we watered the chickens.

"Here Black Boy," he coaxed.

Black Boy walked up to the trough, smelled of the moonshine, kicked his feet and growled. But he wouldn't drink it.

"He's almost in a notion," Finn said. "And I know what will put him in a notion."

Finn ran to the cellar and came back with a crock of sweet milk. He poured the gallon of sweet milk in the trough to mix with the moonshine. And Black Boy went to the trough growling and kickin the pine needles with his hind feet. He started drinkin the milk-and-moonshine. Black Boy gorged himself to hold the gallon of sweet milk and the pint of moonshine whiskey. He licked the trough clean as a pawpaw whistle.

"We're goin to see somethin happen," Finn said. "I don't know what it will be. But somethin will happen!"

Black Boy got down on the pine needles and rolled. He opened his big mouth as he looked at us with eyes that sparkled with livin fire. Black Boy growled as he wallowed on the ground. Then Black Boy jumped to his feet like he was a young pup. He ran circles around us with his tongue out.

"That tonic is workin on 'im," Finn said. "He's a happy dog. It's doin 'im good."

Then Black Boy made a beeline toward the barn. He leaped over the gate like a red fox. He took down the path that leads from our barn to the big pasture field. He was out of sight under the trees whose pine needles looked good in the moonlight.

"Where's that dog goin?" I asked Finn.

"He's goin to hunt," Finn laughed.

"He's got so he can't smell a track when the ground is damp," I said. "I know he can't carry a track dry as it is now."

We hadn't stood there talkin five minutes until we heard Black Boy bark treed.

"What did I tell you," Finn said. "Black Boy's got somethin. Listen to that music won't you!"

"He's barkin to a bunch of poplar leaves," I said. "That dog's drunk. He doesn't know what he's doin."

Finn started runnin toward the sound. I followed Finn out the path by the barn and under the oaks and pines to the far pasture field. We saw Black Boy jumpin up on a small sourwood at the edge of the pasture field, barkin every breath.

"Sure he's got somethin treed," Finn said.

"I believe he has," I said. "I believe he can see it. Probably a house cat."

We ran across the field.

"House cat," Finn laughed as he got to the tree first. "It's the biggest groundhog I've ever seen."

Tall, bean-pole, freckled-faced Finn reached high on the small tree and with his big hand he gave the tree a shake. The groundhog tumbled to the ground. He hadn't more than hit the ground until Black Boy had him. He gummed the groundhog to death with a throat hold.

"Let's take it to the house," I said.

"Hell no," Finn said. "You go to the house and get a mattock and two coffee sacks. Black Boy is runnin in high gear tonight. Let's stay with him. It may be his last great hunt!"

Before I got back with the mattock and the two sacks I heard Black Boy bark treed. When I reached the pasture field, I saw Finn with the groundhog in his hand, lookin up the black gum where Black Boy was barkin. I hurried across the field to the tree.

"He just walked up here and started barkin," Finn said. "May be somethin down in the hollow of that tree. I don't know. Can't see anything from the outside."

"Probably nothin there," I said. "That dog is drunk and you can't trust him."

"Trust hell," Finn said. "I believe there's somethin in that tree."

Finn pulled off his shoes and climbed the big black gum. He grunted as he climbed for it was a hard tree to climb. When Finn got to the top, he looked down in the tree where the top was broken off.

"Have a surprise for you, Shan," he said. "I'll show you something."

"What is it, Finn?" I asked, for I could hardly wait to see.

Now Finn had braced his foot against a black gum limb. He reached down in the hollow top of the black gum carefully. And he pulled a big possum up by the tail.

"Has the drunk dog lied?" Finn asked.

He threw the possum to the ground. Black Boy grabbed it soon as it hit the ground. But I took Black Boy off the possum and put it in a sack.

"That possum had the prettiest bed up in that tree," Finn said soon as he reached the ground. "He was layin up there asleep."

After Black Boy saw me put the possum in the sack, he went off over the hill like a blowin wind. He was goin with his nose high in the air, snifflin as he went.

"He's after somethin' right now," Finn said. "He's windin somethin."

Black Boy hadn't been gone long enough for us to get our sacks and mattock and walk down the hollow when we heard him bark deep in a hollow on the other side of the low ridge.

"He's barkin in a hole," Finn said as he stopped and listened, holdin his breath with his hand cupped over his ear to catch the low sound.

I followed Finn as he made his way through the brier thickets over the low ridge and down into the next hollow. Before we reached Black Boy, we heard him kickin the dirt with his feet. We heard it sprinklin over the dry leaves below 'im. Then we heard him growlin as he jerked on a root with his toothless mouth. When we reached him, he had a hole dug big enough to bury himself in by the end of a blackberry brier thicket. The hole was in the soft loamy dirt and he was diggin fast; he was barkin like he was close to somethin. We made our way through the thicket to him. Finn held Black Boy while I struck a few licks with the mattock. Then Finn let Black Boy loose to clean the hole out with his paws. He rammed his head back in the hole and pulled out a polecat that was black as a moonless midnight. I jumped back. I didn't want its scent to settle on me.

"He can't kill it," Finn said. "He doesn't have the teeth."

But he did kill it. He crushed its head with his powerful jaws.

"What a powerful dog he is today," I said. "How can a dog old as he is crush a polecat's head when he doesn't have a tooth in his head?"

We put the skunk in one end of the sack where we had the possum.

"That's the prettiest polecat hide I've ever seen," Finn said. "That will bring a good price."

"Seven or eight dollars," I said.

Now Black Boy was sick. He wallowed on the leaves. He rooted his nose under the dry leaves on top of the ground down to the wet, half-rotten leaves against the ground. He ran his nose down in the fresh dirt that he had dug from the hole.

"The hunt's over," I said. "He's really sick."

"After a dog gets that polecat scent on him he's through," Finn said. "This may end our hunt."

Soon as we had reached the little hollow below us we saw Black Boy standin to his knees in a hole of clean spring water. Then he left the water and took up the hill as if nothin had ever happened. He was soon out of sight over the hill where there was a beech grove between our farm and Uncle Mel's farm. And soon as we reached the hilltop, he barked in another hole. Wet with sweat, and tired of keepin after Black Boy, we hurried down the hill. Black Boy was barkin in the end of a hollow beech log.

"There's somethin there, Finn," I said as I took the ax-end of my mattock and started pryin away rottin slabs from the log.

"We'll soon know," Finn said as he held the dog back so I wouldn't hit his head with the ax-end of my mattock. "I'll bet it's another possum."

"You're right," I said. "Look!"

I pulled off a slab from over the possum's bed of leaves. He stuck his head out to see what was goin on. Black Boy broke the collar that Finn was holdin him by and leaped three times his length to the possum. I had to choke him loose before I could free the possum to put in the sack with the other possum.

"What a possum," Finn said as I put it in the sack. "Did you ever see this dog do any better in your life?"

"Never saw him work this fast," I said.

Black Boy wagged his tail at us. But he didn't hang around for us to pat his head and rub his nose. He was off like a black flash over the brown leaves to the bluff beyond us. We saw him with his head held high in the night wind, go straight to a little rock. We saw him put his head under the rock; we heard him sniffle. Then he barked. Then he started diggin fast as he could. His hind feet threw sprinkles of loam and wet leaves twenty feet behind him down the steep bluff.

"He's got somethin," I said, grabbin the mattock and one of the sacks.

"You damn right he has," Finn said, grabbin the other sack and followin me.

Soon as we started up the bluff he brought somethin from the hole.

"Phew," Finn screamed. "It's a damned polecat sure as the world."

They came rollin end over end down the steep bluff toward us. And soon as they reached the bottom of the bluff, the polecat's legs stretched out limber. It was dead. Black Boy had crushed its skull with his jaws.

"It's a broad-striped polecat," Finn said, tense with excitement.

Finn put the polecat in the sack while Black Boy rooted his

nose down under the dry leaves to the wet half-rotten half-loam leaves. Then Black Boy made for the little fresh spring water creek that flowed from the steep bluffs to drink water. He wallowed in one of the little deep holes against a fern-covered bank.

"Two livin possums in one end of this sack," Finn laughed. "Two dead polecats in the other. It's gettin heavy."

"Wonder when the herbs will die in Black Boy," I said.

"When they die in Black Boy," Finn said, "his huntin will be done for tonight."

"Maybe forever," I said.

"But this is wonderful," Finn said. "I've never seen anythin like it."

Now Black Boy left us. He went down the creek toward Ragweed Hollow. And we followed the cattle path down to the fence. We didn't hear from Black Boy. He didn't return to us nor did he bark. Tired of runnin after him and carryin the game, we sat down on a beech log to rest. But we didn't rest long. We heard Black Boy bark in a hole on the hill across the hollow. We started runnin toward him. When we climbed the hill, sweaty, tired and out-of-breath, we found Black Boy in a dirt hole in a little drain.

Finn poked a long stick back in the hole and told me where to dig down to strike the hole. I soon put a hole down for it was shallow down to the hole. Then Finn put the stick back again and told me where to dig. I put down another hole and then another. When Finn put the stick back, he felt a bed of leaves.

"It's a groundhog or a possum," Finn said. "I feel it."

He twisted with his stick; then he pulled it out.

"Red hairs," Finn said, examinin the hairs on the end of the stick in the moonlight.

"Let Black Boy loose before somethin jumps out," I said.

Soon as Black Boy put his nose in the hole to sniffle, he yelled. Then he started fightin.

"Somethin bit 'im," I said.

"A young red fox," Finn roared as Black Boy and the fox tangled.

"What do you know about that," I said. "Who ever dreamed of a fox bein in a dirt hole?"

"He's found him a rabbit in that hole," Finn said. "He was havin a good meal when Black Boy found him."

"He's finished the fox," I said.

"We'll just carry it outside the sack," Finn said. "It would take too much room in a sack."

"This will about end our hunt," I said. "Black Boy is gettin tired. Look at his tongue. It's dropped down like a shoe-tongue."

Finn carried the sack of possums and polecats and the mattock; I carried the fox and the groundhog. It was like carryin a full-grown hound-dog pup to carry the fox. Now we made our way off the hill. Black Boy walked in front of us. But soon he disappeared.

When we reached the foot of the hill, we started up the Ragweed Hollow jolt-wagon road for home. We were tired now; we were wet with sweat—our clothes looked like we had jumped in the river. And the load of game was gettin heavier every step we took.

"I hope he won't find anythin more," I said.

"Listen," Finn said turnin his head sideways for his ear to catch the sound. "I hear 'im! He's got somethin!"

We hurried toward the sound. By a log pile at the upper side of the field where Doore's had had tobacco, Black Boy had found another polecat under the log pile. He had it killed when we got there and he was wallowin on the tobacco-patch dirt. He was rootin his nose in the ground like a hog.

"It's a narrow-stripe," Finn said. "He's crushed its skull."

"Another damned polecat," I said. "You can put it in the sack or we'll leave it. I don't aim to put my hands on it."

"It's got wonderful fur," Finn said. "Sure, I'll put it in the sack."

Finn opened the sack and put his dead polecat with the other two. He tied the sack and grunted as he swung the sack across his shoulder with one big heave.

"Some load," Finn said. "But there's money in these hides."

"Thank God this hunt's over," I said. "Look at Black Boy. He's sick enough to eat grass."

Black Boy was eatin stems of dead crab-grass that he found in the tobacco balks.

"You can't tell about Black Boy," Finn said.

And Finn was right. As we were slowly trudgin toward home, weary under our heavy loads, Black Boy let out a blast of barks that came hard and fast.

"He's treed," Finn screamed. "He can see it! He's close to it!"

Even with our heavy loads, we broke out in a slow run. He was barkin on Doore's bluff just above the road. We had a good road to get to him.

"Look up there at that groundhog," Finn laughed.

The groundhog was up a little sassafras saplin. It was bigger than the first groundhog that we had caught. We hurried up the bank to the tree. Black Boy was backin off and runnin toward the tree, then leapin up and barely missin the groundhog.

"He's got plenty of pep left," Finn said.

Then Black Boy tried to climb the tree but his toenails wouldn't hold in the sassafras bark. Finn shook the sassafras. When the groundhog hit the ground, it hit the ground runnin. But before it had got many steps Black Boy grabbed it by the throat and choked it to death. It made my load heavier. Two big groundhogs and a fox for me. Three polecats and two possums for Finn. And he carried the mattock. Now we called Black Boy and started home. The October wagon-wheel moon beamed on us; the night wind rustled leaves on the trees dry as oakchips. But now we were goin home to show Pa the game we had caught with Black Boy before eleven o'clock.

Before we reached home Black Boy barked at somethin in the bottom.

"You go to him, Finn," I said. "Leave your sack here and I'll watch the game. We can't carry all of this and follow that dog."

Finn walked across the bottom where Black Boy was barkin on the creek bank. Soon as Finn reached him, I heard him laughin.

He came back across the bottom carryin a big black bug that had pincers.

"Back to his old age," Finn said. "The herbs have died in 'im."

And just as we reached the hog-lot bluff, Black Boy barked treed somewhere upon the bluff. I went to him this time and Finn watched the game. Finn heard me laugh when I saw that he was barkin at a cluster of leaves lodged in the forks of a shell-barked hickory. The herbs had really died; Black Boy had been livin in his old world. Now Black Boy was livin in another world where he was an old dog.

"My God! Black Boy is going back to his prime," Pa said as he looked at the pile of game. "That's the way he used to hunt when he's a young dog."

"Thirty dollars worth of hides," Finn said. "And enough groundhog hide shoestrings to lace our boots for a couple of years."

Black Boy laid down that night soon as we had skinned the game and stretched the hides. Next mornin at sunrise when we went to feed him he couldn't get up. But he ate a little layin down. His eyes were not like embers glowin in the night; his eyes were glassy.

"It's probably a tough hangover," Finn whispered in my ear so Pa wouldn't hear him.

But Black Boy's breath grew shorter; his great panels of ribs didn't heave when he breathed like they always had. And today was his nineteenth birthday. Before the sun had set, Black Boy had gone to the Great Huntin Ground where there was plenty of game. Pa was up on the barn logs with his hand back in the hay huntin for his medicine to break his October cold when we told him that Black Boy had finally breathed his last.